ACCLAIM FOR
Shiva Dancing

"Skillful . . . The author has created such appealing characters and
has done such a good job of portraying her heroine's longings and
uncertainties that we are kept guessing . . . Kirchner's descriptions
of domestic customs are richly suggestive, adding color and
flavor to an already evocative novel."
—*Christian Science Monitor*

"Kirchner adds the right amount of spice to this palatable debut."
—*Seattle Weekly*

"*Shiva Dancing* echoes the work of Alice Adams . . . Interesting,
cosmopolitan characters."
—*Booklist*

"An auspicious debut . . . A light, romantic tale, [*Shiva Dancing*]
is also a deep, questioning look into the immigrant soul, the
warring within, the confusion and guilt, the nostalgia and hope."
—*Earth Times*

Born in India, BHARTI KIRCHNER worked as a software systems engineer for many years before becoming a prizewinning cookbook author
and novelist. Her second novel, *Sharmila's Book*, is available in a
Dutton hardcover edition. Ms. Kirchner lives in Seattle.

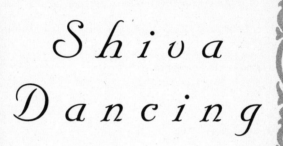

Shiva Dancing

Bharti Kirchner

A PLUME BOOK

PLUME
Published by the Penguin Group
Penguin Putnam Inc., 375 Hudson Street, New York, New York 10014, U.S.A.
Penguin Books Ltd, 27 Wrights Lane, London W8 5TZ, England
Penguin Books Australia Ltd, Ringwood, Victoria, Australia
Penguin Books Canada Ltd, 10 Alcorn Avenue, Toronto, Ontario,
    Canada M4V 3B2
Penguin Books (N.Z.) Ltd, 182–190 Wairau Road, Auckland 10, New Zealand

Penguin Books Ltd, Registered Offices: Harmondsworth, Middlesex, England

Published by Plume, a member of Penguin Putnam Inc.
Previously published in a Dutton edition.

First Plume Printing, April, 1999
10 9 8 7 6 5 4 3 2 1

 REGISTERED TRADEMARK—MARCA REGISTRADA

The Library of Congress has catalogued the Dutton edition as follows:
Kirchner, Bharti.
    Shiva Dancing / Bharti Kirchner.
    p.   cm.
    ISBN 0-525-94367-6
        0-452-27882-1 (pbk.)
    I. Title.
    PS3561.I6835S48   1998
    813'54—dc21   97-34054
                                                      CIP

Printed in the United States of America
Original hardcover design by Eve L. Kirch

PUBLISHER'S NOTE
This is a work of fiction. Names, characters, places, and incidents either are the products of the author's imagination or are used fictitiously, and any resemblance to actual
persons, living or dead, events, or locales is entirely coincidental.

To my family in India
and to Tom
for all that I am

Acknowledgments

Writing a first novel is a daunting task and I couldn't have done this book without the support of family and friends. My sincerest thanks to Dick Gibbons, Diane Ste. Marie, Barbara Galvin, Leon Billig, Peter Holman-Smith, Daniel Goldsmith, Bruce Dodson, and Barbara Craven of the Seattle Writers Association. Also to the regulars of the Monday morning group—Ann Adams, Tom McGovern, Pat Trammel, Mike Simonton, Stever Ladd, Wally Lane, Jean Seideman, and June Dragger. And to Lynn Bursten, Alle Hall, Suzanne Greenberg, Marie Herreras, and Candace Dempsey. Your comments and suggestions have helped shape this book.

To friends Gary Boynton and Judy Boynton, for giving me encouragement.

To the Artist Trust and the Seattle Arts Commission for supporting portions of this work.

To Nancy Pearl for making the C. K. Poe Pratt Writers Room available.

To Michael Anthony for driving me through Rajasthan and answering my questions.

To Kakababu for having faith in me.

To my husband, Tom Kirchner, for all the help and understanding. This book is as much his as it is mine.

And finally to Jane Dystel, Miriam Goderich, and Rosemary Ahern, professionals all. I am fortunate to have such a strong publishing team.

I owe much to all of you.

Book
One

Seven, her people had always believed, was an auspicious number. One's life began anew every seven years. So it seemed quite natural to Meena Kumari that she was to wed Vishnu Chauhan on her seventh birthday, the night of the full moon. Named after the Hindu god of nurturing, Vishnu was also seven. They had grown up together in Karamgar, a small village of less than a hundred mud houses scattered along winding dirt paths at the edge of the Great Thar Desert in Rajasthan. They had been friends and playmates ever since she could remember, spending hours playing hide-and-seek in the low-lying rocky hills, smelling the marigolds and chasing the wild peacocks that foraged for food in the village streets.

On the morning of her wedding Meena watched her mother, Gangabai, sweeping the warm brown mud floor of their house with a bamboo broom as she did every morning to remove the overnight accumulation of windblown sand. Their round, thatched two-room hut was just a camel's spit away, as Grandfather would say, from the encroaching sand dunes. Gangabai looked tall against the door, pretty in her long full skirt, matching blouse, and half sari. Her presence gave a glow to the room. She knew all there was to know, all that had to be done.

Meena looked up and asked, "Mataji, do I get to come home with you afterward?"

Mataji stopped to smile down at Meena. "Haven't I told you so enough times? You two are still too young. You won't move in with Vishnu until you're fourteen." She laughed. "You'll have a lot to do then. Their house is twice the size of ours. But you'll get used to it. I did when I moved in with your father and his parents. And that's the way it's been in our family as far back as anyone can remember."

Fourteen, that's another seven years, another life away, Meena thought. And in the meantime she'd be living only a short walk from Vishnu's house. What more could she want?

Meena went over to the window. On this day in March, which was also her birthday, the sun was brighter than usual and it bathed her in its yellow light. What was Vishnu doing now? she wondered. Yesterday after school at this time they had walked to the edge of the village, giggling, shyly holding hands. When she found a pretty pebble in a reddish brown shade by her feet, she slipped it into Vishnu's trousers pocket and told him always to keep it. Then at a place where the sand dunes skirted the road they stopped to play hide-and-seek. As they kicked at the sand, a lizard came out of its hole. They decided "lizard" would be their code word for passing secret messages to each other through friends. This was in case Vishnu was actually sent to a better school in another village, as his mother had so often threatened. Yes, and yesterday they had raced from the sand dunes to the sweetshop located in the center of the village. Meena won, but the shopkeeper wagged a finger at her.

"Girls don't run," he said. "And they don't beat the boys."

Meena avoided his glance and eyed the rounds of *laddoo* in the showcase. Her favorite confection was made of ground chick peas and had an orangeish gold color. Vishnu must have noticed, for he bought her one with the little money he had in his pocket. She popped half of it in her mouth. Her teeth first sank into the tender exterior, then down into the part from where sweet juices flow. She shoved the other half in Vishnu's mouth. She wouldn't share such a treat with anyone but him. She didn't get it all that often.

"Meena," Mataji called out on the wedding day.

"I'm coming." Meena rushed to the bedroom. She could hear Grandfather, who had a cold, snoring in the other room.

Rummaging through an old bureau drawer, Mataji produced a jar of henna powder. As she mixed it with water, she reminded Meena that red was the sacred color for weddings and that three parts of a bride's body must be stained red: the soles of her feet, the palms of her hands, and her nails.

"But wash your feet first," Mataji said. She sang a snatch of a wedding lyric with a high, happy note, a tinge of sadness at the edge.

Using water from a huge earthenware pitcher Meena rinsed her feet and dried them. She settled herself on a stool, the only one in the house, and watched as Mataji painted the soles of her feet with the brown paste. It felt cool and she wiggled her toes from the tickling sensation. Her feet were soon turning red. "A sure sign Vishnu loves you," Mataji said.

Her touch was soft as she next tinted Meena's palms and nails a deep crimson. Her love seemed to move up Meena's feet and hands to engulf her entirely. Meena wished she could get up and dance.

"Time to get dressed," Mataji said.

Meena would later recall slipping into an ankle-length flared silk skirt in scarlet decorated with tiny octagonal mirrors and a matching short-sleeved bodice. The ensemble was nothing like the simple cotton clothes she wore every day. Mataji had saved and saved to buy the material and had sewn it herself. Meena wore an anklet of tiny silver bells that made a ringing sound when she moved, and her arms were encircled by glass and conchshell bracelets. An intricate tiara of hand-worked gold inset with rubies trembled on her forehead.

Then Mataji fastened a gold necklace with a locket around her throat and Meena felt its weight pulling at her neck. "My mother gave me this on my wedding day," Mataji said. "I thought of selling it so many times when I ran short of money. But for the life of me I never could do that."

Finally Mataji draped a sheer muslin veil tinted in a melange of pink, yellow, and orange splashes over Meena's head. As she did so, she recited the ancient wedding blessing, "May this veil bring you joy and happiness all your life."

At the sound of footsteps Meena flounced across the room in a rustle of silk and went to the door. There stood Auntie Teelu, Mataji's cousin, a plain-featured woman with a busy mouth, the self-appointed leader of the village women. She was making her daily round. A harmless old gossip, Mataji had often called her behind her back.

Yawning and scratching his head, Grandfather joined them.

"My dearest little child." Auntie Teelu bent close to touch Meena's head with her right palm and bless her. Then, turning to Mataji, she said, "You know, Meena's the prettiest bride of all." Today nine pairs of girls and boys were to be married in a common ceremony and Meena knew them all.

"Big green eyes," Auntie Teelu gushed on as she gazed at Meena. "Shiny black hair. A face like the goddess Sita's. You must be proud, Gangabai." She sat on the stool and for the next half hour rattled on about the news: how the villagers were rushing around preparing food, pressing their finest clothes, and tuning musical instruments. After all, such a ceremony happened only once a year. How nice, Meena thought, that on this day everyone was able to shed all cares and celebrate.

"I need to get ready myself," Grandfather said, "wash up a bit." Peering inside the pitcher, he added, "Not a drop left."

"Meena, did you use all the water?" Mataji asked.

"I didn't mean to, Mataji," Meena said, ashamed of herself.

"I must get water," Mataji said to Auntie Teelu and rushed out toward the village well.

Auntie Teelu left, humming a tune as she went. This evening would end with music and dancing and a joyous party, Meena knew. She could hear her neighbor practicing a *bhajan*. It sounded like a thin wail rising and falling with the gusts of wind off the desert. Meena started chanting herself.

Mataji was gone longer than usual and after a time Meena became impatient. When Mataji returned, her brass pot was only partly full, her face distorted in pain. "I fell and twisted my ankle," she said. "That's what took so long."

Poor Mataji. She had worked so hard for this wedding. No rest for months. And now this. Meena rushed to her, held her hand, and helped her settle in a chair. "How can I help you, Mataji?"

"I'll be fine, my precious one," she reassured Meena as she bandaged her swollen foot.

Grandfather frowned as he looked down at Mataji's feet. "I don't like that."

"What do you mean?" Mataji asked.

Meena wondered why her heart beat faster.

"Nothing," Grandfather mumbled. "Nothing."

Neighbors drifted in and out with offers of assistance. "Never mind," Mataji told them all, "it's just a small sprain." Soon the house became quiet again.

By now Grandfather had dressed himself in a white tunic-and-pants set, trimmed his mustache, and wound an elaborate five-colored turban on his head. It didn't escape Meena's attention that he appeared a little somber.

"You look great, Grandfather," she said, trying to cheer him. "And you, too, Mataji." Mataji was now resplendent in a fine white cotton sari reserved for special occasions.

Turning to Grandfather, Mataji said, "I wish my husband were here on our only child's wedding day." Tears glistened on her cheeks.

At that moment Meena experienced an overwhelming sense of loss. Her father had died from malaria when she was still a toddler. She had known him only as an imposing figure who moved in and out of her limited world unpredictably. Mataji had often expressed regret that he suffered from fever for weeks before dying a painful death because the proper medicine failed to arrive in time.

"And we're on our way," Grandfather said, leaning on his cane.

It was late afternoon when they headed down a winding dirt road toward the wedding pavilion about twenty minutes' walk from the house. Along the way, the baby goats nodded toward Meena and the buffaloes groaned. The old temple and the conical roofs of houses turned golden under the yellow desert light and lifted her spirits.

The road ended in an emerald green field of millet rippling in the breeze. And Grandfather, as he always did, passed the time by telling Meena tales of Rajasthani kings and queens. "Little Meena, you must remember our illustrious heritage," he began. "This is Rajputana, land of the children of warrior kings."

Of course he was repeating himself, but Meena didn't mind hearing the stories again. Grandfather's voice had energy, his face looked animated, and he pronounced each word carefully so it seemed weighted with history. "Those kings ruled us before the British took over India," he continued. "Although we got our independence more than two decades ago, not much has changed for us. We still don't have much land or money. But remember we're Rajputs, children of kings." He twirled the ends of his mustache. "And you, Meena, are a Rajput princess about to be married."

She'd better take dainty steps, as would befit such royalty, Meena told herself.

"On my wedding day," Mataji said with teary eyes, "I hardly knew your father. He was from another village. I was frightened. But you

and Vishnu are best friends—much better that way." She halted, then
tugged at Meena's elbow. "Look, child."

And there, down a slight slope, was a large gold-embroidered
canopy standing against the vast desert sky. Stretched over four
wooden posts and held in place by ropes and stakes, the wedding
pavilion was a tent without walls that dazzled Meena's eyes. The
whole village was paying for the cost of the weddings. Grandfather
gestured toward the marigold braids wrapped in spirals about the
posts. "Those bright yellow flowers are our offerings to the sun god,"
he explained solemnly. "We're descendants of the sun."

Meena's throat choked with joy, excitement, and fear. This was a
grand affair. But when she raised her eyes, she noticed the charcoal
clouds above her that filled the sky to the west and hung low over the
village. She had never seen so many dark clouds.

"That's why we Rajputs are such strong, energetic people," she
heard Grandfather saying. "Your great-great-great-great-grandmother
led the entire village against the Muslim invaders. Her husband was
killed in the fight. She herself was wounded by an enemy sword. But
she didn't just sit and cry. Her last words were, 'I'll give every drop of
my blood, but not my land.' "

The phrase still echoing in her head, Meena entered the pavilion.
With a swish of her skirt, she sat down on a cane mat next to Vishnu,
her husband-to-be. He wore light-fitting white trousers, a pearl-
buttoned white shirt, and a shimmering indigo vest embellished with
tiny mirrors. A red turban towered above the thick arched eyebrows
that bridged his aquiline nose. He looked older, more dignified, no
longer her fun-loving playmate of yesterday. And Meena remembered
that Mataji had instructed her not to look into his eyes until the end
of the ceremony, as dictated by Hindu wedding custom. That was
just as well, because she was feeling shy.

Sixteen other bejeweled and elegantly dressed children, looking
like a collection of desert blooms, sat facing one another in two rows.
Janu, the girl across from Meena, leapt up from her mat and rushed
to her mother, who consoled her before returning her to her place.
Poor Janu hated her bully of a groom who pulled her ponytail constantly, Meena knew. The match had been made by Janu's mother.
How lucky Meena was. Of all the boys in the village Vishnu was
the finest.

Auntie Teelu along with three other women came forth with trays heaped with pure white jasmine garlands. She draped one about the neck of each child. Meena savored the sweet scent of hers as she listened to the haunting notes of a *shahnai*, a tubular flutelike instrument favored by the gods. By now grownups had sat down all around the children in two circles, palms together, thumbs against their chests in the Hindu gesture of reverence. A few women carried babies at their breasts. Everyone Meena knew was there, all except Uncle Arvind, Mataji's younger brother, a grain merchant who lived in the next village. He was habitually late.

Meena looked up to see the priest—Pundit, or wise man, he was called—make his entrance swathed in a floor-length saffron wrap of cotton. Acknowledging no one, he strode to the dais at the head of the two rows of brides and grooms and settled himself in the lotus position. His head was shaven, his chest bare except for a sacred thread looped diagonally from his neck down across his upper body to mark his status. On his forehead was a slash of white sandalwood paste that indicated his priestly calling. Meena was awed. She had never seen a more important personage.

Solemnly he began the ceremony by speaking of the creation of the world. How Lord Brahma created man, then fashioned a woman out of

> "*The gentleness of the morning dew,*
> *The meekness of the deer,*
> *The will of a lioness,*
> *The vengeance of a tigress. . . .*"

Pundit bellowed out the words. How good it was, Meena thought, to be a woman. Mataji had said that women were held in high respect in ancient India.

Eyes closed, Pundit began to chant wedding prayers to Lord Ganesh, the elephant-headed god.

> "*O Lord of good fortune . . .*
> *Preside over the giving away of a pure-hearted maiden*
> *To an honorable groom. . . .*"

Every few minutes Pundit opened his eyes, dipped his fingers in a bowl of clarified butter, and flicked a few drops of the ghee into a ritual fire before him. The fire, a deity named Agni, was to be the witness. The ghee sizzled; the flame flared up and burned brighter. A nutty aroma rose in the air and mingled with the musky fragrance of sandalwood. Meena inhaled deeply of the heady mixture.

His invocations to the gods complete, Pundit asked each bride and groom in turn to circle the fire together seven times. He knotted the hem of each groom's shirt with the loose end of his bride's long veil to symbolize the marriage bond. Vishnu was to walk in front the first three times and Meena the last four. This was so she would have the upper hand in the marriage, Pundit explained. Meena began her seven revolutions, gaining vitality from the fire as she completed each.

"By taking seven steps together," Pundit pronounced the vow for them to repeat, "you become my companion for life. We shall combine our hands, minds, and hearts in all our actions. . . ." Pundit's incantations became blurry at the last go-around. Meena was glad when he asked them to return to their seats.

"Now, take the hand of your bride," Pundit instructed the grooms. "This is a sign of your pledge to support and protect her."

Vishnu enfolded Meena's palm in his slender fingers. Her bracelets jingled and she trembled inside. His delicate touch, tentative yet reassuring, would be etched in her mind forever.

Pundit continued chanting. It must have made Meena drowsy, because Vishnu leaned into her and squeezed her fingers and that brought her back to life again. "Now, children," Pundit said finally, "you may exchange garlands. In doing so, two become one."

Eagerly Meena draped her wreath around Vishnu's neck. As he raised his around her head, a blossom fell to the ground. She shivered, knowing it was a bad omen.

Pundit now bid them to look into each other's eyes. At that moment, all the figures around Meena vanished and her senses became suddenly sharp. There was only Vishnu, magnificent Vishnu. A halo of love and warmth radiated from him. It seemed as though she were setting eyes on him for the first time.

"You're now married." Pundit blessed them with a shower of turmeric-stained rice and rose petals and thus brought the wedding ceremony to a close. Meena rose, and clicked her bracelets with those of Janu and the other brides. As if on cue, the setting sun broke through the clouds and suffused the faces around Meena with a soft golden glow. She watched as Mataji, along with all the other mothers, began a high-pitched ululation of joy, punctuated by the ringing clash of cymbals.

Just outside the canopy Vishnu's father struck the dholak with his palms, announcing the postnuptial festivities. His fingers were a blur as they played out a staccato rhythm of joyous rapture. As a counterpoint, Janu's father played a sad tune on the one-stringed ektara. A marriage, Meena knew, was both a happy and a sad event for the bride: happy to be joining her husband, sad because she would leave her parents.

Amid the singing of a *bhajan*, Auntie Teelu and a band of boys stepped forward with large platters heaped with sweets in each of the seven colors of the rainbow. Meena's hand reached out for a milk fudge flavored with cardamom. At the first bite, the creamy morsel melted in her mouth like a whirlpool of pleasure. Would Vishnu like a piece? She turned to him, but his eyes were glued to a group of folk dancers just beginning an intricate bit of footwork. At other wedding ceremonies Meena had attended, she got out there and danced barefoot. But on this day she was the bride. She was disappointed that today she could only watch.

By this time it was dusk. People were beginning to drift away in small groups toward the village and Meena wanted to go home too.

"Don't stay out late, Gangabai," Auntie Teelu warned Mataji as she picked up her belongings. "Bad things can happen after dark. And there are a lot of clouds in the sky."

"Arvind is supposed to pick us up on his camel," Mataji replied. "We really should hang around. I can't walk too well. Please don't wait for us, Teelu. We'll be fine."

Family after family left. Meena watched as Vishnu waved a goodbye. He fixed his eyes on Meena as he joined his parents, who were already on their way. Even as he followed them Vishnu kept staring back as though he was reluctant to part with her. She'd see him tomorrow, Meena knew for sure.

Half an hour passed. A few people still remained, cleaning up the debris while singing a farewell song. Meena fidgeted. Grandfather coughed. And Mataji's ankle was so swollen that she could barely keep her sandal on. Still no sign of Uncle Arvind.

"That worthless brother of mine." Mataji snorted. "Didn't show up for the wedding—and now making us walk. Probably busy making a deal."

Dust rose skyward in the distance. Two cameleers were approaching. Could they be Uncle Arvind and his friend? "Look, Mataji!" Meena gave her a poke and pointed to the west.

"That's him," Mataji said.

They started walking toward the men on the camels with Mataji grimacing at each step she took. Grandfather hobbled along on his ancient legs, jabbing the dirt path with his cane. On the far horizon, lightning struck like the yell of a witch and thunder broke as though the sky were releasing demons. The two men on camels, now in full view, came toward them. Both wore beaded black vests that glistened in the sudden light over their khaki shirts. It had been months since Meena had seen Uncle Arvind and his friend. She couldn't recognize them.

Mataji grabbed Meena's arm and held it tightly.

The men stopped their camels and slid down less than a house length away. The first man, tall and muscular, hastened toward them, rolling his sleeves up as he walked. He looked down at Meena over a huge nose and tried to grab her. They were bandits, Meena now realized.

Mataji caught Meena with one arm and struck out with the other, slashing the bandit's bare arm with the sharp edges of her silver bracelet.

"You old crow," the tall man snarled as he saw the blood. He swung his riding stick at Mataji's head. With a groan she fell to the ground and lay there moaning. He struck her harder across her chest with his stick. She was now silent.

"Mataji!" The cry came not from Meena's throat but from somewhere deep inside beyond the reach of language. Mataji raised her head slightly, her eyes unfocused, then fell back. A shudder racked her body and she went limp. Brilliant red blood oozed from the side of her forehead where the first blow had split her skull. Her lotus-white sari was stained yellow from the dust.

"You finished her," the short one growled.

Mataji dead? How could that be possible?

Grandfather cursed the bandit in a barely audible voice as he fell to his knees to attend to Mataji. The short bandit, his tattooed forehead partially hidden by greasy curls, turned to Meena with a gap-toothed leer. With huge rough hands he pushed her to her knees and snatched the ruby tiara from her forehead, nearly toppling her with his force, though he missed the gold necklace that was hidden under her bodice.

He stuffed the tiara in his pocket and barked to his camel, "Down." Groaning in protest, the cream-colored beast sank to its knees and lowered itself on its haunches. Before Meena knew it he had seized her by the arm and thrown her onto the camel saddle. He climbed up behind her, but not before Grandfather struck him on the hand with his cane.

The bandit wrenched the cane from Grandfather's hand and sent it flying into a bush. He smirked at Grandfather. "Go home, old soldier. Your war is over." He pulled the rein, urging the camel to its feet.

"Let me go," Meena cried. She turned to face him, pounding his chest with her fists. But the bandit only laughed. The camel rose to a standing position, balked, and began to move. She could feel the metal handle of the bandit's dagger pressing against her back.

"Mataji . . . Grandfather . . ." Meena cried, her body bouncing with each step of the camel. She looked back past the bandit. The tall man had remounted and was following them. Mataji was lying on the ground, a blotch of white against the red earth. *If only I hadn't used up the water,* Meena thought to herself with anguished remorse.

She saw a man run from the wedding canopy toward them, but he couldn't keep pace now that the camels were moving away from the village. Soon the thatched huts, the temple, and the grain-storage bins grew smaller and disappeared from view. Why didn't the entire village come out to pursue the bandits? She grew confused. Then she knew. No one there owned a camel.

It seemed to Meena that they had ridden forever under the full moon over a flat and barren land with only an occasional babul bush to break the monotony. A hot dry wind blew with increasing intensity, driving a cloud of gritty sand before it. Meena found herself jouncing up and down and had difficulty staying mounted. The camel behind began to make a grunting noise. The tall bandit shouted to make himself heard between gusts of wind. "A dust storm is coming."

Meena remembered the story of a neighbor who had been caught out in the desert in such a storm and was never seen again. "Put your veil over your face," the short bandit now commanded. She noticed that both the bandits had covered their noses with handkerchiefs.

Meena squirmed and pulled a corner of her veil over her face, her heart reaching her throat in fright. With each breath she took in so much sand and grit that she felt she was about to suffocate. All at once, a blast of wind snatched her wedding veil away. The pretty patch of color floated in the air, then flew behind her and disappeared from sight. Meena's heart sank again at the loss of her wedding veil.

After a long time the wind subsided and the moon reappeared. Eventually the camels emerged from the desert onto a paved road. By then the last petals had been blown from her jasmine garland, leaving only a string around her neck, a reminder of the joyous part of the day. Sitting on the camel's hump so far above the ground, Meena felt small and alone. This was the first time she'd been away from Mataji. Meena would do anything to get back. Could she escape by dropping off the camel? No, she was afraid of the height. Despair took hold of her until, from deep within, she heard Grandfather's gift of words: "We're Rajputs, children of warrior kings." Meena reminded herself she was a valiant princess. She sat upright and prayed to her ancestors that she could live up to tradition and find her way back.

The stars were all still out when they arrived at a train station swarming with passengers. "Well, we've made it to Bikaner, at least," the tall bandit said from behind. He ordered the camels to sit. The short bandit dismounted, gripped Meena with his filthy hands, and pulled her down.

With wide eyes she took in the scene around her in the station yard. Never before had she visited a town so big and noisy or seen so many people all at once. Her quiet village of Karamgar had a population of only a few hundred. She gawked at the yellow sandstone buildings and was dazzled by the electric light. She listened to the thunder of motor scooters and the screech of car wheels, sounds that were new to her. She almost forgot she had been kidnapped.

A third man, also in a beaded black vest, met them. After exchanging a few words with the tall bandit, he took the camels and disappeared.

As a train chugged into the station, its noise punctuating the night, bursts of steam enveloped Meena. She had only heard stories about trains. It looked like Ravana, the demon who stole Sita in the tales of the *Ramayana*.

"I want to go home," she whimpered.

The short bandit put his grimy hand over her mouth. "Quiet, bad child, or I'll . . ." He pointed to the dagger on his belt, chuckling at the terrified expression on her face.

Escape was out of the question for now. She'd have to wait.

She screamed and kicked on her way up the steps as the bandits hustled her onto the crowded train, but the passengers busy trying to get a seat took no notice. Inside the compartment, the men forced her to sit between them on a cushionless wooden bench against the side of the car facing two rows of benches down the middle. She didn't know it then, but it was the low-priced third-class compartment. The seat was hard, her body ached from bruises, and she was thirsty. But she wouldn't cry. After all, she was a Rajput and Rajputs don't cry.

The short bandit took off his vest and pulled his shirt over his head. This lifted his bangs and exposed the word "thief" tattooed in Hindi letters on his forehead. She realized he had been convicted of robbery before. Noticing her curious gaze, he pushed down his hair to cover his forehead again. Drops of perspiration fell from his back. A smell like week-old rice floated from his body. It was obvious he had not bathed in days.

The tall bandit, whose eyes had the yellowish cast of a rotten fish, congratulated his sidekick. "Nice piece of luggage you got there, soldier." The cut on his arm, with blood drying around it, had turned purple. It was the wound inflicted by Mataji.

Piece of luggage. Meena knew that was slang for a woman. Only rowdy boys in her school ever used such a word.

The short bandit grinned. "Let's see how much we can get for it in Delhi."

Delhi? Meena's breath caught. She'd heard tales about bandits selling village girls in big cities. Those that didn't cooperate were killed. She felt as though all the blood had been drained out of her. But again she reminded herself she was a Rajput. Somehow she must escape before the train reached Delhi.

The three of them occupied an entire bench that seemed big enough for five. A lad clutching a bundle tried to squeeze in at the end, but the tall bandit elbowed him to the floor. His lips curled. "Get out." The boy scrambled to his feet and disappeared in the crowd.

Meena surveyed the scene in the compartment. Passengers, mostly men, were sitting or standing wherever space was available among grain sacks, rolls of bedding, and fruit-laden baskets. She could make out the sweet smell of mangoes. A young boy slept in the luggage rack up above her head, oblivious to everything. A man spat on the floor and was immediately cursed by those about him. Another sneezed nonstop. Still, in Meena's eyes, none were as filthy and mean as the two bandits.

The night wore on. Occasionally a passenger would catch her gaze fleetingly and whisper to others. They must suspect something. Could she jump out of her seat to get their attention? The short bandit seemed to have noticed. He hissed between his teeth and pressed her shoulder down. His angry eyes slashed her face. The tall one slid in closer.

By now she was unbearably thirsty. She drifted into a dream state, in which she recounted the story of the evil bandits to Grandfather. For a change she was the storyteller. He listened, nodded, and said, "They can't keep you for long, those two rotten ones. You're stronger than them." He receded into the distance.

The train pulled to a stop at a station. *"Chai,"* called out a vendor from the platform. Oh, how she would like a cup of tea now, Meena thought. She sat up, hopeful they'd buy her a cup.

"You pay," the short bandit ordered the tall one.

"Didn't get any cash this time," the tall captor grumbled. "Only jewelry." He extracted some coins from his pocket and stuck his hands out of the window. Meena raised her head to see a vendor, a young man in a white cotton dhoti, standing on the platform dispensing tea in clay cups.

None for her. Meena simply sat, while the bandits swirled the precious liquid in their mouths, savoring it before swallowing it. Her throat was parched and she couldn't help but give a longing look toward a shrunken old turbaned man who sat across from them with a basket of mangoes at his feet.

The old man asked the tall bandit, "Wouldn't your daughter like some *chai*?"

"She doesn't want anything."

The old man smiled. "But it's so late and she's little. Surely she could use something."

"Peetaji." Meena put a plea in her voice as she called the tall bandit her "respected father." To use the suffix "-ji," a deferential form for addressing one's elders, made her feel ridiculous.

The old man stared at the bandit, who grudgingly nodded.

The old man paid the vendor and handed Meena a cup with shaky hands. His wrinkled face and loving eyes were just like Grandfather's. She guzzled the tea. It was deliciously sweet, every drop of it. Following the example of other passengers, she threw the empty vessel out through the window. It hit the platform with a cracking sound and shattered into pieces, the sound drowned out by the whistle of the train as it got under way.

The warm brew calmed Meena. She closed her eyes. Her head fell against the shoulder of one bandit and she drifted off to sleep. Much later she was jolted back to consciousness as the train shuddered to a halt. The two villains were asleep, one snoring with open mouth. In the faint compartment light her gaze met the old man's and a look of understanding seemed to grow in his eyes. He began to shout, "The conductor is coming," over and over again until at last the bandits awoke and rubbed their eyes. Meena could tell the old man was up to something.

Ticketless passengers gathered bags and parcels and pushed their way toward the door all at once in a mad rush. The bandits began to whisper to each other. "Didn't think they checked tickets on the night train," the short man said. "Will the conductor throw us out?"

"He'll want a bribe," the tall one said. "And he might ask about the 'luggage.' Let's get out and catch the next train." He started for the door.

"Quick, girl, out!" the short bandit ordered. He grabbed her by the back of her bodice and shoved her ahead of him to the door and out onto the steps.

"No," Meena cried. She ducked, hitting him in the groin with the sharp edges of her armlets. Several of her glass bangles broke in pieces. That startled him enough to make him lose his balance. A passenger took this opportunity to hit him in the back with his fist.

The bandit doubled over, his face contorted with pain. "Ah-h-h . . ." He tumbled forward onto the station platform, his sack of jewelry flying out of his hand. At the same time, another passenger threw a basket of mangoes over their heads. Both bandits were now on the ground, splattered with mango juice and pulp.

"You'll regret this when I get through with you," the tall bandit cursed Meena as he sprang to his feet.

"Ungrateful little bitch," muttered the other as he wiped pieces of the pulp from his cheek.

Rubies sparkled in the station light. Meena's tiara, a family heirloom, lay on the ground. The bandits scrabbled to recover their booty, but it was being scattered by hordes of passengers shoving their way toward the exits. In their greed, both seemed to have forgotten her for the moment. Here was her chance. Standing on the train steps, she stretched her hand out to retrieve her tiara, but it was just out of reach.

A pair of arms dragged her back inside. "Let the tiara go," the old man said.

In the scuffle, Meena struck her forehead on the door. Dazed and limp from the blow, she felt a bruise forming just above her eyebrow. But she was safe, surrounded by a human wall of villagers.

The tall bandit tried to reach her through the crowd. The other passengers pushed him back out onto the platform. "Very mischievous, this daughter—" he shouted, but he was cut off in midsentence by the screeching of the train as it lurched into motion.

"Get lost, you scum," a scrawny one-eyed man yelled back from the compartment.

The train began to pick up speed. Meena could see the tall bandit through the window. He waved his arms as he ran along beside the coach, but whatever he was saying was drowned out by the taunts of the villagers and the sound of the accelerating train. Soon he fell behind and gave up the chase. Meena sagged onto a seat, breathing so heavily that she didn't feel the motion of the train.

The conductor, a mahogany-skinned man with a black mole on his nose, made the rounds of the compartment, punching each passenger's ticket. Finally he regarded Meena. "Whose child is this?" he asked.

The other passengers crowded around him, babbling excitedly.

"One at a time." The conductor's voice stilled the air.

"She's the bandit king's daughter." A wispy man gestured with his hand nervously. "I mean Krishan Dev, who's wanted by the police. Can't you see the strong resemblance?"

Meena was about to speak up but was interrupted by a young man puffing a *bidi*. "Can't fool me," he said, removing his hand-rolled cigarette from his mouth. His matted hair smelled of coconut oil. "She's Jaya, the youngest princess of Bikaner. Those bandits were holding her for ransom. Look, how else can she be so pretty and dressed in such fine silk? How else could she have green eyes? If you'll permit me, I'll return her to the royal family."

Green eyes? Mataji had told Meena that she had inherited them from her father, a Pathan from the Northwest Frontier.

"I didn't get a good look at those bandits," the conductor said to the crowd. "But I know who they are. We'll catch them the next time." He motioned to Meena with a gentle wave of his hand. "Come. I'll find you a better seat." He opened the steel door and they slipped into the adjacent coach.

Here the passengers were dozing, one mumbling in his sleep that his goats hadn't come home. Finally, after walking through several cars, they came to one with roomy cushioned seats. It was cool and empty except for a middle-aged couple seated together.

"This is the first-class compartment," the conductor said. "Sleep here tonight. No one will bother you. In the morning, when we get to Delhi, we'll go to the police station. We'll help you find your family."

Meena sat down, noticing for the first time that her skirt was torn, her bodice soiled. How sad that her pretty wedding clothes were in such a sorry state. Slowly she became aware that she was being watched. She raised her head. Two pairs of eyes, the color of a rainy sky, peered down at her. She had never seen blue eyes before.

They were fair of skin, must be Europeans. She had only seen pictures of Europeans in books. The man was taller than Grandfather and balding. The woman, rounder than Mataji, wore a flowered dress and had glasses on. Her lips were hibiscus red, her curls the color of wheat straw with gray touches. A pale wool shawl, much like that worn by the women in Meena's village, was wrapped around her shoulders. Who were they? They were speaking to the conductor in English. Although Meena knew the English alphabet and a few simple words, she was unable to follow the conversation. She became more uneasy every time they stared at her.

The woman reached into her black bag, extracted a confection, and offered it to Meena. It felt rock hard as she held it between her thumb and index fingers, and it was wrapped in a shiny silvery paper so beautiful she couldn't take her eyes off it. She finally opened the package and popped the contents into her mouth. Before long she lay down and fell asleep, lulled by the rhythmic motion of the train, a gingery taste in her mouth.

In the morning, it was the shrill whistle of the train slowing into the Old Delhi station that awakened Meena, not Mataji's usual gentle touch. There was a gray-brown haze outside and the morning was cool. Then she noticed. The woman's wool shawl was spread over her body. It had kept her warm all night.

The couple seemed to watch her every move. Meena avoided their eyes and peered through the window at the scene on the long station platform. Children slept on straw mats unaware that ragged coolies were rushing about with heavy trunks on their heads. Sitting on a bench, a mother somewhat resembling Mataji braided her daughter's hair. Hawkers pushed carts of everything from toys to almond milk, all enticing looking. A beggar with no arms twisted this way and that on the ground, making Meena shiver. So this was Delhi. It was chaotic, overwhelming, terrifying.

The conductor returned. "Were you able to sleep?"

Meena nodded. She was hungry. But even more than nourishment she wanted her family. "When can I go home?"

"As soon as we find out where home is." He talked to the couple for a few minutes, then turned to Meena. "They'll take us to the police station," he said. "Their driver is waiting with a car."

While the conductor finished his duties, Meena waited in the station with the couple. A hawker walked past, his dark eyes peeking from under the large flat woven basket on his head, singing out, *"Jilebi."* Her mouth watered at the smell of the squiggly fritters dipped in syrup. The couple must have noticed, because they called him over and asked for a portion. It was served on a small plate made of interwoven strips of bamboo leaf. Meena broke a *jilebi* apart, stuffed a piece into her mouth, finished the plateful, and licked off every bit of sweetness from the tips of her sticky fingers.

The police station, a drab three-room brick house with a flower garden in front, bustled with khaki-uniformed men, some with rifles over their shoulders. The four of them sat on a hard bench as they waited their turn. At one point the conductor rose, went outside, and returned with cups of tea purchased from a street vendor.

Much later, a police officer emerged from an office and signaled for them to come in. Meena saw a large desk with five glass paper-weights but no paper, several rickety chairs, and ledgers piled haphazardly on the warped floor. A big clock ticked away on the wall. The officer dusted a yellow register, opened it, and began to ask questions.

He spoke first to the conductor in Hindi, which Meena grasped, then to the couple in English, which she couldn't follow. He recorded their answers.

Finally he turned to Meena. "Can you tell me what the bandits look like? Neither the conductor nor this couple have seen them."

Meena began describing them. The officer listened quietly, nodding his head every now and then, finally saying disgustedly, "Those two are up to their old tricks. We'll get them one of these days. What village are you from?"

"Karamgar," she said proudly. "It's in the desert."

"That's northwestern Rajasthan," the conductor added.

"You've come a long way, my dear child." The officer pulled a drawer open, drew out a map, and examined it for several minutes before shaking his head. "There's no such place on the map. Are you sure that's the correct name of your village?"

Of course she was. Meena was about to say so, but the officer cut her off.

"There are over five hundred thousand villages in India. I don't see any post office with that name."

She didn't know about post offices. Mataji didn't get letters.

The officer got up and motioned them to remain seated, saying, "I'll be back shortly."

The clock struck eleven times. Meena grew anxious. Who would help Mataji wash the clothes, pound the grains, and prepare lunch today? Who would pour water in Grandfather's tumbler? Would her teacher think that she skipped school intentionally?

They went through a second round of tea. At last the officer reentered, closed his ledger with a sigh, and said to the conductor, "Here we go again. Another lost child."

"Can't you do something?" the conductor asked.

"No phone, no post office. We can't spare men to search for a village that's not on the map. She can stay here until we can find her an orphanage."

The conductor and the couple began arguing with the officer. Enough of it was in Hindi for Meena to gather that they were trying to persuade the officer to devote more effort to finding her village.

At last the officer held up his hands and said in Hindi, "We just don't have the resources. And her family might not take her back. She has been kidnapped." He paused, glanced at the couple, and said to the conductor, "She would be likely to end up on the street if fate had not brought her to this couple." He conferred with the couple, then handed them forms to sign.

Just like that, everyone stood up. Meena did the same.

The woman squatted next to her so that their eyes were level. She smiled.

"This is Mrs. Gossett," the conductor said to Meena. "And this is Mr. Gossett."

The man looked down at her with a twinkle in his eyes. He and the woman seemed tall and remote and strange. Meena shrank back against the wall.

"These fine people are from America," the conductor said. "They live in Delhi just now. You go with them. They have no children. You're very fortunate."

"I want my Mataji."

"That's not possible," the conductor said. "But don't worry. Mr. and Mrs. Gossett will take good care of you."

Meena looked at the police officer, whose eyes seemed to say: What can we do? This is the best chance you've got.

Meena bristled with rebellion. You can't take me away for very long, she thought. Mataji wouldn't know what to do without me. Vishnu would be broken-hearted. Everyone in the village would miss me. I was born there. I'll get back there before I die. You see, I'm a Rajput.

Book
Two

2

Meena's first day back at work after Mom's death was turning out to be a nightmare. A three-week backlog of paperwork was overflowing from her In basket all over her huge oak desk and the computer monitor in front of her was showing a list of e-mail messages several pages long. The phone rang again.

"Software International," she answered and automatically reached for a notepad. Her telephone cord caught memos and assorted documents and knocked them to the floor. She stifled a long sigh of frustration, swiveled her chair to face the window of her tenth-floor office, and gazed down into the glass and concrete canyons of San Francisco's Financial District. "Meena Gossett here," she said calmly.

"Tomorrow's your big three-five, isn't it?"

Kazuko's ever cheerful voice caused Meena to smile in spite of all. How like Kazuko to remember a friend's birthday. Work could wait. Kazuko was just the person she needed to talk to. Meena relaxed and leaned back in her chair, ready for a long conversation. "You know, I almost forgot."

Saying it made Meena realize how quickly a year had passed. She glanced at her reflection in the glass wall that separated her office from the workstations of her staff. The woman who stared back cut a rather severe figure—aloof, professional, controlled. She hadn't smiled much in weeks. Yet she was somehow glad that she still had her waist-length black hair, her big green eyes, and her bronze coloring.

"Thirty-five is important," Kazuko was saying. "I read in the Berkeley *Bulletin* that we have a new body every seven years. It's like we've shed our— *Oops*. Another call just came in. I'll be right back."

Thirty-five. Five times seven. Could Meena have already passed through five such cycles? On her seventh birthday, the first cycle, she had been married in Karamgar in the shadow of a dust storm only to be kidnapped at the end by bandits. At two times seven, she had won the science award at Lick Wilmerding High School in San Francisco and blossomed into one of the school's "top five" female runners. Mom's feelings had been mixed—being both smart and athletic didn't make sense to her. At three times seven, to Dad's clear delight, she was starting Stanford's graduate program in computer science— and head over heels in love with a motorcycle racer. Mom and Dad didn't understand that part. Meena wasn't sure she did either. At four times seven, she had already been a lead designer at SIC, Software International Company, for five years. Her career was definitely on the fast track and shortly thereafter she was promoted to project manager in charge of COSMOS, a database development system. And now came five times seven just when Mom Gossett, in many ways Meena's only anchor in life, had passed away after a long illness. Yes, her life was in a state of flux.

Suddenly the air-conditioned atmosphere crackled with a certain energy. The black cloud of grief that surrounded her parted. She visualized herself boarding a train that was about to leave the station: destination undetermined, adventure in the air.

"A word of warning." Kazuko was back on the phone. "There'll be a party at my place tomorrow night and you're the guest of honor. Henry and I have been planning it for weeks. It'll be a full house."

Her petite, exuberant friend with the pageboy haircut and three jade studs in each ear was quite her opposite in appearance. But Meena had always had a fondness for Kazuko. Flip at times, Kazuko had heart to spare. She had been there for Meena these nine, no, ten whole years. Even after her marriage to Henry, Kazuko had continued to stay in touch.

Marriage—how single and alone that made Meena feel. Her eyes fell on the gold-framed photo of Charles and Abby Gossett on her desk. Standing close but not touching, each affected a cultivated smile. Her adoptive parents wouldn't be celebrating this one with her. The Polaroid had been taken at their beach cabin just before Dad died eight years ago. Always a background person, he looked thin and a little stooped, his face alert, hinting at the keen intellect within. Mom still had her stiff posture, though she had become stocky as she aged. And those square shoulders. Growing up, Meena had looked at them often when she was afraid to meet Mom's stern eyes. That was usually during a confrontation over some transgression on Meena's part of her strict rules. Mom's expression seemed to have softened. Or was it that Meena had matured and come to understand that she, as an adopted Indian child and strong-willed to boot, wasn't easy to deal with either? How frail and helpless Mom looked in her hospital bed. With the need to exert authority gone, she was far more accessible. Meena finally did achieve a sense of intimacy with her that had been impossible when Mom was younger and more authoritarian. Now Mom's strong presence wouldn't be there anymore to see Meena through life's occasional dark periods.

In a half-conscious effort to distract herself from a depressive line of thought, she reached for a #2 pencil from the tray behind the paper clips in her central drawer.

"I haven't thrown a party since Thanksgiving."

Kazuko's voice brought Meena out of her reverie back to her high-rise office with its ever present subliminal hum of hidden machinery and eye-popping bluish-white fluorescent light. "What should I bring?" she asked.

"Just you, for God's sake. It's your birthday. I've invited the whole gang and, oh"—Kazuko sounded as though she had an afterthought— "Henry's asked a couple of his buddies to show up. No problem, I trust."

Kazuko, samurai matchmaker, had slipped it in smoothly. She had the habit of asking her guests to bring someone "interesting," and then maneuvering the "compatibles" to the same table of hors d'oeuvres. Meena had met at least one nifty guy that way—Carlos came to mind. Nonetheless she said, "Don't do me any favors."

"Why not, Meena-san?" That added "san," the Japanese formal term of address, was a bit stiff for Meena's taste.

"If I get another aerobics teacher who does a headstand on the sidewalk, I'm going to be single for the rest of my life. And that graphoanalyst—his idea of an exciting evening was showing me his interpretation of the handwriting of convicted criminals. The more bizarre the crime, the bigger charge he seemed to get out of it. I think for him it was better than sex."

Kazuko giggled. "You didn't meet either of them through me."

"Maybe I'm just not cut out for California men."

"California is a big state."

"Actually, right now, I don't want to get involved. With Mom gone, I find myself thinking about India. . . ."

"Come off it, Mee-chan," Kazuko said. Meena liked the more intimate "chan" better. "You went through the Indian phase in your teens," Kazuko said.

"The Indian phase," dabbling in things Indian. Yes, but today something different had begun.

"You remember how cold it was for Mom's funeral?" Meena asked. "That was the coldest day of winter."

"Was it? It didn't seem—"

"I hadn't felt that alone since the day I was stolen. Memories kept coming back. I relived my wedding day. Vishnu was beside me."

"Vishnu?" Kazuko sounded incredulous. "You were only seven when you married him."

"But what became of him? Does he remember me? Would he accept me as his wife if we met?"

"Mee-chan!" Kazuko laughed. "He's ten thousand miles away. For sure he has remarried. Maybe she's a widow by now."

"I'd like to track him down," Meena said. Again she looked at her image on the glass wall, touched her cheek, smiled. It was quite an alluring smile. "I keep thinking about him."

"Aren't you about thirty years late?" Kazuko could be tough on idle daydreamers, but Meena knew she aimed to protect. "Don't you think it's time to let go?" Kazuko added.

Meena didn't feel quite so alone. "You know, Mom always had a problem with me returning to India," she said. "She thought if I went there I might catch the plague or something. I told you, her only son died in India in a bus accident. It seemed pointless to upset her."

"What in the world would you go back there for?" Kazuko sounded perplexed. "And how're you going to find Vishnu? India is huge."

"Where there's a will," Meena said impishly, "there's . . . e-mail. Laxmi has lots of contacts. She's an Indian classmate of mine from Stanford. I've gotten occasional e-mails from her since she went back to Bombay. She says the Internet's quite the thing in India."

"Meet Vishnu in cyberspace?" Kazuko said. "That sounds like you.

But what do you know about him?" Her voice had a dark edge of warning. "Look, I'll tell you about Asian men. Japanese men, I should say. You remember my ex, don't you?"

At that point Meena figured she had better end the conversation. Dave Williams, her lead programmer, was standing at her door, program listing in hand. He would have problems for her to look at. "Let's talk later, Kazu-chan," she said. "Someone's here to see me. See you tomorrow night."

"Seven sharp."

Meena said good-bye and motioned Dave to come in, but her mind wouldn't focus on the business at hand. She kept flashing back to her village in India: the mud huts, the well, the colorfully dressed people. Kazuko's advice rang true. But while Meena knew that India was emotionally and culturally light-years away, it was still a promised land to her.

Birthday or not, it was time for a run after work. Meena needed to loosen those knots in her back that came from sitting in her office all day and to put the fragments of her self back together again. Tonight there would a party in her honor and she wanted to be at her best.

She left her apartment at Twenty-fifth Avenue and Fulton, trotted up to Kennedy Drive, then turned east, easing smoothly into full stride. She chose her favorite running course: a bridle trail that wove its way through Golden Gate Park. There was always something new here—a mushroom, a bird's nest, a wildflower patch. The park regenerated itself constantly; it too had its natural cycles.

As her eyes roamed to check traffic, she noticed an artist sitting on the grass sketching a patch of forget-me-nots and a woman in a deep plum sari sweeping past him. How differently women moved in a sari. So much fluidity, control, and grace. Meena felt her own movements were too sharp and angular in contrast.

The sari had been her outfit of choice during her teenage years—her "Indian phase." It was Auntie Bimla who taught her how to wrap herself in a sari as well as to prepare spicy Indian dishes and perform the Hindu religious rituals of *puja*. Meena eagerly went to performances featuring musicians playing ancient instruments like the sitar, sarod, and veena. She watched Kathak dancers as they told tales with nimble fingers, undulating bodies, and subtle facial expressions. Mom's disapproval finally wore Meena down. She didn't have any Indian friends of her age to turn to for support. Thousands of Indians made the Bay Area their home now, but not back then. So saris returned to the bottom drawer of her dresser. Shorts, sweats, and tee shirts came back up on top. Only in the last year or so, had Meena begun to wear saris again, albeit only for the infrequent special occasions.

She rounded a corner and loped into the Rose Garden, a favorite spot to jog through. There was always something to admire here: a perfumey yellow blossom as big as a grapefruit, a tiny red bud delicate as a seashell, yet another with the sheen of a silver spoon. She recalled the last time she had strolled here. It was with Kazuko and their respective dates just before Kazuko met Henry. How long ago that seemed. Double-dating had been fun. They dined, went to shows, and kicked up their heels on the dance floors as though the night were endless. Then Mom became ill and Meena spent every evening in the hospital from seven to ten. The creative flame of software design burned her days. Her only escape was running. Kazuko still called or came over. And now Meena wondered whether she could have gotten through that terrible period without Kazuko's animated support.

Meena took a turn onto a narrow trail carpeted by pine needles. She glided past a pansy bed and through a eucalyptus grove richly permeated with the odor of camphor. She experienced a sense of release and ran effortlessly. The feelings of grief in mourning, which had suffused her consciousness only moments before, dissipated in the breeze. Work woes that had hung over her head evaporated. She felt light, glorious, exuberant.

As usual she'd finish her run with a final lap on the dirt track at the Polo Field. She approached the field just as the late afternoon fog, a predictable event at this time of the year, was descending. Good. It would be cooling. She burst onto the track, picking up her pace, and was soon dripping with perspiration. Dozens of runners of all sizes, shapes, and fitness levels were sharing the track. She passed several as she accelerated into the final turn, but her speed and concentration reduced them to a blur. Just the same, she felt unified with them. We're all equal, she thought. We share the road, the effort, the pain, the ecstasy. How different from the abstract, lonely world of cyber-space where she spent her day.

Now, sprinting all out down the home stretch, she nearly collided with a runner going in the opposite direction. She had a brief impression of a tall, broad-shouldered fellow running powerfully, but clumsily and in the wrong lane. She was distracted and in that moment was outkicked by a cocky high school jock who had perceived her as a challenge. Damn—no way. But it was too late. He beat her by a stride. Then she stopped thinking about it as she spotted Hal, the septuagenarian diehard, shuffling toward her. His white tissue hair and his peculiar gait made him easily recognizable from a distance. Hal had always encouraged her in her running. She smiled warmly and waved at him. The big grin on his face said: I'm happy to be still moving.

Meena slowed to a walk, wiped her face with the bottom edge of her tee shirt, and eventually came to a halt as her breathing returned to normal. A sense of being cleansed came over her. Running had put her mind back in her body. Feeling at peace with herself, she meandered back along a misty path through a stand of eucalyptus toward her apartment.

Skin still tingling from the invigorating needles of the shower, she opened her closet door. Corporate suits, in grays, blacks, and dark blues, took up most of the space, allowing barely enough room for only two fancy dresses and a set of running gear. She settled on the boat-necked three-piece silk dress in apple green, whose color washed her with a feeling of rejuvenation. With its fitted bodice, straight skirt, and matching boxy jacket, the outfit had a tailored look relieved by the lushness of the fabric. She knotted her waist-length hair in a chignon, drew a lipstick across her lips, took a peek at her image in the mirror, jammed a lip balm and her keys in a beaded evening purse, and was out the door in minutes.

It was sunset as Meena drove north on Twenty-fifth and then east on California Street with its rows of pastel houses all the same height pressed together like toy train cars. Kazuko's two-story, five-bedroom golden stucco house was always easy to spot because of the Japanese rock garden in front. On the sidewalk Meena stopped momentarily to contemplate the moss that had grown over a boulder and watch one of Kazuko's cats do a luxurious stretch. She heard the merry laughter that rippled from an open window, like bells announcing the arrival of good times. She inhaled the sharp pungent odor of ginger sizzling in hot oil. Kazuko sure knew how to throw a party. She had the knack of finding a theme, pulling together the right people, hiring the best caterer, then stepping back and letting things take their course. Tonight would be Meena's night. Friends would welcome her with big hugs and ask her about her life. In her current mood, she'd love the attention, though in the back of her mind there lurked a sense of misgiving at something yet unknown. She hadn't attended a party or dated in a while. Could she still make eye contact, greet people, engage them in small talk? She braced herself, drew in a deep breath, decided to have a grand time, and strode through the door with a smile.

They were there, all of Meena's friends plus a few new faces, standing, jostling, circulating in Kazuko's living room. Candles, flower vases, and trays of tidbits were placed at every corner. As Meena crossed the threshold, a hip-length blue kimono painted with clouds and chrysanthemums pushed toward her on a pair of legs in black velvet jeans. A fashion designer might want to copy this ensemble, Meena mused, not surprised to find it was Kazuko. Her footfalls were butterfly-light; only her toes touched the floor. In one arm Kazuko held a platter of ultra-thin stuffed mushroom canapés; with the other she gave Meena a hug. There was a reassuring closeness in her touch.

Behind her came her husband, Henry. Garrulous himself, he was still glad for Kazuko to open the way. His Brooks Brothers suit was probably put on only half an hour before, but it was already a little wrinkled. As usual the blond, red-cheeked insurance agent was smoking. In an hour he'd fill an ashtray. His puffing habit annoyed Meena, but he was good for Kazuko. Ever since their marriage, Kazuko hadn't stopped smiling.

Henry removed his cigarette long enough to press his lips to Meena's hand and whisper, "Happy birthday, Meena." That was all. The words somehow sounded impersonal. Meena had never felt connected to him.

"Meena!" she heard and looked up. From the far corner of the room Carlos blew her a kiss and went back to looking suave. A linen blazer accentuated his olive brown skin. His gelled, designer-cut hair resembled a museum statue head. His most astonishing feature, though, was his erect stance. He was proud of being Carlos. And proud always of his latest flame. Tonight he was arm-in-arm with a woman wearing maple red hair coiled atop her head and a slinky white gown.

Kazuko put a hand in Meena's arm and steered her toward a tall Nordic woman, not *People*-magazine pretty but a commanding presence with short hair, impenetrable eyeglasses, and a smart gray suit.

"Remember the seal painting in the North Beach Gallery?" Kazuko asked. "Here's the artist, Anna Christiansen." She made the introduction.

"I hear you're having a new exhibit," Meena said to Anna, as Kazuko, always the good hostess, faded away and gave the two women a chance to talk.

Presently a voice floated to Meena over her shoulder. "You look fabulous tonight."

There stood Carlos. "Keep that smile." He grinned, pecked her cheek, then was off with his companion.

Typical Carlos, Meena thought. She had known him for five years. He was charming and always great company, a special friend. No romance between them—Carlos was a little flighty with women. Meena knew any love relationship with him would be temporary, but a camaraderie could be forever. She told herself again she preferred the latter.

Kazuko reappeared and took Meena by the hand. Kisses and smiles descended from all directions as Kazuko led her to the dining room. No one else was there, Meena noted with relief. Already overwhelmed, she needed quietness, time to collect herself. She hadn't known how it would feel to be out in a crowd so soon after Mom's death.

The long dining table had been covered with linen in a shade of green that made all food look extra appetizing. The centerpiece was African violets with neat purple petals peeking from a row of identical brass pots. Oddly, for Kazuko's house, they looked a little droopy. On the left were finger foods, from sushi to stuffed grape leaves. On the right were tulip-painted porcelain teacups, pink sugar cubes, and lemon wedges wrapped in yellow muslin. Bottles of vintage champagne cooled in a silver tub of ice. Meena remembered how Kazuko had so often talked of perfection being ingrained in her as a young girl growing up in a Japanese-American household. She had arranged the table just the way Meena liked, simply and elegantly. "It's beautiful!" Meena exclaimed.

She wondered, though, why Kazuko had led her in here. Did she appear as hungry as those wilted violets that could use a big gulp of water?

Another guest was at the front door and Kazuko dashed to greet him. Meena took the opportunity to slip into the kitchen to fetch water. She returned to find a lone man standing pensively before the table. She had seen him somewhere, this fortyish Anglo-American, tall and solid but not heavy. His mass of walnut brown hair was fashionably disheveled. Other men his age must envy him his hair. Clad in a checked poplin shirt and khaki trousers, he was certainly the most dressed-down man at her birthday party. But he seemed perfectly sure of himself. He had presence. She wondered who he thought he was.

She stepped up to water the violets, pretending to be concerned only about their condition, but half noticed the platter in his hand.

"Do you see a place for this?"

Was Mr. Tall and Confident asking this because she was a woman? Or was he bewildered by the wide array of delicacies, as single men sometimes were? Meena pushed silverware aside to make room and said, "Maybe right here."

She was ready to return to the living room to be with her friends, but was stopped by a spicy warmth floating in the air. It came from the platter he had just set down. Chunks of rosy potatoes coated with brown spices, splashed with green. Auntie Bimla had made this dish. *"Aloo chaat,"* she found herself saying. "I haven't had *aloo chaat* in ages."

He fixed his blue eyes on her. She had to notice them. Eyes that had seen much and stored it all. Eyes with a hint of suffering in the downturned corners. Meena mentally searched for that shade of blue. Sapphires, blueberries, forget-me-nots. None were a match.

He said, "I was taught how to make *chaat* in Jaipur."

The capital of Rajasthan. He knew her home. Well, almost. And they were alone in a room. Conniving Kazuko had a hand in this, Meena was sure.

She asked casually, "Oh? When were you there?"

"It's been twenty-plus years," he said. "There was a *chaat* stall right in front of the campus of the University of Rajasthan. Every morning I used to stand there and watch a man named Pillu toss boiled potatoes with black salt, chili pepper, and everything else. That was breakfast and lunch. I used to tell him, 'Pillu, if you came to America, you'd make millions.' "

He went to college in India? Ate from street vendors? Learned to prepare *chaat?* There were more layers to his personality, she guessed, and he was showing only the top. She felt warm, tingly, and tense. Was it sexual tension, the vitality he oozed, or that the window needed to be opened to ventilate the room? She stroked the two bobby pins beside her ears that anchored her hair.

He asked, "You're from India, aren't you?"

She nodded a yes.

"When did you come over?"

"When I was seven." And an image of camels flooded her mind. That had never happened before. "I'm from Karamgar," she said. "In the western part of Rajasthan. Near the Great Thar Desert."

"I didn't travel there. I hear the desert's beautiful." He offered a hand. His grip was warm, solid, and tight. "My name's Antoine."

Antoine. French. An unusual name for this all-American type.

Antoine must have read her unspoken thought, for he said, "I was born in France. Dad was teaching there. Mother liked everything French. So she named me Antoine."

"My name is Meena."

"Did I see you in the park wearing a Bay-to-Breakers tee shirt?"

Oh my God, that threadbare tee, blotched with sweat. She flushed. "Yes, I run in the park."

"You're a speedster."

"I did cross-country in school. Do you run too?"

"Run?" He laughed. "I slow-jog. I'm just getting back after a long layoff, doing a couple miles every few days. I need to up my distance." He patted his belt. "I live in Marin. Way too much food there—"

"Food has replaced sex in Marin County." Henry had appeared, holding a cigarette box in his palm. "I read that somewhere."

Antoine's lips widened in an amused smile. His eyes took on a deeper shade, a crystalline blue, now that he was playful.

"Have you two been introduced?" Henry asked. "Meena, I'd like you to meet Antoine Peterson, my friend from when we were kids. I'm sure you've heard of his latest book, *Parallel Lives*. Last week the *Chronicle* raved about it. Antoine, meet Meena Gossett, software expert, guest of honor of this party."

At the mention of software, Antoine seemed to wince. "I'm afraid I use a computer only when absolutely necessary. And I'm probably the only person here who's never been near the Internet."

Ah, Meena realized, an author. Good God. How could she not remember the name Antoine Peterson? She asked, "Did you write a poem in *The New Yorker* about begonias forgetting to bloom one summer?"

"You read poetry?" Antoine said. "You're an endangered species."

"And your book?" Meena asked. "Is it a thriller?"

His confidence seemed to melt in a shy smile. "A literary novel, I'm afraid."

"I have to read it," Meena said. "I'm spending far too much time on computer manuals."

Henry said, "You'll have to forgive our Nethead—"

Nethead. Meena didn't like that label, one of many she seemed to have acquired. She was preparing a riposte when Anna, the artist, came up to say, "Carlos is looking for you, Meena. He wants to dance. The samba. Excuse us."

With that Anna took Meena's hand and steered her out the door. Meena could feel Antoine's eyes on her back as she left. She wasn't ready to leave him either. At the same time, she sensed Henry didn't want her there.

In the next room brisk bouncy samba music reverberated from the walls. As usual women were clustered around Carlos. Three of them this time.

"Forward, side, together." Hips swaying, eyes flashing, Carlos was demonstrating the steps. He was crisp and elegant. Worth watching, Meena had to admit to herself.

"One and two, two and two—" Carlos spotted Meena. "Want to do some moves, señorita?" He winked. "No dance, no life."

Meena laughed. "Remember the dance-a-thon I went to with you, Carlos? Tell me what happened."

"You broke your foot."

"I couldn't run for three months. I'd rather just watch."

Carlos took his jacket off, pulled a red bandanna from his hip pocket, tied it around his neck. "My dad always says, 'You have to break a toe or something once in a while. How else would you know it was there?' "

"Remind me not to dance with your father either."

Later Meena drifted to the dining room to find Henry and Anna discussing wine, Carlos and his date orbiting the table, and Kazuko mingling with other guests. Meena floated along, sampled a cheese cube and a grape, then found her hand reaching to the *chaat* plate. With a pick she speared a chunky potato and popped it into her mouth. Oh, the tang of lime, the pleasant bitterness of roasted cumin, the pungent jolt of cilantro! Where was the *chaat* connoisseur now? She wanted to compliment him on his cooking, talk to him more about running, poetry, India. She glanced about the room, smiling at her friends, all the while checking for Antoine's tall frame and brown hair. He didn't seem to be around. Why, with all the friends who were here, did this disappoint her so?

Kazuko burst out from the kitchen with a layered chocolate cake ablaze with tiny candle flames. A folly was a better name for it, garnished as it was with green pistachios, dried cranberries, and fresh raspberries. Kazuko glowed with pride as she showed it around.

Henry and Anna became quiet, Carlos stopped munching, and everyone turned toward Meena. Carlos took her hand and started singing "Happy Birthday." Meena flashed a smile. She held a secret wish in her mind as she blew out the candles.

"O-tanjobi omedeto gozaimasu." Her voice merry, Kazuko gave a slight bow.

"Many happy returns," came from Henry.

Carlos said, *"Felicidades."*

"Joyeux anniversaire," said his date, adding that French was her favorite language.

This made Meena think again of Antoine. Her eyes scouted the room once more. Had he left? she wondered. Why so soon? Wasn't that rude? Anyway, why was she worrying at this beautiful moment?

Champagne corks popped. Carlos lifted his glass. "To Meena."

She cut the cake and placed the wedges in scallop-edged dessert plates, saving a big piece for herself. With a forkful in her mouth, she shut her eyes. Silky smooth, gooey sweet, pleasantly bitter at the edges. The cake took away all other sensations for an instant. It tasted even better than Kazuko's last cake.

Suddenly Meena sniffed the air, opened her eyes. Tobacco smoke. Henry of course. He was standing a few feet away, a fresh Marlboro in hand. Meena started to cough. She needed fresh air.

She made her way through the study, then down the hallway to the living room. Carlos was standing over the CD system alone, nibbling on his cake and tapping his foot to the Mexican music playing. The rich strains pulled her. Carlos had played the same music at Kazuko's Thanksgiving party, Meena remembered.

"Meenaji," Carlos said, taking her in his arms. "Let's dance." She liked that -ji, an Indian honorific that he had learned from her.

He danced rather well, and now that she was in a better mood, Meena found the offer hard to resist. "Where's your date?" she wondered aloud.

"She had to leave early." Carlos moved toward the side table where two sombreros sat. He seemed to have come prepared. He settled one onto her head, then the other one on his own. "Follow my steps," he said with a tilt of his head, putting on a Spanish accent, assuming the manner of a coach.

Hands on hips, she followed his controlled, elegant gestures. Now and then she let her attention stray from the dance floor to the door, hoping for Antoine to emerge. Which was a bit silly, she admitted to herself, especially with Carlos being so attentive. Palms clasped behind him, he now whirled around her, leaning slightly forward. Sparks in his eyes, a radiant smile on his lips, he watched her as if entranced. Was this a dance of courtship?

The music increased its tempo and Meena was transported by its rhythm to a vast open place with moonlight, a benign breeze, and bare earth. Suddenly she was a young Rajasthani girl, dancing shoeless on warm sand. She stopped thinking and just moved, giving herself to the movements, becoming one with the rich dense sounds. By the time they stopped, she was sweaty, exhilarated, spent but full.

"I could stay up all night dancing," Carlos was saying.

Meena's mind snapped back to the room. "Thanks, amigo." She stared at her watch. "Oh my, it's midnight. I need a glass of water." What she really needed was to get away, to absorb this experience, to linger on its pleasure.

In the kitchen an aproned Kazuko was loading dishes into the dishwasher. Smiling, she examined Meena's flushed face. Meena noticed how keen Kazuko's eyes were even at this late hour.

"Did you meet Antoine Peterson?" Kazuko asked offhandedly.

"The hot novelist? Yes, briefly. He just seemed to vanish into thin air."

"He had to take his friend, Liv, to the airport. She flies to New York a lot on business."

"Friend?"

"Partner, fiancée, liaison, whatever the latest word for it is. She lives down the street. I've met her a couple of times. Henry knows her better than I do. He seems to think they make a good pair. But if you ask my opinion, she's not the right one for Antoine. What did you think of him, by the way?"

The floor wobbled under Meena for a moment and there was a ripple in her stomach. It had not been easy for someone of her natural reserve to open up to a stranger, especially after so many months of solitude. But she had done it—only to discover he was committed to another. She should have expected that of someone like Antoine, who was famous, a little arrogant, and not at all bad-looking. Yet he had acted like he was available. . . . For reasons she didn't fully understand, she was drawn to him in a powerful way. And look where it had led her. A relationship that was history before it even got started.

The next moment her practical self took over. So what was the big deal? Weren't Kazuko's parties always a trip to Fantasyland? A late morning daydream, the frothy top of a cappuccino, a surprise flower bouquet at the door. In a few days he'd be just a dim memory, just one more interesting conversation at a party. Actually she should be grateful to savvy Kazuko for hosting this one, Meena said to herself. At least it had gotten her out of her funk. She hadn't been in such high spirits since Mom fell ill. To Kazuko Meena said, "Well . . . his *chaat* was pretty good."

"He cooks a lot of Indian dishes," Kazuko said.

Just then Carlos burst in. "Meenaji, let me walk you to your car."

Meena embraced Kazuko and murmured, "How can I ever thank you?" She stepped out the door, Carlos beside her. The night was cool, clear, and still. The moon veiled part of its face like a coy maiden. At her car Meena reached down to unlock it.

"May I give you a birthday kiss?" Carlos asked. The glow in his dark, liquid eyes accentuated by the moonlight gave the question a slight sense of urgency.

Before Meena could respond, he drew her closer, his lips meeting hers lightly at first, then more boldly. Gently Meena pushed away. She had a compartment in her heart for Carlos, but not the one marked "passion."

"Every kiss is a message, amigo," she said. "I think I know what you want. That's not meant for us to share."

"What about our dance?"

True, she had put her body and soul into that dance. But she wasn't dancing for Carlos, she was back being a young girl in Rajasthan. "I was just dancing, Carlos."

"And superbly," he responded. "It makes you even more attractive, Meena. And more of an enigma." After a pause he added, "What are you looking for?"

4

"I have no choice but to fire you," P. Sen said.

The words hit Vishnu Chauhan like a vicious blow to the stomach. Sitting in the cramped, windowless executive office of *India News*, he stared blankly at the wall beyond Sen's shoulder, bare except for a faded calendar from last year and an alert little lizard that regarded him impassively from one corner. The heat on this spring day was so intense that one could fry an egg on the footpath outside, Vishnu thought.

P. Sen, his boss of three weeks, was a tall, imposing, patrician figure educated at Cornell University. He came from one of Calcutta's richest families. Vishnu had yet to learn what the letter "P" stood for. Could it be *paapee*, meaning a sinner who would acquire bad karma? Vishnu's mother had taught him that important word when he was a child.

Even though his head was still reeling and his throat felt like blotting paper, Vishnu decided he'd try to reason with P. Sen. "But how can you fire me, sir?" he asked. "I know this newspaper from the ground up. After ten years here, covering everything from politics to sports, I've built up a wealth of contacts. That has served the paper well."

Vishnu knew that as a journalist he was well respected. But he was also aware that the charge against him had nothing to do with his competence. Rather it was his honesty that had done him in. His weekly column, for which he spent hours of his own time investigating, was devoted to ferreting out corruption and abuse of power by government and business officials. It was avidly read by Calcutta's English-speaking elite.

Last week's column had been an exposé of Best Ghee, a manufacturer of vegetable shortening, in which he had detailed the company's sordid practice of adulterating its product with low-grade oil and harmful chemicals. The ghee looked shiny and appetizing, but it had proven to be dangerous when consumed. There were numerous reports of children and the elderly becoming mysteriously ill. Vishnu had discovered that the common thread connecting these reports was the use of Best Ghee. Yet through flashy packaging and clever advertising the company was outselling other similar, but possibly more pure, products on the market. It was especially outrageous since cooking oil was one of the most basic items in a family's kitchen.

Vishnu was about to become a victim of his own success. For several days rumors had swirled through the office that the president of Best Ghee, a wealthy industrialist named Patiala, had met with P. Sen and demanded Vishnu's resignation. The rumor further said that Mr. Patiala was considering buying a controlling interest in the newspaper, whose sales lagged behind its only rival, the *Calcutta Times*.

"I can prove from my interviews that Best Ghee has substandard ingredients in it," Vishnu continued hopefully.

"You should know that I've talked to some of the workers you interviewed." P. Sen's close-set eyes narrowed to tiny black slits. "They all deny speaking with you."

Vishnu wished his previous editor, Bal Murti, hadn't retired. Bal had approved this article. In fact, the column had been his idea to start with. He had stood by Vishnu through similar sticky situations uncovered in his past columns. There was the case of sexual abuse by the proprietor of a girls' hostel, and the one involving a top government official who had charged a servant with jewelry theft and left him languishing in jail even after his wife admitted locating the missing items. Yet another case involved a woman being fondled in a crowded Calcutta bus by the head of a rape prevention squad, the infamous "Eve-teasing" scandal.

But all Vishnu's previous achievements apparently meant nothing now. Looking at P. Sen, Vishnu saw an enormous ego. The man wanted to surround himself with his own people. For all Vishnu knew, he might have been set up.

"But . . ." Vishnu stammered, still trying to placate his boss, "the story boosted our sales. And my job is to report the truth."

"I'm sure you're aware that Best Ghee is one of our biggest advertisers," P. Sen said. "Next year a good ten percent of our advertising income will come from them."

Then this was truly the end? The cold reality and its ramifications began to sink into Vishnu's consciousness. No job meant no money. Well, he'd manage—but his mother, the only parent he had left, and her relatives in Rajasthan would suffer. The substantial money order he sent her every month supported them all. He was also financing the building of a new temple in his village. A twinge of pain ran through his chest. His palms became wet.

"You can check the topics I've laid out for the rest of the year, sir—"

P. Sen interrupted. "I didn't think you'd be this upset."

Of course Vishnu would be upset. This job wasn't just a way of earning a living, it was his life. He investigated and exposed corruption and injustice, saw himself as a friend of the oppressed. Coming from the obscure settlement of Karamgar, he felt a deep sympathy for the voiceless commoners who suffered because of the callousness of the powerful. He had built a solid career on writing about the wrongs that could be righted, or so he had made himself believe.

Abruptly P. Sen stood up behind his desk. His lean frame reminded Vishnu of a whip about to descend. "You have half an hour to clear out your desk. Stop by the cashier. I've given you an extra month's salary."

Vishnu stumbled out of P. Sen's office, his head floating, almost disjointed from his body, but still up. He knew what he had done was right and he'd continue writing the same way. But now he'd be known as a controversial reporter, one who could jeopardize a publication's income. He doubted that the other English paper in town, the *Calcutta Times*, would hire him.

Vishnu ignored the greeting of a colleague who was sipping tea at the standup counter of the office canteen and pretended to be rushing out on a research trip. He stalked his way across the large room equipped with computer monitors and returned to his own desk, which was hidden by stacks of paper, paperweights, and files. He had no box to pack his belongings. Why would he need one? He slipped just a few newspaper clippings in an envelope and strode out into the hallway. He could write anywhere about anything just using a pen and paper and his wit. He made no farewells. It was better that way.

At the wrought-iron gate, he turned to look at the large brick building built during the days of the British Empire. Every morning the huge block-lettered sign on top of the building, INDIA NEWS, had welcomed him to his own little kingdom. Now for the last time his eyes caressed the smooth rounded Corinthian columns. The gate latch clicked shut like a chord containing a wrong note. The promising career that had made Mother and his village proud was ended.

The day passed slowly. Vishnu sat in his tiny apartment, fixed in a sunken armchair like a fly stuck in a bucket of molasses. Then the next day, and the next. He didn't answer the phone, couldn't concentrate on reading anything serious. The endless week dragged on. Finally, when boredom replaced numbness, he thumbed through the classifieds in the paper. It appeared as though companies wanted systems analysts, programmers, or receptionists, not a journalist.

He pushed the paper aside and picked up a copy of *CineBlast*, a trashy magazine for movie fans he had bought several weeks ago to keep track of who's who in Bollywood, the Bombay film industry. This might amuse him. Or maybe not? On the cover a muscular male actor, his body barely covered, sat on a motorcycle with what cinema jargon called a "devil-may-care smile." Ugh. Why would any man want to resort to this kind of modeling? Was it only money? He flipped to a page inside. There, beneath a color shot of a bosomy actress, was a small advertisement.

EDITOR WANTED
Leading Women's Erotica Magazine seeks an
open-minded editor
Man or woman with "experience"

He shoved *CineBlast* aside. Rubbish. He couldn't believe he would even consider a position with a magazine that advertised here.

It took only three days for him to change his mind. By Saturday the idea came to him that perhaps he was being too particular. The idea of an erotic magazine for women was new. He didn't want to admit it, but in time its circulation probably would surpass that of the *India News*. He began working on his résumé, chewing the end of his pencil—an old habit from school—as the hours rolled by. At long last he took it to the postbox. As soon as he slid the envelope in, he bit his thumb. He loathed himself for being so desperate.

The next day a friend called to inform him that the *Calcutta Times* wasn't hiring, but that a correspondent job in Kashmir had opened up at the Delhi office of the *Hindustan Times*. Vishnu frowned. Kashmir, the Muslim-majority state in the northern region, was still the Indian subcontinent's undecided territory. Once it was a beautiful land of glass-clear lakes, quiet snow-laden mountains, and cheerful merchants in red turbans. Now separatists were demanding an independent state and planning to boycott the next general election. Arson, bombing, and riots were everyday occurrences there. Still, he mailed his résumé to the *Hindustan Times*. After all, he had applied to an erotic magazine.

What to do next? Vishnu had always lived simply and had little in his apartment to occupy himself. A bed, two chairs, a table, and some books were the only amenities. He picked up a teak box inlaid with brass wires that his mother had given him, the only knickknack he had. He invested important papers, family pictures, and a sandstone pebble from Meena in this "memory box." As he opened it, his mind returned to the old days—days that, in contrast to the present time, seemed gentler and certainly more colorful.

It was dawn, the day after his wedding, and he was only seven years old. An agitated voice awakened him. His eyes flew open to Mother, who sat by his bedside with tears on her eyelashes like morning dew on grass. "Meena's missing," she cried.

"You're lying." He leapt out of the bed and slapped Mother on the face. He had never done anything like that before.

Mother seized him by the arms, controlled him, and slowly broke the rest of the news. Meena's grandfather had returned to the village alone and recounted the story of the girl's kidnapping.

Within the hour the whole village poured in through their door, bearing fruit, tea, incense, and comforting words. But an argument soon broke out. Janu's mother screamed at Vishnu's parents for deserting Meena and her family and held them accountable for Meena's mother's death. Half the village sided with her. "By now Meena must be dead, too," they declared. "It's a tragedy. They are both martyrs."

The other half of the village insisted that Meena had been sold to a pimp. "She has ruined her family's reputation," they maintained. "She'll be an outcast from now on. If you mention her name, you'll have to rinse your mouth with water from River Ganga."

Partly to protect herself, Vishnu's mother joined the latter camp. She didn't refer to Meena by name anymore.

Only Pundit, the priest who had married them, discounted both versions of the story. "I had a dream last night," he offered. "Meena was sitting on a sandalwood throne in a grand palace, a gold crown on her head. She was happy and smiling. Her *atma* is too powerful to be destroyed at this young age. Believe me, she'll return one day. We'll all be so proud. Take good care of her. I might not be here to receive her then."

Auntie Teelu concurred with Pundit. "She'll never forget her home. She'll be back. I know she'll be back."

The whole incident so shocked Vishnu that for the next several days he felt neither hunger nor pain, only emptiness.

Within a month both Meena's grandfather and Pundit died—of heartbreak, many were sure. Some neighbors boycotted Vishnu's family, stoned their windows, and refused to sell them rice. One night the family barn caught fire from an unknown cause. To compensate, Vishnu turned to his studies and became the brightest boy in his class. He forgot all about Meena until he reached fourteen. Then his best friend, who had been married the same day, had his wife move in with him. Vishnu sank into a dark mood again.

"It doesn't matter," Mother said. "We'll find you another bride, just as beautiful."

When those words didn't work, she contacted a relative in the next village whose cousin's son-in-law lived in Jaipur, the capital of the state, and shipped Vishnu off there. He arrived at the Jaipur bus station with a relative and was overwhelmed by the racket, the crowd, the blade-sharp jolt of the unfamiliar. In the days that followed, he scanned the face of every pretty girl he chanced to meet. "Meena?" he would cry out. But each time it was a stranger who looked at him oddly.

During his college years, he appealed to plenty of girls. Though dating wasn't common in those days, girls and boys mingled together in groups, exchanged glances, breathed heavily in each other's presence. Occasionally he'd pair up with a girl, slip out to the cinema and hold hands after the lights were dimmed. There would be a few kisses after the intermission. Little by little he buried Meena—a precious pearl of a pain—deep within.

Upon his winning an essay contest on the subject of the future of computing in India, Vishnu was offered his first job by the contest sponsor, *India News*, an English daily. That position would take him to Calcutta, a megalopolis in the east clear across the country where "intellectual" Bengalis lived. Vishnu knew the city boasted many English readers, but he didn't want to relocate to a place so far away. He was quite happy in Jaipur. He had always lived in this state. But the only newspaper in Jaipur was the Hindi regional *Patrika*, with a limited circulation. His teachers advised him that he shouldn't pass up this opportunity to improve his command of the emerging world language, and so he finally accepted the offer.

At his new job in Calcutta he was assigned a desk next to a woman reporter coincidentally named Meena. She was older than him and so overweight that the gold chain she wore disappeared in the folds of her neck. She yelled at the teaboy for spilling tea on the saucer. But there was something about her. It was the name. Meena. Ruby tiara and red silk skirt; yellow marigolds and juicy *laddoos*. Meena.

His memories weren't as hidden as he thought. He'd begin researching a story and find himself instead paging through old newspaper files for information on kidnapped and missing persons. He mentioned this to a relative, who told his cousin, who informed Mother in Karamgar.

"Forget her," she wrote to him. "After all these years. Sometimes it's better not to know."

Vishnu never took Mother's advice, believing Meena was alive and that someday he'd rejoin her, make it up to her. Like many of his college-educated classmates he had turned away from religion. He did, however, believe in the meaning of his own name. Vishnu, the god who preserves.

And yet he and his family had failed to save Meena.

At the end of a workday, his head aching from too many facts, the incessant clicking sound of the keyboard, and dealings with irritating colleagues, he'd see the absurdity of his urban life. His village of Karamgar had metamorphosed too. The population had doubled. The place now appeared on local maps. There was a post office. Yet life there still consisted of the basics. What would it be like, Vishnu occasionally wondered, to live there again? To come home to a small brick house. Meena dashing about. Tall and thin and vivacious, her lower eyelids outlined with kohl, her shiny long tresses hanging loose down her back. Their children scampering about her feet—a boy for sure and, oh yes, a girl too. A goat for milk. A well for water. A mango tree named after his boy.

All this wasn't just a pipe dream, Vishnu believed. Such a life could materialize for him, if only he could overcome the obstacles placed in his path—like his separation from Meena.

A deep burning desire formed inside him and, oh, what happiness it promised to bring.

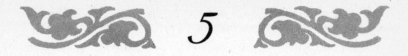

5

The week after his dismissal from *India News*, Vishnu decided it was time to go out into the town. He changed into a white short-sleeved shirt and fawn-colored trousers and surveyed himself in the mirror. He wasn't the kind of man who had a terrific build, straggly hair, and wore a leather jacket and rode a motorcycle with a proud helmet on his head: the kind women swooned over these days. He was slender, with medium dark skin, no more than average height, strong of leg from having played soccer in school. His features might be said to be handsome. A woman friend had told him in a tender moment that a look into his eyes made her want to "turn into a rose."

This morning the postman had left him two letters: an aerogram from his mother and an envelope from the erotic magazine. He crammed the first in his pocket and breathlessly opened the second. The printed stationery had a nude couple as its logo and the words "Flaunt Your Body, Expand Your Mind" as the footer. The typed note read "Does not meet our needs." He crumpled the sheet into a ball and threw it into the dustbin in the courtyard.

"Vishnuuu . . ." he heard a woman's voice call behind him. His neighbor Asha? Couldn't be. At this time of the day Asha would be attending classes at Presidency College. It was another young woman, the one with a sullen mouth from the floor above. Not half as pretty as Asha, but he knew she was interested. She let her washing, including her brassiere, hang just over his window. He put his palms together to greet her, but spared no words, then with today's *India News* under his arm he emerged onto the Ballygunge Circular Road.

The morning fog was just lifting. The neighborhood was coming alive with the jingling of rickshaw bells and clatter of buses. For ten years he had lived here. He strolled up the block.

"*Salaam,* Vishnu-sahib." The white-bearded herbal doctor, the tassel on his fez bouncing, bowed a greeting to Vishnu from his shop. Gazing at the herb bottles on the wall shelf, the doctor added, "You look pale. Perhaps you should come in for a checkup. I have herbs to lower cholesterol, roots to cure impotence—"

Vishnu smiled. "I wish my problems were so simple."

He saluted and took a few strides down the road only to meet an emaciated woman with a filthy infant in one arm. She extended her stick-thin hand, beseeching money in a quavering voice. The boy's lower eyelids were smeared with kohl to keep away the evil spirits. Poor as the mother was, she loved her son enough. Feeling sympathy, Vishnu rummaged in his pocket, found some coins, and placed them on her palm. She looked at him, touched her forehead with the coins, uttered a word of appreciation, then moved toward another passerby.

The clothing shop owner across the street stood in his doorway, tilting his face to a sky obscured by a gray-brown haze. Palms together, he saluted the sun, mumbling a prayer for a prosperous day. When Vishnu neared, the shopkeeper waved at him. "Come here, Vishnu-babu. What's the hurry?" With that came an offer to make trousers at a discount. "Want to look like a cinema star?" the man said. "I can do that in a day's time."

"If I get that bonus—" Vishnu answered automatically. It was a game the two of them played every day.

He crossed the street. Along the footpath a fruit vendor was arranging pineapple, papaya, and coconut. He gestured to Vishnu. "Coconut water, babu-sahib?"

The water inside the coconut, kept cool by its hard shell, would be a sweet, refreshing beverage on this already warm spring day and possibly the most pure that could be found in the city. Besides, the man needed the business. But Vishnu was on a tight budget. "Maybe later."

"I'll hold one for you."

Vishnu had never been above talking to the street people, those ignored by the upper class and the educated. For that reason this simple man from a nearby village liked him and always saved an extra juicy coconut for him.

Calcutta's heart dwelled in these neighborhoods. Even a bachelor like Vishnu living alone was part of the community. Calcutta was for real. This was his city.

A car slowed alongside him. "Taxi?" the driver called.

No, Vishnu indicated with a gesture of his hand. During his years as a reporter, he hired taxis all the time to get quickly around the sprawling metropolis. How secure, important he felt then. Today he took the subway and a bus.

He got off across from Presidency College. For thinkers it was the center of Calcutta, a warren of schools, colleges, and bookstores. He glanced, as usual, along the stalls lining the footpath carrying English-language books of all sorts. He'd like to browse. But first, a cup of coffee and the newspaper to relax. The Coffee House, the gathering place of Calcutta's intelligentsia, stood before him. He trotted up the worn stairs to a large high-ceilinged room badly in need of paint but with the grace of a once-noble older woman. The smell of rich strong coffee roamed the air.

At a table by the entrance a happy cluster of young people, possibly students from Presidency College, discoursed in fluent English on the mathematical meaning of infinity. How he, Vishnu Chauhan, would like to be a student again! At other tables scattered about the room writers, artists, and politicians congregated, speaking in a babble of Bengali, Hindi, Tamil, Marathi, English, and who knew what other languages or dialects. Vishnu spoke Hindi, Rajasthani, and English, but he liked listening to some of the other cadences: shrill, guttural, like speaking with a marble in the mouth. Hearing them spoken was like taking a foreign trip without having to carry a passport.

Over there, a pale-faced, blond Westerner, his backpack propped against a chair, scribbled on postcards, wearing a smile that said he had left the obligations of his real life behind. How did he manage to do that?

Vishnu settled himself at a table in the rear. He'd have his privacy here. A familiar waiter, magnificent in a white tunic and turban, approached. "Coffee, sir?"

The waiter returned with a small cup on a tray and set it down on the table. Vishnu began sipping the dark, potent brew slowly. Normally a tea drinker, he drank coffee only when he visited this establishment. Today he felt the caffeine strike his chest. Now that he was sufficiently alert, he drew Mother's letter out of his pocket.

The postmark indicated that it had taken two weeks to arrive from Karamgar. Oh, that village post office, still not keeping a regular schedule. He could tell by the handwriting that the scribe this time was his mother's cousin's wife. Mother didn't know how to write. He ripped open the aerogram and unfolded the single sheet. The thin paper crinkled in his hands, sounding like Mother's bangles rubbing against each other.

> My dear Vishnu,
>
> Three days ago, I slipped and fell in front of our house and broke my right hip. I have been bedridden since. Having spent your last month's money order on the wedding of my cousin's daughter, I had to borrow a thousand rupees to pay the hospital and hire a full-time servant. Could you wire me some money right away? And please add an extra thousand rupees for whitewashing our new temple.

His severance pay wouldn't cover both. Vishnu put the letter on the table and rested his eyes in the cradle of his palm for a second before continuing to read.

> Son, I hope your health is good and your job is going well.
>
> How I wish I knew English, for then I would be able to read your articles. I run my fingers over the clippings you sent me. It feels like touching your hand. Did I tell you I keep them locked in my trunk along with my jewelry and my best saris? I show them to relatives when they come to visit. I am so proud of you.
>
> > Your mother

Vishnu read the letter again to listen to her voice, folded it, and put it back into his pocket. He wouldn't answer her quite yet. She wouldn't understand his situation. To her, unemployment of any duration was shameful. And, Vishnu shuddered to think, with the job market being the way it was, it could take him months to find a journalist's position of similar status.

He took another swallow of coffee, unfolded the newspaper, and skimmed the column on the third page. It had been written by his replacement, Sukumol Mitra. Convoluted phrases. Poor diction. Pure gibberish. How did this baboon get to be a reporter? Clearly the newspaper needed better writers.

Vishnu closed the paper and picked up the coffee cup. It was then that he noticed a man watching him from an adjacent table. With reporter's eyes Vishnu gathered the details about him quickly. Age about thirty. Cheeks pitted by acne marks. A scar down the right side of his forehead. Spice brown trousers. Blue-checked shirt. Slanted eyes and high cheekbones. He must be a member of an aboriginal tribe from near India's border.

The man glided his chair closer, greeting Vishnu with pressed palms. "Vishnu Chauhan? Do you remember me? I'm Pradip." He spoke in a mixture of Hindi and English. His English accent was more small-townish than Calcutta. "I was there when you interviewed Karun Dhotia, our party chief, three years ago. I sat by him. Your article in *India News* about our Jai Shiva Party was excellent."

An intrusion on his thoughts. Still, to ignore the man would be rude. "Oh yes." Vishnu nodded. He recalled Karun Dhotia, the leader of the Moxan tribe, the man with the foolish idea of a separate state, Moxanland. The interview took place in a low-rent office filled with musty-smelling papers and cockroaches running over them. Dhotia was large. His throaty voice reverberated in the small dark space. He seemed quite sure of what he wanted: control of the local economy, his own police force, schools taught in the Moxan language, Tihili. And now Vishnu remembered Pradip too. He was most cordial at the meeting. He brought tea, even stirred the sugar for Vishnu. Both Dhotia and Pradip answered all his questions fully, which made it easier for him to write the piece. "What's Mr. Dhotia up to these days?"

"He is reorganizing the Jai Shiva Party."

Vishnu remembered that this tribe worshipped the Hindu god Shiva.

"Our new party logo is Lord Shiva in his Nataraj dancing pose," Pradip said. "Shiva has many hands and legs, many powers. When he dances, the world moves, shakes and changes."

Vishnu pictured the pose: Shiva with four extended arms carrying weapons, his enemy under one foot, his other leg raised and crossed over, forming the circle of the universe. Shiva, who destroyed before recreating. There were many interpretations of that pose. "We were inspired by Tagore," Pradip said.

Vishnu had read much of Tagore, the Nobel Prize–winning Bengali poet, who died half a century ago.

Pradip kept on. "Speaking of Shiva he said, 'In His dance, freedom finds its image, dreams their form.' "

Freedom, that must be the Moxan byword, then. Vishnu shivered.

"We have a new office, north of here in Shambazaar," Pradip said. "Now that we've moved in, Dhotiaji wants to run a newspaper." Glancing at *India News*, he lowered his voice. "I got the news from a friend. Their loss. You were their best reporter."

Vishnu folded the paper. "Thanks."

"But are you safe?"

Vishnu looked directly into Pradip's face.

"I don't mean to scare you, my friend, but—" Pradip looked around, then whispered. "There's a rumor that Best Ghee has thugs watching your moves. He's mean, the company president, Mr. Patiala. We don't care for him either. My little niece got sick when she ate Best Ghee with her rice. And Patiala wants to take over one of our villages to build a factory. He makes fun of us tribals. He calls us 'uncultured.' "

"How can a fired journalist threaten him now?" Vishnu demanded with a brave face. "And doesn't Mr. Patiala have enough problems already?" The next moment he pictured the narrow, winding lane that led to his apartment building and hired men waiting for him there at night. He pushed his chair back, leapt to his feet. "I appreciate your stopping by, Pradip—"

Pradip remained seated. "We might have a job opening for you if you'd be so kind as to consider it."

Vishnu sat down again.

"Dhotiaji's launching an alternative newspaper in English. A weekly that would be a four-pager to start with. We'll call it the *Tribal Express*. It'll cater to the lower-caste people and tribals. Not just Moxans but Nagas, Bhils, Khasis. So many tribals live in Calcutta now. They're college educated. They want to be heard. And they want to know what's going on with their brothers and sisters around the state. Dhotiaji's interviewing for an editor's position. It would be just right for you."

This might just be a propaganda paper. "Really, Pradip, I—"

"We've talked it over. Nothing but the best for our cause. I've been sent to ask you to interview for that position. I called you at home, but you didn't answer. I thought I might see you here."

"Why me?" Vishnu asked. "My political views don't match Mr. Dhotia's. India should remain unified and he's working to split it up."

"Perhaps you're not considering all the facts," Pradip shot back. "Wasn't India a loose federation, a bunch of kingdoms, before the British?"

"I don't really want to get into a political discussion."

"In independent India, my tribe has nothing. Nothing." A deep cry seemed to lurk behind Pradip's words. "Our ancestors are the *adivassis*. They're the original inhabitants who lived in India before the Aryans came. They lived on small plots of land doing whatever they could. They kept getting pushed nearer the borders by the invaders."

"I know," Vishnu replied. He felt their suffering—but not enough to side with them.

Pradip continued. "And we're being driven out again. Ajmeer Paper Mill put their main plant in our district, Sran. Immediately there was a huge migration of workers from other states for jobs. We used to be more than half the population there. Now we're less than a third. A minority."

"But the paper company built schools for children, didn't they?" Vishnu pointed out. "And a college. Don't they employ many Moxans?"

"Do you know what it's like to be a minority in your own land? Our language, culture, tradition are all gone. Our kids learn Hindi and English in school. They won't speak Tihili to their parents at home. They are embarrassed to sing and dance."

Vishnu remembered the "de-Hinduize" movement of many of the tribes. They wanted to retain their own language, food, and clothing style—a separation that had led to a lack of unity with other Indians. Vishnu preferred a common way of life to bring all citizens together. The key to that was, of course, education. "What about the educational funds given to Mr. Dhotia by the state government?" he asked. "What has he done with that money?"

"That pittance!" Pradip spit the words out. "We don't want money. We want our language and culture. We want our land back. We won't stop at anything."

Vishnu remembered the terrorist activities some ethnic groups had engaged in: riots, kidnapping, looting. He pictured blood on the streets. His jaws locked and he couldn't speak.

At that moment a familiar laugh and the sound of gold bangles colliding drew his attention. It was Asha, his neighbor, who glided into the restaurant with another young woman. Her wispy sari had a blue-and-white cloud pattern and seemed as light as the sky. With each step she took, her long braided hair swayed across her slim waist. She put her textbooks down on a table and waved at him. He felt his face soften, his eyes come to a gentle focus, his mouth begin to widen, hinting at a happy smile.

"I've read your column," Pradip continued, leaning across the table, trying to catch Vishnu's eyes. "And I know about you. You're a Hindu, a Rajput. You're part of the majority. But you're not a rich boy. You come from a poor village nobody has ever heard of. You sympathize with the rest of us. Your mind is open. And you're a fighter. We need fighters. You can still write about Best Ghee or whatever else you choose. And we'll protect you from thugs."

Eyes still on Asha, Vishnu said, "I appreciate your concern, Pradip, but . . ."

Pradip bounced to his feet, fished around in his shirt pocket, found a card, and handed it to Vishnu. "Give me a call if you change your mind." With that he strode away.

Vishnu put the card in his pocket without even looking at it.

"Vishnuda!" Asha approached his table with a smile that dimpled her cheeks. Her lips were naturally rosy. "Father's been asking about you, and here you are."

The suffix -da indicated Vishnu was older and to be respected. Today he did feel his age. "I stayed in most of last week," he said. "Which is why I didn't run into either you or Mr. Das on the stairwell like I usually do."

"That's what friends are for," Asha said, "for times like this." Her voice swelled with concern. She had the nurturing instinct of someone far more mature. Asha, the name meant "hope." Vishnu appreciated her simple intimacy. He realized he was staring at her. He dropped his eyes.

"Would you like to come up for dinner tonight?" Asha's eyes brightened; her voice rose as if something grand was going to happen. "I'll ask Mother to make mustard fish."

Mustard fish, the Bengali classic. It must have been six months since Vishnu had tasted the thick pungent sauce of freshly ground mustard.

"You can edit my English essay afterward," came from Asha a moment later. "You promised that weeks ago."

"I did, didn't I?" Her cheerfulness and her mother's mustard sauce appealed much more than the simple *poori* and potatoes he had eaten all week. "What time?" he asked.

"Seven o'clock," replied Asha. "We eat late, you know. After it cools down. Now if you'll excuse me . . . I have to compare my math answers with Smita's."

Vishnu watched as she rejoined her friend at the other end of the room. He stretched his arms out, inhaled deeply, and looked out the window, only to find a blue-orange afternoon sky smudged with ashen clouds.

6

It was six a.m. Meena woke to the chirping of sparrows crowding against her window. She listened to them for a moment, threw back the down comforter, sat up in her queen-sized brass bed, and let her eyes roam around. Unlike her living room, where she strove for clean lines and bold color effects, the low-ceilinged bedroom was decorated in muted hues, rounded shapes, and textured surfaces. The radiator had clicked on, taking the chill off the early morning air. The walls which she had color-washed herself gave off a warm peach glow even on this gray morning. Leaving this sensuous nook for work wouldn't be easy. She hopped out of bed, her toes wiggling in the plush carpet. Her eyes came to rest on a photograph of Auntie Bimla on the dressing table taken eighteen years ago. Meena picked a fresh daffodil from an enamel jug on the same table, placed it before the picture, and bowed. Suddenly Auntie Bimla came alive.

A handsome woman, not much for clothes or ornaments, her best feature was the gentleness that exuded from her face. One would hardly expect Auntie Bimla to be so serene, for her life had been filled with misfortunes. Meena had heard over and over again how as a teenager Bimla was married off by her family in India to a prosperous man fifty-five years old. He was fat, crude, and ugly with a disposition to match. Unknown to her family, he was a chronic drinker and gambler. He soon lost all his money and took to beating her. One night he came home drunk, got hold of her wedding jewelry, and threw her out, accusing her of failing to bear him a son. Her family, being of lower status in the village, blamed her for everything and disowned her. Like many in her predicament, she migrated to New Delhi and joined the Women's Auxiliary, a support organization that took in displaced women and gave them vocational training. Fluent in Hindi and several other Indian languages, Bimla soon acquired a working knowledge of English as well and, in her spare time, functioned as an interpreter for an American family. The Gossetts, who were stationed in New Delhi at the time, met her through friends and hired her as Meena's nanny. Later, when asked to accompany the family to San Francisco, Bimla agreed readily.

Only seven then, Meena's heart still ached for Mataji, and she told Auntie Bimla all about her. Mataji, who had persevered in the face of so much adversity only to be hit by the bandits—Meena's eyes would burn with rage and grief as she recalled the scene. Mataji, poor and not schooled but happy and loving, her lean silhouette outlined in a long flowing skirt, a play of colors, and a veil coming down to her nose. She would squat in their yard every afternoon to make an open cow-dung fire. She sang "one, two, three . . ." as she pounded the wheat dough, refolding it to make it more pliable and to knead her affection into each layer. She'd scoop out a ball and hand it to Meena to roll into a circular shape. With pride on her face, Mataji would say, "That's a perfect round. You have the hand for it, my dear." She'd puff the breads over the fire, fetch a pot of spiced vegetables from the kitchen, and arrange the food on a reed mat. They'd have a picnic, watching the sunset and the camels passing by.

What a contrast Meena's dinners with the Gossetts in their San Francisco home were. She sat on one side of a long dining table with a white cloth while Mom and Dad occupied the two end chairs. Mom set the table with the perfection of a hotelier that Meena admired even at that age. They were served pot roast and boiled vegetables with no embellishments. Sauces were "too French" and Mom never prepared them except when company came. The dinner conversation came mostly from her. "We have a little sad news today." In a slightly nasal voice she'd announce the resignation of her favorite gardener. She was well spoken; her words were precise, with boundaries around them. Not a stray hair on her temple, not a silly notion in her head, very little laughter. That was Mom.

And she was all for form. Silverware must be used at the table, even when peeling an orange. A torture, since Meena liked touching her food. Mom was never harsh, never said, "You don't do that." Only her eyes got rounder and became red when she disapproved. One such look from her was enough to make Meena slump down in her chair and lose her appetite.

Afterward Meena would sneak into Auntie Bimla's kitchen for a second dinner. Little by little Auntie Bimla became her surrogate mother. Meena was the child she could never have. Like Mataji, she was strong and protective, always there in time of need. Meena began to trust her.

Those first six months in San Francisco were a time of terror. Meena had difficulty eating, drinking, sleeping, even playing. She'd run from room to room, from the front of the house to the rear, as if being chased, but refused to answer a question if asked. Years later she'd know she was still dealing with the anger and fear of being kidnapped, of being displaced from her home and her country. Mom gave up on her. It was the infinitely patient Auntie Bimla who murmured Hindi phrases of comfort in her ear and tried to make sense out of Meena's every syllable. Because of Mom's strict orders, Auntie Bimla spoke only English the rest of the time.

At night Meena would lie awake for hours. The moment she dozed, she'd have a nightmare of riding in a train with the bandits. She'd jump out of bed screaming. Auntie Bimla, who slept in the next room, would rush in to hold Meena in her lap and stroke her hair while humming a devotional *bhajan* or telling her an Indian parable in a soft, soothing voice. Auntie Bimla never seemed to exhaust her supply of stories. The most favorite was the tale of a thief who came to steal a dessert from a family kitchen, but instead slipped a coconut shell over his head. He just couldn't get out of it. He ran around the village like that. Children followed him everywhere, laughing, calling him "coconut head." Meena would laugh too. Gradually her fear would subside and she'd fall asleep cradled in Auntie Bimla's arms.

One weekend when the Gossetts were out of town, Auntie Bimla ambled into Meena's room. "Let's burn the bandits," she suggested offhandedly.

"Do what?"

"Come." Auntie Bimla took Meena by the hand and led her to the backyard. She built a small charcoal fire and asked, "What did they look like?"

Meena described them.

Auntie Bimla cut figures from cardboard and newspapers to make effigies. "Get 'em," she said in her imitated American accent.

Meena threw them into the fire. The flames rose as if in anticipation and enveloped the two characters, who writhed in agony before crumpling into ashes.

"They're gone, destroyed," Auntie Bimla rejoiced. She raised her thin right hand, poised an imaginary dagger, and made stabbing motions toward the embers. *"Khatam,"* she intoned—the Hindi word for "finished."

Meena pranced around the ashes, laughing wildly.

Auntie Bimla gathered the ashes in a small cardboard box and sealed the top. They rode the bus to Ocean Beach. They stood at the edge of the water and, as Auntie Bimla instructed her, Meena relaxed her fingers. The box bobbed on the waves a second before sinking from sight.

"That's the end of that," Auntie Bimla said.

Auntie Bimla never revealed where she got the idea of "burning the bandits" and it didn't matter. That night Meena slept well. She held back the whole incident from Mom, however.

Over the next few years Meena made friends, got mostly A's in school, spoke only English, frequented hamburger joints—in short, became a normal American kid. It was clear Auntie Bimla's job was done. She could return to India if she wanted. But she never did. She had no one there.

Auntie Bimla was a stay-at-home. Her single weekly excursion was to the grocery store for her vegetables. She prepared and ate her simple vegetarian meal alone, except when Meena joined her.

Meena remained close to Auntie Bimla. It was as if they were made of the same flesh and blood. Meena could sense when Auntie Bimla was out of sorts. They could talk for hours or share a silence together. That suited Mom fine, though Meena suspected she resented Auntie Bimla a trifle. Mom pursued her volunteer work and, for several years, was on the board of SFMOMA.

Meena still remembered the afternoon when she tiptoed into Auntie Bimla's room, her first report card with a B in hand. Auntie Bimla sat at a table sipping lemonade, flipping the pages of a magazine.

"You got a B in history?" She took her glasses off, wiped them, put them back on, and read the report card again. She flung it onto the table and overturned the lemonade.

At Auntie Bimla's instigation, Dad talked Western history with Meena at dinner; Mom lectured on art history at breakfast. Auntie Bimla herself got busy tutoring Meena in Indian history, though that was never in the school curriculum. In time she taught Meena the Vedas, the Hindu mythical stories of the *Ramayana*, the translated poems of Kalidasa, the concept of "dharma" or devotion. She invoked the word "karma" often. It literally meant "work," but implied that every deed gave rise to an effect equal or greater in weight. Her karma, Meena knew, was to study history.

She managed an A in history the next semester but hated the subject just the same. And she found the two modes of teaching to be incongruent. But she had long ago learned to split herself in two. A school essay she started began with the sentence "In my house, there are two homes."

History, Meena concluded years later, was a problem subject because she didn't like switching back in time. The past was painful.

During her teenage years, her primary source of emotional support was Auntie Bimla. If Meena was confused when a boy first kissed her, or wanted to know what to wear to her first dance, it was Auntie Bimla she went to. But as she began to date, she clashed with Auntie Bimla too. Having grown up in India, her old nanny was unfamiliar with the practice and to her it reeked of immorality. Whereas Mom and Dad seemed merely cautious and didn't screen Meena's boyfriends, Auntie Bimla looked them over minutely. Most were either corrupt or not good enough. "They're wild," she'd declare when all they had done was to hold Meena's hand. "Meena can't stay out after nine," she would whisper sweetly to them.

How could Meena upset Auntie Bimla? At the same time, Meena resented not having the same freedom as her classmates. She felt smothered. For a time she refused dates, acted shy, and was called an "ice goddess" behind her back. A romantic at heart, she secretly craved warmth, wanted to form relationships with boys. She could only daydream.

It was Thanksgiving of her senior year in high school when Meena brought a college track runner home. He was handsome all right, but Mom raised an eyebrow at his track shoes. Dad grew silent when he found the star athlete couldn't pronounce two consonants placed next to each other, saying "nu-cu-lar" instead of "nuclear."

"He runs?" Bimla mouthed her disapproval in private. "That's how he wants to make a living? What else can he do?"

Meena smirked.

"Don't trust a man who moves too fast."

Auntie Bimla proved to be right. The track star sprinted in and out of Meena's life. She soon met another boy, a scholar this time, but couldn't erase the track star from her thoughts. That is, until she remembered Auntie Bimla's burning trick. One day when no one was home, she built a fire and went through the same ritual. The flames swallowed the "track man" in no time.

Would there ever be a way, Meena often wondered, to repay Auntie Bimla for her devotion? Auntie Bimla didn't need any material goods. Her life consisted of basics—a walk in the park, tea with the family, an occasional card in the mail and she was happy. She never once seemed to feel limited by her mundane life. The word "sacrifice" was prominent in her vocabulary. She gave all of herself to others.

Then came the day when Meena graduated from high school. "Now I can go back to India," Auntie Bimla said, tears sprinkling her cheeks. "You, my dear child, are going to move to the dormitory at Stanford in the fall. Who would I have here? Mr. and Mrs. Gossett are rarely home."

"I'll go to India with you," Meena said eagerly, "for the summer."

They spent the rest of the day planning their trip without Mom knowing it. Early the next morning, Meena prepared *chai* just the way Auntie Bimla liked it, rich in milk and extremely sweet. Cup in hand, Meena knocked at her door. Today they'd discuss their plan with Mom, get her permission, and call the travel agent.

No response. That was unusual. Auntie Bimla rose early. Meena pushed the door open.

There was Auntie Bimla stretched across the bed, eyes shut, silent. Meena touched her hand. Cold as a tile, with a grayish cast. "Oh no, Auntie Bimla," Meena cried. "Don't leave me here alone."

Auntie Bimla had died in her sleep of a heart attack. Her face in repose had tranquillity. No regrets.

Alarmed by Meena's cry, Mom and Dad came rushing in. They

couldn't believe it. Auntie Bimla had never complained of any ailments.

For days after her death the house seemed to have lost its spirit. Auntie Bimla had treated all human and inanimate objects with care. "Everything has consciousness," she would say. "They all have their stories. Even this chair." Those loving hands with chipped nails and calluses that dusted and swept constantly were now sorely missed. The rooms no longer gleamed. The chill in the stairwell was unbearable, the crack in the wooden floor unsightly, the dust on the windowsill too grim. Nobody was listening to their stories.

Meena knew her parents couldn't tell how traumatic Auntie Bimla's death had been for her. They did, however, realize that their daughter was a stranger. Dad put Meena on his To Do list twice a week. Mom scheduled Tuesday nights with her to munch on popcorn and play Scrabble. Mom who lived and breathed art encouraged Meena to try her hand at it. Meena was much too restless to spend quiet hours at an easel, though she did manage a few charcoals and watercolors. Athletic by nature, she gravitated toward competitive sports, especially running. Mom and Dad never quite grasped her fascination with being "out in the elements." Like many parents, they tried to make her a replica of themselves: reserved, cerebral, cultured. They read the right books. Every word, every action was refined and controlled.

The bond between Meena and them was more verbal and intellectual, less of the heart, though they loved one another very much; Meena could never be silent with them. That would be too uncomfortable. To be sure, there were times when Mom would speak spontaneously, share her sentiments. But within minutes her manner would become guarded and she'd stare at Meena in a curious way, trying to evaluate her response. In a second the mood of intimacy would dissolve and Meena would retreat into her shell. Then too, their busy lives and material possessions and the importance they attached to social status proved to be barriers. They were well meaning and provided for her material needs, but never really understood her.

And yet, over the years she learned to accept them and eventually she achieved a sense of connectedness. Finally she was less of a guest, more a part of the family.

"You've been very loyal," Mom had said on her deathbed. "I

couldn't have asked for a better daughter than you. I know I made a lot of mistakes raising you, but I tried, Meena. At least I had sense enough to hire Bimla."

This morning as she showered and dressed, Meena reflected on whether Mom and Dad ever did replace that sari-clad guru, that loving guardian, that slayer of bandits. No, they occupied separate chambers in her heart. How different life would be today if Auntie Bimla were still alive.

7

Meena looked up from the software report on her desk to see Joy walking through the door.

"That's a nice suit you have on," Joy said. With zero makeup, droopy hair, glasses that kept sliding down her nose, and a jumper that would be more appropriate for a housepainting job, she could have modeled for a "before" picture in *Glamour* magazine.

"I got hold of this yesterday." Meena showed her the cover of the manual, entitled *A Comparative Study of Database Systems*. "A well-researched piece of work. I read most of it last night."

"I'd fall asleep in five minutes," Joy said.

Joy's appearance and her casual remarks didn't tell the whole story. Even with a minimal background in software technology, she had risen through the ranks of SIC and was now Meena's peer as project manager. Joy had accomplished this, Meena believed, through an uncanny ability to perceive where the power resided within an organization and seek favor with those who exercised it. Rumor had it that she was also not above a well-timed "cleaver in the back" to eliminate potential rivals. "Well, I didn't," Meena said. "COSMOS is mentioned here in great detail."

"I heard on the grapevine that Brett wants to take over COSMOS."

Brett Watson. That pompous MBA, her other peer, was a real pain. Brought in to manage the development of an electronic banking package, he had immediately set out to build an empire by swiping functions and resources. Now he was nibbling away at Meena's sphere of responsibility.

"He has no software background," Meena said, not even trying to hide the sarcasm in her voice. "He can't control his own projects, let alone something as complex as COSMOS. I'm almost tempted to let him try and watch him fall on his face."

Joy adjusted the frame of her eyeglasses as if focusing a camera lens. "It's all a big game, you know. Why did you become a manager if you don't want to play?"

Meena sat silently. At times like this she wished she were still a programmer. As a freshman at Stanford, she had enrolled in a programming course mainly out of curiosity. By the end of the semester, software had become her all-consuming passion. Whether it was ambition or intellectual challenge she didn't know, but she was fascinated by all aspects of computer software, especially programming. Caught up in an abstract design problem, she'd become oblivious to the flow of time and forget her problems. Oddly enough, she found afterward that she understood herself better, was more at ease with herself. Soon programming became a major part of her identity. Later, as a new hire at SIC, she spent long hours at her keyboard, her mind absorbed in the intricacies of program logic. She'd get a new insight into a computer language, a shortcut to do a function, and that would make her mood incredibly light. Egos, jealousies, backstabbing, and lies had had no place in her life then.

For now she responded to Joy by saying, "I think for a project this technical, a manager has to have a technical background to be effective."

Joy sniffed. "Being a techie isn't everything."

Meena knew where Joy was coming from. They used to be lunch buddies until a couple of years ago when both became contenders for the position of COSMOS project manager. Because of her computer science degrees and a decade of programming experience, Meena got the job. Joy was given another project as a consolation prize, but it fulminated in her ego. Meena sometimes wondered how she had escaped Joy's knives. Only recently Joy had admitted that the COSMOS project would have been beyond her abilities. Still she seemed compelled to needle Meena every now and then. Just the same, Meena had a certain respect for Joy. Underneath that frumpy appearance, she was extremely shrewd and managed to get what she wanted in the corporate environment. And she had a warmth that didn't always surface. Like the time after Mom's death when Joy came to visit Meena with a bouquet of flowers. Besides, Joy was the only other woman manager in her division. Why couldn't they be friends again? Meena wheeled her chair to the window and murmured to herself, "I am beginning to wonder about this techie bit." She asked inwardly when was the last time she'd seen a play or had friends over for dinner.

Joy seemed to have overheard the comment. "Why don't we do lunch," she asked casually, "and talk about my project? I could use some help setting up test cases."

"And I could use a break." Meena tapped some keys on her keyboard. Her daily calendar opened before her, filled with appointments and meetings, even a double booking. She identified one open slot. "How about eleven-forty-five today?"

"Could you make it eleven-thirty? I get here before seven. By midmorning I'm famished."

Oh really? Why, Meena wondered as she keyed in the lunch date on her calendar, did Joy come to work so early? She never seemed to have that much to do.

A break at lunchtime was a luxury Meena could seldom afford, so today, with an hour to spare, she felt super-rich, if only in time. To her, having grown up in San Francisco where nearly half the population had an Asian heritage, Asian food was as familiar as a hamburger. She was excited to be back at the high-ceilinged River of Sand restaurant, a Hong Kong–style eatery in Chinatown. Joy smoothed the hem of her jacket, pink seersucker and a size too small.

They squeezed into a window table where a thin pane of glass separated Meena from the chaotic energy of Broadway. An endless stream of people flew by as if on parade, along with vehicles making countless decibels of noise. Meena pictured herself out there too, browsing among the stands of exotic fruits and vegetables in a stunning array of shapes and colors. The narrow street was lined by sorbet-colored buildings, lion heads on their facades protecting all from evil. A trash can on the street corner overflowed, an ugly sight.

But as raucous and littered as Chinatown was, it gave off a feeling of exuberance that always caused Meena to think of India.

"This is my first time at a dim sum place," Joy said, watching her keenly. "I don't get to Chinatown very often. The last time I was here was with you for Christmas shopping three years ago. Remember the noodle place we went to?"

"I sure do," Meena said. A good start, she thought. She needed some allies in the office. Besides, lunch was a way to disengage her mind from the infinite details and abstraction of software design work. She was already beginning to feel transported to another world from inhaling the smoky sesame oil wafting from the kitchen. She asked, "What was it you wanted to talk about?"

Joy stared at the white carnations that burst out of a Ming-style vase placed next to her. "I'd like a COSMOS test database for my system testing."

"That's easy," Meena said immediately. "I'll have Dave come and see you."

Joy began sipping water. Meena listened for a long moment to the clatter of chopsticks against the background of dozens of conversations in different languages, then wondered if Joy might not be hiding something.

"A vacation condo is what I need," Joy was now saying. "But I don't have the money. Maybe I should moonlight. . . ."

Meena hadn't put her roots down enough yet to buy real estate. While half listening to Joy's scheme, she surveyed the room. It was crammed with a largely Asian clientele who hovered over their plates, communing as much with their food as their tablemates. The walls, freshly painted swan-white, reflected a sense of peace that Meena breathed in. Sensing Joy had exhausted the topic of condos, Meena switched the subject. "Who have you been reading lately?"

"I picked up a whodunit by an unknown author at the supermarket yesterday," Joy said. "The first chapter starts with the police finding the body of a busboy inside an industrial oven turned on high. I couldn't put the book down. I was up all night."

A white-coated waiter wheeled his cart to their table. He bowed, then began lifting the lid of each bowl with a gloved hand and showing the contents like a magician getting ready for his act. Meena ordered pork buns and shrimp dumplings and, as always, egg custard tartlets to finish the meal.

Joy cut a piece from a largish bun before saying, "The mystery has made the best-seller list."

That brought Antoine to mind. Meena asked, "Have you read anything by Antoine Peterson?"

"The heartthrob who lives in Marin? I read the one he wrote about his divorce, *Terminal Case of Love*. Literary, but actually I kinda liked it. He has a poetry collection, too. You read any of his stuff?"

"Nothing except a poem," Meena said. "Must have been a year ago. It was about a time in his life when he couldn't even grow begonias."

Joy's eyes widened. "And you remember him from that?"

Meena hesitated before saying, "Well, I ran into him at my birthday party."

"Really? You always get the breaks, Meena. Does he look like his picture?"

"Didn't notice. He was tall. His eyes seemed expressive."

Joy helped herself to three dumplings. "His new novel, *Parallel Lives*, is supposed to be even better. He's reading this Thursday at the Bookworm in Corte Madera. Say, wouldn't it be fun to go together? You could introduce him to me. And on the way we could discuss our next week's meeting with the marketing department."

Meena poured jasmine tea into both their cups. Her fingers trembled and her pulse rate jumped as she said nonchalantly, "Let me think about that." If they left work before five, it would take less than an hour. They could have dinner before the reading. The plan all but finalized in her mind, she said as if in afterthought, "I do want to read more novels."

"Tell me," Joy said, "about your birthday party and Antoine Peterson."

Meena took a bite of her egg tart, letting the velvety custard melt sensuously in her mouth. "Not much to say. I barely spoke to him. And he didn't stick around."

"Sure that was all? In the office you only talk about bits and bytes. Today I'm seeing a different side of you, Meena."

"I haven't thought much about dating lately, to tell you the truth."

"Who has? You're always so well put together. I'd die to look like you. And even *you* can't meet somebody!"

Meena checked her watch quickly. "My work is all I know. Right now I'm married to COSMOS."

"No doubt about that," Joy agreed. "COSMOS is the company jewel. And you guard it as closely as if you owned it."

What was Joy implying? Meena remained composed. If she was offended by Joy's comment, she wasn't going to show it. "I came up with the idea of the database package," she said. "We never had an offering like that. These past two years—I've given the project everything. I'm going to stay with it until it's done."

"Well, I'm sure COSMOS is so close to being done, anybody could wrap it up." Joy smiled, showing a perfect set of polished white teeth. "I know how careful you are. You needn't worry about keeping the details a secret."

Was this another attempt to needle her? Best to ignore Joy and maintain a professional manner, Meena thought. "I'll be shipping COSMOS-1 shortly," she said with pride. "Now I'm hammering out COSMOS-2."

An expression of ridicule crossed Joy's face. "Doesn't leave much time for anything else, does it?"

"I manage to find time for other things," Meena said, now thrown off balance. "But I don't really have time for a relationship at this point." She tried to summon a smile as she poured more tea in Joy's cup, knowing all the time Joy was probing, seeking a flaw she could exploit.

"My father says men don't appreciate women who are so self-assured."

"I'm not sure of everything." Meena began to seethe. "Believe me, I've got plenty of loose ends in my life." She pushed the plate away from her only to have it nearly hit Joy's water goblet.

Glancing up, Meena caught a hint of glee in Joy's eyes. "I have to get back," she said as she struggled to her feet. Her fingers fumbled with the double handle of her purse. She could feel her back muscles beginning to knot.

"The dim sum was great," Joy said.

8

Asha opened the door and turned away, her voice singing, "Vishnuda, come in. I'm setting the table." With hands as delicate as an Odissi dancer's, she unfurled a lacy white tablecloth.

Vishnu let his eyes follow the curve of Asha's trim figure. She was wearing an aquamarine *salwar-kameez*. Tight pants, a high-necked knee-length tunic, a matching chiffon scarf flung over the shoulders. He was taken by the shimmer of the fine fabric framing her face. "That's a nice color," he observed.

"Wish I could say I had it stitched in Delhi," Asha said. "That's how some of my rich classmates talk." She giggled, as though she were letting him in on secrets of her feminine world. "But no. This is off the racks of New Market."

Vishnu laughed. He loved the way her hair swept up off her forehead. Like a soft mass of rain clouds. It reminded him of someone, he wasn't sure who.

Mr. and Mrs. Das entered the room. Vishnu found himself smiling naturally. Asha's parents were what Indians called "plain living, high thinking" people, a breed slowly becoming extinct. Mr. Das, who was gripping a cane, must have been a handsome man in his youth with a finely chiseled face. Now with dry skin, baggy eyes, and hair receding at the temples, he looked tired and helpless, yet refined and dignified. His pure white *kurta* and matching trousers were freshly laundered.

"So good to see you, my son." Mr. Das spoke in English, as Vishnu wasn't well versed in the regional Bengali language that the Das family spoke. "Come sit down." He motioned as he eased himself into an armchair, wincing with pain. Mrs. Das helped him settle in.

"Where are my sandals?" Mr. Das asked his wife.

Mrs. Das fetched her husband's sandals from under a bookcase, saying to Vishnu, "All last week we didn't see you once." Kindness and regret were etched about her eyes as though she had accommodated everyone and everything, all except her own wishes. She veiled her hair, as traditional Bengali women do, with the edge of her ivory sari. Now middle-aged, she had given up wearing bright colors. Her married status was indicated by a vermilion blob on her forehead and an identical smudge on the part of her hair. She was sturdy but graceful and had a proud posture.

"I'm fine, *mashima*." Vishnu addressed her as "dearly beloved aunt" and folded his hands at his chest to greet her. He watched as Mrs. Das and Asha glided across the room to the kitchen.

Mr. Das, a state government official, opened the conversation with a discussion of the recent heat wave and how much cooler this evening was. Thank God, Vishnu thought, Mr. Das hadn't inquired about his dismissal. He let his shoulders relax.

"Do you know what our dear Petroleum and Natural Gas Minister Samir Gupta is up to?" Mr. Das was chattering about politics. "He sends his children to school in Switzerland. Where does the money come from, can you tell me?"

Vishnu shook his head, meanwhile listening for Asha's voice in the kitchen. The whirling noise of the ceiling fan and the crash of pots distorted her words. He could smell the onion that she must have been sautéing. He could hear a snatch of her ringing laughter. He wished Asha were sitting with him.

Mr. Das continued. "I don't know if you've read in the paper they are opening up the northeast to tourists again."

Being a business and industrial sector reporter, Vishnu hadn't kept up with the political unrest in that part of the country. He knew that a number of tribes lived in that area besides the usual mix of Hindus and Muslims. He shook his head no.

"Things seem to have calmed down," Mr. Das said. "You don't hear much. Except for the Moxans."

Vishnu's ears perked up. "Moxans? What's going on with them?"

"They have a new office in a five-story building in North Calcutta," Mr. Das said. "It's right across from the vegetable market in

Shambazaar. There's a big sign: Jai Shiva Party Headquarters. That's a lot bigger space than the one-room office in South Calcutta they had before." A scowl clouded his face as he added, "I hear they've got computers."

"Do you know who's funding them?"

"Possibly guerrillas from Myanmar."

Vishnu asked, "Is that an official view?"

"No. My own. My guess is the guerrillas are coming over the northeast border and infiltrating the tribal organizations. They need medicine, bicycles, and God knows what else. They smuggle in diamonds and rubies to buy things. A lot of money changes hands. Before you were born, people used to call the whole northeastern part of India 'witches brew.' The tribes living there realized they were Mongolians, with no ties to either Hindus or Muslims. They wanted their separate state."

"Where do the Moxans fit in?"

"The Moxans lived in the forest for many years and kept to themselves—until our government started cutting down the mango and jackfruit trees to build roads. The trees were their livelihood. They couldn't support themselves anymore. Their leader Karun Dhotia formed Jai Shiva twenty years ago by recruiting unemployed young Moxans. Now I hear they have a Moxan Students' Federation, a Moxan Mothers' Association, even a Moxans for the Muslims Group. I sympathize, but we can't go on breaking up India, can we? Dhotia is making noise again—"

"I interviewed him several years ago," Vishnu ventured. "He speaks well."

"I hear young Moxans are dissatisfied with his talk. They want action."

Asha emerged from the kitchen with two glasses of lemonade. She put them on the coffee table next to a novel by the revered Bengali writer Bibhutibhusan Bandopadhya, and departed. Vishnu picked up his glass carefully, as if Asha's touch were still there.

Mr. Das glanced at her back, sighed, pulled out a handkerchief from his pocket and dabbed the perspiration off his forehead. "I want Asha to get married as soon as she graduates," he said gloomily. "My health isn't good."

Vishnu nearly choked.

Mr. Das went on. "Asha's mother and I are old-fashioned." He pronounced the name Asha with tenderness. "We want a Bengali son-in-law, so we can keep our culture. I bet your mother has picked out a Rajasthani bride for you."

Vishnu shook his head. How could Mr. Das indulge in such narrow, provincial thinking? Was he saving for a dowry too? Totally absurd. An arranged marriage for Asha with someone of her own caste? Didn't Mr. Das know young Indians did away with the caste and regional barriers? Vishnu stifled a cough and a desire to get up and leave.

"We have a new chap in our office," Mr. Das gloated. "He comes from a good Bengali family. He's well mannered, works hard, doesn't smoke or drink or take drugs. I want to introduce him to Asha. I hope they will hit it off."

Vishnu couldn't bear it anymore. He began to rise.

Asha burst in. "Dinner's ready."

Relieved, Vishnu sat down at the table with Asha and Mr. Das. His eyes went over the rice, lentils, and vegetables arranged attractively on a shiny brass platter. He began eating with his fingers, as did the Das family, and sipped only water. Many Indians now indulged in alcohol; not this family.

Like a good hostess, who wasn't supposed to take her meal until everyone was finished, Mrs. Das hovered about. She poured water in their tumblers every few minutes and regaled them with stories. "When I was a young bride I didn't know a thing about cooking," she said. "On my first day my mother-in-law asked me to fry some *potol*. That's a vegetable dish all Bengali women are supposed to know how to cook. Well, I didn't. So what did I do? I went to my neighbor. He was a seventy-year-old man. He got an old cookbook out, *Pakpranali*, something of a classic. Between the two of us we figured it out." She turned to Mr. Das. "You're lucky you ate that day—"

"You fried the *potol* well," Mr. Das interrupted his wife. "It was the rice you burned." He then commanded, "More rice for me and Vishnu."

Mrs. Das, unfazed, immediately scooped out steaming rice onto their plates. The pearly grains were tender and distinct—a sure sign, Vishnu knew, of a good cook.

"Can't eat as much as I used to," Mr. Das added, taking his third helping.

Vishnu was perturbed at the way Mr. Das took his wife for

granted. He busied himself putting a ball of rice in his mouth, picking out a bone from the Hilsa fish and placing it on one corner of his plate. His lips tingled from the pungency of the bright yellow mustard sauce. "Excellent fish, *mashima*." The memory of last week's simple meals disappeared as fast as the food on his plate.

Mrs. Das radiated pride as she spooned a second helping of fish for Vishnu. "Asha made it for you."

Asha, lovely Asha. Vishnu sneaked a look at her. "You've become a good cook."

Asha cast a respectful glance at Mrs. Das. "Not like Ma. I'm more concerned with getting through school." She held her zestful eyes on Vishnu a bit longer than usual. "Wish I had more free time. I want to learn to make new dishes."

That glance told him what he desired to know: that she wanted to build a home with him. As the meal proceeded he pushed his anxieties to the back of his mind, leaned against his chair, and watched the family—Asha saying to her mother she had to rise early the next morning to study, her mother asking what time she would like to have her tea served, her father insisting that Asha keep the table fan next to her tonight to keep herself cool, Asha arguing that he needed the fan more and that she herself could sleep just as well with the windows open.

They wound up with a chilled rice pudding. Vishnu's palate was awash in a creamy sweetness.

"My younger cousins want cakes on their birthdays," Asha said, scooping the last bite from her brass bowl. "But our family custom has always been to serve rice pudding on all special occasions."

"That's a custom I could get easily used to," Vishnu said.

Mr. Das licked his spoon, then excused himself to take his medicine. Mrs. Das went with him, leaving Vishnu and Asha seated face to face. Vishnu clasped his hands to keep from touching her. All he could think to say was, "Enjoyed your hospitality very much."

"Father enjoys talking to you," she said. "He doesn't go out much. It's good that you came over."

"After this delicious meal," Vishnu said, withdrawing from the table, "I don't think I'll be able to give your paper as much attention as it deserves. Shall we meet at the Coffee House tomorrow?"

"That would be better for me too," Asha said with a lilt. "I'm pretty useless myself after a big dinner. And I like the coffee there."

"At eleven then." He moved to the door.

Mr. Das hobbled in slowly. "You're leaving so soon?"

"Need to catch a few winks before it starts to get hot."

At the doorway Mr. Das stopped over his cane. "Hope it won't be too long before we see you again, Vishnu. Come anytime you feel lonely. I'm always good for a cup of tea and some gossip."

Vishnu gave him a smile and a wave, then drifted down the staircase, quite content.

That night Vishnu dreamt that his apartment was burning. The heat was so unbearable that he rolled out of bed, dressed, and rushed out the door in less than a minute. He raced along the hallway, down the stairs, and onto the ground to watch a hungry fire that had by now engulfed the whole building. It was shaped like a *trisul*, Lord Shiva's three-pronged weapon.

"Shiva's angry," a voice suggested from somewhere. "He's destroying."

Vishnu dripped in the intense heat, his face seared by the glare of fire. He shook in fear. Neighbors bunched around him, everyone searching for family and friends. A mother pushed through the mob to wail at him, "My baby, where's my baby?"

Where's Asha? Vishnu's eyes fastened on the open window on the top floor. There was Asha, and another woman who looked somewhat familiar. Both seemed to be trying to escape. Suddenly Asha screamed. He rushed into the building, followed by the mother in search of her baby. The scorching air and heavy smoke stopped them both from going far. It was impossible to breathe.

"Meena!" Vishnu heard himself shout.

Just then he awoke, his clothes soaked, his heart thudding. He jumped up, rubbed the nightmare from his eyes, but couldn't make sense of any of it. Fire, chaos, women, and Lord Shiva, all at once.

Might Lord Shiva be warning him of an impending danger? Mother had told him that Shiva appeared before her in dreams prior to major upheavals in life. That was superstition. He had always prided himself on being a modern man. Tonight he wasn't so sure.

He gazed out of the window. The street below was deserted and a dim light from the lamppost cast a jagged shadow on his wall. Shiva's shadow? Vishnu couldn't tell.

9

Meena had reached the last few pages of the revised COSMOS-2 design specifications. They were looking good. But her concentration was interrupted when the phone rang.

"Meena, I'm ready to start showing your mother's house." It was the real estate agent's voice on the line.

"I have a few more things to remove." Meena sighed. "I'll reserve Saturday for it." She hung up.

She had been avoiding returning to Mom's house. Everyone she had grown up there with—Mom and Dad and Auntie Bimla—was gone. The house had taken on a stillness that she found difficult to bear.

She poked a pencil through her hair, as if to dislodge from her head the unwelcome prospect.

"My, but you look busy this morning." Her boss, Alex Lester, a corpulent man with bushy eyebrows and dark hair slicked back, was standing in the doorway. She had known Alex, who called himself a "lifer," for the entire twelve years she had worked for this company. Only ten years older than Meena, he seemed to belong to an even older generation in taste and manner and had become something of a father figure to her.

"Busy? Me? With nothing to occupy me but COSMOS-2?" Meena said, then experienced a feeling of apprehension. Alex's usually jovial expression was absent as he plopped into the chair across from her. There was a faint tic in his left eye. What was bothering him? "How was your meeting with Gamma Solutions?" she asked, remembering his morning appointment with that key client.

"Depressing as hell," he said wearily. "Gamma wants early access to COSMOS-1 to verify that their spreadsheet application will function smoothly under it. They're threatening to switch to Graymatter's GALAXY software if we refuse. They're panicky because Sawoya is releasing their new spreadsheet system using GALAXY. Gamma can't afford to come in second."

Meena was flabbergasted. "But my project's on time—just as we've announced." She went over the timetable in her mind before continuing, "Next week, our three designated companies get their early copy of COSMOS-1 to pretest for glitches. They'll give COSMOS a thorough shakedown and notify me of any problems they run into. My staff will correct the bugs. Then and only then does COSMOS-1 get put on the market. That's standard procedure in the industry. Gamma could have been part of the advance testing group. They felt they couldn't spare the staff and the computer resources. At the time, they said they were comfortable with our April release date. Besides, COSMOS is going to be a generation ahead of GALAXY—that's worth waiting for."

"To Gamma, that's a the-check's-in-the-mail response."

"But, Alex, we can't afford to release untested software," Meena persisted, fighting a rising sense of alarm. "We're known for the reliability of our products. It's one of the main things that distinguish us from our competition."

Alex examined the fingernails of one hand in silence. "I heard you had problems with COSMOS testing when I was on vacation."

"Yes, during that power blackout. We lost a small amount of program logic that had been coded since our last backup of the system. And a file directory too. It took us a little time to recover, but we got back on track in a matter of days. The good news is," Meena added brightly, "the incident proves how COSMOS can recover from a power failure."

"There's no question about you knowing your stuff," Alex said. "But I seem to be hearing a lot of complaints lately. It's more a matter of perception, I guess. Some people find it difficult to relate to you. They think you're a bit too technical."

"Of course I'm a techie," Meena responded quickly. "My entire background is in computer science. You need it to tackle a project as complex as COSMOS. How can you lead if you have no clue what your programmers are doing? Respect, in this industry, is based on technical expertise. As far as getting along with people, just ask any of my staff if they like working for me or not."

Wrong thing to say, she realized in a flash. Alex had managed to rise through the ranks at SIC, all the way from the mail room to division chief, through a combination of people skills and cunning. Like her two peers, Brett and Joy, he had no experience as a software programmer or designer. And like them, he harbored lingering feelings of jealousy and resentment toward the technical wizards who made SIC a leader in the industry. These days, rumors of layoffs were in the air. Could it be perhaps that he felt threatened?

"I already have," Alex admitted. "You demand a lot from your staff, but you treat them well—you're protective of them. Overprotective, some would say."

"What really is the problem here, Alex?"

"Brett thinks we need to concentrate more on marketing and finding out what our customers need if we're going to grow the company. And keep ahead of the competition. That requires a broader, less technical perspective, you see."

A surge of anger coiled up from inside Meena like a cobra. She tried to keep her voice steady. "Is that why Brett's nosing around my area lately?"

"He's analyzing all departments in our division to assess their potential for supporting this type of effort." Alex didn't meet her eyes as he said that.

"And he has yet to come up with any good ideas," Meena countered. "I, who have a narrow vision, proposed COSMOS. Isn't it going to be our flagship product for the foreseeable future?"

The tightness in her chest, Meena knew, was a direct reflection of how disturbed and threatened she felt. In the months leading up to and immediately following Mom's death, she had been at loose ends, adrift, badly in need of an anchor for her life. She had thrown herself totally into the COSMOS project, becoming so identified with it that her future in the company had become intertwined with it. Had she made her peers, perhaps even her boss, jealous?

"I'll be going to Europe next month," Alex said abruptly. "To check out new marketing opportunities. While I'm gone, Jean will be in charge of the division."

Meena was stunned. How could Jean be an acting division head? A mere office manager nicknamed the Pencil Czar, Jean hoarded office supplies and questioned every expenditure. Her entire focus was a nitpicking attention to insignificant details. Meena knew the company's entire bank of products well. She'd have liked to be appointed the acting boss even if, given her workload, it wouldn't be smart to take on any more. But at least he could have asked. She stared at him in silence.

Alex smiled sheepishly, heaved himself to his feet and, with a deep sigh, shambled out of the room.

Meena remained seated for a few minutes, struggling to get her thoughts and feelings under control. Something had gone badly awry; she sensed impending danger. To see COSMOS to a successful conclusion and keep her career on track, she'd have to get to the bottom of it quickly.

Alex was clearly playing both sides, hers and Brett's. For what purpose? She knew what Auntie Bimla would have said at this instant: "You can hide a rotten egg, but you can't hide the smell."

10

On Saturday Meena parked her car in front of Mom's house in Pacific Heights and entered through the cedar gate with a packing crate in hand. From the northern edge of the property she could get a view of the Golden Gate Bridge, hazy as usual. She wandered through the grounds, now a little shaggy around the edges because the gardener, with no one to supervise his work, had gotten careless. He no longer mowed the lawn and pruned the rosebushes on schedule. She passed the flowering cherry tree, the bougainvillea trellis, the nasturtium vines that tangled at her feet and looked up at the house. The two-story, four-bedroom stucco she grew up in blended slate, metal, and wood details and had "good bones," as Mom used to say. Now it was empty. Mom had already sold most of her furniture and belongings before she died. Meena had hired a professional mover to haul away the household items she wanted to keep and donated the rest to charities. Today she was going around to pick up the few remaining books and a trunk whose key she'd had to fetch from Mom's safety deposit box.

In the entranceway Meena stood, struck by the dust, invisible until she touched a surface. There never used to be a speck of dirt anywhere. Now the place seemed small without the imposing effect of art and furniture, dead and unbearably silent without the bustle of the family members.

And then suddenly it was twenty-eight years ago. She was seven, walking up the front steps for the very first time.

The big house was palatial by the standards of her native village.

So much ground, so many corners to hide in, such a variety of art displayed in various niches to look at. But it was difficult to adjust to. The food was bland, the weather frigid to her tropical skin. People looked and acted strangely. Meena was obliged to speak English to everyone, but she couldn't figure out what people were saying most of the time. And she was still feeling freshly her loss of Mataji, Vishnu, her grandfather, and her village. This existence was so different that her insides churned, just like a washing machine, one of the many new gadgets she had to get used to.

Meena had liked Dad from the beginning. He was the easier of her two new parents to take to. This morning as she turned left to what had been Dad's study, her steps echoing in the carpetless hallway, she longed to see him seated in his leather cushioned chair. The oak-paneled room where he hid had an auburn cast from the leather-bound volumes that crammed the shelves on the wall. His quiet presence permeated the air. The chessboard would be there too; Dad had taught her to play chess. Every Saturday morning she'd appear in the doorway of her professor father. He'd interrupt his administrative paperwork to ask, "How was school this week?"

The school semester had already started by the time Meena arrived in San Francisco. On her first day she found herself in a huge labyrinth of a building. In the hallway young teachers with silver hoops in their ears chatted between classes. Children ran about, some stopping to gawk at her. What a contrast to her one-room village school. Children sitting under the shade of a tree with slates on their laps, chalk in hand. A stiff, graying teacher asking questions from a textbook. Failing to answer correctly meant you'd be put inside the room. How casual and at the same time intimidating her San Francisco school seemed in comparison.

Mom had dropped her off at school. Mom—Meena used the word, though she asked herself how Mrs. Gossett could ever be her mother. But at the moment even that stern woman seemed like a bosom buddy.

Meena's teacher, a woman with bad skin and huge eyeglasses, made the introduction. "This is Meena Gossett," she said, then, turning to Meena, added, "I want you to tell the class where you're from."

Her Rajput face immobile, Meena shot up from her chair and in her limited formal English vocabulary replied, "I come from the desert of Rajasthan, where there are camels and bandits . . ."

"Baloney," said the class clown, a kid with chubby cheeks and two ink dots for eyes. The other kids snickered and whispered.

The teacher tried to restore order. Meena sat down, but that episode dampened her spirit. How could they make fun of a newcomer? She was glad when the day was over. She gathered her books and put on her jacket, then found that the zipper wouldn't close. She had broken it.

At home she rushed straight to Auntie Bimla, whose loving welcome lifted her heart.

"What did you have for lunch?" Auntie Bimla asked.

"A hot dog," Meena chirped. "It was soo good."

"Oh, my god!" Auntie Bimla cried. "You ate beef?"

Mataji and Grandfather, as Meena would recall it then, wouldn't have approved of her eating beef either. That was a religious taboo in her Hindu family. But how could Meena help it? It seemed like today she had done everything wrong. She ran to her room with a flushed face and stayed there the rest of the afternoon.

In the days that followed she tried hard to fit in. Under Mom's strict orders, Meena spoke only English—with an accent, as everyone would remind her—except to her stuffed polar bear who would listen to her Hindi phrases. And when something went well, the Hindi word *achcha*, well and good, would come out of her mouth automatically. Before long she lost her accent. Mom proudly pointed it out at dinner one evening. That night Meena cried in her room, feeling as though she had thrown part of herself away.

Her family, the camels, and the blazing colors of Karamgar soon became pictures in a storybook painted in her heart with blood. She never again mentioned them in school. She even wondered if that wasn't a past life and she had been reincarnated from it. And Vishnu became a tender secret buried in an inner chamber of her heart, remembered only when she was alone at night.

Dad was ever the supportive one. "I saw your poem in your school magazine," he'd say to her in her teen years. "Very nice." It took some adjustment to get used to his delicately pale, almost translucent complexion, but when he spoke, his face glowed with an opal light.

She talked poetry with him. He'd take his glasses off and look closely at her, listening to her verse. Finally they'd switch to his pet subject—foreign affairs. He'd voice concern about a war or famine someplace. They'd discuss the goings-on in the world for hours. As computers became her major interest in college, he delved into them himself. In his last years, he was involved in a UN-sponsored project called Peace through Computers, one that took cybereducation to children all over the world.

Leaving Dad's study, Meena turned right to the breakfast nook, still cheery with the morning sun. The sliding glass doors led out onto a garden sprinkled with patches of yellow marigolds and blue lobelias, now that it was springtime. As a teenager she'd put on a baggy sweat suit on Sunday mornings—she liked being comfy—and join Mom at a small round rustic table for breakfast. Mom wore her trademark pearls and beige angora cardigan. Her salon-coiffed hair, flat on top, failed to balance her square jaw, but her fingernails were perfect little scallops colored a sensible pearl pink by a manicurist every week. She would set down her scones, bullet hard, and the *Chronicle* between them. Auntie Bimla would come rushing out from the kitchen with a pot of *chai*— that was the only time Mom would allow Indian tea to be served. Meena would savor her cup while Mom talked art, sprinkling words and phrases such as "eye" and "energy," and "going beyond time." With a short stubby finger, she'd point to a Mondrian piece from a SFMOMA catalog. "Harsh colors. He's playing primitive, you might say. But if you look beyond the surface . . ." Her face would shine as she went on about how an artist related to the universe. How excited Mom became then. Meena got into art mostly in an attempt to understand Mom. Meena guessed she couldn't get the tenderness she wanted from Mom because that was reserved for her art. Dad hinted some years later that Mom was, deep down, an artist manqué.

Mom's two cookbooks were lying on the black marble counter in the kitchen: one an early Julia Child tome and the other *The Joy of Cooking*. Mom would take these books out whenever company was invited and read through the recipes carefully, as if they were sacred inscriptions with hidden meanings. Then she'd proceed to overcook everything. Meena placed the books neatly inside the packing crate.

She climbed the skylighted stairwell to Mom's beige boudoir, now bare but for its soft lacy curtains. She crossed the room, opened a window overlooking the backyard, and stood there breathing deeply of the chilly spring air. Then she went over to the huge closet. Mom's trunk was pushed into a dark corner. As a child Meena knew it as a catchall for all manner of junk. She pulled the trunk out into the light, unlocked it, and raised the lid.

She came up with something hard lying on top. A bundle of diaries, some with velvet covers, others plain notebooks, all more than twenty years old. Mom had said she kept journals of all her trips. Had they been left here for her? Or did Mom just forget to dispose of them? Meena hesitated to peek into them; a diary was so private, it would be like putting a stethoscope to someone's soul. There was one marked with the year she was adopted. She reflected for a moment, then picked it up. From inside, a dried red petal of a rose fell out. The flimsy paper, browned with age, gave off a musty smell. Meena held her breath as she flipped the pages.

Here was Mom in New Delhi. Much younger then, Mom's handwriting was tight, bold, almost calligraphic.

> *March 5. I'll never forget the trip to Bikaner this past weekend. The desert town was quaint, and we spent hours visiting a grand 16th-century fort made of yellow sandstone. I was stunned by the gorgeous marble statues, the gold and silver work on the ceilings and the lavish Moghul paintings. But the biggest surprise was on the return train to Delhi when the conductor brought a beautiful seven-year-old girl named Meena, Indian of course, to our compartment. She was wearing the prettiest silk clothes and a gold necklace, but no shoes. He told us she had been kidnapped by bandits from her village, but had somehow managed to escape. He left her with us until we got to Delhi. She's a darling child. A strong one. All through the night she didn't cry once.*
>
> *Once we arrived at Delhi, we took her to the police station. The officer there was obviously not too interested in finding out where she belonged. She's a spunky girl. Answered all his questions. But to him she was just one of thousands. He seemed to think the area was infested with bandits and we would be in considerable danger if we drove out there on our own.*
>
> *We have a big enough bungalow here in the Janpath neighborhood. Plenty of room for Meena. So we gladly brought her home. The house seems more alive now that we have a child here.*

March 6: Today I passed up my club luncheon to buy clothes and shoes for Meena, the same style wealthy Indian children in our circle wear. What fun to dress her up and comb her hair. Poor girl. She looks so sad. I sat with her at the dinner table. She took one look at her plate of pullao rice and chicken curry, which I assumed would be banquet food for her. She pushed it away, ate only the flat bread and some potatoes.

How I wish I spoke Hindi, so I could comfort her. Our cook and servant understand her, but they're quite busy. I don't like to admit it to anyone, but I've never been good with languages. And I'm embarrassed to speak the few Hindi words I know. I'd pronounce them all wrong.

March 25: I canceled my beauty salon appointment and spent the morning reading to Meena from picture books. She enjoys this activity, even if she doesn't understand English. I believe she's exceptionally bright and will learn the language soon. I can't imagine her in an orphanage. Those filthy places. What would become of her? She'd be wasted there. I can see her growing up to be a poised young woman, getting a Fine Arts degree like me and becoming an art teacher.

Though we've only been given temporary custody of Meena, I think if we try, they'll let us adopt her. We have wanted to adopt a child ever since Lance left us. Yes, I must work on Charles.

April 15: Meena was just sitting here with me in the study. With her big eyes she kept looking at the books and magazines on the shelves. She speaks some English now and reads a little too. She ran outside to the garden when she heard a mynah bird crying. I have so many different sentiments when I hold her close. I feel motherly, but also a little worried that we don't seem to connect well. Meena dulls my craving for a child, though I doubt if she could ever take the place of Lance.

April 30: Lance, my dear son, I miss you so much. Today would have been your 18th birthday. You stayed with us such a short time. You said good-bye to me to go on that bus trip and I never saw you again. Part of me is buried with you. I still see you all around me. I hear your voice. I look up and find the room empty. I cry. Why did you have to leave so early?

May 7. This evening I'm sitting in the garden with my diary. Too hot to be anywhere else. A few mosquitoes are buzzing around, as usual. My maid, Chitu, just brought me a gin and tonic (oh, do I need one) and my slippers. She's watering the rose-bushes now. Her eight-year-old is standing next to her. There is a closeness between the two, poor though they may be. I envy that. I'd like to have that kind of bond with Meena. But I'm afraid I'm a bit of a loner and have always stood apart from other people.

May 30: Charlie seems to get along great guns with Meena. He adores her. She runs to the door to meet him when he comes home. Why doesn't Meena feel that way about me?

There is something about Meena that draws me to her. I think I'm coming to love her. Maybe in time she'll feel differently. I must be patient. I'm not the cold person she thinks I am. There are a lot of warm feelings inside me. I just can't let them out the way Charles does. I try to show my love for Meena by doing things, but that doesn't seem to be enough. Maybe I've forgotten what it's like to raise a child. I was so much younger when I had Lance. Maybe my heart has hardened since Lance's death. Am I afraid of being hurt again?

June 15: Strangest thing happened this week. A police officer phoned Charlie and said they have located Meena's village, but that we have to take her back. He suggested catching a train to Bikaner, then hiring a chauffeur-driven car to get there.

My heart sank. Charlie and I talked about it at length last night. What's going to happen to this beautiful child? She'd have to live in a primitive village with bandits running around nearby. No, we can't take her back. It would be like abandoning her.

Besides, both Charlie and I have grown terribly attached to Meena and the thought of letting her go is simply unbearable. I don't think I can stand to lose another child. We also think we can offer Meena a much better future. So we decided in the end that it'd be best for all concerned if we didn't take her back. I know we're doing the right thing.

June 30: I'm a little more relaxed now that I've hired Bimla as a nanny for Meena. She was recommended by someone Charlie knew at the American Embassy and came with good credentials. What's most important is that she's multilingual in English, Hindi and Rajasthani. Meena has perked up a bit since Bimla came.

Meena's still having difficulty adjusting. She eats very little, jumps at every sound and has nightmares. Who could blame her? But she doesn't cry. She's got to cry.

I asked Bimla to talk to Meena. Bimla tells me Meena is a Rajput and Rajputs don't cry. There is so much about this culture that I don't understand. I feel like an alien, helpless and on the sideline.

....

July 2: The police officer paid us a visit today. I panicked. I didn't want Meena to see him. So I took her quietly away to a neighbor's house through the back door. I told Charlie to tell the officer, "The girl doesn't want to go back."

Thank God. The officer accepted our answer and didn't argue. He got a big bakshish on condition that he'd keep his mouth shut.

Meena shut the diary and stumbled to the window. Her eyes filled with tears, her breath came in gasps. She felt empty inside, as if some vital organ had been snatched from her. *The girl doesn't want to go back?* How could Mom do that? God, she'd have returned to Mataji in a minute. Who knows whether she'd have been accepted in her community or not? But by eliminating that option, Mom had cut her off from her very life source.

After an instant she wiped away her tears and looked across to the Golden Gate Bridge. The fog had finally cleared a little. She could see the red tips peeking through a misty white curtain.

How could Mom do that? Mom seemed to think she had done her a favor, that the life she had given Meena was the best possible. But was it? To be sure, she had had material comfort and freedom of choice. But was that equal in price to the rich tradition and human warmth she had missed? She didn't know the answer. Most of all she resented Mom for presuming to decide the course of her life.

Meena rummaged through the rest of the trunk. Her long wedding skirt, still a lush red silk, was carefully wrapped in tissue inside a box. She ran her fingers lightly over it, experiencing a tingle of pleasure in its cool smoothness. Tucked among the many folds was her gleaming gold wedding necklace—she'd often wondered what had happened to it—and a picture of her taken during her first year in San Francisco. She was wearing the same wedding dress (the bodice now too tight), her conchshell bangles and the necklace, but not her ruby tiara. The bandits had stolen that. No smile floated on her lips, and her large expressive eyes still held a hint of pain. She had never seen the picture, though that afternoon photo session was still vivid in her memory. Mom had dressed her in her wedding finery and put a crimson mark on her forehead. Meena remembered stamping the first few steps of a Rajasthani dance with her feet, just to hear the bells on her ankles jingle. She then abruptly struck a formal pose for the picture before Mom could ask her to stand still.

All these years and Mom had never shown her that photo, never said a word about it. And yet she had saved it in the trunk. Had she known how important these memorabilia would someday be to Meena? Had she been trying to suppress Meena's soul to make her transition to being an American easier? Did she think Americanizing Meena was the only way to be close to her? Meena would never know for sure. What she knew was that she belonged in neither culture—adapted to one, but not at home in it, wanting to belong to the other, but too long away from it.

She thought of the woman she could have been, sharing life with Vishnu in an obscure village. She'd hand-shape the millet breads and bake them over a fire made with dried cow-dung patties and, for sure, raise his many children. Life bordering on austerity, one drought away from disaster, but lived with intense emotions and close personal relationships born of mutual dependence. It would have been a different Meena, but one who was whole and who experienced life more fully. For the first time in her life, she found herself missing the simplest joys.

She had fulfilled Mom's expectations, but not her own. At first came a feeling of outrage, then of letdown, finally of—freedom.

Perhaps it wasn't too late yet.

She strode out of the room with an incredible feeling of lightness, pausing as she passed the floor-length mirror in the hall. A thin band of sunlight reflected in the glass highlighted her features. In slim jeans and a tee shirt, she looked every bit the smart, modern, carefree Western woman she was, possessing more than necessary and still not able to grasp what made life complete. But inside she was filled with a newfound confidence and purpose.

11

On her way to a meeting, Meena passed by the rows of cubicles inhabited by her programmer staff. Her eyes located Dave Williams in front of his computer monitor. He was pale and lanky and so shy that he blended with the white wall. But he was brilliant, and she had made him lead programmer on the COSMOS project. She said good-morning to him.

Dave stopped keying, swiveled his chair around, broke into a grin. "How goes it, boss?"

"Okay. Later today I'd like to talk with you about the new comparative study on database systems. Looks like our COSMOS will be a winner." Dave would be pleased to hear that, she knew.

But no, he was hesitating, his ears were reddening. Glancing about as if to make sure no one else was within earshot, Dave whispered, "Watch your step." Silence and then, "Brett came down here yesterday. He pretended to talk about football, but he was looking over my shoulder to see what I was doing. I think he was on a fishing expedition."

Brett again. Anger built up in Meena like steam. Few managers would have the gall to go snooping around a programmer assigned to another group. Not Brett. He was making good on his threat of taking over her project. "I'll keep my eyes open," she said. "Thanks for the warning."

"By the way," Dave said, "we start integrated testing later this week. We might need your help."

"I'll be available," she said reassuringly. Just before walking on toward the conference room she hesitated, half turned, and added, "Don't forget to lock your desk at night."

She had trusted Dave from the day he began working for her. Only a few years ago he was stuck in an entry-level position in another division. At their first meeting she realized how hardworking and dedicated he was and arranged for him to take a programmer aptitude test. He turned out to be bright and scored full marks. So she offered him a programmer trainee position and transferred him to her unit. He learned to code fast, showed complete loyalty to her— and related well to other programmers on his team too, a quality rare in a profession where hotshot coders often became prima donnas. Dave was, in short, Meena's dream employee.

Only a month earlier, a reporter from *PC* magazine had asked Meena during an interview, "What has been your greatest accomplishment so far?"

"I've recruited people with great potential," Meena had replied, "then given them challenging opportunities and watched them rise to the occasion." Dave wasn't the only one. She had hired Arthur from the UC Berkeley campus; Karen from a software company that had closed its doors; Judith, who was a secretary with uncommon energy. Under her guidance, all had become highly competent programmers. She motivated them by letting them perform challenging work. When they did well, she rewarded them with raises and promotions. She had helped build careers.

Late that afternoon when Meena returned to her office, she clicked the mouse to cruise the Net even before sitting down at her desk. As she waited for the computer to respond, her finger reached a tab divider in her slimline address book. There she dug up the e-mail address of her Stanford classmate Laxmi, who was now settled in Bombay. Glad that she was allowed personal e-mail in the office because of the long hours she worked, Meena composed a message.

Dear Laxmi:

Greetings from San Francisco. Hope all is well with you and your family. How has life turned out for you in Bombay? Do you still play the sarod? I remember when you, Ravi, Joseph, and I used to double-date. We had so much fun at Ravi's apartment. Are you at all in touch with him? Joseph and I didn't make it.

On a more serious note, Mom died several weeks ago. It was quite traumatic for me. So far I've managed to keep my spirits up, but it's been pretty hard sledding. I've been back to work for only a short time and am slowly easing back into my normal routine.

Here at SIC I'm managing a team responsible for developing a new database software package called COSMOS. Ten talented programmers work for me. We've added many features to make COSMOS perform better than similar products on the market, but couldn't incorporate all the bells and whistles in this first version. Nevertheless, it's been an exciting challenge for me.

By the way, could I ask you a favor? I know you travel throughout India on business. If you should ever happen to find yourself in Rajasthan, could you possibly make a detour to a village named Karamgar, northwest of Jaipur? It's sort of an oasis in the desert, not on the map and I can't give you any directions, but I know you'll find it. Please ask the village elders about a Vishnu R. Chauhan, now thirty-five. Would appreciate any information about him.

I have had very little downtime this past year, but with COSMOS-1 going out the door, I'll be able to take a breather soon.

Please write when you have time. I'd like to stay in touch with you.

Meena

The next meeting with the marketing department turned out to be an extended session. The large conference room was filled with a quorum of representatives from all divisions. Meena found a seat at the back and listened as someone brought up the subject of Write Now. The old word-processing package was a cash cow for SIC. A customer had complained that a macro facility in the latest version wasn't working.

"We've got to get the problem fixed soon," someone from marketing said.

"I can easily debug it," Meena said. "I was part of the team that wrote the original package ten years ago."

"Meena knows all about programming," Brett said. "She's from India. That's where all our jobs are going." With a short, quick laugh he tried to make a joke out of his cutting remark.

"Let's move on," the chairperson said to Brett, who now made himself a little smaller in his chair.

Lately this type of Meena-bashing had become routine. Best to ignore it, Meena thought. Still, it was difficult to focus on the rest of the meeting. All those years spent in this place: nine in programming, three as a manager. She had attended industry conferences, read computer journals in her spare time, developed a network of professional contacts—all in preparation for the job of designing COSMOS, a database offering that the company hoped would become its bread and butter. The project had been so well managed that she and almost everyone else considered her a shoo-in for a vice presidential position. That is, until Brett joined the company and turned things sour. A born manipulator, he seldom missed an opportunity to discredit her accomplishments. Meena realized that he'd try to ease her out, take over COSMOS, and claim her success as his own.

Meena reminded herself she had been steeped in the lore of her Rajput ancestors in childhood. The Rajputs sacrificed their lives to protect their families and their land from invaders sweeping into northwestern India. First came the Aryans, then Alexander, then the Mongols, and finally the British. None had succeeded in subjugating her clan. Nor would Brett. Her warrior heritage surfaced in response to the threat. No way, she resolved in her mind, would she allow Brett to destroy what she had achieved over the last twelve years.

12

That evening Meena went home ready to Wite-Out the workday from her mind. She cheered up when a neighbor, Ahmed Rasul, got in the elevator with her. Over the past two years, she had become a friend of the Muslim immigrant from India and his family. They were her only contact with the local Indian community. Like most expatriates, they retained their traditions in food and manners and the way they approached life, and that was fascinating to Meena. He owned Ahmed's Video and Spice Center located on O'Farrell Street. She shopped there all the time.

"They're still living in India," Mom sneered when she first met the family.

"They've done well here," Meena remembered saying to Mom. "Ahmed is a successful businessman. You'd never know that, he's so humble. He's taking care of his mother and raising a beautiful kid too." Sure, tradition could be a burden at times, Meena admitted to herself, but it seemed to anchor the Rasuls, making them more accepting of circumstances. There were times when Meena felt the lack of a stable base. And so, through the Rasuls, she experienced India secondhand.

Ahmed pushed the button for the sixth floor for both of them. "Want to watch a video with us this evening, *behenji*?" As usual, he called her "respected sister" in Hindi. But since she had forgotten much of that language, they usually conversed in English.

"Not Sadhna in another 'wet sari' movie, I hope," Meena said, laughing. The Rasul family watched Indian videos often as part of their attempt to stay in touch with the culture they had left behind, to feel as though they were in India if only for a few hours. Meena was often invited to join them. Though Hindi films were long and over-dramatic with improbable plots, they were a form of relaxation for her. "The last one we watched together, Sadhna sang and danced through pouring rain the whole time. If it were me, I'd catch a serious cold."

Ahmed's face dissolved into a grin. "This one's an art film from Calcutta, *behenji*. Not a 'spectacular' but a family story. It's so popular I can't keep it in the store."

"I'll be over in an hour," she said.

Once in her apartment, Meena changed and then retreated to the sanctuary, a huge walk-in closet outfitted with a meditation rug hand-woven in India. With sandalwood sticks burning in an incense holder before her, she eased into the classic full-lotus position taught to her by Guru Kailash a year ago. Eyes closed and spine straight, she gazed inward to watch her breath. The clutter in her mind dissolved like wisps of morning mist. A quiet confidence in herself arose from deep within, as though she were becoming part of a larger being, one that was stronger and wiser. Silently she repeated the mantra the guru had granted her. The vibrations of those words rang clear inside her, dispersing the last tendrils of negative emotion that blocked the path to inner peace. All the scattered parts of her being began to coalesce. Her exhalations became longer than her inhalations. Her conscious-ness expanded beyond the space around her, beyond this building, out to an indescribable infinity.

She had fallen into meditation quite by chance a year ago when she'd arrived early for a personal-computer convention at the Hilton Hotel. She wandered into an auditorium filled with the guru's fol-lowers. An Indian man approached her.

"I'm afraid I'm in the wrong room," Meena remembered saying to him.

"I bet you're not." The man flashed a wide smile. "You're here to meet Guru Kailash."

"Who?"

"Guru Kailash will plant a seed in your mind. That could change your life. He comes from a long line of yogis in India. Tonight's meditation could be a very special one."

Meena was skeptical. She vaguely remembered Grandfather in India meditating. She didn't practice it herself then, being too young to be taught the ways. But she had a half hour. No harm listening while she was waiting. She settled herself in the last row. Everyone was buzzing as Guru Kailash climbed onto the stage, a homespun cotton shawl wrapped around his thin shoulders, a rose garland around his neck. Sea-foam-soft hair cascaded about his plain lined face. His age was indeterminate. But his eyes, ancient as they were, danced with the mirth of an innocent child. An aura of peace emanated from him as he took his place. Instantly the whole room fell silent.

Guru Kailash proceeded to guide the group in a meditation. When Meena opened her eyes again, the clock on the wall had advanced a whole hour. To her surprise, the colors in the room, which she had barely noticed before, vibrated. The objects around her took on sharper outlines. Even the faintest sound was magnified. Oh, how alive she had become. More than relaxed. Meditation was for her.

At the end of the program the guru held a special initiation backstage for three people he selected at random from the audience. Meena didn't know why she was chosen, but was glad of it. She never got to the computer convention and didn't regret it.

Since then, computers and meditation complemented each other in her life. Where one left off, the other picked up. Once months later Dave, her ace programmer, had approached her with a glitch in his coding. The problem was obscure. Meena plugged away at it for several hours, then gave up and went home stumped. That evening just before she finished her meditation, the cover page of a computer manual, one she hadn't considered for this problem, flashed before her. She rushed to the office right away and pulled the book out of her drawer. By the time the clock struck midnight, she had the answer.

Meditation was part of her daily routine now. Yet tonight, for the first time, Guru Kailash materialized before her. His clear figure was a presence so powerful that she felt the floor vibrating. She saw the lively eyes, the peaceful countenance, the one outstretched hand ready to comfort. His smile was warm and radiant and erased all petty grievances from her heart. A feeling arose within her that he was holding a candle at the doorstep, inviting her to take a step outside. As she reached out to touch his hand, he vanished. She opened her eyes, feeling solidly centered and ready to face the world again. The twenty-minute ritual had restored her better than a two-hour nap.

After showering, she tied the sash of her bathrobe around her waist and sat at her dressing table. As she powdered the shine from her nose, she hummed a melody half remembered from an Indian film. The meaning of the Hindi words escaped her now.

She pondered what to wear and found herself drawn to a sari. The flowing apparel had always felt kind to her skin. In Western clothes she acted assertive, just right for the daytime. A sensuous sari was meant for the night.

Tonight's selection of a luminous yellow silk complemented her dark complexion and instilled in her an attitude of expectation. She wrapped the six yards of fabric around her waist, leaving just enough to drape over one shoulder. Standing in front of the full-length mirror, she struck various poses. What had happened to manager Meena? The same dark eyes, the same burnished skin, the same dimpled cheeks, yet she had become subtly different. She was a woman, an Indian woman to whom much could happen.

Something was missing. Jewelry. She moved softly to the closet, opened a small wooden jewel case lined with red velvet, took out a pair of gold earrings. Now, hair. She removed the pins from her hair and let it fall to her waist. One strand bounced over her face, as if glad to escape the confines of her professional demeanor. She picked up her boar-bristle brush and ran it through all the way to the end. A gentle fragrance of the herbal shampoo she had used that morning wafted about her. Her tresses were her pride. Suddenly she realized why she kept them long, even during busy periods in her life when short hair would have been more convenient. Mataji wore her hair the same. She'd be gray by now, but would still possess thick, silky knee-length hair. Meena was merely keeping to family tradition.

She picked up a hand mirror to get a back view. Too casual, she thought. Perhaps she should braid it the way Indian women do. So she plaited it into a long braid, tying the end with a neat gold bow. She slipped on a pair of sandals to complete her Indian look. Finally ready, she walked down the corridor to Ahmed's apartment.

Sonny answered the door. "Auntie Meena." A smile flooded the seven-year-old's face. "See my new kite." He held a butterfly-shaped fighter kite.

"I flew the exact same ones in India when I was your age, *bhai*," she said, addressing him as a little brother. "Glad to see they're still making them."

Except for an expensive brick-red Bokhara rug on the floor and a

large television set, the living room was simply furnished: an upholstered couch, a few more or less matching chairs, a dented coffee
table. No plants, flowers, pictures, or great view to impress a guest.
But this family of three generations was close, as was evident from
the babble of high, happy voices, the smell of cumin and coriander
that escaped from the kitchen, and the total disregard for the television news.

Ahmed's wife, Shaheen, who had just drifted in from the back,
stared at Meena for a moment. "Very pretty. You have the figure for a
sari." Shaheen pulled up a chair for her. "You look Indian, like us."

Meena received the compliment with a smile, but the meaning
behind the words stung her. Was the sari indeed just a veneer? she
wondered. Was she, an American, posing as something else?

Ahmed's mother, the elder Mrs. Rasul, came into the room, made
straight for her usual end of the couch, and began cooling herself with
a palm leaf fan. Light-skinned—Indians would call it "fair"—hair
frizzy from dryness, and lips pinched together, she looked slightly out
of sorts. As always she smelled of talcum powder. Meena could picture her in India on a sultry evening seated on a verandah, covered
head to toe in her sari, attended by a retinue of servants, complaining
about mosquitoes.

"Such a pretty face," chirped Mrs. Rasul as she looked up at
Meena. "But dear, you have dark circles under your eyes. You need a
vacation. How many times have I said you work too hard?"

Better than being asked why she wasn't married yet. That question, which came frequently from Mrs. Rasul, embarrassed Meena
because she didn't know the answer.

"It's hard to live alone, isn't it?" Mrs. Rasul didn't wait for an
answer. "Ahmed's new assistant is single. The chap is a little shorter
than you are and chubby, but he makes a good living. Doesn't smoke
or drink. Would you like Ahmed to introduce him to you?"

Shaheen emerged from the kitchen with a platter in hand and
interrupted her mother-in-law's matchmaking. "Have some *dalmut*,
Meena."

Meena took a handful of the mixture and popped it into her
mouth. Peanuts, raisins, roasted lentils, and crispy noodles dusted
with red chili powder—oh, the flavor, the aroma, the crunch.
"Mmmm. These are hot."

"This is a new brand," Shaheen said. "Customers who come to

rent Indian videos always pick up a packet of *dalmut* to munch on. Just like in India. You have to have *dalmut* to watch a show."

Ahmed interjected. "Did I tell you, *behenji*, we might be going to India for vacation in late spring? Just before the general election."

"Will there be a Hindu-Muslim riot like last time, Daddyji?" Sonny asked.

"No," Ahmed said. "Indian elections are getting more orderly. Less interesting."

Meena asked him, "Is spring the best time to visit India?"

"It starts to get hot in spring," Ahmed replied. "Fall and winter are the coolest seasons. But for me, anytime is fine."

"It's hard to know where to begin when I visit India," Meena said. "There's so much to see and do. It's a living museum."

"We always start our trip in Bombay," Sonny said. "This time we're going to visit the caves. Why don't you come with us, Auntie Meena?"

"Quiet, the movie is starting," Ahmed said, adjusting the knobs on the VCR.

They pulled their chairs to make a semicircle in front of the TV set. The film from Calcutta, known internationally for its low-budget, high-quality movies, turned out to be a comedy. It was about an expatriate Indian returning home with his two young children, both born in England, after twenty years. At first, the man was at odds with everything. His children adjusted better. Slowly he began to see the values of his ancient culture. The story was set in Calcutta and showed the sprawling city, a hospital, a park, and a vegetable market.

Meena and the Rasul family laughed at all the jokes as they ate their way through the *dalmut*.

When the movie ended and the credits rolled, Shaheen remarked, "Wasn't the hero crass?"

"They exaggerate in movies," Meena said mildly.

"That man was a caricature," Mrs. Rasul said. "He was caught between cultures."

"Like me," Meena said. "I have great respect for the Indian way of life, but if I ever went back . . ."

"I can see that man's point," Ahmed said. "I didn't appreciate India half as much when I lived there." His eyes had a dreamy look and his voice seemed to come from another continent. "Now, India is in my blood. When I go back everything seems wonderful. I don't notice the noise, the crowding, the cow dung on the street. The roses in our garden in Bombay seem bigger and more perfumey than what I can buy at Union Square. And my relatives are so hospitable. We spend hours drinking tea and catching up."

"I like the sweets." Sonny's eyes grew large. "*Sandesh, rosgulla, ros malai.* They are all so tiny, but so good."

"I spend the entire time with my mother," Shaheen said. "I follow her around like when I was a little girl. All my wanderlust goes away. Mother makes my favorite *saag.* I take a bite and I cry. I feel like I've come home."

Mrs. Rasul wiped away a tear. "San Francisco is nice, but I'd like to spend the last days of my life in Bombay. I'd look out at the mosque from my room upstairs; hear people speak Marathi on the street. That beautiful language. It's music to me. Ahmed, would you take me there when the time comes? Then maybe my soul would rest in peace."

"You've got some good years ahead of you, Ji." Ahmed, now misty-eyed himself, addressed his mother respectfully. "And you have the best of both worlds. Your blood pressure got lower here. You can fly to India whenever you want. But you won't find such a cool pleasant evening in Bombay even in winter."

Slowly Mrs. Rasul raised herself from the chair. "Well, if you'll excuse me . . . it's my bedtime. Meena, hope to see you again soon." She shuffled out of the room.

"Auntie Meena, can I show you my other kites?" Sonny beckoned Meena to his room and she stayed with him until his mother asked him to go to bed. Meena kissed him good-night, thanked her hosts, and returned to her apartment.

She unwound the sari, changed into her nightgown, and felt more at ease. She had been Indian for the evening, but not the way the Rasul family were. To them India was the mother with an enormous hold on them. They were connected to her by a bond stronger than anything she had ever known. To them life in the U.S. was pleasant, yet their homeland was something greater and more magical.

To Meena India was just the germinating seed of a memory. She must help bring that tiny sprout to life.

13

Corte Madera was about a half hour's drive from the city. Meena crossed the rainbow arch of the Golden Gate Bridge and entered Marin County. Her tape deck was playing a ridiculous song: "Loving a Stranger." She turned the music off, but couldn't turn off her misgivings about this trip. Driving up to a reading by a semicelebrity or jerk she had met for five minutes at a party—and one who was engaged, at that—good grief, Meena, she said to herself. It would have made more sense if her colleague Joy was with her for this literary excursion or ordeal, whatever it was going to be. But then Joy, who had bubbled about Antoine's first novel over lunch last Tuesday, had canceled at the last minute.

Meena walked through the Town Center, casting glances at the upscale mall's usual mix of glossy boutiques, trendy restaurants, concrete walkways, and cyclamen beds. On this balmy evening the stores were almost empty and only a few scattered shoppers lingered at the lighted windows. But she found the tiny auditorium at the back of the Bookworm absolutely packed with women.

"Can't put the book down," a blonde woman was saying to her neighbor as Meena slid into one of the two remaining back-row chairs. The woman had on denim vest, jeans, and boots, all matched, and several strands of beads. "His images are so evocative."

"He's huge," the woman next to the blonde burbled. Long boat-shaped earrings dragged across slender shoulders with each turn of her crew-cut head. "I'm getting several copies autographed for Christmas presents."

Meena felt stiff, programmed, and out of place. There had been no time to change after work. She was in her business uniform—navy linen, pumps and all. Her feet hurt and she hadn't read any of Antoine's books. She looked around. Here was her competition. Now where did that thought come from?

The room hushed. Antoine strode before them to the stage, exuding confidence in a navy sport coat, his walnut brown hair tousled as ever. That was his "look," Meena now knew. His mien was artistlike, his forehead high and prominent, a sign of intelligence. Dark circles under his eyes hinted at more than lack of sleep.

The bookstore manager, very Marin in cutoffs, a tee-shirt, and curly blond hair, tapped her microphone. "We have with us Antoine Peterson, Marin County's own author. . . ." While she made the introduction, Antoine's eyes roved across the room seeking familiar faces. He flashed a smile at several before noticing Meena. There was a glimmer of surprise, a slight squaring of shoulders, a parting of lips. Or did she hallucinate all that?

He took his place behind the podium. Voice measured, he described *Parallel Lives*. "It's a tale of twin brothers," he said, "one a renowned polar explorer, the other in jail for writing bad checks." He opened his book and slowly began to read. "They met in the visitors' room of the prison." He spoke as though he were delivering these lines for the first time instead of finishing up a three-month book tour. "Walt looked at his mirror image clothed in rumpled prison coveralls. He wanted to embrace his brother, but . . ."

Meena found herself pulled, like a puppet, every which way by strings of images. She alternately felt love, disgust, and compassion for the characters in the book. She was both anticipatory and uncomfortable. Antoine read his work with passion, as if this was the only thing he could possibly do. His protagonist was someone who lived fully, embracing life's joys and sorrows in turn, one who extracted the last drop of meaning from each experience. As she listened, the distinction between the story and Antoine blurred. It was hard to tell where one left off and the other began. She was seeing into his soul with a sense of intimacy akin to making love. And apparently the effect was not limited to her. The blonde in denim was gazing rapturously toward the podium and the crew-cut woman's breathing had become audible and a bit ragged. A photographer moved in and snapped a few shots. Antoine didn't blink. He was one with his story.

Quite suddenly his voice stopped. Meena drew breath, felt her cramped back against the hardness of the chair and her sore feet pressed against the floor. The audience was laughing, clapping, and surging toward the stage. She glanced down at her watch. Forty minutes had passed.

Meena retreated, avoiding the rush of adoring fans, and threaded her way to the table where the manager now sat behind a cash register and several stacks of Antoine's books. Minutes later, when she wandered back toward the stage with both his novels, she was last in line. She was sure Antoine didn't notice her shuffling forward. She felt a little foolish having to wait.

But Antoine was a pro and the line moved quickly. Finally the woman in front of Meena bent over the table showing lots of tanned skin and murmured, "I take you to bed every night."

Antoine had a polite smile on his lips as he jotted words down onto the page. Up close his face looked weary, revealed a few more lines. "Thanks," he said. "Maybe I'll see you at my next reading."

The woman fluttered her eyelashes, attempted a seductive grin, then stepped back. An older woman with a humorous look about her. Meena decided she was just joking.

Meena held out her two books quietly. As he looked up, his eyes widened in recognition. "Well, hello, Meena. Sorry I had to leave your party early," he said, while his hand wrote "To Meena."

Hers was not a common name. Quite often she had to explain to people where it came from and how it was spelled. But he penned her name as easily as a familiar one like Mary or Susan. As he returned the books to her, his hand brushed against hers. She felt a surge of pleasure. Deliberate? She dismissed the thought. Here was a complex man, she had gathered that much after listening to his reading, and attractive too. Probably almost impossible to figure out. She wasn't sure if she would care to take on a challenge of that magnitude even if offered. She smiled faintly, thanked him, and turned to go.

"Would you have time for tea?" Antoine called out from behind her.

Meena swung around quickly. She hadn't liked his overconfident manner even at their first meeting. Now she was definitely annoyed. "Thanks, but I should be going. I have several hours' worth of work to do."

"Actually I'm a bit hungry. Have you eaten yet?"

"No, but—"

"Do you like *chai?*"

"I love *chai.*" The words slipped out on their own.

"Let's go have a bite to eat, then. I know a little Indian place around the corner. The food's excellent and they make good *chai*, too. Won't take long. I promise."

"All right."

My God! Her spontaneous pleasure and excitement at spending time with Antoine had overcome her natural reserve and the nagging fear that of late she was becoming a rigid corporate automaton. Underneath the surface she was a flesh-and-blood woman after all.

The store manager waved at Antoine and said, "See you over the back fence."

Antoine stopped to thank her. As Meena waited at the exit, she glanced across the courtyard and noticed a trendy women's dress shop named Paint the Town Red, closed by now. A mannequin, bent slightly backwards in a suggestive pose, modeled a long white dress with a beaded neckline. Meena pictured herself in a flowing gown like that, twirling across a dance floor with Antoine. What a silly thought, she said to herself as Antoine rejoined her.

"She's my neighbor," he said as he held the door for her. "My house is two blocks north that way." He pointed toward the road that ran parallel to the mall.

That would be Tamal Vista Boulevard. She couldn't see Mount Tamalpais in the darkness, but knew the mountain formed the backdrop for this arty, laid-back, affluent village.

Antoine walked beside her, their shoulders almost touching. He was easily five inches taller. She groped for something clever and intelligent to say. "Actually I'm glad you invited me." That came to her ear as mundane. "I didn't get a chance to tell you how tasty your *chaat* was." Hey, that wasn't so bad.

"I make it on special occasions," he said. "That was your birthday. You're a year older."

"This is going to be an important year for me," Meena said. "I'm starting my fifth cycle of seven. Thirty-five is a junction. I look back over my past life to see where I've been and forward to see where I want to go—"

"Sounds like you're getting ready to make some changes," he said.

"I'm forty-two, at the midpoint, and still haven't sorted everything out." Something in his voice conveyed a sense of regret.

Antoine the celebrity was shedding his aura. She liked him better as a regular guy with regular worries.

A few feet down the street neon lights flashed the name of a restaurant: Ganesh's Whim. "Good old Ganesh, the elephant-headed god with a human body—he's my favorite Indian deity," Antoine said. "He's a big eater. Isn't he?"

Not many people possessed such detailed knowledge of India. Meena laughed to herself, remembering how Auntie Bimla treated her gods like they were part of the family. She wanted to impress Antoine in turn. "Yes," she agreed. "My nanny used to make all kinds of sweets in the days leading up to Ganesh Chotourthi every fall. She loved festivals—and sweets."

"The owner's name is Ganesh too. He's the cook at night. No fixed dinner menu. It's all according to his mood."

They stepped into the small eatery furnished with chrome tables, fluorescent tubes, burning incense, and paisley walls—a curious mix of fast-food efficiency and old-world charm. A strong chili pepper fragrance emanated from the kitchen's service window. Meena drew a glance from the cook, who paused to stare at her for a second before resuming his chopping.

The waiter came out from behind the cash register. He was a tall, lean Indian whose dark complexion was set off by a soft white turban. "Good evening," he said to Meena. Then, turning, "Antoine, where have you been lately?"

"I'm house-sitting Liv's place in the city four days a week," Antoine told him. He added to Meena in an undertone, "I have my dinner here a couple nights a week."

When they were seated Antoine stretched his arms above his head, then brought them down gradually as though gathering back the energy he had spent at the reading. Music started up in the background and filled the silence between them. The subdued beating of the tablas swirled about her. The traditional paired Indian drums, so subtle yet insistent, entered her body through that place on her forehead where the third eye was, gave her mood a lift, then spread a feeling of restlessness to her extremities. Almost unnoticed a sitar joined the tabla and Meena felt the tug of another place, another era.

She touched the bobby pins behind her ears and took several sips of water.

Antoine leaned slightly toward her across the table. "It's easy to like Ganesh. But his father, Shiva, is almost as remote as Brahma. The only one of the main gods I can relate to is Vishnu."

Vishnu. The sound of that name came as a shock. Just in time the waiter returned, poised to take their order.

"What's Ganesh cooking tonight?" Antoine asked the waiter.

"Ganesh bought organic peas and potatoes in the market today," the waiter replied. "With those he has prepared especially fine samosas."

"Excellent. *Chai* and vegetable samosa for two," Antoine ordered the waiter.

"See how he orders?" the waiter said to Meena. "Just like an Indian."

Antoine chuckled. It was obvious the waiter teased him often. Meena liked it that Antoine had taken the trouble to cultivate a friendly relationship with him.

After they had been served, she decided to show off a bit herself. "You can always judge a cook by his samosas." She cut into the triangular pastry. It split open, revealing a stuffing of peas, potatoes, and whole cumin seeds and exuding a spicy aroma. She spread a little mint chutney of bright green color on it, took a small bite, then resumed talking. "Whenever I try a new Indian restaurant, I order samosa first. If they have a knack for that, they generally have a knack for other dishes. This one passes inspection. It passes my test for watered-down Indian restaurants." Oh, my God, she was talking too much. She was so nervous.

With a laugh he said, "I appreciate the tip," and turned his attention to his own samosa. He fell silent for a time, obviously hungry from the way he emptied his plate. He gulped down his *chai*.

A hint of cardamom scent rose from her cup and summoned a feeling of animation. The drums throbbed faster, the sound reverberating inside her in an urgent way. What should she say next? She asked, "Have you been running much lately?"

"No." His eyes were steady on hers. "I've been pretty inconsistent. It's always that way when I run alone. How about you?"

She said, "I've been pretty regular. I'm training for a race, actually."

"Which one?"

"The Kimochi Cherry Blossom Run." She tried to keep her voice casual, though the race meant a lot to her. "It'll be my first race of the season."

"Is it a tough one?"

"Sort of," she said. "It's only a five-mile course, but mostly uphill. It fools a lot of people. Only a month to go. There are plenty of races during the summer, but the Kimochi's my favorite. They have a big bash following the race, which is a nice opportunity to meet with friends."

"Do you train a lot?"

"Oh, an eight-mile loop in Golden Gate Park several times a week."

"I'd like to run the Kimochi," Antoine said wistfully.

"Have you ever run a race?"

"No. I saw a friend finish a marathon once. When he crossed the finish line he looked mesmerized. Like he was in a state of ecstasy. I'd like to experience that feeling someday. I don't care much for being a spectator." He paused, pushing his hair back from his forehead with his fingers. "Liv doesn't run. . . ."

Meena had forgotten about Antoine's woman friend. "How does she work out, then? Nautilus? Aerobics?"

"She doesn't."

How dull it must be, she mused, to share life with a physically lazy companion. Life was movement, a sprint, a dance.

"How long have you lived in San Francisco?" Antoine asked.

Meena welcomed the shift in the subject. "All except the first seven years of my life," she said. "My American parents brought me here from India."

"Must have been quite a change."

The tabla beat rose to a frenetic crescendo. Breathlessly she was caught up in the rhythm until it stopped for a meaningful pause. "Yes, it was," she said. "But I was very young then. I got used to the food, learned English, made friends. Still, at times I felt very lonely, very sad. Some days I didn't want to leave the house. I preferred sitting in my room and staring off into space. My Indian nanny helped me a lot. What also saved me was Indian music. In Rajasthan, working or playing, people sang. A good singer could make the rain fall or the sun shine. I used to think the buffaloes gave more milk if you sang to them and, of course, the crops were better. . . ." She stopped, embarrassed at how much she had revealed to someone she barely knew. He was listening with his whole being, from the way he was leaning toward her.

"I wish music came that naturally to me," Antoine said. "I sing only in the shower. Do you play ragas at home?"

"Yes, often."

"They have the structure of Western classical music and the free-ness of jazz. I had to listen to them for a while before I got to like them."

"Mom brought a pile of records from India, but she didn't play them. My Indian nanny and I did. The sitar, the veena, the tabla took me back to the desert, to my village home, to my family." She lapsed into silence for a moment, flooded with memories of music that pen-etrated the nape of her neck, her skull, the very roots of her hair. "What I couldn't verbalize, I always felt in music."

"Music must go back before developed speech," Antoine said. "Back to the time when man was close to nature and imitated the howling of wind, the sound of waterfalls, the cry of birds."

Meena nodded thoughtfully, impressed with his insight. "I can't speak Hindi or Rajasthani anymore," she said with a sigh. "I wouldn't be able to talk to my relatives even if I could locate them. They won't speak much English. Oh, sure, if I spent any time there at all, I'd regain my fluency. But in the meantime, music would bring us together."

"I'd like to go back to India myself," Antoine said.

Meena fancied arriving at her village. A clear sky, a brilliant sun bathing the desert landscape in its marigold yellow light. Bells ringing in the temple, people chanting, relatives approaching with open arms from a distance, the women arranging their veils to leave a tiny slit open so they could peer out at her. One of them would have to be Mataji. And oh, what a surprise—Antoine there beside her.

"What fun it would be," Meena said, "to hear the *bhajans* and the temple bells, standing on the grounds of our house like I used to."

"I'm trying to talk Liv into honeymooning in India."

"Oh?" Her tea tasted cold and weak. She set her cup down, trying to keep her hand steady. The tabla music reached another crescendo, then ended abruptly, the last few beats clawing at her heart.

"How about a run through Golden Gate Park this week?" He

breezed on, as if oblivious to her reaction. "Now that I'm staying in Liv's apartment, I'm only five minutes from the park."

Why didn't I see it? she thought bitterly. He wasn't sincere. He was just taking her as another woman fan grasping at him. And he was so smooth. The rational side of her mind countered that he was only being friendly and that it was she who had blown the whole evening up out of proportion.

"Oh, you are?" she said in a neutral voice.

"I like running the flats."

A wave of humiliation was followed by a surge of anger. "How many miles do you usually do?" she asked.

"I could keep up with you, oh, maybe for three or four miles."

No, she didn't want to run with him. It wasn't that she was frigid or heartless or had developed an aversion to men during her recent period of solitude. Quite the contrary. Of late, she had begun to crave male companionship with increasing intensity. But with the need came vulnerability, painfully evident in the presence of this attractive yet self-absorbed man. It was almost too much to bear.

Anyway, she rationalized, his mileage was a lot lower than hers. She'd have to split her eight-mile run, doing the first half alone and then joining him for the second half. It made no sense. She barely had enough time left before the race to train properly. She remained silent.

He opened his wallet, withdrew a card, and handed it to her. "Give me a call next Tuesday. That's a day I have free." His deep blue eyes, conveying perhaps a sense of uncertainty, seemed to search hers for a definite answer.

The card still held the barest warmth from his touch. She forced a smile and stood up. "Well, thanks for the *chai*. I really have to get home now."

He escorted her to the parking lot. She climbed into her car, allowed him to close the car door, and watched his receding figure in silence. As soon as he was out of sight, she crushed his card and tossed it into the litter bag, then shook her head angrily as tears backed up in her eyes.

14

Vishnu found Asha seated alone at the Coffee House, crisp and cool in a cotton sari the color of candlewax. Bent over a pile of papers, her face had the quiet energy of a slow-passing deer. A thick braid of lustrous black hair was draped over her shoulder. She raised her head and a happy smile gave her eyes the shine of a full moon.

He chose a chair and sat facing her. "Been waiting long?"

"Just ten minutes." She must have noticed the distraught look on his face, for she added in a voice thick with concern, "You don't look well, Vishnuda. Is anything the matter? I sure hope it wasn't my cooking."

"I don't think so." He leaned his cheek on his hand. "I had a crazy dream last night." He didn't quite want to tell her about it. But Asha seemed eager to listen, from the way she was gazing up at him. His mind drifted from image to image and he found himself recounting the fire scene and his trying to rescue two women—Asha and Meena.

"Who's Meena?"

"My child bride," Vishnu said. "I was married when I was seven. People in my village married young in those days. And they still do sometimes."

"You are married?" Asha's question was laced with hurt, surprise.

"I was. You might find it hard to understand," Vishnu said, "growing up in a modern city like Calcutta. Here people are marrying later and later. But Rajasthan is different, still very traditional, especially in the villages." He went on to say that Meena was the prettiest girl around and that they were inseparable until their wedding day when she was taken by bandits. He noticed how Asha's face had turned grayish, how her eyes had lost their luster. He hastened to add that his "marriage" had begun and ended on one afternoon nearly three decades ago. Still Asha said nothing.

He suppressed a sigh and asked, "Where's your English paper?"

She put the loose sheets in order and handed them to him. "I hope I did this right. Maybe you'll laugh at my sentence construction. You know how proud we Bengalis are of our own language. At home we speak nothing else, never Hindi or English."

He scanned a paragraph. "Your English is good. Just needs some tweaking." He was an expert editor and could certainly help her with that. He flipped through a few more pages with a practiced eye, aware that she was sitting close, within arm's reach. For the moment he let go of any thought of Meena and the nightmare. He felt light and airy, even hopeful. He only pretended to read.

Someone brushed past their table. Vishnu raised his head and spotted a smiling Pradip strolling off. Vishnu stared at the back of his garish plaid shirt, asking himself why the Moxan was here again.

But then, why not? Coffee was fast becoming a fashionable drink and this haunt served the best. Vishnu returned to the essay mindful of his unemployed status. When Asha asked him how he liked the paper so far, he replied "good" with only half his attention.

In half an hour he finished and handed her back the edited essay. Asha took the paper from him carefully, as if his touch had made it special, or so he conjectured. With a flip of her braceleted hand she slid the pages into a large envelope, then consulted her watch.

"It's almost one. I have to run to the chemistry lab. You've helped me a lot, Vishnuda."

Vishnu listened to the ringing of her bracelets for an instant. "It was nothing," he said. "When do you finish your exams?"

"This Friday. Two more days. What a relief that will be."

Vishnu hated to see her leave. She was the afternoon sun—direct, clear, and constant. "Want to go for cutlets this Friday?" he offered a little hesitantly. "There's a Muslim place just around the corner from here. *Kabiraji* cutlet, they call it. Would you like to try it?"

"Oh, yes. That sounds marvelous. I know they use a secret spice mix in their famous cutlets. I've never had it." She leaned across the table and whispered, "Just don't tell Mother. She'll be disappointed if I refuse her evening meal."

"Promise."

He watched her stand up and turn. Eyes glistening, she tossed a good-bye smile over her shoulder. Her two-inch drop earrings whipped. The loose end of her sari pleated vertically over her back made a zigzag pattern in space. He didn't know he was holding his breath until she waved from the door.

Vishnu remained with his newspaper, turned to the classifieds and scanned them, but found himself daydreaming about Asha. A nagging awareness that Pradip was at a table nearby, watching his moves, was in the back of his mind. When he lifted his eyes and caught a figure clad in pink-and-purple plaid approaching him, he tried to ignore it.

"Have an hour to spare, Vishnu-babu?" Pradip asked in a jovial voice. Vishnu knew the suffix -babu, meaning an upper-class gentleman, was added to flatter him. "I'd like to show you our new office."

Vishnu could either accept his invitation or study the Situations Vacant column some more. He didn't relish the idea of being pulled into the Moxan circle and knew that even a jaunt to their premises might not be safe. But the classifieds bored him so. And as a journalist he was interested in digging into this tribe's situation. He supposed he could always back out.

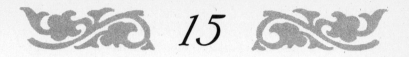

15

Karun Dhotia sat at an immense desk. He was just as Vishnu remembered him, a large balding man in his early fifties with heavy jowls, a full-lipped mouth, and laser-beam eyes. He exuded a kind of magnetism that simultaneously attracted Vishnu and repelled him. He looked up at Vishnu's knock and his face broke into an oily smile of recognition. "Please come in, Vishnu," he said softly. Then, motioning toward a chair, "Do sit down." The polite words were, nonetheless, a command.

Vishnu smiled diffidently and eased into a chair in front of Dhotia's desk. The freshly painted room was furnished in a mixture of new and old. Heroic posters adorned one entire wall. LORD SHIVA PRESIDES, proclaimed one in a flashy script beneath a gyrating image of Shiva. In the next one, MOXANS, AWAKE! trumpeted a fierce-eyed tribesman with a red bandanna around his forehead and brandishing an assault rifle. The third declared INDIA IS MANY VOICES and featured adolescents in a variety of ethnic garb walking hand in hand.

"It seems I've lost a whole morning interviewing." Dhotia sighed, shoving a stack of papers to one side of his desk. "The most qualified candidate for our editor's position so far is a young man whose father has promised to make a donation to our party in the event of a successful interview. Unfortunately the boy has no writing experience."

"But Vishnu does." Pradip laughed as he patted Vishnu on the shoulder. "His writing was powerful enough to get him fired. People listen to what he says."

"I like that. Fire! Passion! Conviction!" Dhotia called out as if invoking three deities in support of his cause. The walls seemed to vibrate. "Words that make people shake off their lethargy and inspire them to sacrifice for the sake of their cause."

Vishnu recoiled, intimidated by this intense speech, yet admiring the fiery leader. After all, Dhotia had given the last twenty years of his life for his people. Even so, Vishnu wondered if their cause could be his cause. And now Vishnu felt the weight of the wallet in his pocket. It was ever so light. His rent was due next week. He hadn't sent his mother a money order in many weeks. In a state of inner turmoil, Vishnu stammered out, "I'm not sure I'm ready to take on a responsibility of this magnitude just yet."

Dhotia's smile widened, exposing tobacco-stained teeth. "Ah, of course, you need time to think. It's after all a great responsibility. That's what you're saying. We're holding a regional party conference next Monday at the Carlyle Hotel. It would be an excellent opportunity for you to meet more of our people."

It was an attractive suggestion, for it would enable Vishnu to find out what really was going on with this tribe. He was familiar with the Carlyle Hotel. It had been fashionably ritzy twenty years ago. But now Sudder Street, where it was located, was known as a haunt of drug dealers, prostitutes, and petty criminals. Why there?

"Whoever is hired will be well paid," Dhotia continued encouragingly. "You see, we have good funding." The next moment his forehead creased in a frown. "Of course, if you're concerned about the authorities, you can use a pen name."

That would be cowardly, an implicit admission of guilt. Surely there would be other options open to him. Vishnu rose from his seat, saying noncommittally, "I'll think it over."

"Let me show you our computers on your way out." Dhotia led him down the hall to a large room. Several Moxans sat at workstations, staring intently at their monitors.

"You'll have your own e-mail ID," Pradip said. "You could talk to the whole world."

At the door, first Dhotia and then Pradip shook his hand warmly. Dhotia said, "Let us hear from you soon."

Out on the boulevard, the blazing sun blinded Vishnu. A motor scooter whizzed by, narrowly missing him as he jumped quickly back from the curb. The driver had on sunglasses and a black leather vest.

He looked evil. Might this be a thug hired by the ghee baron he had insulted?

Vishnu steadied himself against a lamppost and took several deep breaths. When he recovered, he found his mind was vacillating between two unappealing choices: Do I take this job? Or do I get killed?

16

Days had gone by since Meena and Antoine had tea, but she had been unable to stop thinking about him. Now, sitting in her living room, she recapitulated her conclusions one more time: There was no point in spending time with someone who was in a relationship about to culminate in marriage. Forget him. Let his novels collect dust. Reading them would only weaken her resolve. Yet in the next moment a vision of the attractive man at the podium at the Bookworm insinuated itself unbidden into her consciousness. The tall lithe frame, the warm resonant voice, the deep-set eyes hinting at a capacity for suffering. And again a small voice inside her whispered: But what if he doesn't really love Liv?

So much for conclusions.

At work today, Joy had brought a copy of an interview with Antoine. "Thanks, Joy, I'll read it later," Meena had said, not wanting to appear too interested, and put it away in her purse. The day had proved to be busy and she never did find the time to look over the page-long article in her office. Now finally she had a chance to read it.

She trembled as she unfolded the page. How silly to get so worked up over a publicity write-up, she thought. But the question-and-answer piece turned out to be excellent.

Here was Antoine on India: "India is complex, frightening and beautiful all at the same time. There's no place on earth where I feel more connected to my fellow human beings."

On writing: "The writing process is a dragon, at once both terrifying and fascinating. I don't know if I'll ever be able to tame the beast completely."

On women: "Relationships are definitely the most difficult aspect of my life. As many times as I have tried and failed, I have come away feeling that I have grown personally and that I'll be able to make the next one better. But no two ever work the same way. Eventually I find myself back at square one, wondering where I went wrong."

She was seeing another side of Antoine, a man who explored his inner self as intensely as distant places on earth. Maybe she'd finish his *Parallel Lives* after all. But not at the expense of other fun activities in her life. First and foremost, she must tend to her patio plants, which were beginning to show signs of neglect. Her tiny garden of flowers and herbs, six stories above street level, was important because it gave her a sense of connection with the earth. She could hardly wait to read this month's issue of *Flower Garden* magazine, lying on the coffee table next to *Parallel Lives*. And she must not forget that her volunteer day for the Bay Area Mountain Reforestation Project was coming up next Saturday.

She worked her way around her gallery of plants, watering each one as needed. She felt tender toward the silvery sage bush that would soon be covered with fragrant flowers and attract a crowd of bees and butterflies. With gentle hands she pinched back the growth tips of an aster, fertilized the pansies cascading out of a hanging planter, and mulched the soil around the stocky stems of a large pot of tulips. She replenished the bird feeder with sunflower seeds, millet, and corn and listened to the birds that fluttered around her, twittering and chirping. This was her moment of perfect peace. Yes, she might finish *Parallel Lives*, but it would have to compete for her attention.

A thick evening mist had by now obscured Golden Gate Park just across the street and was drifting in her direction. Darkness descended with the moon making only a cameo appearance. A chill came into the air. Meena shivered and went inside.

She propped her head up against a pillow on the sofa, held a glass of mineral water in one hand, and opened *Parallel Lives* with the other. On this damp, foggy San Francisco evening punctuated by a foghorn beyond the Golden Gate Bridge, she didn't need an excuse to curl up with a book.

She read a paragraph first silently, then aloud. Antoine's style was elegant. His words were silken threads woven into richly textured images which in turn merged into a complex tapestry of human pathos.

The phone buzzed. The clock said it was ten o'clock. Three hours had slipped by without Meena noticing.

"We had dinner tonight at Ganesh's Whim, Meena-san." Kazuko sounded as merry as a theatergoer at the end of a play with a happy ending. But she never called this late.

"I've been there," Meena said. "What did you have?"

"Lamb kebob and tandoori bread. I thought I had died and gone to heaven."

"What took you to Marin?"

"Henry had to drop something off at Antoine's place."

Why was something or someone always reminding Meena of Antoine? "I love their *chai*," she said. "Makes me want to go back to India."

"Still thinking about Vishnu?"

"Yes. Often."

"Mee-chan, it's not like you to get carried away." Kazuko's voice now deepened in concern. "But lately when you speak of India you don't sound very rational."

"India is an important part of my life."

"It was a long time ago. By the way, Antoine said—"

"You saw him?"

"Yes. He said you went to his reading. How did you like it?"

"It was good," Meena said after a moment. "I bought both his books. I can lend them to you, if you haven't read them already. I'm about halfway through one of them."

"You liked him too? How strange." Kazuko laughed. "He couldn't stop talking about you. So when are you two going to run together?"

"I wasn't planning on it at all," Meena said. "I'm training for a race. I had a late start this year. If he's slow like he says he is, then he won't be able to do as many miles as I like to do. That'll set me back even more."

"Henry's been friends with Antoine since their sophomore year in high school. Henry says Antoine used to be quite athletic. He put on five pounds writing his last novel and badly wants to lose that extra weight. He's motivated. I bet he'll try staying at your pace."

Meena turned to the back flap of the book jacket and gazed at

Antoine's photo for the umpteenth time. He wasn't overweight; he only had a little sadness in his eyes.

"Weren't you looking for a training partner?" Kazuko asked. "It would be good to have someone with you. Especially after dark. Do you know that last week a woman runner was mugged in Golden Gate Park?"

"That's odd." Meena tried to deflect the conversation. "Why would someone attack a runner? We don't carry money with us when we go jogging."

"Don't you think Antoine is fascinating?"

The question caught Meena off guard. She almost said yes, but stopped herself. All she needed was another complication. Mom dying, work falling apart, and . . . Antoine. She remembered breaking up with Joseph, the motorcycle racer, in her first year of grad school. She couldn't study for weeks, her grades dropped, she lost weight and ended up seeing a psychiatrist. She put the book down on the coffee table and said, "It'd be different if I were in my early twenties. I might be mooning over him. But now that I've had my heart broken a few times—no, I don't want to get involved."

"Henry says Antoine knows a lot about India," Kazuko said. "He lived there for a while. He still has friends there. If you want to locate Vishnu I bet he could suggest ways. . . ."

Meena didn't want to use him for that. Still, she had to admit, something pulled her toward him. And Kazuko, who was a good judge of character, had never given her bad advice. Perhaps Antoine could be a friend like Carlos was. She and Carlos went to the theater, to ball games, to restaurants. They spent hours chatting about nearly anything. Clearly Antoine was a writer with much insight into people and places. So why not spend a little time with him? "You're right, Kazu-chan," Meena said. "Running alone is hard. It's true, the cliché about the 'loneliness of the long distance runner.' I guess I could train with him a few times. Now that he's in the city, it would be convenient. And it won't be for long. He's moving back to Marin soon, isn't he?"

"In three weeks."

Meena could keep a rein on her feelings for three weeks. And if he was a jerk, she would be repelled even sooner and that would settle the whole issue. "I was angry with him that night," she whispered. "I threw his number away." Kazuko would keep her secret safe, she knew.

"Here, let me give it to you."

Meena jotted the number on a memo pad, tore off the sheet, and propped it up on her dressing table to remind herself to call Antoine in the morning.

Who was she kidding? She wouldn't need a reminder. She already had the number memorized.

17

What a glorious afternoon for running, Meena mused as she arrived at Golden Gate Park. She walked across a field, a voluptuous green under a silvery blue sky, to the Polo Field track where she was to meet Antoine. This was their agreed-upon time, but he wasn't here. A gray squirrel came out of a bush, looked toward her, and scurried away. A light breeze sprang up, raising small clouds of dust. She shivered in her workout gear of shorts and a tank top. Runners circled the dirt track once, and once more, and yet again. Still no sign of Antoine.

After stretching her hamstrings for the fifth time, she glared at her watch. To run with Antoine today she had cut her mileage by half and now he was already fifteen minutes late. That was two lost miles. She was vexed, wondered if she should wait for him any longer, then decided she would. He wasn't much of a runner, probably wasn't familiar with running etiquette. Be prompt for a running date or else your partner goes on without you. She'd make an exception this time. She began her backward bends.

And there was Antoine, wearing a white tee shirt, cutoff jeans, and a blue headband, coming toward her at a slow jog. She straightened.

"Sorry I'm late," he said. Yet his body language showed no sign of embarrassment: no hasty steps, no searching eyes. He must have taken it for granted that she'd wait for him.

"I was about to give up."

Now he asked, "Well, shall we give it a whirl?"

She was tempted to reply, "No, frankly." Instead she said, "Let's do an out-and-back."

They headed west toward Ocean Beach on a trail carpeted with conifer needles. It bordered Kennedy Drive and was lined by cedar and spruce trees and escalonia shrubs with shiny leaves. Meena set a comfortable pace at the start. A blackbird flew out of a thicket in protest, bent on protecting its nest. Meena lowered her head to avoid being hit by the bird and, in the process, sneaked a long look at Antoine. He was holding his arms tight, working his shoulders too much. But she wouldn't correct his gait or slow down. Not yet.

As they waited for a traffic light, he asked abruptly, "Do you make hot curries?"

"I don't cook much," she said. "But I make a mean lentil stew sometimes when I have friends over." The light turned green and they took off again.

His breathing was becoming labored from the unaccustomed effort. He said, "I like my curries very hot. Hot enough to make me sweat." His words came in short bursts as he worked for more air. "My hair . . . stands up."

Meena found it difficult not to laugh. Three male runners, park regulars, glided past in the opposite direction. One of them called out to her, "Looking good."

She smiled back, then cast a sidelong glance at Antoine. A slight frown. Jealous? She hoped so. His face was flushed; he was obviously in oxygen debt. Poor thing. No longer the cocky male. Perhaps she should slow down a little.

A large friendly collie emerged from the bushes and attempted to keep pace with her. She petted its head while maintaining her stride. The dog's owner ran up and put it on a leash against its evident wish. Meena's laugh entwined with Antoine's.

"You like dogs?" Antoine asked.

"Yes," she said. "But I don't have one right now. I had a collie when I was growing up." She felt lighthearted now. The anger toward Antoine was entirely gone. "At the crossing ahead we'll be about a mile from where we started." She flicked her wrist to check the time on her watch and asked, "Want to go farther?"

"I don't think I can," Antoine panted. "Stayed up too late last night. I'm paying for it now."

Goodness, he did need coaching. "Sure you can," she said. "Let's do a run-walk. We'll walk a couple of minutes, then run a couple more. We'll go on like that for a while. I'll time it."

"Okay," he said miserably.

She led him in a run-walk for another mile. He managed that well. "That was mile two," she said. "Want to head back?"

"No," he said. "I'm enjoying this. Let's do another half mile."

"Relax your shoulders," she said. "Shake out your arms."

And he did.

They reversed direction after a time. Steps in synch, she could harmonize with him now and share the experience. His legs seemed looser and he even speeded up a little. He could be a good runner if he were more consistent in his training, she thought. "You know, you could finish the Kimochi 8K race?" she said.

"Oh, yeah?"

They drew nearer to the spot where they had started. "I'll sprint the last hundred yards," Meena said as she accelerated her pace. "That's my finishing ritual."

"Go ahead," Antoine said as he followed her at a jog.

Eventually she slowed to a walk. He joined her for a cool-down that would soon return their heartbeats to normal. Her lungs full, her mind clear like an empty monitor screen, Meena felt exhilarated. "That was five miles," she said, "same as the Kimochi distance."

"I can't believe I ran that far." He pushed his headband up his forehead to stop sweat from rolling into his eyes. "This run-walk thing works," he said in a voice still soprano from running. "Would you have time for something to drink?"

She was thirsty and eager to spend more time with him. They had barely talked during the run. Her computer mind rationalized that every opened session must be closed properly. "There's a small café on Cabrillo Street," she said. "They don't seem to mind sweaty runners. I often stop there after a workout. Want to try it?"

"Sounds good to me," he said eagerly.

The café was a spotless, functional place with bare walls and a stainless steel service counter. It was practically deserted. The owner, a high-cheekboned Korean woman, nodded to them in welcome. Antoine picked two bottles of mineral water from the display case and paid for them. The woman returned the change with a slight bow but no words, afraid perhaps to make a mistake in English.

They established themselves at a small table by the window,

overlooking a circular patch of yellow daisies in a grayish concrete pavement. As Meena watched, Antoine opened the bottles with an easy twist of rough fingers. They weren't soft city-boy paws. He probably knew how to fix a garage door and weed a yard.

He lifted his glass to her. "To our first run."

Meena raised hers, waited a second until the water became de-fizzed and took a deep swallow. Crisp chilled water. All these years of being away from the arid deserts of Rajasthan, but water never lost its appeal. She drank water when she was tormented, confused, bored, or elated, not merely thirsty. She took several more sips and, in between, glanced at Antoine's face, which was slick with sweat. It made him look quite virile, she was embarrassed to think. "Water is precious to someone from a place like Rajasthan," she said. "I go through a lot of it."

"Rajasthan is the best part of India," Antoine said. "But finding pure water was a problem. In Jaipur I drank Fanta or Campa Cola or tea, rarely water. I hear India has a better water system now. Tap water is safe in most places."

"Soda pop in Jaipur?" Meena said. "I never heard of soft drinks in Rajasthan."

"I was thirsty the first night I was there." Antoine hunched a little, cupped his palms around his glass, holding it close like a memory he wanted to preserve. "God, it was hot. I was twenty, an exchange student traveling alone and still feeling awfully disoriented. My hosts, Mr. and Mrs. Naj, and their two children lived in a bungalow. Their son, Deepak, was my age. At dusk, like about this time, we were all sitting on the patio and I was on my fourth glass of limeade. A neighbor came to visit with her two kids. Her head and mouth were covered with her sari. Only her eyes were showing. I thought she looked mysterious and exotic." He laughed. It was quite a marvelous laugh, low, rich, and comforting. "The baby was bundled on her lap and the toddler sat beside her. At first the baby cried and the toddler tried to chase a mosquito. Then someone's goat wandered into the yard and broke a bougainvillea shrub. Through it all I was trying to engage Deepak in small talk and doing badly." He sat back, stretching his hands behind his head for support. "Then Deepak's sister started tuning her sitar. In not too long, music filled the patio. Each note took on a life of its own. Time didn't move. Children fell asleep. Everything became still. I stopped being thirsty."

The image was so lovely that Meena sat quietly for a few seconds and held it. She could see the house, hear the raga.

"In my village," she said, "I'd be out in the yard in the late after-noon, watching a train of camels on the horizon." Vishnu's face formed in her mind's eye. "I'd perch myself on Grandfather's lap. He'd bounce me on his knee and tell me stories of kings and jewels and bandits. Repeats, of course, but each time his characters took on different names and faces and the stories ended with a different twist. My mother would return from the well with water, humming a song to welcome the night."

Antoine clinked the ice cubes in his glass as though the sound would shake his thoughts loose. "I took some incredible pictures there. The best was when I caught a group of Rajasthani women in a dust storm. I'll have to show it to you sometime."

"Dust storm?" She flinched. "On my seventh birthday there was a dust storm. That day I was kidnapped by two horrible bandits." Why was she saying this? she wondered.

"Kidnapped?" he said.

"The bandits came on camels. One had eyes like a dead fish. The other had filthy hands. He forced me onto his camel. They hit my mother. Hit her and hit her . . ." Her voice choked.

Antoine's face softened and for once he seemed at a loss for words. His eyes filled with compassion as they held hers for several moments. Finally he said, "I had no idea. You've lived through something that's almost beyond my imagination."

"I'd like to find my village again." She surprised herself by saying that. "But India's so big. No one can keep track of all the villages, not even the government."

"Deepak might be of help," Antoine said. "His father is a retired chief of police in Jaipur. I believe he still has a lot of contacts. He helped my dad in his tropical plant research."

"Vishnu Chauhan, my classmate, might be living in Jaipur now," Meena said. "His mother was planning to send him there to school. It would be great to get back in touch with him."

"I'll be sure to ask Deepak about him," Antoine said.

Meena looked out the window at the encroaching darkness. She wanted to go on, but her sense of propriety said no. And her water glass was empty. She checked her watch and shot to her feet, saying, "I really need to get back now."

Antoine stood up too. "Let's run again soon. Latter part of next week. Would Friday work for you?"

Meena considered that. "It might. If you're serious about running an 8K race, though"—she laughed as she said it—"you'll have to run more often and go farther than the race distance."

"You're what I need," Antoine said. "I really want to run the Kimochi. I won't be as fast as you are. I'd be happy just to finish."

As they headed for the door, the Korean woman waved at them. "Come back again." Her English wasn't bad after all.

"Same time Friday?" Antoine asked Meena.

"Yup," Meena said. "And same place. But be on time. Next time I won't wait for you. Serious runners don't."

Antoine shook her hand. She noticed he held it for a few seconds longer than necessary. She felt a tingling sensation, edged with a momentary thrill that came from inside her.

Out on the pavement, fallen pink and white dogwood blossoms made an incandescent pattern in the light of the setting sun. She picked up a petal and examined it. It was as perfect as a Georgia O'Keeffe painting. She crossed the street, paused long enough to breathe the smell of mown grass in front of a house, then headed back to her Fulton Street apartment, an evening raga still swirling in her head. The lightness in her step, she well knew, wasn't just from a workout.

18

Antoine had his faults, Meena could see that. He had annoyed her by trying to change her training schedule at whim. Last week he had left her six messages on six different days with specific times to meet and had at the last moment canceled every single one of them. Today's message was no different: "Can't run. Let's just meet in our place. I'm bringing a Frisbee."

It was irritating. Why was he so capricious? This afternoon she had gutted through a tough eight-miler, alone. Afterward she debated before deciding to drop by Café Cabrillo, the place run by a Korean woman that Antoine had called "our place." There he was, seated at a table, apparently lost in a skein of thoughts. She joined him and for the next hour they had a good chat about everything from Tagore to trains. She didn't talk about work and only in passing mentioned her twice-a-month volunteer work at the Internet Literacy Center across the bay in Berkeley. She knew he wasn't comfortable around computers and wouldn't relate to the technical world in which she was immersed every day.

"I'm glad you're not angry with me," Antoine was saying now.

"Well, I was, to tell you the truth," Meena said. "But not anymore. Somehow I don't seem to be able to stay angry with you for very long."

"Ellen would have had a fit."

Suddenly he opened up and began to talk—really talk, all about his broken marriage and how devastated he was when it failed. He went on for a while, then said, "I don't regret knowing her. But the marriage was a mistake. . . . Why do relationships go wrong?" He raked his fingers through his hair in a gesture of frustration, almost as though he was hoping to find an answer there. Then with a sigh he continued, "I should have known. It was up and down from the beginning, even when we were dating. This is different."

So he enjoyed her company? Meena allowed herself to savor that, and as she did, a surge of well-being came over her. And yet—

She summoned the courage to murmur softly, "And Liv?"

Antoine shifted and looked away. After a time he said abruptly, "Let's go throw the Frisbee, shall we?"

Under the park lights they flipped the Frisbee back and forth a few times. Noticing him moving rather stiffly, Meena suggested, "Why don't we warm up with a few stretches?" And she showed him her stretch routine.

"Much better," he said after a few minutes of practice. "Now my back is looser." And then with a smile, "You know what I like about you? You are so in tune with your body. I'm too much into my head."

"Wait till you get more into running," Meena replied. "Then you'll feel your whole body as you move, as you do anything."

"You still want to run with me, Meena? I've been such a screw-up." His head, carried so erect, just a moment ago seemed to sink between his shoulders. His face now looked boyish and defenseless. Meena hated to admit it to herself, but she felt a real affection toward him.

"Only if we can make it every other day," Meena said firmly. "No excuses. There's no point in training unless you're consistent."

"Yes, ma'am." He chuckled. "I promise to stick to the schedule, starting tomorrow."

They walked in comfortable silence up to the Fulton crossing, where he gave her a warm grin and bid her good night.

"See you at the track tomorrow," Meena said cheerfully before turning the corner.

The sky was bleak, her knees stiff from the tough training, but as she glanced up she saw the dazzle of a single star wedged between wind-ruffled clouds.

19

It was late morning when Meena stepped into the small tenth-floor conference room for the division's weekly project managers' meeting. A rectangular table stood at the center of the room with six leather-covered chairs placed around it. Sunlight streamed in through the room's only window, casting shadows of the saucerlike leaves of the potted rubber plant on the wall without warming the room. Alex, the boss, settled himself at the head of the table. He had on a three-piece suit, white oxford shirt, and gray rep tie. He stirred his coffee with a small straw, looking down at the bottom of the cup as though something interesting was hidden there.

Brett, dressed just like Alex, slid into the chair to his right, the "power" place. He was of medium build and would have looked like a hundred other men on the street but for his large flared nose. A transplant from Illinois, he had skin of a peculiarly indoor quality that the California sun hadn't yet managed to burn away.

Meena recalled how she was Alex's favorite until Brett was hired. But Brett, younger and less experienced, posed no threat to Alex. Soon they became chummy, talking by the water cooler, lunching together, playing tennis after work. Would it surprise anyone if Alex was grooming someone who reflected his own image?

Her ample body ill-concealed in a blue and white jumper, Joy marched in and took the chair on Alex's left. Three seats remained empty. Meena settled into the end chair facing Alex.

"I'd like to talk to you after this," Brett murmured to Joy. "I'm doing performance evaluations. Some of my people worked on one of your projects."

"Let's have lunch," Joy said. They traded a glance and possibly an understanding.

An alliance was definitely forming. Meena tried not to squirm in her chair.

Alex started the meeting, his eyes roving over all the faces. "You first, Meena."

Meena reported on the COSMOS project and the latest milestone it had reached, then became excited as she described her staff's test results. Alex filled a page with notes. Both Brett and Joy sat woodenly and neither commented.

Meena tried to bring some life to the room. "If there are any questions . . ."

Alex put his pencil down. "Thank you, Meena. Next." He turned to Brett.

Brett stirred, cleared his throat, reached into his pocket and pulled out a pack of cigarettes, then put it back. Perhaps, remembering that Alex didn't smoke, he didn't want to endanger his status as the fair-haired boy. "Did anyone watch *Mariel* last night?" As Brett began describing a sitcom, both Alex and Joy gave him their attention and laughed often. Meena doodled. Even with her head down, she could tell Alex was watching her occasionally. She drew a camel, then an elephant. A quick look at the wall clock. Five minutes had slipped by, nothing accomplished. Her camel took on one passenger, then another. Another minute crept slowly by. Finally she lifted her eyes from the notepad.

"Did I miss something?" Turning to Brett, she said, "Could you repeat the status of your project?"

"You in a hurry?" Brett's eyes narrowed.

"Meena's right," Alex said. "Let's move things along."

"The main module is, uh, done," Brett fumbled for words. "I mean it has been tested with sample data." He cast a sideways glance at Meena. "Well, there's not much more I can do if Meena's COSMOS is not on time—"

Meena had a powerful urge to tweak his huge nose. "You weren't listening," she said. "COSMOS is ahead of schedule."

"Of course, it would be. It's a simple little software package." Brett gave a short laugh that had the dismissal quality of a wet mop.

Meena said, "Do you know how many thousand lines of code COSMOS has just for—"

Alex cut her off. "Let's proceed. Thank you, Brett. Joy?"

Joy gave her spiel to Alex and Brett, ignoring Meena.

The coldness of her peers numbed Meena. She had been at SIC long enough to know that the time-honored method of getting rid of someone was simply to freeze them out.

"No meetings the next two weeks." Alex held up his notepad. "I'll be in Germany. Call or e-mail me at my hotel if you need anything. Jean will know my schedule."

Brett and Joy left the room together, chatting.

Alex smiled at Meena. "See Lou Cassidy in case of an emergency."

See the president of the company for a project problem? Not likely. Meena got up and moved toward the door.

Alex trotted after her saying, "Cassidy was asking about you."

Meena spun around and stood still. When Lou Cassidy inquired about you, it was either very good news or very bad. "What did he have to say?"

The left side of Alex's face twitched. "He heard a rumor that you might leave the company. He's worried."

"A rumor?"

"Cassidy read an excerpt of the talk you gave at the last National Database Conference." Alex had changed the subject. "He thinks COSMOS will become a big revenue earner for us."

"We'll get their attention with the first version," Meena said warmly. "The next version is the one that will bring us market share. We're going to wipe out most other database systems on the market. If Lou ever wants to see a demo—" She saw that Alex was staring away stonily.

"Just make sure it doesn't have any bugs."

"All software has bugs of one kind or another, Alex," Meena said. "But we'll fix them as soon as they're reported. By the way, what did you mean by a rumor?"

Alex mumbled something.

"Will you talk to Mr. Cassidy before you leave, to squash the rumor? Tell him I'm definitely not leaving."

"If I get a chance. Let me know if you need anything else." Alex turned away abruptly and strode toward his office.

That was lip service, Meena knew. Alex didn't support her. Her peers undercut her. SIC was supposed to be a family. Sure—a dys-functional one: weak father, kids out of control. Why was she sur-prised that her brainchild COSMOS, which had enhanced her status and reputation, should also raise the level of jealousy? Her love had become her nemesis.

When evening came, Meena was more than glad to exchange the office for the Internet Literacy Center, where she taught two evenings a month as a volunteer. In a room filled with computer monitors she was demonstrating how to use an Internet "browser" program to a cluster of students, mostly folks in their sixties, when—lo and behold—who should appear at the back of the room but Antoine? Head slightly down, obviously ill at ease, he barely caught her eye. So the Internet Innocent, who wrote longhand and had his secretary transcribe his manuscript onto a floppy disk to send to his publisher, was interested in computers? Meena smiled to herself inwardly. Though she was pleased to see him, she wouldn't show it in her manner. Antoine was doing his best to remain inconspicuous, but his height alone made it difficult. He gave the appearance of listening, though at times she caught him intently staring at her. Her heart pounded, but she carried on normally.

Finally, to her relief, it was time for hands-on practice. The stu-dents began to seat themselves at the monitors with only one chair remaining empty. A sprightly woman in her seventies looked know-ingly at Antoine and said, "You sit here. You're the handsome one."

Antoine reddened and sat down with seeming reluctance. After making a point of answering all the questions from other students, Meena casually came over and stood behind Antoine to watch what he was doing.

"This mouse doesn't seem to work, Ms. Gossett," Antoine said.

Talk about uptight, Meena thought. "Let me try it," she said and performed a couple of routines. "You just have to click it like this." She took his hand and showed him how to press the mouse correctly, then added, "Well, Mr. Peterson, now that you know how to ask questions, would you care to find out if your books are mentioned anywhere on the Internet?"

"You mean I can do that?"

"All you have to do is direct the computer to do a search using your name."

He keyed in his name laboriously using one finger, clicked the mouse, sat back and waited. Soon, twenty summary items on the topic flashed on the screen: book reviews, including one from the *New York Times*, a magazine interview, a profile in the *Chronicle*. With a throaty chuckle he said, "I'm beginning to see the benefit of using this." He was like a little boy with a new toy.

"And you can research your next book, too," she said. "For instance, you can search on words having to do with subjects you're interested in." She watched with amazement as he typed "Turkish women."

She showed him how to use a browser, then said, "Now you're on your own," and left him to attend to her other students.

When the hands-on hour was over, the students began to file out individually. All except Antoine, who remained absorbed in the screen before him. After a while Meena came over and stood quietly behind him. Aware of her presence, he switched off the computer with obvious reluctance.

He turned to her with a sheepish smile. "Thank you, Ms. Gossett."

"Welcome to the cyberworld, Mr. Peterson. There's more to come . . ."

20

This evening Antoine had kept his promise and Meena was glad to have trained four excellent miles with him. Afterward she continued on her own for another couple of miles while Antoine cooled down. When she finished, they walked over to Spreckles Lake.

Now the ducks were crowding each other, their raucous noise breaking the quiet as Meena scattered some bread. Antoine was stretched out on a lakeside bench behind her. Half-turning, she said to him softly, "All sorts of animals were a part of our life in India." He listened with attention when she recalled her Indian past in a way that Mom and Dad never had. "Goats, buffaloes, wild peacocks wandered in and out of our yard," she added. "The line between animal and human was not drawn as clearly as here."

"I remember peacocks jumping from fence to fence in Jaipur." Antoine sat up. "And cows were everywhere. They even had a square dedicated to cows. People brought vegetable peels from home to feed them. They'd bow before 'gou-mata.' Cow-mother. I liked to watch that."

"You must have been a Hindu in a past life," Meena said jokingly. This evening was a Popsicle that she wished she could go on licking.

"I have a mantra, too." Antoine half smiled. "It's 'Kimochi.' Do you think I'd be able to finish that race?"

"Of course, but you've got to train a little bit harder," Meena said. "We only have a couple of weeks left."

He seemed to have fallen into a dreamy silence under the lunar light. Feeding the ducks more bread crumbs, Meena wondered if all couples shouldn't begin their relationship with a sport in common, something to dissipate the aggressions and frustrations of the day, leaving them mellow, receptive, open to one another. She told herself they probably couldn't be this comfortable together otherwise.

Her relationship with Antoine was definitely becoming more serious, she acknowledged. And she liked its progression. They were becoming friends first, finding common ground; in time she was sure they'd be lovers. There were subtle sexual sparks between them, like the way he had brushed against her during their run today.

She was beginning to look forward to their meetings with increasing anticipation. Only once before had she felt this way about somebody, and that was with Joseph the motorcycle racer.

It was her first year of graduate studies at Stanford. She blushed now as she remembered how naive she had been. Five years older than Meena, Joseph was quite different from the people she had previously associated with. He was the first of his family to finish high school and knew nothing of art, music, or literature. She liked his casual, irreverent attitude—he called his mother by her first name, Grace. He had the flattest abdomen in California and he danced like Travolta. He moved in quickly.

A sexual athlete by his own admission, he was the catalyst who brought the passion deep within her to the surface. His first kiss melted her. She was forced to realize that she was a flesh-and-blood animal, that her healthy young body craved a pleasure she had denied herself all this time. Away from home and with Auntie Bimla gone, she finally freed herself from the tentacles of Indian tradition, which held that a woman must be a virgin until marriage.

At semester break when she came home, Dad gave her a keen look and said, "My, Meena, you seem different. Very grown-up."

She remembered turning away and blushing.

Her love affair with Joseph had been too intense, too fiery to last. In the years that followed she had other affairs. Then for the past six months Mom's illness had left Meena with little time for outside interests. Only now, after meeting Antoine, had she begun to feel the familiar desire beginning to stir deep within. Insistent yet subtle, with a range and depth that none of her other male friends had shown, Antoine had insinuated himself into her life, surprising and delighting her with the quick turns of his mind.

Her bread bag now empty, Meena sat next to Antoine on the

bench. Soon their talk drifted to the lot of women in Rajasthan. "Women worked awfully hard every day," he said, "except on Teej when men did all the chores. I remember setting up a swing on the terrace of the Naj house so Mrs. Naj and her daughter and other female relatives could sit and watch women folk dancers who had been hired to perform for them. The dancers had sticks in their hands and bangles up to their shoulders. They made wonderfully graceful symbols and designs in the air with the sticks, and a jangling noise with the bangles as they danced barefoot. They were stunning in their costumes—red and gold and green."

She shifted her eyes upward to the sky and saw the moon bare its face. "Teej is celebrated at the full moon, isn't it?"

"That night just as the dancers took a break, the moon came out. Mr. Naj said, 'Now our American friend is going to perform for us.' I didn't know what the hell to do except a scene from *Merchant of Venice* that I vaguely remembered. 'In such a night as this . . .' Later the girls told me I seemed as passionate as a romantic movie star. We laughed a lot that night."

He was sitting an arm's length away. She read the desire in his face and his eyes, sensed the tension in his powerful body. After a moment's silence he rose from the bench with a sigh, said good-bye, and walked off into the darkness.

Meena sat for a few minutes, lost in her thoughts. If life was a pie chart, hers had an empty quadrant, the one labeled "companion." No, not just any companion. One with whom to build a life of shared experiences. One to confide in. One to give her love to. Antoine showed promise of filling that role—when he was around. She emerged from her introspection acutely aware of the empty seat beside her on the bench.

At noon the next day Meena picked up her phone and dialed Joy's number. After their ordeal of a dim sum lunch, she had pretty much written Joy off and avoided her as much as possible. Then Joy had brought her that newspaper piece about Antoine and much had happened in Meena's life since then. Though she didn't want to admit it to herself, she was dying to tell someone what Antoine was like, now that she was getting to know him. Kazuko had been on vacation all month. There was also—something she wanted to admit perhaps even less—her growing sense of isolation at SIC and the need for human contact within the company.

Why not give Joy one more try?

"Hi, Joy, like to go get a sandwich? We could talk about those test cases."

"Can't make it," Joy said. "Sorry, I'm swamped. I'll call you another time. Thanks for asking."

Joy sounded more polite than usual, but from the tone of her voice Meena knew she wouldn't call.

Meena had a sudden vision of Mataji and how well she bonded with the women in her village. When the men worked in the fields or went off to the town to trade goods, the women and their children got together. They sang, danced, and told jokes for hours. Her village was poor. The women had little to give each other except love, trust, and time. For women friends there was always time.

But in corporate America the product came first, people second. To survive, one was constantly required to assess people and situations and manipulate them to one's advantage. How could Meena expect SIC and its employees to operate otherwise? Still, she yearned to return to a place where people were valued simply for what they were and not for their utility. She'd never find it in a consumer-oriented society, which placed the highest value on the production of objects. She'd have to look for it in the towns and villages of a so-called underdeveloped country such as India.

Meena smiled inwardly. It was her Indian self lecturing, the one she thought had been lost forever.

21

Meena was arranging a bunch of stark white calla lilies in a tall vase in her living room when the phone rang. She examined the shape of each lily, a spouted cup, a delicate receptacle, as she lifted the phone.

"I'm staring at a day-old pasta salad and can't seem to get excited." The voice, rich, smooth, and hypnotic like a DJ's from a midnight radio program, was Antoine's. This afternoon he had skipped his workout and she had jogged alone, so his call was a pleasant surprise.

She laughed. "I hate leftovers, too."

"Since I started running with you, I've lost five pounds," he said. "But now I'm hungry all the time."

"Well, if you run regularly, you can eat without guilt," Meena said. "That's one of the side benefits, you know."

"Have you been to Mamma Mia on Polk Street? It's Italian. Supposed to be good."

How did he know about this place that had special meaning for her? "Mom and Dad were friends of the owners," she said immediately. "They used to take me there on my birthday and holidays." She remembered how she'd always wear her best skirt and blouse, put a bow in her hair, and be ready at least an hour early.

Antoine's voice came through her thoughts. "The *Examiner* gave it two and a half stars."

"It's a good restaurant," she said. "But for me the fun was the store next door, a place called February Thirty-First. The same people, the Canavinos, managed both. I used to call Mrs. Canavino 'February

Mamma.' The store was one of those quirky Polk Street joints with odd toys. I bought a flying cockroach there one time. It looked so real that Auntie Bimla jumped when I opened my palm and let it fly up in the air. The restaurant is still doing well. February Thirty-First is gone."

"I'd like you to have dinner with me." His voice grew bolder.

She lowered herself onto the sofa. Her mind raced with all the possible meanings of this invitation.

Antoine continued, "I have news from Jaipur that you might be interested in."

"I'd love to go."

"Great," he said. "I'll make a reservation. Pick you up in forty-five minutes."

She showered, then slipped into her coral *salwar-kameez*. The two-piece ensemble of Indian brocade was comfortable, yet stylish enough for dinner. She had bought it a year ago, while browsing through an import shop down on the Peninsula. The store clerk had told her that, once, only women in northern India wore the *salwar-kameez*. Now, with young women all over India riding motor scooters, marching in the streets protesting one governmental decision or another, and sitting in offices giving orders, this functional tunic-and-pants set had become their preferred daily wear, with the traditional sari reserved for special occasions. Meena liked the loose cut of the outfit. And the textured fabric gave her a feeling of sensuality that was missing from her utilitarian life. At the last minute she clasped a silver chain around her neck for an added touch of elegance.

An hour passed. What could take so long? Just when she thought he had learned to be punctual. To occupy herself she went back to her chores. Her living room was sparsely furnished and required little tidying. She fluffed the throw pillows on the ochre sofa and the two Scandinavian chairs a few too many times and straightened the frame of a large abstract painting, one of her own, titled *Options*. Once she had loved to express herself in color and form; now she never found the time for it. She dusted the bookcase on the opposite wall and became aware that she had barely touched any of the novels in more than a month. Briskly, she pushed the garish computer manuals closer together to frame her limited edition Bauhaus teapot. Its smooth curved side and striped black and white body was a visual treat that showed to best advantage standing alone.

She paced the hand-knotted Kashmiri carpet back and forth, allowed herself one Pepperidge Farm Sausalito cookie to take the edge off her hunger, and finally began to worry about him.

The door buzzer sounded.

"Sorry I'm late," Antoine said, standing stiffly. "Are you ready?"

She nodded as she locked the door. She sensed an undercurrent of agitation in his manner.

En route to the restaurant Antoine appeared to concentrate on his driving, though Meena could tell half his mind was somewhere else. For once he hardly said anything. She stared out the car window at the familiar views of the Richmond District, her part of the city. To tourists, San Francisco was synonymous with trendy areas like the Marina, Fisherman's Wharf, and the Embarcadero. To Mom and Dad, born San Franciscans, an upscale area like Pacific Heights was more desirable, and Meena had grown up there herself. But personally she liked to hang out in flat and foggy Richmond. The district ran west to the Seal Rocks bordering the Pacific Ocean, north to Lincoln Park and the Presidio, and south to Golden Gate Park. Its streets, "the avenues" as they were called, were dotted with restaurants, bookstores, and clothing boutiques, offering opportunities for whiling away spare hours either alone or with friends like Kazuko and Carlos.

The Russian deli on Eighteenth Avenue was where she had breakfast on Saturday mornings. It was a lively place filled with savory smells. She'd hear stout Slavic grandmothers in babushkas chattering with the counter person in consonant-rich Russian as they made their purchases of blini, piroshki, and black bread. They would remind her that Richmond was originally settled by Russians. Next door was a used bookstore that boasted the city's best selection of "predigested" classics with clever comments by previous owners. Just beyond, Clement Street was dominated for nearly a mile by Asian restaurants, mom-and-pop Asian groceries, and Asian tailor shops. Small wonder this section of Richmond had been renamed New Chinatown. Though less glitzy than the original Chinatown, it was every bit as lively and the food was, in Meena's opinion, better.

They turned onto Geary, the vibrant main artery awash with traffic, jammed with motels and appliance outlets. Tucked in among its industrial buildings was an art movie house that Meena frequented. Eclectic Richmond pulsed with raw crisp energy. She could live here and not miss the rest of the city.

They arrived at the restaurant ten minutes past their reservation time. February Mamma, grayer now and top-heavy as always, bounced into the waiting area and greeted them with a broad smile. Then she recognized Meena. "What a surprise! I've been meaning to call you." She reached up to hug Meena, almost crushing her, inspected her appearance, and nodded approval. "Lovely outfit, Meena dear. You look so Indian. So attractive." Words gushed from February Mamma's mouth like torrents of rain. Her overly arched eyebrows gave her a theatrical look. She was onstage as always. As far as Meena could remember, February Mamma never did anything in a small way.

"I'm so sorry about your mother," February Mamma said. "She always looked so young. We miss her."

Last time Meena had dined here, it was with Mom. That seemed only yesterday. Meena sighed, then introduced Antoine.

"You're the writer?" February Mamma asked. She glanced at him with narrowed eyes, as though she was ascertaining if he met her criteria or not. "I read about you in the newspaper."

Just the same protective way Mom and Auntie Bimla would act. Meena was embarrassed. She didn't mean to put Antoine on the spot.

Antoine smiled easily.

February Mamma resumed. "And here you are, a famous person in my restaurant with my little Meena. Follow me, please." She led them through a dining room with recessed ceiling lights amid a muted burst of piano music to a table by the window. The smoky rose color of the linen matched the wall. Two fresh orchids of brilliant purple hue tangoed in a slender glass vase. A candle flickered in a small wooden stand. Potted palms on top of chest-high dividers acted as walls and made Meena feel as though she were in her own private space.

February Mamma handed them each an oversized menu. Leaning slightly toward Antoine, she confided, "I've known Meena since she was a little girl."

Antoine gazed up at her with eyes that said, Tell me more.

"She used to come here, a lovely girl with beautiful long hair. And she was such a good child—never gave her parents any worry. Not like my boys." February Mamma glanced beyond the window as if her sons were still out carousing around somewhere.

Meena asked about Paolo and Vito. February Mamma talked for another minute before bustling away.

Antoine was wrapped in an embryo of silence. Meena wished she knew his password, the open-sesame to his mind. She nibbled at a piece of bread, listened to the piano music that drifted about her, and studied the menu. The restaurant's specialty used to be veal scaloppini. When she came here with Mom and Dad, wearing her best clothes, she'd be afraid of getting the brownish sauce on her blouse. Ah, the veal scaloppine was still there, she noted. Several of the other entrees were new. Perhaps she should try one of the new ones.

Antoine skimmed his menu, closed it, and said, "You order for me. You're the expert."

"Hard to choose," she said. She reached for more bread, still ravenous.

"So, how's life and work?" he asked finally.

"Life's interesting sometimes. My work's endless. Always."

"Pretty intricate, I imagine."

"Yes, it's very detailed work. But not all that different from novel writing. We create our own universe. I program computers in their special languages. The coding is structured, like your plots. Then I add various subroutines. They're like your subplots."

"Wish I could be as dedicated as you are," he said as he fiddled with his fork. "I'm focused one day, distracted the next. Henry told me you were featured in *PC* magazine. You're a heavyweight in the industry."

She laughed. "I've been stereotyped. Disciplined . . . overachiever . . . hard-working . . ."

He nodded, leaned forward into the glow of candlelight, and locked her eyes with his. "But the real Meena is passionate . . . intriguing . . . very tender."

He had never spoken to her in so intimate a fashion. It unnerved her a little. She was seeing the artist he was, one who captured her essence with a few brush strokes. She reveled in the beauty of the moment. His eyes seemed to catch a certain light. Did his remarks reveal his true feelings? Or was she merely projecting her own expectations about him? She realized her breathing had stopped.

The moment ended. He drew back from the table, resumed toying with his fork, and lapsed into a pensive mood again.

"Liv called from New York just before I left the house," he said after a moment. "That's why I was late."

Liv. So she was for real. That Rebeccalike creature was now a person, coming between her and Antoine.

"When will she be back?" Meena could barely recognize her own voice.

"Tomorrow." He parked the fork in its place, knocking the salt shaker over in the process. He set it back up and glanced around the room. "Deepak, my friend in Jaipur, returned my call last night. He said he's heard of a Vishnu R. Chauhan."

Meena closed her eyes. Any other time, she would have welcomed the news. But now it was just Antoine's way of once more changing an awkward subject. When she opened her eyes again, she saw their waiter, a tall blond, coming up to their table—or to be more accurate, making his entrance.

"Would the signore prefer to ponder the menu a little longer?" His words grated on Meena. "Our specials today are . . ." And he recited a long list of dishes with unfamiliar ingredients as if they were poetry in a foreign language, one dish running into the next.

Meena couldn't remember a thing except the last item. She ordered pasta with wild mushrooms for both and red wine. The waiter departed.

Meena forced a laugh. " 'Ponder the menu?' He must be a part-time actor."

"I was once one myself," Antoine said without looking at her.

She waited for him to go on, but he was silent again. Nothing seemed to be going right between them tonight. This wasn't the same affable Antoine she had been jogging with. "So that's why you read so well," she tried.

He massaged his temples with his fingers as if trying to release a tiny demon of stress. "Is your friend a journalist?" he asked.

Friend? Oh, Vishnu. "Don't know."

"Apparently there's a well-known newspaper reporter in Calcutta by that name. He writes for an English daily."

Meena and Vishnu were the two top students in their class. Vishnu could certainly make it as a journalist. It delighted Meena to think that he had. "It might be him. Even the middle initial matches. We played together from the time we were two. He was my best friend. He was very bright, even as a seven-year-old. But Calcutta is quite a ways from Rajasthan. Why would he move there?"

"I've asked Deepak to try and contact him. See if he's the person."

"Oh, Antoine, thank you." She sought out his eyes, but they were somewhere else. Scrabbling in her purse, she pulled out a card. "Here's my e-mail address if your friend ever gets hold of Vishnu." She handed it across to him.

Antoine seemed to stare at her loose sleeve trailing over the table surface. "God, that's a beautiful fabric," he said in a dreamy voice. "I remember once walking through a meadow in Jaipur. Wind blowing over the grass. Rows of clothes drying on vines and clotheslines, flapping in the breeze. White dhotis. Saris, skirts, and scarves in bright blue, green, purple, magenta. Living colors. Swaying like flowers under the sun. I had just turned twenty."

He paused and started again. "I remember thinking that was a special washday. Then the laundryman, the *dhobi*, showed up, wearing a pink turban to protect himself from the sun. He had a patient face. His fingers were corrugated from being in water. He spoke a little English, told me that washing clothes was his daily routine. It was his life work, his dharma, his religion. I was fascinated. I decided then and there I would be a writer. Writing would be my dharma, so to speak."

Antoine's story struck Meena like one of those Indian parables Auntie Bimla used to recount. A vivid tale that ended with a revelation. Listening to it she felt she was becoming a part of his life.

Antoine continued, "The *dhobi*'s teenage daughter was with him. She was slim, had on a long skirt, blouse with bare midriff, and a veil. Lovely girl. Her eyes were large, innocent, curious. Even the way she moved—" Antoine half glanced at Meena. "She said something to me in Hindi. I tried to figure out what all she said. But the moment she realized she'd spoken to a strange man, she blushed and pulled her veil over her mouth and ran away."

And if Meena were that peasant girl? Would she have lingered? What a silly thought, she rebuked herself—and just when she was about to locate Vishnu.

At that moment the waiter brought their dinner. Butterfly pasta, crowned with a pesto sauce and three types of mushrooms arranged like a still life. Tonight she had a "terminal" hunger, a huge void that needed to be filled.

Antoine seemed preoccupied again. He picked at his food as if his appetite had flown off somewhere. She wished that he would resume his story. She had things to tell him too. But he sat like a computer monitor whose light had burned out.

She was relieved when February Mamma came up to them. Her beaming face, her jerky walk, her hoarse voice broke through the stifling atmosphere.

"How was everything?" February Mamma checked their plates.

Meena smiled. "Delicious, as usual."

"Dessert?" February Mamma intoned. "It's on the house. Tonight we have—"

Meena was still hungry, but desserts were meant for happier times. "Nothing for me."

Antoine patted the corners of his mouth with his napkin. "It was a lovely meal. I couldn't eat another bite."

Outside the restaurant, the wind was picking up, moving from a benign breeze to hair-ruffling gusts, typical of a San Francisco spring evening. Meena settled into Antoine's car and they drove in what seemed to Meena to be a nail-biting silence. Then the electronic beep of the car phone cracked the quietness.

Antoine spoke in a low voice, ending with a sharp "Call you back a little later," and hung up without looking at Meena.

Must be Liv, checking. The whole evening had been a fiasco because of that woman. Meena stared through the dirty windshield, not seeing anything.

Antoine parked his car on Fulton Street in front of her apartment building. He helped her out and silently escorted her to the top floor. His gait was heavy and he seemed alone. The rapport that had grown up between them in the last few weeks had evaporated.

She was at her door before she noticed a glossy package beautifully wrapped in yellow-gold paper, a long-stemmed red carnation placed atop. Antoine bent down and picked up the package. "A secret admirer," he said.

Meena unlocked the door, reflected a moment, then asked, "Won't you come in?"

As he handed her the package she said, "Make yourself at home." Antoine examined the painting on the opposite wall, then eased himself onto the sofa while she put the carnation in the vase along with the lilies and examined the effect. A swirl of red petals among the white. A dash of excitement in a serene setting.

Package on her lap, Meena curled up in a chair across from him. She stripped off the wrapper to find a small wicker basket filled with shredded green tissue. She combed through it and located a large yellow mango with streaks of red. There was a gift card bordered in gold with the words "That's what friends are for," signed by Carlos.

"What a perfect mango!" She looked up at Antoine as she cradled the fruit in her palm. Smooth-skinned, heavy for its size, fragrant. A sticker said, "Eat fruit when soft to the touch," which it was, but it would keep at least another week in the refrigerator. She fantasized sharing this fruit with Antoine—pictured them biting into the succulent flesh, sweet juice running down their chins.

Antoine stared at it, and then at her, like this was all very strange.

"It's from Carlos." She lifted the mango in her hand appreciatively. "He must have really searched to find a mango this size."

"You should watch that guy." Antoine had a slight furrow on his forehead. "I met him at Kazuko's house."

"I've known Carlos for years," Meena said softly. "He's my friend and knows how much I love mangoes." She pronounced the word "mungoes," like Carlos would.

"So I'm a gringo and don't know mango from samba." His voice bordered on sarcasm. "Would you like a serenade and flowers?"

Antoine was jealous. That was funny. How was he to know she and her friends often exchanged little gifts for no reason—cards, fruits, theater tickets—as tokens of loving attention? And it was sad. Antoine had been slipping away from her all evening. She got up to go to the kitchen.

He rose from the sofa and padded after her. "Perhaps I should leave," he said in a constricted voice.

"A mango is just a fruit, Antoine."

She opened an overhead cabinet, reached for a large crystal bowl, and placed the fruit inside. The colors reflected from the transparent sides of the bowl like a sun bursting. Aware that he was watching her, she said, "Carlos and I are friends, the way you and I are."

"I'd like to be more than friends."

She looked up. She'd been waiting to hear those words. But not even a sound came to her lips. There was Liv—and something else too. No, someone else. Vishnu. That was why she had never found someone to marry. She turned, her back jamming against the counter as she faced him.

"I'm sorry," he said. "I'm not making much sense tonight. I'm upset."

"Want to talk about it?"

"I have at least ten things on my mind. My new book, life . . . Liv coming back."

Her chest ached to see him suffer. She wanted to listen, be a friend, help him sort things out. "Aren't you happy about Liv coming back?" She was expecting a yes answer, hoping for a no. She waited breathlessly.

He looked away, rubbed his forehead, and finally said, "Of course. Well, I should be."

She watched his sturdy shoulders for a moment. She could smell the faint fragrance of cologne emanating from him.

"Her father died a couple of months ago," he continued. "She's gone through a lot lately. She was very close to him." Antoine ran a long forefinger with a square-cut nail around the rim of the bowl. Was the circle he was drawing symbolic of the trap he found himself in? He had never revealed this much about Liv.

"Her father wanted us to get married," he continued. "It seemed like a good idea at the time. Liv and I were getting along splendidly. My second novel was released to excellent reviews. The publisher went all out to promote it. I had an idea for another novel that was accepted. Things were going great. I was on top of the world. And now Liv's gone half the time, my writing isn't going anywhere, and . . ."

"Is there something else, Antoine, something a little closer to home?"

He looked into her eyes.

So he did like her company. Hope was swelling within her, but with that came an edgy feeling. He seemed abstracted, irresolute, not at all his usual confident self.

"I like spending time with you, Antoine. Somewhere in our core we're very much alike. But—"

Antoine's voice softened. "I know. I've watched you all this time. God knows how I've battled with my own feelings." He paused. "Look, I'm having trouble working on my new novel. It's set in Germany. But I realize that's not where my heart is. I'm in pain all the time. I'm lost. Then when I see you, I think I have a chance. . . ." He cupped her face in his hands with eagerness.

She looked deep into his eyes and detected no reserve. It was as if she had known him forever. She could feel everything he felt. Her heart soared in exultation. She was getting the world's best gift—Antoine.

He seemed about to speak. Instead he drew her closer and leaned down, putting little diamonds of kisses on her lips and eyelids and murmuring words with the softness of a dove's back. The moment was nothing but possibilities, her one hand caressing his face, the other reaching for the stars. Her legs went foolishly weak under her. She lost herself, aware only that she was tasting more than his mouth. Their hearts were touching, their skins craving each other; they were breathing in unison.

He kissed her harder now. She was ready to give herself. Yes, she would. Never mind the big invisible hand pulling her from behind, the silent voice reminding her that—

The shrill of the phone jarred her eyes open. She took a ragged breath, another. Who—? Carlos? Never mind Carlos either. She'd call him back tomorrow. Or next week. Or next month.

The ringing stopped. The warm wetness of Antoine's lips was still smeared on hers, but the mood was shattered. She saw him draw back slightly. For her too a trace of caution resurfaced. Think this out, Meena. What is it you're doing with Antoine? And why are you trying to get in touch with Vishnu?

She managed to stammer in a husky voice, "Let's think this over," as she pulled away.

Antoine stood there, still holding her with those strong hands and staring into her eyes as if searching for ways to restore what had been broken.

"Antoine, I—we—" she stammered, "we have to know what we're jumping into. It breaks my heart, Antoine. But—"

"Meena, Meena. I want you so much."

"And I want *you*. But I don't want—for me it can't—can't just—be a casual thing. And I don't think it can for you either. We're both serious. So if you—if, after seeing Liv, you still feel this way about me, then, well . . ."

"You're right." He released her abruptly. Hurt and disbelief narrowed his face into an elliptical lean form. "I got carried away. I'm sorry."

"When I met you," Meena said in an already regretful tone, "I wasn't dating or even thinking about it. But—one thing happened after another. And now I don't know what to do. Maybe it's the timing. We both have unfinished business."

"Unfinished business?" Antoine's voice was suddenly charged with anger and mistrust. "Yes, of course," he said after a moment. "I know how busy you are. I must be going."

So—he was taking this as a rejection. And, she could guess, he was jealous of Carlos. He must have figured the call was from Carlos and that had ruined everything.

Antoine stalked to the door, then swayed. The color had drained out of his eyes, leaving them vacant. "Good luck in the Kimochi race," he said as he walked toward the elevator.

Meena was crying inside. This was no way to say farewell.

She heard the hum of the elevator car descending. She flopped down on the carpeted floor and hugged her knees. Through the open door to the kitchen she could see the mango still sitting on the counter. But she had lost all taste for it.

22

When Meena got to work at seven that morning, she glimpsed the tall figure of Dave Williams through the glass pane of the SIC entrance. He seemed lost in his thoughts as he hurried along the passageway. Strange. Where was he rushing off to so early? She flew in through the door and called, "Dave!"

He peered into her face with alarm. His jaws were clenched tightly like the blades of a scissors. His ears went ruby red.

"Is something wrong, Dave?" she asked.

He bobbed his head in an affirmative way.

"Let's go to your desk," she said.

They crossed the hallway to his cubicle. Inside, he pulled a chair for her with stiff hands and settled himself at his desk, his earth-colored eyes intense. "I think someone has made a copy of my COSMOS design spec," he said breathlessly.

"Don't you keep it locked?"

Dave pushed his blond hair back with his fingers. "I came in around six-thirty. Hardly anybody is here then. I went to get a cup of coffee across the street. Left the folder right here." He pointed to the top of his desk. "Opened to a certain page. I was gone ten minutes at the most. When I came back, the whole thing was gone. I found it by the copying machine. I knew someone had taken it, then didn't have time to put it back. I e-mailed you right away."

Meena said, "You know the specs are always supposed to be locked in your desk when you're not there."

Dave nodded a yes. The red of his ears deepened.

Meena rose, saying, "Let's talk about this later."

A bit later, back in her office, she was interrupted by one of Brett's pro-grammers, who asked her a few technical questions. That handled, she opened her e-mail box. There were nine new messages. On most morn-ings that would have overwhelmed her, but today Meena was glad to be buried in a pile of work. The administrivia helped her keep from thinking about Antoine. She zipped through the first eight, mostly memoranda from other managers of the company. The ninth one was from Laxmi, her Stanford classmate, who now made her home in Bombay.

> Meenaji:
>
> The name Vishnu R. Chauhan rang a bell, but for days I
> had no clue. Then I came across an old computer article
> that I had clipped from India News. Guess what? It was
> written by Vishnu R. Chauhan. He's a columnist, very
> popular with the subscribers.
> I called the paper's Calcutta office right away and asked to
> speak to him. The woman who answered said there was no
> Vishnu there. I kept probing. She barked at me and wanted
> to know if I was a marriage broker or from the police.
> Will keep looking for Vishnu's name in other publications
> and asking around. In the meantime, I am snail-mailing
> you the article.
> My company is looking for someone to fill the director's
> position. They are especially interested in candidates
> from the States. I've talked about you. They seem keen.
> We're one of the biggest software houses in India. If
> you're interested, you can mail me your resume.
>
> Laxmi

So Vishnu really was a journalist. That fit with what Antoine had said. And Vishnu covered the computer industry. So there was a common interest. A most favorable sign. And a job possibility in India was surfacing for her, too. No harm sending a résumé. She could air-mail it separately from home. For now she composed a reply.

> Laxmiji,
>
> Thanks for all your help finding Vishnu. If you do get hold
> of him, give him my love and my e-mail address and
> mention our code word "lizard."
>
> Meena

With great elation she hit the Send key. Then she went about her day in good spirits.

Much later she sat down at her terminal and again checked for mail. Up popped a bright green note on her screen. It was from James A. Lanigan, a senior programmer at Gamma Solutions. The bulky man was nicknamed "Attila the Hun" but more readily answered to Jim. Meena had first met him five years ago at a computer conference, then bumped into him periodically at various professional gatherings. In his early forties, the man always wore a plain white shirt and narrow tie, got thicker glasses every year, and had an absentminded look about him. Computing was Jim's first love and it was hard to stop him once he got started talking about it. She knew he'd be ready to test his graphics application under COSMOS the minute it was released. Now she was eager to get a report on his progress.

> Captain COSMOS,
>
> Glad your database software will have a Fast Call feature.
> It'll make my job so much easier. I've burned some
> midnight oil testing my application and trying to make it
> run faster. It's ready to roll.
> BTW, are you racing the Kimochi 8K next weekend?
> Claudette says she's going to. Do you know Claudette
> Dain? She's our office manager, a top runner in the Bay
> Area. Your age. The thirty-five to thirty-nine group.
> Best of luck.
>
> Jim

That BTW—"by the way" in Netiquette—was a surprise. The name Claudette Dain was familiar from the rumor mill: she was Brett's girlfriend. Meena couldn't think of being outdone by Brett's girlfriend in the race. Last year Meena had placed fourth in her age group. This year she had better finish higher.

What flabbergasted her more was the mention of Fast Call. That feature, her brainchild, was embedded in COSMOS-1 code, but Jim wasn't supposed to know about it. It was being billed as a "future objective," one that would be released with COSMOS-2. This information was classified "top secret." She put her head back on her chair. Sweat beads were forming on her forehead.

The third surprise was Jim's statement that he was about finished with his application. He couldn't possibly be at that stage unless someone had supplied him with the COSMOS interface code. But COSMOS was proprietary, "closed." Only her programmers and the early test sites had access to such information. How had the confidentiality of her project been compromised?

She reached for her glass of water, took a long sip, and thought back to this morning's encounter with Dave and his suspicion that the COSMOS design specifications had been copied. She had dismissed it then. As long as the information stayed in-house, it didn't matter much. But now she saw the problem was bigger than she had imagined. The specifications document contained important information that competitors and clients would love to get hold of. And at least in the case of Gamma, it seemed they had. Who had copied it? All her programmers had signed an agreement of confidentiality. Her pulse quickened as though she were running sprints on a track. She could take only shallow breaths.

Dave came over to her door. "Guess what we found out?" he said excitedly.

"What?"

"When I got back to my cubicle after lunch I couldn't find my desk key. Art tried his key on mine and it opened. Just as an experiment we kept trying other desk keys and found several that could open mine. And my key opened both Art's and Karen's desks."

Thank goodness for the daily meditation practice. Meena could make herself not just appear calm but *be* calm, cool, clear-thinking. She processed the information in her head, then said, "I was under the impression the locks were one of a kind."

"Not so." Dave kept on speaking as he took a chair. "But wait. Things aren't as bad as they could be. The document that was copied isn't the latest version. My current file was unmarked and hidden at the bottom of my desk. That was untouched."

"I'm still concerned," Meena said. "I'm going to order a safe for our group. We'll store all our confidential files in one place and have limited access. Just a couple of people will know the combination. In the meantime, store any confidential material in my file cabinet." She pointed to the cabinet at the back.

"I'll tell the other programmers." Dave leapt to his feet.

Meena got up too and headed for Alex's office to tell him what had happened. But the room was empty. He had already left for Europe. She continued down the hallway, remembering that Jean the Pencil

Czar was filling in for him. Jean would have to approve funds to buy a safe. Her cubicle was two doors along.

The Pencil Czar turned her swivel chair around to face Meena. Her thinning gray hair and shapeless flowered dress suggested an old-maid manager of a secondhand bookstore instead of an office, Meena thought. Her oversized Sophia Loren eyeglasses were perched midway down her nose and she glanced at Meena above them. She had a way of looking at people as though she knew every bad thing they had ever done and was waiting for the next one to happen.

"Hello, Jean," Meena said. "How're you today?"

There were no words of welcome, just a freezing silence.

"I'm afraid we need to buy a safe," Meena said. "Looks like we have a security exposure here. A COSMOS document was picked up from a programmer's desk and copied by somebody. We also found that the same key can open many desks. My suggestion would be to get a safe right away."

The veins on the Pencil Czar's temples stood out and she popped like a firecracker. "A safe? We don't have the budget for it."

Meena backed away a couple of steps, but relaxed her face. "Our documentation is confidential and important. There are legal implications if it gets in the wrong hands—"

"Does Alex know about this?"

Fire blazed through Meena's veins. A low-level clerk like the Pencil Czar trying to second-guess her? Damn you, woman, she thought. "I can't talk to Alex," she said. "He's in Europe. And it's not something I'd care to put in a fax or e-mail. If I talk to Lou Cassidy, it could cost you your job."

"This is the first I've heard about it," the Pencil Czar squealed. "You and your programmers are always in such a hurry for everything."

"So when will we have it?" Meena asked.

The Pencil Czar narrowed her eyes. "Let me call a few places." She pulled her address book from a drawer and placed it on the desk. "I'll let you know by this afternoon."

Meena returned somewhat unsteadily to her office, settled into her chair, clutched her glass of water, and stared through the window that overlooked the Bay Bridge. From her vantage point, the traffic on the bridge rolled smoothly along, a contrast to the turmoil inside her. She feared that the COSMOS document problem might just be the visible edge of an about-to-tip boulder overhanging the road. The worst might yet come rolling down.

To calm herself she opened her desk drawer, pulled out a thin, well-thumbed book of haiku, and flipped to a page at random. A line caught her eye. "A swan, a pool, floating leaves." The image renewed her. She closed the book gently and put it back.

A safe was delivered early the next week and that morning Meena breathed a little easier. She picked up the phone and dialed Jim's number at Gamma. She hadn't answered his e-mail yet. A brief recorded message directed her to punch the pound key for the receptionist.

The call must have rolled over to yet another extension, for a female voice answered. "Office Administration. Claudette."

Wasn't she Brett's girlfriend? The runner extraordinaire who would be her competition at the Kimochi race this weekend? Meena hesitated to answer.

"Can I help you?" the other end said. The cheerfulness in that voice was artificial, like a saleswoman's during the Christmas season.

"May I speak to Jim Lanigan?" Meena filtered her voice through a layer of professional smoothness.

"Sorry, he's on vacation."

On vacation? But he just—then it struck Meena. He had gotten information about the COSMOS interface early from somewhere, tested his application, and was finished with his project.

"When will he be back?"

The woman's voice had taken on an edge. "I wouldn't know."

Could Jim be having a problem with the company? "I'll try again later." Meena put the receiver down. It was a setback, but she'd find a way to talk to Jim eventually.

She decided to stroll over to Brett's office, bring up Jim's name to catch him off guard, watch his reaction. She wouldn't mention Claudette.

Brett's office door was ajar. He was hunched over his phone, scratching his head with a fleshy thumb. His hair was shaggy on the nape of his neck, past due for a haircut.

"Look, I've been out of town—" she heard him say in a rising voice. She knew he was lying. Was he talking to a woman? Someone he wanted to avoid? He slammed the phone down.

Talking to Brett now would be a wrong move, Meena knew. Quickly she turned and walked back to her office. She'd have to come up with another means of unraveling the mystery of the missing COSMOS document.

23

It was sunny, fifty-eight degrees, and a perfect day for the Kimochi 8K. Walking to the race, Meena stopped to stretch at a pond surrounded by a lush meadow with a eucalyptus grove beyond it. Petals from rhododendron bushes made a mandala pattern on the grass. The spot had special meaning for her. Many times now she had jogged with Antoine in this part of Golden Gate Park.

She eased along toward Kennedy Drive. The road was closed to traffic today and, for a distance of two city blocks that she could see, it was filled with runners. All were waiting behind the starting line ready to hammer the five-mile course—destination, Japantown.

It was difficult to wade through the milling people, but Meena was in a racing mood, only a little tense because her training hadn't been as consistent as in previous years. She would be satisfied just to place in her age group.

"Fifteen minutes to go," the race director boomed through a loudspeaker.

She lifted her head to look for the starting line.

"Meena," a cracked voice called out from behind.

Here was Hal, the septuagenarian runner, standing erect on the sidewalk clad in jeans and a lambswool sweater. A beret tilted on his head gave him an eccentric yet stylish look. He had often said his road-racing days were behind him, but he faithfully attended the events to cheer on fellow runners like her.

"I was hoping you'd come," she said.

"How do you feel this morning?"

"I'm ready."

"I've watched you train, Meena," he said. "You're dedicated. You'll do well."

"I'd really like to break 33:20, my last year's time."

"Would that be a personal record on this course?"

She nodded.

"See that woman over there in orange?" He pointed to a figure on the other side of the street. "That's Claudette Dain. She wins a lot of races. You're in the same age group this year. She wants to do a PR too."

Meena turned to take a good look at Brett's girlfriend. Compactly built with long hair done in corkscrew curls, she seemed out of place in Lycra. She had piles of makeup on, as though for an important date. And who should she be with but Brett himself? He was in street clothes, wearing his usual foolish grin. He obviously wasn't a runner.

"Good luck, Meena. See you at the finish line." Hal walked away.

Now feeling a little more jittery, Meena jostled her way to the third row behind the national-class speedsters invited for this event. Brett had brought out the fighting spirit in her. At work he had recently had the upper hand, but running was Meena's territory. At least, she resolved, she'd beat his girlfriend, that wonder runner Claudette.

"Five minutes to go," the race director yelled.

Meena continued to warm up by stretching her calves and hamstrings and running in place.

A jazz band in the park played something raucous. Unintelligible directions came through the loudspeaker and only made Meena more nervous. She told herself to return to her center, direct her attention to one point. She closed her eyes and touched the area on her forehead between the eyebrows to open the "third eye." Feeling calmer, she got into position by placing her right foot ahead and lowering her body slightly.

The runner next to her pranced and puffed. "What am I doing here?" he complained. "It's Sunday. I could be in a warm bed."

Butterflies in the belly and all, Meena said, "I want to be no place else." She was feeling strong.

At the sound of the starting gun Meena surged ahead, a pump of adrenaline pushing her forward. The only sound now was of rustling feet. Rounding the first turn, she glanced behind her to see an ocean of heads bobbing up and down. In that moment of inattention someone elbowed her on the arm. She quickly moved to one side, pushed her way ahead of the pack.

Within a couple of minutes the crowd thinned out and she found herself running alone. But not for long. Claudette fell in right behind her, matching her pace. She'd be a tough competitor. Meena didn't want her so close.

At the one-mile mark a volunteer called the time: "Six minutes, forty seconds."

It was slightly faster than her usual pace at a running event. Meena smiled, pleased with herself. If she could maintain this pace, she should be able to gain a lead over Claudette.

Miles two and three came and went. Friendly bystanders cheered and whistled and called out, "Way to go." Claudette was still tucked in just behind her. Meena ran on in a fluid, easy motion, and now entered a meditative state. There was no past or future. Only this moment, the big sky, and running.

At the four-mile mark she found her left toes were jamming against the front of her racing shoe. Oh no, a blister, she could feel it forming. She pushed on. One more mile to go. Claudette was still behind her.

The big banner in Japantown came in sight. Meena started to make her move, but skidded on a pebble. Claudette pounced on the opportunity and unleashed her own final kick, drawing up even with Meena. They dueled side by side. Meena reached deep into her reserves, but couldn't draw up that last ounce of extra energy. Just before the finish line, Claudette inched ahead. A half second later Meena heard the applause from the crowd, which came to her as both a thrill and a humiliation. The finish-line clock overhead read thirty-three minutes, five seconds, her best time on this course yet. But she had not beaten Claudette.

A race volunteer wrapped a shiny silver thermal blanket around Meena's shoulder. She sucked in air for a few moments and cooled down by walking around until her heartbeat returned to normal. Then she went over to the rest area, where refreshments were set up on tables. She took a can of mineral water and a few orange slices and watched the other finishers pour in.

"Congrats, Meena," Hal was calling out. Claudette was with him. "Let me introduce you two."

Meena felt her mouth drying. She was trying to get over being bested by Claudette.

"Claudette, this is Meena."

Claudette shook Meena's hand. "Enjoyed racing with you," she said, smiling. "You have a good steady pace, so I stuck behind you. I didn't think I could keep up with you the whole time."

Claudette had the approachable quality of a woman not terribly impressed with herself. And she had unleashed a strong kick at the end. "You were good for me," Meena said. "I haven't trained that much this year." She laughed. "But it's my best time yet."

"A tight finish," Hal said. "You two were splendid to watch, running neck and neck. I haven't finished an 8K in that kind of time in more than twenty-five years." Hal took a step back. "Good to see you, Claudette. And you, too, Meena. I'll be looking for you in the park." He excused himself and left.

"That last mile was a killer," Claudette confessed, "now that I've put on a little weight. I'm having problems with my partner, you know how that is. It's making me a compulsive eater. Dove Bars are my downfall. Do you mind walking over to that table? I see some Dove Bars there. . . ."

As Claudette scoffed two ice cream bars, Meena chatted about her training schedule, the courses she liked to jog, the races that topped her list. She noticed Claudette's eyes flickering around the field.

"Oh, here comes Brett now," Claudette said.

"Congratulations, Claudette." Brett joined them. "So how're you, Meena? How was the race?"

His words made Meena seethe.

"You two know each other?" Claudette looked up at Brett in wonder.

"Meena and I are both managers in the same division at SIC," Brett said.

"She runs really well," Claudette told him, suddenly condescending. She added, "How far can you run, Brett?"

Brett scratched his head and turned. "I see somebody I know over there." He disappeared in the crowd.

Meena and Claudette kept chatting until the loudspeaker interrupted to call them to the award ceremony. They hurried toward the stage, where a clutch of spectators had gathered. Starting with the youngest, the top three finishers in each age group were called up to receive their medals. Meena held her breath as the turn came for women thirty-five to thirty-nine.

"First place: Claudette Dain. Second place"—now Meena's heart was beating at the speed of light—"Meena Gossett . . ."

The clapping and cheering dimmed out the rest. Meena climbed the stage. The race officer put the medal around her neck. It was a moment when flowers blossomed and no dark clouds could be seen in the sky. Wish I could hold on to this feeling, Meena thought. She shook hands with the third-place winner, hugged Claudette, then got down from the stage, her feet barely touching the ground.

Meena watched the other medals being awarded. Claudette stood beside her, smiling at first, then surveying the spectators and frowning.

"Where the hell's Brett gone?" Claudette whispered after a while. "That jerk. He promised he'd take me to lunch—" Her voice caught. She groped for a tissue, adding, "I have to go."

"Wish we could have talked more," Meena said.

"Same here," Claudette said. "I've heard so much about you. You're the rising star, Brett told me. You're different than I thought. Maybe we can run together sometime. I don't have my card with me. You can call me at Gamma."

They parted with an embrace. A promising encounter, Meena reflected. Claudette could become a friend and a running partner. With Antoine out of the picture these days, Meena had been running alone. Claudette was a talented athlete, if a little undisciplined. Running together would help them both, Meena figured.

"The last two runners are coming," came the announcement. Meena decided to walk to the finish line to cheer them on. She was only fifty yards away when she saw someone familiar cross the line. A man breathing hard, his chest heaving. Just then a tall woman in a black dress and leather boots stepped out from the sidelines and started kissing him fiercely.

Good God. It was Antoine. With Liv? If he saw Meena what would he think? She hurried to blend in with the crowd before he could spot her.

It was too late. "Meena," Antoine called, staggering over the grassy field toward her. "Wait."

Meena turned, feeling effervescent, and waited for them to come closer. Right away Antoine looked at the medal between her breasts.

She blushed as he bent to read the inscription. She could hear him breathe.

"Wow, Meena." He wheezed. "A medal. In such a big field. That's quite an achievement." He gave her a quick hug, then jerked back.

Antoine, oh Antoine, Meena lamented silently, remember how it used to be. Even that brief touch transported her back to when they were friends: running together, talking for hours at Café Cabrillo, watching the ducks on Spreckles Lake. Meena looked into his eyes with both question and expectation. He blinked as though to deflect any private communication, then nudged Liv's shoulder in a familiar way.

"Meena, this is Liv."

The woman in black dress and boots remained impassive for a moment, then reached into her storehouse of charm to force a smile onto her mauve lips. Meena looked her over. Liv was taller and heavier, but pretty just the same. The aloofness about her came not from depth of character but from consciousness of her status in the business world. Her perfume, sweeter than a lily, made Meena want to sneeze. Liv looked odd next to Antoine, who had on a tee shirt and skimpy running shorts and was glowing with perspiration. Though Meena hated to admit it, they made a handsome couple. For the first time she faced the corporeal evidence that Antoine wasn't hers, never had been.

Meena cleared her throat and said, "Pleased to meet you."

"Liv, I told you about Meena Gossett. Without her coaching I wouldn't have finished this race."

"Thanks so much for running with Antoine while I was gone," Liv said with a slight smile.

Meena was still too dumbfounded to be saying much, but she noticed how Liv was watching Antoine's every gesture. "Perfect weather for a race, wasn't it?" she said to Antoine.

"The weather was fine," Antoine said in a normal manner. "It was my legs that weren't. They cramped at the third mile. So I stopped at the rest station, drank water, stretched. After that, I ran-walked like you taught me, Meena. I was slow, very slow, but I did manage to make it to the finish line." A happy grin bloomed on his wet face.

"I'm so proud of you, Antoine," Liv said.

Meena said, "Congrats on your first—"

Liv cut her off. "We have to go, darling. We're meeting George and

Paula for brunch. And you have to shower and change." She locked her right fingers in Antoine's left hand and started to turn away.

Antoine raised his eyebrows to Liv as if asking why she couldn't wait a minute. Liv moved a short distance away but, Meena noticed, kept half an eye on them.

A private moment with Antoine. Meena hoped to hear that he wanted to jog with her again soon and meet at Café Cabrillo afterward. Instead he was saying, "My cousin's getting married. Won't be running for the next few days." As if his whole relationship with Meena was based only on running. As if the other night in her apartment had never happened. She knew her face was no longer cloaked in cheerfulness. Her lips were crimping from disappointment. Out of the corner of her eye she saw Hal approaching.

"They want you for a group photo, Meena." Hal was waving her over.

"Oh, I shouldn't keep you. Good to see you, Meena," was all Antoine said. He stared into her eyes for one more heart thump, then he and Liv drifted away.

Meena stayed for a moment. Alone, quite alone. The whole field with hundreds of runners seemed empty. Well, so much for a reunion with Antoine. At least she had this medal. As she examined it, the silver-plated disc glistened in the abundant California sun. The blue velvet ribbon felt warm around her throat. A glorious day, but no one to share it with. She had been both a winner and a loser, mostly a loser, in today's race.

24

Another soggy spring day in San Francisco. Meena was glad to get out of the rain and gusting wind and into the lobby of her apartment complex after work. Absentmindedly—she was still puzzling over a COSMOS-1 problem—she pressed the button. Just as the elevator door began to close Shaheen flew in. She was bundled up in a trenchcoat, typical San Francisco wet-weather attire, thrown over her *salwar-kameez*. On one palm she had inscribed in Arabic script a few words of what Meena guessed to be a verse from the Koran, in a natural orange dye that contrasted with her dusky brown skin. Her other hand was clutching a jute shopping bag. After taking a look to ascertain that the sixth floor button had been pressed, she turned to Meena and asked, "Working late again, *behenji*?"

"Yes," Meena said. "I've been working on a software bug all day. Time just flew by."

"What a pity," Shaheen said. "You work so hard. But at least you live alone. Now you'll be able to go to your own place and relax. For me, the evenings are the busiest time. I have my family to take care of." Yet her genial expression told Meena that Shaheen wasn't complaining. The life she had chosen suited her perfectly.

"I just went to the store to get some gingerroot." Shaheen lifted a thick buff-colored gnarled root out of her bag. "You see, Ahmed has a cold. I'm going to put shredded ginger in his *chai* to warm him up. It's a traditional Indian cure."

"With your care, I'm sure he'll get better in no time at all," Meena said as she stepped out of the elevator.

"We're having *khichri* for dinner, that's our rainy-night stew, and playing Carom Board afterward," Shaheen said. "Please come join us if you can. My mother always said a good *khichri* solves most problems. It might be just the thing for your software bug."

"Thanks, Shaheen. I'll see."

In her living room the red light on her answering machine was blinking.

"Meenaji, Carlos here. Would it be okay to stop by your place this evening?"

Meena could feel a load lift from her shoulders. Last week she had called to thank him for the mango and had talked only to his answering machine. He hadn't returned her call as quickly as in the past. Why not? she wondered. Of course, she would be delighted to see him, and she left him a message saying so.

The mango Carlos had given her had continued to ripen, sitting on the butcher-block table in her kitchen. And every time she noticed the bowl, she brooded about Antoine. Somehow she couldn't bear the idea of eating the fruit that had unlocked Antoine's feelings. Finally she moved the bowl into the refrigerator.

She replayed in her head one more time last weekend's meeting with Antoine and Liv at the Kimochi race. Wasn't there a spark in the farewell look he gave her, one that said, I'll be back. Or was she mistaken? She hadn't heard from him since. With Mom's death, she had lost a sense of belonging anywhere or to anybody. Now she was beginning to think of herself as what people in database lingo refer to as a "dangling child," existing in a social vacuum, unconnected to family or friends, a lost soul.

Carlos would understand. He had moved to the Bay Area ten years ago and made himself part of the singles set. His father was a wealthy politician in Mexico City with vacation homes in Aspen and Lucerne. Meena sensed that Carlos wasn't in agreement with his father's political views, although the subject never did come up. Even though he had long since adapted to the lifestyle of his new home and spoke the language fluently, he still felt a frequent longing for the ways of his native Mexico. At home in either, belonging to neither. This dilemma he had discussed often with Meena, and it had come to form a bond between them.

Now, as she waited for him in her living room, she pulled Antoine's *Parallel Lives* from the bookshelf almost without thinking.

She stretched out on the sofa, comfortable in fleece-lined sweatpants and a matching sweatshirt with a hole in one armpit, and let her loose hair drape over the end of the sofa. She hugged the book tenderly for a moment and pictured Antoine's face before opening it. It was silly, she admitted to herself, but she'd been reading the book slowly, a few pages at a time, afraid that when it was finished she'd lose what little connection she had with Antoine. It was like holding a preserved plum in the mouth, savoring its bittersweetness to the end.

Slowly she flipped to the bookmark; a hundred more pages to go. She read a paragraph, then found herself daydreaming about Antoine. She closed the book, put it on the coffee table, and peered at the shelf for a few seconds before picking another.

This one was the *Ramayana*, the ancient Indian epic, a story that was part of her growing-up period in India and with Auntie Bimla. As an adult she continued to read it, and each time she did, she arrived at an answer to some question she hadn't even asked. In moments the story took her back to India. Soon she was smelling the dust, hearing the thunder, feeling the desert wind knife through her. On a night like this she'd be sitting on Grandfather's lap as he spun the familiar story of Rama. Vishnu would be there too, half lying on the mat, gazing up with O-shaped, curious boy's eyes.

The doorbell sounded. With the book in her hand, she hastened to let Carlos in. His bearing was still proud, but he looked visibly exhausted. She could see fatty deposits under his skin. He must have partied far too late last night.

"*Amigo!*" Meena kissed him on the cheek.

He stared at her face for a moment, smiled with affection, took her hand and kissed it tenderly.

"Come on in." She motioned him to the sofa. "Coffee's made."

"No," he said. "Sit down with me first."

She sat in the armchair opposite him.

"Is this how a beautiful woman spends her evenings?" he asked. "With a book?"

"It isn't just any book," she said reasonably. "And I've always loved reading. As an only child, books were my best friends."

"I have no time to read," he said.

"You're never alone, it seems."

"I'm seeing a woman." The smile that traveled across his face was a shade naughty. "Simply exquisite, utterly enchanting, and just a bit married."

"Carlos!"

"This one's serious." He laid a hand over his heart. "You know how much I love sushi."

Meena could feel her eyebrow rising. "Six months ago you were living with a Soo Fong-Lee and you swore by Kung Pao chicken."

"She wanted out. I didn't."

"But a married woman? You could get yourself in trouble."

"Oh no, it's all right. She's from Japan. Visiting relatives. Her husband flew in from Tokyo yesterday. Yoko and I went to the airport to meet him."

Just imagine a husband being greeted by his wife and her new lover.

"He's a businessman," Carlos said. "Very cool. They are separated right now."

"Sounds like he took it well."

"I want to marry her."

"You want to marry every woman you meet, Carlos." Meena did perhaps notice something different about him this time: his shining eyes, his high, happy voice, the slight distance he was keeping from her.

"I'm not as shallow as you think," he answered. "I need to settle down. I've moved eleven times in the last ten years." Yes, there were tiny lines around his eyes, a tinge of sadness etched in the creases, Meena could see. "I'm a permanent transient," he added.

"You just visited your family in Mexico, didn't you?"

"Surprise," he said. "I ran into your colleague Joy there. She's just bought a condo in Oxaca. Did you know that?"

"No. Joy never told me."

"I saw a lot of my family," Carlos continued. "My brother came to visit. Brought my nephews and nieces with him. They're all grown and they don't know me very well. Mamá served me flan. Papá talked politics as always, but so much has happened to me that at first I didn't have much to say—I thought I'd stayed away too long. Then after a few days it seemed like I'd never been away."

"But it's hard to leave San Francisco for good, isn't it?"

"Yes. It's *the* city. I love selling. We both have done well here." His eyes swept her living room. "We drive fancy cars and live in nice places. But are we satisfied? No—deep in our hearts we're pining for our country, our people, our culture. And something more that I can't pin down." He paused. "Why don't you go back to India? See your own people? Get to know your motherland?"

"I will."

"Why wait so long?" Carlos asked.

She glanced up and there it was, a snapshot of Mom and Dad on the occasional table. "I don't know. Has to do with Mom and Dad . . ."

"They kidnapped you. You know that?"

The truth seared her chest like a burning iron rod. "Yes," she said after she regained her composure, "on a jeweled throne. Pity, they never understood India. In New Delhi they lived in a posh neighborhood. All they could talk about was the poverty. Dad learned a little Hindi but wouldn't speak it. Mom never bothered with the language. When I told them what my village home was like, Mom said, 'How could anyone live there?' Too bad none of the beauty reached them. But my nanny, Bimla, taught me all about India."

"It's nice that she gave you that."

"Auntie Bimla would take me to Indian concerts in Berkeley. She'd buy me books on India. But Mom and Dad wanted me to be an American."

"Is that who you feel you are?"

"I used to," Meena said. "I did most everything an American girl would do except cut my hair." She brushed a strand of hair back from her forehead and touched her bobby pins to keep herself from crying. "But now I feel split in two. When I was younger I didn't think about my homeland. I had everything here—parents, friends, running, work. All those things are falling away."

"What do you mean?"

She broke into nervous laughter. "Maybe I'm feeling this way because I'm not in a relationship."

"Oh?" Carlos stared at Antoine's novel on the coffee table. "So you're reading him. The hot author. Charming, good looking. Moody, if I may say so. He lived in India. Sure, you'd find him attractive." Carlos winked at her. "And he probably lusts after you."

She smiled wryly to herself, thinking Antoine had suggested the same about Carlos. "Antoine was here when the mango came."

"You're going to get your feelings hurt, *amiga*," Carlos said. "I hear they're looking for a house."

No, that couldn't be. She knew Antoine and Liv were supposed to get married, but somehow . . .

Carlos said, "Face it, he took advantage of you."

Mired in depression and hurt, Meena couldn't respond. Carlos was right. She heard the sound of raindrops beating against the window.

"How do you feel right now?" Carlos asked.

She hid her face in her hands for a second, blocking everything from view, thinking she'd made an obvious fool of herself. But then she lifted her head and indicated the other book on the coffee table. "I've been rereading the *Ramayana*. Sita, the goddess, is a role model for Rajput women. We Rajputs are supposed to have descended from her." She sighed. "After her marriage she was abducted by Ravana. And there she ran into all sorts of problems. Her husband, Rama, fought to get her back, and in the end she was returned to him safely."

"And?" Carlos asked.

"And Rama asked her to take a fire test to prove her purity. Sita felt humiliated. She was in pain. She called out to Mother Earth, 'Save me, o dear Mother.' " Meena paused to take a long breath. "Thunder clapped, the sky lit up, the ground cracked open. Mother Earth came out on a jeweled throne and took Sita on her lap. The throne went down and the ground closed after them. Sita was never seen again." Meena fell silent. Finally she said in a small voice, "I feel humiliated like her . . . I just want to disappear."

"Don't take it so hard, Meena," Carlos urged. "It's not the end of the world."

She nodded slowly. "You're right. This is modern-day America. Unlike Sita, I have options."

"And believe me," Carlos muttered, "Antoine isn't that great a catch."

"Actually, there's a man in India I'm trying to get in touch with. Through the Internet." She saw Carlos frowning. "He's a friend from my village. A journalist for a major paper in Calcutta."

"You want to see him after all these years? Good God, Meena. Why would you be looking for him now?"

"I should tell you my big secret. I was married to Vishnu when we were both seven. Maybe that's why I never got married here."

Carlos choked, but recovered in a moment. "Sounds every bit—or should I say every byte?—romantic."

Laughing, she rose to her feet. "Let me get you some coffee."

"No." He stood up. "I told Yoko I'd take her to an old Elvis movie."

At the door he reached out and held her hands. "Call me if you need me. I'll be here."

When he was gone Meena drifted to the occasional table where his card saying "That's what friends are for" was sitting. Next to it stood a framed photo of Mom and Dad beaming out at her. She brooded over a fragment of conversation she had had with Mom when she was about nine.

"Mom, why don't we ever go back to India?"

"I don't know, honey," Mom said tentatively. "Don't you like your home here?"

"I do, Mom. But kids in school ask me about India. I can't tell them much. I have forgotten my village, my family. But I dream about them almost every night—"

"You're an American now, my dear. This is a great country. There are plenty of kids in India who'd love to trade places with you. If you went back there you might catch malaria. You don't want to get sick, do you?"

Meena tuned out the memory of the rest of Mom's talk. She sank onto the sofa and shut her eyes. At the moment she had lost all sense of peace. It was bad enough with trouble brewing at work, and Antoine gone. But now Carlos had made her face issues she didn't even want to consider. Good God, why do your best friends have to do that?

She rose, padded into the kitchen, cupped the mango in her hands. She'd never be able to eat it, but she didn't want to waste it either. It was a symbol of her feelings for Antoine. All of a sudden she knew precisely what to do. She walked resolutely down the corridor and knocked at the door of the Rasul family.

Sonny was still up and met Meena at the door. Meena offered him the mango and was rewarded with a warm smile. "Auntie Meena, can I cut Mommyji a slice? She loves mango."

Meena stroked his black hair, gazed into his large innocent eyes. "You do with it whatever you like, *bhai*."

"Go show it to your daddy." Shaheen had just appeared.

Sonny squeaked a thank-you, gave Meena a quick hug, and scampered into the living room.

"When we were newly married," Shaheen said, "Ahmed and I shared a lot of mangoes. Ahmed called it 'lovers' fruit.' I believe he was right—I got pregnant with Sonny right away." She smiled shyly. "Now we divide a mango three ways. It's become a family tradition."

Returning to her apartment, Meena did her bedtime ritual of massaging night cream on her face and drinking a glass of hot milk. She turned off the lights and got in bed. It was past ten, but her mind, a maelstrom of conflicting thoughts and sentiments, churned like a computing machine. She lay awake tossing and turning.

She wondered whether her life course would ever stretch clear before her. She wondered whether she would ever be dividing mangoes three ways.

25

It was five o'clock. Quitting time. Meena wished she felt better about the way the day had turned out. But things were still unsettled at work. In fact, the only positive development of the past month was her new friendship with Claudette, the office manager from Gamma Solutions. Gamma was located only a few blocks from SIC. It had been easy to meet Claudette after work in the evening for a jog along the Embarcadero. Claudette was on her way to becoming the friendly colleague Joy once was and the running partner Antoine had been. Meena locked her desk and dialed Claudette's number.

"I've been waiting to hear from you," Claudette answered cheerfully.

"I was going to call you for lunch today, but it got pretty hectic around here," Meena said. "But today's Thursday and the stores are open late. The Sun Shoppe is having a sale of tropical plants. I'd like to check it out. Want to come along?"

"I'd love to," Claudette said. "Let's hit Neiman Marcus afterward. I have a taste for a truffle."

"Fair enough," Meena said. "It's set, then. Meet me in front of the Crocker Galleria." She put on her jacket, said good-bye to Dave, and called it a day.

Market Street was jammed with single-lane traffic because of construction work. They were always fixing the roads here. Meena strode to the designated corner and waited. She watched as people poured out of the office buildings, a few of them casually attired but for the most part buttoned-down types—women in navy suits and bow-tied white blouses, men in pinstripes. Claudette stood out from a distance in her bright purple two-piece ensemble. She was walking leisurely, swinging an alligator purse. Her hair was pinned up on top of her head and a few loose strands fell over her rounded cheeks in curly crescents. She was quite definitely her own woman. She kissed Meena's cheek like an old friend. Suddenly the evening seemed a little brighter to Meena.

"So you're a gardener?" Claudette asked on the way to the florist.

"I have some flowers and ornamentals on my patio. I love growing things. Can't wait to water them in the evening when I get home."

"One of these days I'd like to start a garden myself," Claudette said with a hint of envy.

The shop, a lush tropical jungle of potted plants, was moist and warm. Meena studied the selections and read each label as she walked through the rows. "Ah, a ginger plant," she exclaimed. "Always wanted to grow one."

"I buy my ginger from Safeway," Claudette said. "I've never seen a ginger plant before."

Meena asked the florist, "Will it grow well here?"

"Yes, ma'am, every plant has potential." The Middle Eastern shop-keeper's deep voice sounded to her ear like poetry. "Just like people," he added. "Give it room to grow. Nurture it. But don't coddle it too much."

"Does it flower?"

"Yes. This is the flowering variety. The red flowers are very showy."

"I thought ginger only grew in the tropics," Claudette said.

"I'm going to give it a try," Meena decided.

She paid for her purchase, and they headed for Union Square. A blind violinist was playing a happy tune in one corner. A crowd gathered around him, but he looked like he was playing for himself.

"Remember him?" Claudette said. "He played at the Kimochi post-race festivities. I was so upset over Brett that day. But when I heard his upbeat music, I stopped and listened." She added, "I didn't tell you, but Jim Lanigan took me out to dinner on the Pier that evening. You know Jim, don't you? Big guy. Works with me at Gamma. Programmer. He got a divorce recently."

"Sure, I know Jim," Meena said. "I run into him every so often at a computer conference. I rather like him. He's a straight shooter."

"I'm not over Brett yet." Claudette cast her eyes downward. "You know how it is. You go for the one who gives you grief."

"Brett's giving *me* enough grief now." Meena hated saying his name.

"Watch that guy," Claudette said. "You're in his way. He told me so."

"Did he? What else did he tell you?"

"Oh, stuff. I don't remember. Jim could probably tell you plenty more. Brett used to come over to our building to shoot the breeze with Jim. Brett would go past my desk and wink at me. That's how I got to know him."

Meena hoped Claudette would end up with someone like Jim rather than a manipulator like Brett. "Jim's a nice guy," she said. "But why would he want to tell me anything?"

"He's leaving Gamma. Right now he's taking vacation time to interview."

They stopped at a street corner for a light. Meena asked, "Leaving? Why?"

"His boss promised him a raise but never followed through on it," Claudette said.

"How do I get hold of him?" Meena asked quickly. "I'd like to interview him. I could use an ace programmer on my team."

"He lives in El Cerrito," Claudette said. "He's listed. Why don't you buzz him? You could meet him over in the East Bay. He's got custody of his two kids. Doesn't get out too often."

Meena nodded, and resolved to call Jim first thing in the morning.

They stopped at an art store next, where Meena bought a picture—a travel poster, actually—of Shiva, the god of dance. Face serious, his head surrounded by a celestial blue halo, hands wielding ancient weapons, feet twirling on the earth. Intricate wavy lines and pale-to-deep hues gave his picture lifelike dimensions. This would be perfect for that one bare wall in her office.

They were now facing the bright lights of Union Square. Gazing at Neiman Marcus only a few steps away, Meena asked, "Shall we get our truffles?"

Inside the store they leaned over a large glass showcase, dazzled by trays of chocolate nuggets set in gold paper cuplets: mint, hazelnut cream, coffee liqueur, and many more. Meena imagined the intense flavors exploding in her mouth.

"Too many choices," she said.

"Wish I could say that about the men in my life." Claudette made a wry face.

Meena laughed and, suddenly decisive, said, "I'll take the hazelnut."

Next morning Meena arrived at the office humming to herself. The top item on her morning's agenda was to call Jim Lanigan—and not just because he might have a solution to the mystery of the missing COSMOS document. But first she flipped on the computer at her desk to check her e-mail messages. One from Laxmi leapt out at her. The posting time showed it had arrived here last night, already morning in Bombay. She clicked on that message.

> Meenaji,
>
> Good news. I'm expecting. The baby is due in
> September.
> My cousin, who's a college student in Calcutta, met
> Vishnu Chauhan's girlfriend quite by accident in the
> Coffee House. Her name is Asha. She's a lovely young
> woman who insists that she and Vishnu are "just pals." My
> cousin thinks there is more than friendship between the
> two.
> As they say, the plot thickens. My cousin will stay on the
> "case."
>
> Laxmi

A shock wave ran though Meena. So there was a woman in Vishnu's life! He wasn't honoring their marriage!

In the next microsecond she laughed at herself. Why should he? He didn't even know she was alive.

26

Late Friday afternoon Vishnu escorted Asha into the Moghul Palace restaurant on College Street. The sign above the entrance, lettered in Bengali, English, and Urdu, had faded since his last visit here, Vishnu noted. A palace it wasn't. The walls were stained, the cement floor bare, a verse from the Koran in Arabic calligraphy just above the entrance the only decoration. A card tacked to one wall said: "We certify that our food promotes health, vigor and cheerfulness."

Amid the chatter of diners and bustle of waiters Vishnu located an empty booth. He adjusted the curtains and they were in their own private dining alcove. "This place is ancient," he whispered to Asha. "In the old days, it was possible for Muslim women to come here with their families because of these curtains. They'd be covered head to toe in their *burkhas*, which they'd partly remove when they came inside."

They took their seats. The wooden chairs were old and scarred but comfortable. Vishnu felt cozy and secure in the natural light enclosing them. Snatches of music drifted in from the store next door through the open window. A woman's voice belted out

And I will . . . love you forever,
Love you forever,
Love you forever.

Another sentimental film song. Normally Vishnu paid no attention, but today he liked the words, said them silently to himself. Asha quietly rubbed the sapphire ring on the middle finger of her left hand. He regarded her pensive face outlined by soft, shiny hair for a few minutes and finally asked, "Is anything the matter?"

"It's my father." She pronounced the words "my father" with particular respect. "He wants me to marry a man from his office."

Asha being pushed into marriage? Vishnu's throat constricted just the way it had when Mr. Das first told him about it.

"I'm not ready," Asha hurried on. "After I graduate, I want to work for a few years, travel a bit."

She seemed like a frightened little bird, trapped. Had conditions changed much for women since their *burkha* days? Vishnu said, "Listen to your heart."

"I don't find him interesting, Vishnuda. He's the old-fashioned 'rights and duties' type of man. I had tea with him at Flury's the other day. Do you know what he said?"

"What?"

"After we'd talked for only about ten minutes he said, 'When we go on our honeymoon . . .' I was so startled that I dropped my teacup. It broke, of course, and I was terribly embarrassed. The whole arrangement is fine for him, but I don't think we have much in common. He doesn't seem to see that. I guess he just wants to get married."

"Why do your parents want you to marry him?"

"He's of the same caste and subcaste. Our grandparents came from the same village in Purulia. More important, my mother's astrologer says our charts match. Those things mean a lot to my parents. Mother will be devastated if I refuse. She won't say anything to me. But she'll carry the pain in her heart and I'll feel it." She bowed her head and put her hands over her face.

"You're grown up now, Asha, and times have changed," Vishnu said. "Modern women do not have to submit to oppressive traditions that deprive them of the right to determine their destiny. Be honest with your parents. Tell them how you feel about this man. Surely they want you to be happy." He leaned toward her. "You shouldn't marry until you're ready." The next moment he recalled his own childhood marriage to Meena and what it meant to him, and he felt foolish.

His eyes descended on something glistening on the table. After a moment's puzzlement he realized it was a tear. Asha was crying. The weight of that tiny drop had lowered her head. He remembered his mother crying once when he was a child. And he had seen actresses cry in movies. But he had no personal experience of tears in real life. He felt an urge to extend his hand and touch it, but controlled his impulse. He said casually, "How about introducing that man to one of your classmates?"

Asha raised her head, wiped her tears with her fingers, brooded for a moment. "Smita, you mean? Now that you mention it, she's a little like him. And she can't wait to get married either. That might work."

Asha resembled a white champa bud bathed in rain. He was seized by an urge to put his cheek to hers, to hold her close, to taste her lips.

The curtain parted and the waiter cleared his throat.

Vishnu glared at the old man, whose sunken eyes expressed profound tiredness. The man squirmed. Feeling ashamed of himself, Vishnu said kindly, "Two cutlet plates, please."

When the waiter had withdrawn, Vishnu turned to Asha. Her eyes were still swollen, but her face emanated a gentle radiance nonetheless. Vishnu guessed she knew how he felt about her and that had reassured her.

Asha asked, "And what are you going to do, Vishnuda?"

"I might get a job as a correspondent in Kashmir." The words came out of his mouth easily. "The salary's better."

"Oh?" She looked desperate again. "I know a good offer will come your way soon. You're talented. But the Kashmir job will take you away from here. Do you need to go that far?"

He looked into her eyes, trying to reassure her. Asha's face seemed to brighten in response. Suddenly embarrassed, they both looked out the window onto the street.

The waiter came back. His lean old hands quivered from the weight of the plates. He set them down, then hurried away.

Asha broke a piece of the flat bread with practiced hands. "So light and flaky," she murmured. She put the piece in her mouth, then rolled her eyes. "Mmmmm. Good. I wish I knew how to make it."

"My mother could teach you." He wrapped a piece of bread around a chunk of lamb, popped it into his mouth, and savored the spicy richness of meat against the neutral background of the wheat bread. "She's famous in our village for her bread. She can roll a dozen all the exact same size. Her breads are light as a handkerchief."

"I'd love to visit there," Asha said in childlike wonder. "My father says Rajasthan is backward, but I know it's beautiful. I want to see the forts, the peacocks, and of course the camel market."

She seemed to relish each morsel on her plate. Between mouthfuls she gave an account of her college life, her classmates, her eccentric professors. He talked of the Tagore dance-drama he had seen last night and how live theater still flourished in Calcutta.

"I've never been to a play," Asha said.

"Come with me next week to the new comedy," Vishnu said eagerly. "I hear it's hilarious."

"I wish I could take my parents out more," Asha said. "They don't laugh too often. But my father cannot sit for very long. He likes me to tell him film stories. I cut out the love scenes, of course. He wouldn't understand those." She giggled. "Oh, I almost forgot." She fished in her purse, retrieved a piece of paper, and handed it to him. "This is for you."

Vishnu stared at the string of letters and symbols. MEENA@ SIC.COM.

"What's this?"

"Meena's e-mail address."

"Meena," he whispered the name to make it real again. "Meena?"

"I believe she's a woman from your village. Didn't you tell me about her the other day?"

Vishnu stared at the e-mail address again. "Where did this come from?"

"I got it quite by accident," Asha began. "We were sitting at your usual table in the back. A woman came by and asked, 'Do you know if Vishnu Chauhan would be coming here today? The waiter said he usually sits at this table.' I said to her I don't know if he's coming or not, but we live in the same apartment building. The woman said her cousin Laxmi, who lives in Bombay, asked her to try to locate you some time ago. She thought she might find you in the Coffee House—so many reporters have regular tables there. She knew better than to find you in the phone directory. It's such a mess. It turns out this Laxmi went to Stanford University in the United States with a Meena Gossett, who now lives in San Francisco. She's trying to get in touch with you by e-mail."

Could this really be the Meena Kumari he married? Vishnu sat in silence for a time. Images, memories from childhood jumbled in his mind like a tangled reel of yarn. He found a handkerchief in his pocket and dabbed at his forehead.

"Are you all right, Vishnuda?"

"Shocked. I've known her since I was two. We were very close. If it's the right person, that is. Hard to believe she's alive and looking for me. . . ."

"From what I understood, Meena's doing well in the States. She manages a big project in a software house. She's well known in her field."

Vishnu looked away, still wondering if it was his Meena.

"The code word," Asha said, "I was asked to tell you is 'lizard.' "

Vishnu jumped out of his chair. That was his Meena all right. Remembering after all these years the lizards in the sand dunes. He sat down again.

He was most pleased to hear of her success. She was special, he always knew. He drew her face in his head: an oval contour, a delicate nose, gray-green eyes with a haunting quality. How did she dress these days? In a sari? In jeans? What did she like to do in her spare time? He wanted to know everything all at once. But now that he was unemployed, he had no access to a computer, no way to send her an e-mail. Cyberclubs were few and far between, and not affordable. He sighed.

"I didn't realize she was so important to you," Asha said slowly.

Asha's voice brought him back to the room. He said, "Yes, she was. I'll contact her the moment I can get hold of a computer."

He regretted his words when he noticed how Asha's face shrank, how she put her head down and stopped eating. He slipped the piece of paper carefully into his pocket. That was part of Meena. He fretted about Asha too. She must not marry an unsuitable man. Silently he finished the rest of his meal, feeling pulled by both women. He couldn't say a word when he got up and opened the curtain for her.

They left the restaurant and pushed out into teeming College Street. Vishnu was glad to be out of the confined space and into the wide road. Cars, buses, lorries, and rickshaws all honked at the same time, demanding their right to go first. The confusion drowned out his own musings, but he could not miss the longing look on Asha's face.

Do I let the afternoon come to an end like this? He agonized over his options, for he was uncomfortable at the thought of spending any more time with Asha while his head was full of thoughts of Meena.

"I'm going to meet with an old college friend who lives around the corner. Let's get together at the Coffee House next week," he said.

"I'll take you up on it," Asha said eagerly. "And I hope you get a new position before too long. One close to home."

A double-decker bus was lumbering toward them. "See you soon," Asha shouted.

Vishnu watched her get on the bus. He murmured to himself, "Meena, Meena," as he crossed the street.

Book
Three

27

Antoine awoke with another perfect Marin County day facing him. He found himself lacking any desire to get out of bed. He had stayed up late working on his new novel. The story would center on Munich's Turkish immigrants. He had lived in that cliquish yet friendly city during his sophomore year in high school while his father was posted there. Antoine was just fifteen then, a sensitive and emotional kid who laughed easily, was excited easily, cried only when alone. His friend was Homely Henry, an American boy of the same age who lived down the block with his family. They explored the city's trendy areas like Schwabing, but were more fascinated by the Turkish quarter their parents had told them not to go near. Being typical rebellious teenagers, they found their parents' edicts a challenge not to be denied. So they spent countless hours hanging around those forbidden places.

One particular image from that time had given Antoine the inspiration for his new novel. A green-eyed Turkish woman with coal black hair coming out of a building. Just that. She was a few years older, a college student he guessed, wearing a sleeveless summer dress with no ornaments or makeup. But hers was a face that belonged on a magazine cover. She flashed a smile at the two gawky teenagers before walking away. Antoine was instantly aroused. Could she want him? His adolescent mind was consumed with the thought. Homely Henry, standing beside him, had a grin on his face and a gleam in his eyes that told Antoine he felt the same way.

The next day Antoine returned to the neighborhood alone. He

roamed the area near the building, savoring the aroma of spice-perfumed cooking oil wafting about on the summer breeze. He wanted to knock on every door of the apartment building and describe her in his limited German to anyone who answered. Then he wondered, if he found her, what would he do? So instead he stood behind a bush making himself as inconspicuous as he could, hoping for her to emerge. Minutes and hours crawled by. Children frolicked, teenagers strutted, old figures trudged by. He never saw her again.

Last night, more than twenty-five years after the incident, he tried to recapture that "Turkish" feeling, that enigmatic encounter, on paper. The story would be told from the point of view of an American photographer, who eventually found the woman. In Antoine's imagination the two characters met and became romantically involved. But the words wouldn't flow. Over the years he'd found that writing longhand allowed him to connect best with his creative self. But this time it wasn't helping. At two a.m. he finally gave up and fell into an uneasy sleep.

Now this morning, halfway through his second cup of coffee, his mood had not improved. Suddenly it came to him that there was a parallel between Meena and that Turkish woman. Meena had appeared in his life much the same way, like the quick flare of a match that could ignite a fire to burn for an instant or for an eon. Which would it be?

He reminded himself that his life was already charted for him. This evening he and Liv were throwing a party to announce their engagement, to be followed by a month-long trip. They'd be together for his book-tour stop in Denver, then, "killing two birds with one stone" as Liv had suggested, doing more signings and visiting their respective families in Boston and Des Moines. When they returned, it would be time to start the wedding arrangements. A house in the city, take-out food, Saturday night at the movies, season tickets to the opera, another best-seller. Liv had it all planned.

Oh yes, he was content. Liv had been good for him in the period following his divorce. Certainly Liv was as different as could be from Shanti.

Born Ellen Jones, Shanti had changed her name by the time Antoine met her, in an attempt to alter her destiny. As he was to discover in their brief time together, a new name didn't change much. She became more eclectic, if not downright flaky. Shanti tried hard, teaching movement therapy, reading palms, and giving massages. But nothing seemed to work for Ellen Jones for very long, including her marriage. In her own phrase, she got bored with "the game, the routine."

Shanti drove his mother nuts.

"My God," Sybil Peterson would say. "She has a ring in her nose. She drinks wheatgrass juice. She astral-travels. When was the last time she cooked you a real meal?"

Shanti dismissed his mother as "East Coast anxious," but for a while they were happy. They picked wildflowers on Mount Tamalpais, baked bread, wrote their own songs. He still had her granola recipe, which her friend Alice had given her. It was posted in the kitchen cupboard with Shanti's PS: "This recipe does not need to be followed exactly." She brought him out of his narrow, repressed middle-class life. He learned to backpack, grow sunflowers in the yard, and dance naked in the moonlight. The rosemary patch they planted together had grown bushy and now, years later, was still producing a myriad of tiny blue flowers.

But the relationship did not flourish like the rosemary. Shanti had chosen a name that meant "peace," yet she seemed to be in a constant state of turmoil. Her appetite for intimacy and reassurance of her personal worth was more than Antoine could satisfy. He realized it wasn't all her fault and tried to make things work. Her lively, spontaneous nature still appealed to him. But he too was getting tired of her "routine."

What began as vague unease grew into a certainty that she wasn't the right companion for him. Sensitive Shanti picked up on his growing disenchantment, which she rightly interpreted as rejection. "You don't pay attention to me" escalated into "Who needs this?" Then one night Shanti exploded at a party seeing him chat with a woman acquaintance. She accused him of adultery in front of his friends. They rode home in silence. And though he made tender love to her later that night, he knew it was over.

A week later Shanti was gone. He tore through the house, looking in every corner for a trace of her. She had left nothing behind.

He drove to Alice's building, certain Shanti would have gone there, and waited in his car. He could have buzzed the apartment and asked for her, but he didn't. Part of him didn't want her back.

He returned home alone after several hours in a state of depression.

Three weeks later Shanti called to say she had waited for him at Alice's, then given up. In the meantime she had found someone who truly understood her. Antoine felt devastated and relieved at the same time.

And sometime later, he met Liv.

The years blurred in his mind until Meena came along. Her appearance had an unsettling effect on his life. True, she was a little too absorbed in her job and definitely could stand to loosen up a bit. Yet she was competent and creative in a demanding field he had absolutely no grasp of and he admired her for that. She had energy, intensity, and resiliency, as one would expect of a child of the desert. With her beside him, he wanted to plunge wholeheartedly into life. There was much about her he didn't know yet. Had he been younger, he'd have rushed to explore this unknown territory. But now? A twinge of pain in his lower back made him feel middle-aged.

Why was he standing here in front of the phone?

Maybe he could ring Meena at her office. After all, he had made an awkward pass at her the night of their dinner, then chalked it up as one of his moody days. He didn't want to leave her with that impression of him. He'd like to apologize in person. Or would it just make things worse?

Eventually he picked up the phone. "Hi, Meena." All of his senses were finely tuned to pick up nuances in her reaction.

"What a surprise, Antoine. How are you?" Meena sounded pleased on the other end. Her voice was smooth.

"Gosh, I wish I felt as alert as you sound. It's not nine o'clock yet." Antoine smiled broadly into the phone. "I'm still trying to wake up."

"I wish I could say that. I've been at my desk for two hours already."

"I'm going to be in the city," Antoine said. "And I thought if you're free, we could spend some time together. Maybe out at Ocean Beach. A leisurely walk, mind you, not one of your sprints."

"Actually, I'm taking some work home. I have a deadline to meet. But some other time . . ."

"I'm going on a trip," he said. What if, like that Turkish woman, Meena got away? "We won't be back for several weeks." Too late he realized he had said "we."

"Oh? Are you?"

Her voice had lost some of the animation. She would obviously realize he was traveling with Liv. He kicked at the rug on the floor. "I finally dug up that photo of Rajasthan that I've been telling you about. I was planning to bring it along."

"Well, I—"

"Didn't you tell me walking on sand is good for your ankles?"

Meena laughed. "I said running, Antoine, not walking."

Antoine loved to hear her laugh. Hers was a full deep laugh that rose easily to a pair of ripe lips. He had tasted them briefly. Like a corridor with a row of doors and he had opened only one.

Antoine said, "After this vacation, I'm going to start running again." He paused as he gathered his thoughts. "The real reason I asked, Meena, is that I feel badly about the way our last evening turned out. I have some things I need to say to you."

A long silence. Finally a guarded voice saying, "All right."

"See you at five-thirty at the Fulton crossing," Antoine said. "Okay?"

"Okay."

Exhilarated, Antoine rushed to the shower. Needles of water pricked his skin in counterpoint to the tingling he felt inside. To see Meena again! He was back to being that emotional kid of fifteen.

To see Antoine again—what, Meena wondered as she unlocked the door of her apartment, would it be like? It had been so long. But perhaps it did not seem so to him. He only sounded happy to be talking to her.

She stepped into her living room, dropped her bulging briefcase on her coffee table and suppressed a sigh. Her workday had been filled with meetings, employee performance reviews, and administrative details surrounding the shipping of COSMOS-1. She had brought the newest COSMOS-2 design specifications home and would have spent the entire evening on them had it not been for her last-minute agreement to meet Antoine at Ocean Beach. She checked her watch and saw she had no time to spare.

He had been in her mind all day. She had wondered, ever since Liv's return, how things were between them, and now had to conclude they must be getting along fine if they were going to be traveling together for a month. But then why did he call? And sound as if he had to see her?

As she undressed, she thought about the man who had become part of her existence in no time, who had come to dominate her consciousness almost before she was aware it had happened. He was provocative, he stirred her emotions. To be sure, he lacked focus and was at times indecisive, but he was an enormous life force barely contained within a magnificent body. He was intelligent and multi-dimensional, his versatility a source of amazement and delight. He did not shrink from activities—running being only one of them—that would put him at a disadvantage. He was what an ideal mate should be, a nugget of gold found by some extraordinary luck. Their time together was intense and real, at times pure joy, occasionally painful. But each such experience was a little locket of memory that she liked to hug close to her breast.

Seeing him again would be like walking into a thunderstorm, Meena knew. But no matter how bad the knots in her stomach and the tightness in her throat, she must control herself, be cautious, not agree to see him again—not even for running—until she knew for sure his true feelings toward Liv.

She donned a pair of blue jeans and an old sweatshirt, threw an unmatching cardigan over her shoulders. She wouldn't try to look special for him. She locked her door and walked toward the elevator, wondering what the evening would bring.

When Antoine arrived at Ocean Beach the sky glowed with a tangelo sheen. Waves were crashing on the cliffs, dogs were splashing in and out of the water, children were tinkering with their sand castles, and their harried mothers were using the interludes to catch up on the latest gossip.

And there was Meena, standing at the edge of the water, a respectful distance beyond the last couple of beach umbrellas. The rays of the late afternoon sun made her profile strong and clear and gave a gleam to the hair that glissaded down her back. Her long slender legs sheathed in faded denim were arresting. But it was her face that truly demanded Antoine's attention. There was a silence there, a serenity that bespoke a heritage of evolved civilization. How he would love to capture that essence on film or paper.

As he came closer, she turned toward him spontaneously. Her eyes had the clarity of crystal and for one brief moment they reflected the joy that was within.

"Meena, I don't know what to say . . . I . . . I . . . had no right—"

"Please, Antoine," she said with tender eyes.

He opened his arms and enfolded her. There was warmth in her embrace. And truth. He melted and became nothing. Those years of performing on college stages didn't help. The glib talk he was so good at vanished. He realized he was holding his breath until she pulled away.

"Glad you're here." He hoped he sounded ordinary. He looked deeply into her eyes. She was standing so close that he could smell the natural fragrance of her body. "How are things at SIC?"

"It's good to see you—really," Meena said. "Work? Fine. I guess. I'm surviving. Isn't that what we all do?"

"Not always, Meena."

He saw pain lash at her eyes before she averted them. After a moment of uncertainty they drew apart and headed south along the beach. The sun was dropping below the clouds on the western horizon, coloring the crests of breaking waves with a scarlet gleam. Seagulls flew from rocks jutting out of the water, free as Antoine wanted to be.

"I love this time of day," Meena said in a whisper. "Sometimes I wish I had my camera with me. But it would be pointless. I could never capture this on film."

"Speaking of photos—" Antoine felt self-conscious as he extracted a picture from his shirt pocket and offered it to her. He had always been proud of this particular shot in which a battery of Rajasthani peasant women, radiant in red, huddled together for cover in a dust storm under a grayish yellow firmament. The howling wind pressed their voluminous clothing against their body curves. Their faces were wrapped to protect against the driving sand. "Here's one I thought you might appreciate."

She turned toward him in midstep and took the photo, scrutinizing it intently in the diminishing light. "I remember dust storms like this." Her eyes took on a remote look. "My life's so different now. This picture brings back old memories. . . ." Her voice trailed off. She returned the photo and turned to continue down the beach.

"No, please, Meena, keep it. I want you to have it."

The look she gave him then was warm—one that reinforced their bond. She accepted the photo and slipped it into her purse.

They resumed walking in silence. "About your friend Vishnu, in India . . ." Antoine broke off.

"Vishnu was more than a friend," she said. Then, in a whisper, "We were married."

"Married?" Antoine said the word calmly, but he felt he had been cut off from his life support system, from oxygen. All this time he had believed Vishnu didn't matter. And that man in India he was helping her to locate was her *husband.*

"I was married at seven. It was the custom in our village in those days. It wasn't a forced marriage. Vishnu and I were the best of friends. We played together, went to school together, we were never separated. Mataji and everyone else in the village thought we were a perfect match. Of course, my American parents never recognized that marriage, though in Rajasthan child marriage is binding."

The citrus shades of the sky seemed to evaporate before Antoine's eyes, leaving a black void in their place. Could she really still feel an obligation to a childhood husband taken at the age of seven? He had pretty much convinced himself that she was his for the asking. Now it was clear that her relationship with Vishnu was firmly rooted, and bound in ancient, immutable tradition that would not be easily overcome. His confidence shaken, he realized how much he cared about her. . . .

Outwardly he managed to maintain a sense of poise as they continued their stroll down the beach. He hummed, but inside he was filled with turmoil. Another relationship in jeopardy. He told himself he needed to change—to give of himself more, be more decisive.

They found themselves on an area of the beach dominated by kites—kite sellers, kite flyers, kite paraphernalia.

"Oh, I'd forgotten today's the annual San Francisco Kite Festival," Meena said, eying tables laid out with all manner of kites and accessories. "In India we flew kites all the time. That was our biggest pastime. And once a year on January fourteenth, everyone—kids and adults—got a day off to fly kites."

To the left an elaborate kite trailing streamers of neon-bright paper darted back and forth in the gusting wind as its owner teased it skyward. Meena touched Antoine's arm and said excitedly, "Look, that one's a dragon."

They stood for a long minute, following the kite's labored ascent. It fluttered first this way and then that, soaring and diving, but always recovering to continue upward.

Presently Meena gravitated toward an uncrowded table manned by an obviously Indian merchant. Dark and slenderly built, he had alert, quick-moving eyes. With long fingers the man lifted the lid of a wicker basket.

Antoine leaned over and peeked in, saying, "No cobras, I hope."

"Oh no, sir." The vendor's earnest demeanor was part schoolboy, part traveling salesman. He spotted Meena peering at his kites. "You speak Hindi, madam?"

"Thora, thora," Meena said with a self-conscious smile. "I came here when I was little." She indicated Antoine. "And my friend lived in India for a while."

Antoine shrugged. "My Hindi is rusty. I know how to ask for tea. Beyond that I'm lost."

"Allow me to show you my kites," the man said. "They're the old-fashioned kind from India. Not fancy, but easy to maneuver and they go up fast."

His staccato singsong English sounded like a river flowing over rocks. How Antoine wished to speak a tongue other than his own so fluently. Even with a heavy accent he'd have found it easier to express hidden aspects of himself.

The man smiled. "My village near Ahmedabad has the best kites, you know. I've been a kite expert since I was a kid. Even my name, Batash, means wind. My brother's name means water. He catches fish like I never could. My mother told us that we become our names. . . . Do you believe that, sir?"

"My name means absolutely nothing," Antoine said regretfully, wishing that given names in the West had such cultural richness. Then he caught himself contemplating: What if his parents had given him a name that meant "great lover" or "runs like the wind"? Would things have turned out differently then?

"In India we believe kite flying brings out what's in your heart," Batash said. "One of our favorite stories is about a Moghul prince who used to write love notes on his kite to his favorite girl. He'd fly the kite over her compound and cut the string at just the proper moment. The kite would land at her feet as she took her morning walk in the garden." He paused and asked Antoine, "Would you like to try one, sir?"

Antoine reached for his wallet. He paid for both over Meena's protest. Batash handed them each a small, graceful kite and a sleek spool of string. Antoine scrutinized his. The tissue-paper kite was bat-shaped with a split bamboo back. The string was no more than twisted cotton thread. Against the backdrop of roaring surf and gusting wind, it all seemed so fragile. He looked up at the kites darting in the sky. He felt as insubstantial as they looked.

"When I was a kid, we used to glue powdered glass to the strings," Meena told him. "That made it possible to kill other kites, by crossing over their strings and sawing back and forth." She grinned impishly. The brisk wind blew her hair about her face. Antoine's heart thawed in the presence of that bubbly countenance.

"After you," he said.

Following her lead, he held his kite on a short line until there was an advantageous gust of wind. Then he quickly played out the string and let the wind lift the kite, up and up, darting this way or that. He experienced the force of the breeze on his forehead as it tugged the kite higher. He felt light and airy, almost weightless, rejuvenated by a surge of energy transmitted down the string. Childlike, he burst into laughter. Then as the kite suddenly dipped, he cursed, furrowed his brow. The kite soared again and skipped around like a bird. The crisis over, his face eased. How free he felt. He couldn't remember the last time he had experienced such pure pleasure.

He glanced at Meena. She too was laughing.

Almost before he knew it, darkness started to descend upon them like an enormous black parasol. The gusty breeze subsided and he found it difficult to keep his eyes on his kite.

"Walk together," Batash said. "Spin it around. Bring them in quickly." Soon they were able to bring down both the kites without destroying either one.

"Your kites didn't kill each other." Batash smiled. "That has special meaning. You see, I'm also a fortune-teller."

Meena's eyes were low. She appeared to be blushing.

"I have to go," she murmured. "My plants need to be watered in daylight and if I don't leave now it will be dark before I get home."

Unable to speak, Antoine simply nodded. He wanted to ask

Meena to stay, he had so much to say to her, but all he could do was stand there. He felt a knot of discomfort in his throat. It was crazy not to tell Meena about his engagement—completely unfair. But how could he cut himself off from this woman who had rekindled his interest in life? He kept a cowardly silence, shuffled his feet, looked at his watch. My God. He had half an hour to get to Liv's place.

"Please come back next year," Batash said. "I'll have a fresh supply from India then."

They both thanked him and promised to return.

As they headed back up the beach, Antoine heard the Indian merchant's voice from behind. Perhaps the wind and waves altered his last words, but he seemed to say, "May you fly kites together again. . . ."

Antoine rushed to Liv's apartment on Presidio to find guests already arriving. Cassie, Liv's younger sister, smashing in a kiwi green dress, tended the door. Henry leaned against the piano with an adoring Kazuko glued to his arm. Liv held court in the center of the living room beneath a chandelier, stylish in a purple and white dress that looked like a designer affair, conversing with her colleague Peng. The man had a worldly, almost tired look about him. Antoine made a beeline for them and kissed Liv lightly on the lips. Liv responded coolly with a tight smile and slightly raised eyebrows. Antoine mumbled an apology and excused himself. He mingled with the guests, greeting each in turn with a smile and a few personal words, sliding into his social skin. But underneath he was wretched. He could feel the corners of his mouth tightening. To make matters worse, a pebble in one shoe from his walk on the beach dug into his foot, reminding him of Meena.

Gradually the party got lively. Champagne corks popped, Henry shouted a toast, and glasses clinked. Out of the convivial background murmur, congratulatory words floated to Antoine. With an effort he continued to look cheerful. He drifted toward the ring of guests gathered around the lavish buffet table. As his eyes roved over the crowd, his attention was drawn to one late arrival. Liv's boss, D.J., was hard to miss. A flowing mane of silvery hair framed a tanned, crease-free face, giving D.J. a statesmanlike distinction. He seemed to sense Antoine's stare and returned it. His deep-set eyes reflected the flickering light of the brick fireplace with an animal intensity. Antoine was immediately uncomfortable without knowing why. He had been about to walk over and speak to D.J. but found himself heading for the balcony for fresh air. As he looked out over the city lights to the west, his thoughts returned to Meena. One of those far-off lights was hers.

Back in the living room, Antoine stood quietly alone in a corner. The party was going strong with knots of people chatting, laughing, nibbling. Across the room in the hallway leading to the kitchen, Liv and D.J. were standing close together, deep in conversation, the intimacy between them obvious. Typical Liv, Antoine reflected: even tonight working her boss for that next promotion. Liv's face wore a coquettish look. Champagne? The thrill of the engagement? Or . . . ?

Antoine felt strangely detached as he contemplated them. He noticed how Kazuko rolled her eyes as she and Henry passed the twosome. But he himself was devoid of any emotion, no anger, no embarrassment, nothing.

This was supposed to be his party, but he had never felt more like a stranger.

28

After his dinner with Asha, Vishnu returned to his apartment and found a letter from Mother left by the postman, but no response from the *Hindustan Times*. He rang the newspaper office just to be sure he hadn't missed a call. The secretary sounded harried and said the editor was in a meeting.

Vishnu hung up with a deep sigh and opened Mother's letter. He had not responded to her previous one yet. This one had been written two and a half weeks ago. The village post office was slacking off again. The handwriting was neater and more legible this time, perhaps written by the village schoolmaster.

> My dear Vishnu,
>
> Our past monsoon was unusually heavy and brought a bumper crop of millet. I remember how as a youngster you rushed home from school for freshly made millet bread. But the rain also brought mosquitoes and many in our village are now infected with cerebral malaria that the doctors say could be fatal.
>
> The local government must be poor in arithmetic. They report only 40 cases when I know there are close to 200. Our school building was made an emergency medical camp this past week. Some patients don't make it that far. My cousin's wife fainted by the roadside while out walking with her two-year-old son. The boy ate dirt and cried until a

young doctor found them. She is now recovering, but the boy is sick.

So far I've managed to keep well, but I need money to help our relatives and neighbors. Please send a money order as soon as you can. And don't visit me until this epidemic is over.

Your loving mother.

PS. Send more clips from the newspaper so I can show people. I'm always so proud of you.

Vishnu's eyes brimmed with tears. Mother didn't write the letter, yet her presence was there in it. He pictured her slight body in a white cotton sari, several of her front teeth missing. Her seventy-year-old eyes, still clear, were a well of sorrow.

He tried hard to remember their mud house, the dusty road that led to the school building, the after-school snack of sweet *gaujas* waiting for him, his contented father weighing lentils in a hand scale in his grocery store till late at night. The only time Father ever took a day off from work was when Vishnu got married. Years later, when Father died at age sixty, he left no savings. Mother became totally dependent on the money Vishnu sent her.

He folded the letter and put it carefully into his pocket, then contemplated. How long could she survive? Would she lose face if he failed to send her money? And his other relatives? How long could they go on?

He resolved to take up Dhotia on his job offer. He couldn't hold out for a more prestigious position when his people in Karamgar were dying. His professional ethics seemed inconsequential in the face of their suffering. Yes, he'd attend the Jai Shiva Party's conference next week and educate himself on the Moxan political position.

In fact, he was beginning to feel a certain sympathy for that tribe. Whereas the living conditions in most parts of India had improved over the past years, for Moxans they hadn't kept pace. These were tribals, society's marginal people. He decided to help them voice their demands.

Then too, he could use his e-mail privilege to get into contact with Meena. Of course, he could pick up the telephone anytime, ask the international operator for Meena's number in San Francisco and call her. But he felt shy. What if he got tongue-tied, not able to come up with anything clever to say in what would have to be a brief conversation, the price of overseas phone calls being as high as they were? E-mail would allow him the luxury of keying in a note at his own pace. It wasn't as formal as a letter and infinitely quicker—and the price was definitely right.

29

The morning after his engagement party Antoine rolled out of bed, went to fetch the *Chronicle* from the front porch, blundered into the kitchen, and microwaved a cup of water. He dunked a teabag into his cup and squeezed it out. Would Meena scoff at his tea? He hadn't used frothy steamed milk, whole spices, or fragrant loose tea leaves with an estate name attached.

His tea finished, he stood up and extended his arms toward the ceiling in a languorous stretch, half aware of a cobweb on the wall. Abruptly he brought his hands down, knocking Liv's photo from the bookshelf. He picked it up, wiped off the dust, and examined it for a moment. Then he put it back exactly in the same spot to avoid being accused by Liv of moving it. She'd be sure to notice. He had taken the snapshot only last year. Liv beamed at the camera, wearing the usual black dress and laced-up boots. Black was slimming, she always insisted. Not that she was fat. She was quite comely. Any red-blooded American male would say so. But hers was not a face to stay in a man's mind. Not a face that would launch a novel.

Antoine settled on the leather couch with the *Chronicle*. Flipping through it, he found little of interest until he came across a news brief from India buried on the next-to-last page. It concerned the Moxans, a tribal group in the eastern part of the country who wanted autonomy. Antoine had gone through the South Asia Studies program at the University of Michigan some years ago and after graduation kept up on Indian political affairs by subscribing to the weekly *India Today* and through his correspondence with his friend Deepak.

Yet he had never heard of the Moxan tribe. He made a mental note to look them up.

It was midmorning when Antoine sat down to work. He stared at his desk, pen in hand, hoping for a scene with the Turkish woman to emerge in his head. Instead he saw images of Meena, kites, and the beach, then Liv and D.J. at last night's party. Looking out the window, Antoine could see the bright sunlight, but a solid darkness had gathered within him. Unexpressed emotions and ignored truth had conspired to build this block, one that stopped him from writing or going forward in life. If only he could cast aside the safety net underneath him. If only he could pursue what might be a more honest and meaningful relationship. Perhaps then his writing tablet wouldn't remain virginal.

Antoine got up from his chair and began to pace. Sometimes that helped him think. But today it didn't seem to. Nothing did.

At least tonight would bring a welcome distraction: dinner with Henry and Kazuko. Lately Antoine had been craving a real home-cooked dinner—Liv had practically sealed off her kitchen—and Kazuko's meals were always exquisite. Antoine tiptoed around Kazuko a bit because she was Meena's best friend. But her dynamic personality never failed to captivate him.

Between his restlessness and his eagerness, Antoine was twenty minutes early as he parked his car in front of Henry and Kazuko's house just as evening was falling. He had a sudden impulse to pick up some cheese for his hosts. Henry, who had spent his early years in Germany, appreciated fine cheese.

Antoine walked the two blocks to the nearest supermarket and began browsing. Which one to choose? A Brie wedge whose label featured a contented cow? A dense yellow softball-sized Gouda? A creamy white pyramid of goat cheese with a pungent bouquet? He almost settled on the Brie. Picturing it on a table next to nori, umeboshi, and soba noodles, he wavered, started to put it back, then changed his mind again. After all, wasn't Henry eating his sauerkraut with chopsticks these days?

How Antoine envied Henry. They had been the best of buddies for a long time. Antoine was, to be sure, the brighter of the two, better in athletics and all the rest. But Henry, though rather average and not much to look at, was rock solid. Since his settling down with Kazuko this last year, he seemed rapturous as a pan that was bubbling on the stove. Antoine didn't understand why such happiness had eluded him—he was far more experienced with women than Henry and prided himself on understanding them better.

The Brie in hand, Antoine was scanning the adjacent cracker display when out of the corner of his eye he saw a familiar figure in the produce section. Excitement flooded him. Meena!

But—Meena here?

Then it struck him that "here" was Richmond District, her neighborhood. Peeking around the Nabisco and Carr's boxes, he watched her, mesmerized. Her suit was plain black and business-y, but her body knew how to give it shape. Her waist-length hair was clasped back in a silver barrette. He had a strong desire to ease the barrette out with his fingers and watch her hair waterfall around her face and down her back. At the moment she was examining oranges intently as if finding the juiciest one was a most important task, one deft hand squeezing them ever so slightly and feeling their weight before putting them in the basket. Each squeeze of her hand constricted his heart.

He imagined walking over, falling casually into step with her, and a conversation that would go something like, "Had a great time flying kites with you yesterday. And . . . oh yes . . . I got engaged."

Her head began to turn.

He put the cheese down next to a box of wholemeal crackers and fled out the door with the curious eyes of a cash register checker on him. He jogged up the street to the safety of Henry and Kazuko's house. Empty-handed, but with a head churning with visions of Meena, he rang their doorbell.

Meena had just paid for her oranges at the express checkout line at California Super when she spotted Kazuko loaded with groceries and headed toward the door. Meena hadn't seen her in a while and had been meaning to meet her for lunch. She called a greeting, running to catch up with Kazuko just before the exit.

Kazuko gave her a hug and an ardent smile. "It's so good to see you, Mee-chan. I was going to phone you. Lots to catch up on."

"How's Henry?" Meena asked.

"He's great. He wallpapered the kitchen. . . ." Kazuko brought

Meena up to date on Henry's activities, though her happy smile and sparkling eyes would have been enough of an answer. "We're very happy," Kazuko added. "We want all our friends to be as happy as we are. I was saying that to Antoine last night."

Ah? So Kazuko knew of the fun she'd had kite flying with Antoine?

Meena said, "I'm about three-quarters of the way through *Parallel Lives*." She began giving Kazuko her impressions of the book with great enthusiasm.

Abruptly Kazuko broke in. "We went to Antoine and Liv's engagement party last night."

The whole world stopped for a moment. Meena thought there was something wrong with her ears. Antoine, who had insisted on seeing her yesterday, had got engaged to Liv? A burning sense of betrayal ran through her body like molten lava. She wanted to cry out with pain. But no, she reminded herself, she must detach herself, retain her poise. She stood silently.

Kazuko asked, "Didn't you know?"

"No." Meena took a deep breath before adding, "I didn't."

Her eyes downcast, Kazuko said, "I thought you did."

"How was the party?" Meena asked wearily.

"The food was okay, as good as Liv can make it," Kazuko said. "Mike's Chinese-American catered it. The standard fare: egg rolls, wontons, sweet and sour pork. Oh, and Peking duck." Then in a whisper, "I overheard Liv's Chinese colleague joking that a pair of ducks is a sign of conjugal fidelity."

"So who was the infidel there?"

"Take a guess," Kazuko said. "I noticed how Liv was flirting with her boss, D.J. He's a nice-looking man. Tanned, silver hair, well built. Statesmanlike. No comparison to Antoine, though."

"Of course not . . ."

"Poor Antoine," Kazuko said. "He looked distracted the whole time. Like he wished he were somewhere else. I'm sure he noticed it too. I'll bet a dime to a dollar Liv's fooling around with D.J."

"Now, now, Kazuko. You don't know that."

"Nobody can pull the wool over my eyes in these matters."

"Well, maybe they'll work things out," Meena said. "Wish him happiness for me, will you, Kazu-chan?"

"I will. When he gets back from his trip, he'll probably be wanting to jog with you."

"I don't run in Golden Gate Park anymore," Meena said with a sigh. "Lately I've been training after work downtown with a woman runner who works near my office. I do hope Antoine stays with it, though. He's come a long way in a short time."

They chatted for a few more minutes. Kazuko looked at her watch, exclaimed, gave Meena a quick hug, and rushed off.

Meena crossed the street and, as soon as she was alone, felt volumes of tears gathering behind her eyelids, as heavy as the bag of oranges in her hand. She held her face tight. As she opened her car door, she noticed a homeless man going through a garbage can on the street corner. That was a rare sight in this neighborhood. Meena forgot her troubles for a moment and stood there watching him dig up a half-eaten bag of potato chips with glee. On an impulse, she walked over to him and handed him her bag.

He shook the bag, looked into it, and gazed up with incredulous blood-shot eyes. "Lady, you're giving away these good navel oranges?"

"Yes," Meena said. "I think I have a taste for something else tonight."

Antoine leaned on the door jamb as Henry opened the door wearing a pewter-colored turtleneck sweater—no doubt hand-knit by Kazuko. He looked at Antoine and blinked. "Was somebody chasing you? You're out of breath."

"Just . . . getting some fresh air." Antoine felt foolish as he walked into the house.

Henry shrugged, closed the door, and followed Antoine to the living room. "Make yourself comfortable. Kazuko's at the supermarket. I wonder what's keeping her." He paused. "Does a beer sound good?"

Antoine nodded and settled on the nubby white upholstered sofa facing a bay window. His back felt secure against a tasseled silk pillow in blue and rust. A fire in the concrete fireplace threw warmth on his face. A lush sculptured jade plant, which had grown way too big for the urn containing it, soothed him with its greenness. His eyes roved to the television busy chattering the evening news. He tried to concentrate on the aftermath of a tornado in the South. His mind matched the disquiet that flashed across the screen.

Henry returned with two beers and handed one to Antoine.

"Cheers." Antoine took a swig straight from the bottle.

Henry turned off the television and plopped himself into a chair. "What's up? Why so glum?"

"It's my normal face—what can I say?" Antoine knuckled his eyes and smiled. "Getting ready for our trip. We leave tomorrow."

"I'm happy for you, buddy. You've got a good woman. Liv will make a nice home for you. But you look depressed." Henry ended his sentence on a high note as if to turn it into a question.

"Me? Depressed?" Antoine sighed. Depression was his normal state these days.

"Remember our high school algebra class in Munich?" Henry asked. "You understood set theory and I didn't. One evening I asked you to come over to explain it to me. Remember? My parents were out. I got some beer from the refrigerator. And instead of getting into subsets and supersets we shot the breeze—the 'eternal question'— what each of us wanted in life." Henry rubbed his chin with one hand as though he needed time to compose his thoughts. "Aren't we back to the same point? What do we really want?"

"Yes. Only the answers have gotten more complex."

"I'm a simple man, Antoine." Henry leaned forward. "I sell insurance by day. I drink beer and watch TV by night. I like the woman I have. I don't go chasing the rainbow."

Antoine rested his eyes for an instant on his friend's face, a visage he had watched become rounder and more mature over the years. "I see the rainbow and I want to touch it. But maybe at forty-two, my reach isn't as long as it used to be."

"Might there be something else?"

"Yes," Antoine said. "I can't do the book."

"It's more than that. Your distraction is . . . Meena, isn't it?"

"She's who I think about when I wake up in the morning and look out through the window," Antoine said. "And just before I fall asleep at night. She's a pleasant dream."

"I have a confession to make, Antoine." Henry's chestnut eyes were perfectly still in their seriousness. "Kazu suggested I invite you to Meena's birthday party. I didn't really want to. But I went along because I thought Liv would come with you and that would put a stop to Kazu's matchmaking. I guess it backfired."

Antoine pictured the party scene, which he had gone over in his mind many times. And suddenly things fell into place.

"I had no idea I'd be causing you this much grief," Henry confessed. "I apologize, buddy."

"Sooner or later I'd have met her," Antoine said. "It's Allah's will, Shiva's fancy, written in the stars, however you want to explain it. Not to worry, Henry. Rest assured, you didn't cause me this grief. These days I don't know where I'm going with my writing, I don't know where I'm going with my life. I seem to be in a box and I can't see more than a foot away. I think . . . I want out."

"You think too much," Henry said. "Always have. You're complex and moody. Perhaps you don't understand yourself very well. If you ask me—frankly, I wouldn't mess with Meena."

"Why?"

"A table lamp gives me enough light. I don't have to put my hand in the fire to know what heat feels like. Listen, buddy, forget this Meena business. You've known Liv for how long? Five years? You want to throw all those years away?"

Antoine felt his forehead perspiring. "Say, your fireplace is getting too hot."

Henry went over, damped the fire, and eased back into his seat.

"And what does Kazuko have to say about all this?" Antoine asked.

"She says you and Meena would be perfect together."

The fire died down to a few glowing coals. Its pleasant warmth and the beer combined to put Antoine in a relaxed mood. He settled deeper into the sofa.

"Matchmaking's in her blood," Henry went on. "Her grandfather was a go-between in Japan. His job was to match single young men and women. Kazuko told me that once he introduced a wealthy man's daughter to a petty office clerk. Nobody thought it would work. But when they met for the first time in the presence of their parents and relatives, it was love at first sight. Soon they were secretly spending their nights together. Eventually they were found out, and a major scandal loomed. To save face for the families, Kazuko's grandfather suggested they throw a big wedding as if it had been planned all along. It was a stroke of genius and the grateful families made sure he had a seat of honor at the ceremony."

"Kazuko must be as good as her grandfather," Antoine muttered.

The door opened. Shopping bag in hand, Kazuko glided in, her steps ballet-light. "Hello, Antoine. Glad you could make it tonight."

"I was getting worried, Kazu," Henry said. "You've been gone awhile."

"The store was crowded," Kazuko said. "Took longer than I thought. I'll get busy with the dinner now."

"Need some help?" Antoine asked.

"I sure do," Kazuko said. "You don't mind if I borrow Antoine for a few minutes, do you, sweetheart?"

"Not at all, dear," Henry said. "I have to feed the cats."

Antoine followed Kazuko to the newly wallpapered kitchen. A partly open window cooled the room, but brought in traffic noise from the street.

Kazuko started unloading her shopping bag. She handed Antoine a package of shiitake mushrooms, a cleaver, and a large bowl. "Would you mind slicing the mushrooms? We're having *shabu-shabu* tonight."

"What's that?"

"It's an easy dish." She got an electric skillet out of a cabinet and stationed it on the counter. "I'll heat some broth in this. We'll cook at the table. You dip your mushrooms or green onions or beef slices, whatever you like, in the broth with your chopsticks and let it cook for a few seconds. At the end, we drink the broth. It'll be full of flavor by then."

Antoine started slicing the firm dark mushroom caps. "These smell very fresh."

"California Super carries great mushrooms and great cheese." Kazuko took a Brie wedge out of her shopping bag and set it on the counter.

Antoine chopped faster, almost cut his finger.

Kazuko shut the window and the room fell quiet. "By the way, I ran into Meena at the supermarket. That's why I was late."

Without looking at her Antoine asked, "Did you have a chance to talk?"

"Yes. I told her about your engagement party."

Antoine held his breath as Kazuko went on. "She sent her congratulations. She also said you should keep up your running." Now

Kazuko pulled a bunch of slender green onions out of the shopping bag and handed it to him.

Antoine anchored his fingers on the green onions and cut them uniformly, saying casually, "When I get back from this trip, I'll call her. See if we can do a run together."

"Just as I left, Meena mentioned that some software outfit in Bombay is considering her for a director's position."

"She's going back to India?"

"She's thinking about it. In my opinion it would be a mistake. But what can I say? It's her life. She can be very independent, you know. She loves this city, has lots of friends here. But I'm the one who's really close to her." Kazuko paused as though she wanted to stress her next thought. "And Carlos."

"Carlos?" Antoine put the cleaver down on the cutting board, unable to work anymore. He hoped his voice sounded normal, but he knew it didn't.

"He's always loved her. . . ." Kazuko paused, then added, "Meena's still reading your book *Parallel Lives*, you know. She says she reads some pages three times."

"Three times, huh?"

"I don't know if I can say it as beautifully as she does. Let me see . . . the first time for enjoyment, the second time to analyze the author's mind, and the third time to get a glimpse of her own soul through the writing. Much the same as an artist looks at art."

Meena, bright Meena. Antoine had been attracted to her body and her heart—and her mind. He lamented to himself how he had ruined the beautiful intimacy they had built. He said simply, "I'm flattered," but his heart cried.

"Oh, I'm not supposed to tell you all this." Kazuko moved to the other end of the counter. "Don't repeat it. You promise?" The open cabinet door half hid her face.

There was a sudden sound of footsteps. Was someone unexpected arriving? Antoine dropped the cleaver on the floor. As he picked it up, he heard the meowing of cats.

"How long before dinner, Kazu?" Henry asked.

"Looks like we're about finished here." Kazuko gestured. "To the table!"

"Jai Shiva! Hail to Lord Shiva!" a chorus of a hundred voices chanted in Tihili, Hindi, and English.

Vishnu walked toward the dais as Jai Shiva Party members were kicking off their regional party conference at the Carlyle Hotel. Right away he was struck by the sickly green paint on the walls of the conference room. And the heat. An ancient battered air conditioner rattled in one corner in a vain attempt to cool the space. Turbaned bearers in white jackets brushed past, bearing tea on dented trays. The atmosphere seemed to be charged with an excitement hinting at fanaticism, giving Vishnu an uneasy sensation that violence lurked just beneath the surface. An enormous image of Lord Shiva in a frenzied dance hung on one wall. Vishnu glanced at the picture, then turned away and faced the crowd.

Karun Dhotia, the party chief, strode to the podium, his eyes a sleepless red but still shining, his sparse gray hair spread limply across his head. He drew the microphone closer to his lips and, with Vishnu standing by his side, addressed the crowd in Hindi. "Brothers and sisters, fellow strugglers. At long last we have someone capable of bringing eloquence to our story, both here at home and abroad. No longer will the government be able to hide the crimes being committed against the Moxans. Vishnu Chauhan will shine the light of truth on these despicable acts. Please welcome him warmly to our family."

All eyes swiveled in Vishnu's direction. There was muted applause. Vishnu nodded and bowed with joined palms several times, embarrassed and more than a little discomfited. He looked about for a familiar face and spotted Pradip in the front row. Pradip smiled at him and clapped the loudest. At tables scattered around the room Vishnu saw more than fifty Moxan members, handsome young men with almond eyes and skin darker than most of their Hindu brothers. Vishnu was aware they were examining him, many with a critical eye. Suddenly he wasn't sure of his position. His own political views as an educated Hindu didn't mesh with the Moxan tribe's burning desire for self-government. As Dhotia moved smoothly into the main part of his speech, Vishnu sidled along the wall and took a seat at the back of the room.

There were only two women in the audience. One was a roly-poly middle-aged grandmother in a rumpled cotton sari. Her unattractive-ness might have given her an advantage, for she looked totally at ease in the presence of men. The other, a dusky young beauty in a lavender tunic and pants, looked vibrant, in keeping with the popular robust image of Moxan women, and shy at the same time. She was refined enough to attract the attention of a film director in the Bombay film industry—Bollywood, as they called it. Vishnu some-how doubted that she had the slightest interest. She turned around and fixed her penetrating gaze on him for a long moment. He found himself straightening his back.

"First, an urgent matter," Dhotia's voice intruded on Vishnu's contemplation. "The world needs to know what happened last Wed-nesday when our people were brutally attacked by the police."

From habit Vishnu took his pen and notebook out of his pocket.

"All that has been reported is anti-Moxan propaganda." Dhotia put his glasses on and read from a newspaper clipping. "Listen to this. This is from *India News*. 'Five Moxan men in Shatpur village were killed and several others injured in a clash with the police. The vil-lagers were dancing sensuously around an open fire, beating utensils, drinking rice beer, and behaving in an unruly manner. Earlier they had made an animal sacrifice. . . .' See how they lie. Our people were worshipping Lord Shiva. That's how He danced. They make it seem like we're primitive people."

There was a shuffling of feet, scraping of chairs, coughs, mutter-ings, and grumbling. Vishnu felt a flush on his face. He stopped writing and glanced at the floor.

"For years the government has taken our property and oppressed us," Dhotia declaimed. "Now they're physically attacking us. Twenty

Moxans hurt. Five murdered. One missing." He banged the podium with his fist. "Because we are in the way."

The Moxans now lapsed into their native tongue, which Vishnu didn't understand. Dhotia's voice boomed over the uproar. "I met with the Secretary for Tribal Affairs," he said in Hindi. "What does he do? Nothing. He thinks we're nothing. Peasants. Expendable."

A slender boy seated next to Pradip stood up. "My brother was tortured. He came home with one eye missing and wounds all over his body. My mother's heart has gotten worse since . . ." His voice broke and tears streamed down his cheeks.

Pradip spoke to him in a whisper, offered him a handkerchief. The boy sat down, wiped his eyes, then burst into crying again.

A man yelled, "We must take action."

"A *gherao* of the police station," another man shouted.

Vishnu had seen many a *gherao*, a peaceful event in which demonstrators barricaded an institution to prevent the employees from entering and conducting their business. He'd support that.

"A *gherao* for five dead?" came another voice. "No. Five of them for the five of us."

A young man with a beaded necklace around his throat slid to the edge of his chair. "I say bomb the police station!"

"We're not terrorists, we're freedom fighters," an older Moxan with a hump on his back countered. "I carry flowers, not guns." He rose and placed a handful of tiny white shiuli flowers at the feet of Lord Shiva.

Vishnu's discomfort with the charged atmosphere was rapidly turning into fear.

"Our issue here," Pradip summed it up, "is human rights violation."

"We should involve the U.S.," a man said. "The U.S. can pressure our government to stop treating the tribals this way."

"How do we get their attention?" asked a voice that alternated between despair and cynicism. "We have no oil."

"But we shall be heard." The grandmother glanced at Vishnu. "There are two million of us. Our area is rich in coal and manganese. Our literacy rate is sixty-two percent, one of the highest in India."

Vishnu slouched back into his chair and kept his face lowered. The air conditioner clattered to a halt and immediately the room became prickly hot.

The young man in the beaded necklace cried, "I still say a bomb will get everybody's attention."

"Time for a break," Dhotia said. "It's unbearably hot here." He added, "Let's try to resolve this peacefully. Then we win in the eyes of the country and the world."

Looking at the militant young faces, Vishnu wasn't so sure that they agreed. He felt goose bumps along his arms, picturing the destruction and suffering that would ensue if they resorted to terrorism as their means.

Over the heads of the Moxans who were spilling out of the room Dhotia signaled Vishnu. "Let's step outside for a minute. Shall we?"

Together they walked down the corridor, Dhotia draping his arm across Vishnu's shoulders like he was already an insider. That was part of the party leader's charisma, Vishnu realized. To make someone feel included, needed, trusted, and perhaps responsible.

They paused at a tiny verandah overlooking a narrow street. A man sitting on a mat on the footpath below, looking quite content, was repairing shoes. Dhotia lit a cigarette, leaned against the railing, and asked, "So how do you think the conference is going so far?"

"I have my concerns—"

"Now you know enough to understand that we will not be able to defeat the Indian government by ourselves," Dhotia said. "We'll need help from outside. Our difficulties, our struggles, our views are little known outside of India. And that's where you come in."

Vishnu stood in stunned silence. Dhotia was overestimating his reach. He had no international stature. This job was going to be much harder than he had expected. He said politely, "I appreciate your confidence in me, but—"

"I'm sure as a journalist you've made connections."

Vishnu thought quickly. "Perhaps what you mean is that we should get the foreign media interested."

"That's right," Dhotia said gleefully. "Foreign news services like the AP and Reuters. And groups like Amnesty International."

Vishnu thought out loud. "The question is how."

"Jump on the Internet," Dhotia suggested with a bright face. "The remotest part of the world is a 'mouse click' away. Didn't you say that?"

Vishnu looked below to see a street dweller, partially clothed, washing himself at the water pump, the chill of the water making him jump every now and then. Vishnu hid his sigh.

"We may be a primitive tribe, but we too can get on the Internet," Dhotia kept on. "We'll give you your own e-mail ID. You'll be able to contact anyone in the world then. You'll run our website, too."

Suddenly Vishnu remembered Meena. Surely she, a high tech manager in the U.S., would be more familiar with the workings of Internet facilities than he was at the moment. He wouldn't want her to be anywhere near the Moxans, but, ridiculous as all this sounded, perhaps she could advise him.

"I'll do my best," he said.

"You're our greatest hope."

Dhotia's intimate tone conveyed both confidence in him and, Vishnu thought with a shiver, an expectation that results should be forthcoming.

Lunch was served a little later, but Vishnu had lost his appetite. The rice tasted gummy, the mutton curry flat, and the vegetables overcooked. He picked disconsolately at his food, watching the Moxans go back for second and third helpings as he pondered his predicament. Throughout the meal, Miss Bollywood Beauty kept looking adoringly at both him and Dhotia. Vishnu wanted to hear her story, but being the typical village woman she was, she remained quiet and subdued in the presence of men.

When the lunch was finally over, Vishnu noticed a commotion in the far corner of the room where a dozen young members were huddling, supposedly charting an education program for Moxan youth. They were too loud, too excited in their movements. The air vibrated with words like "darkness" and "rubble" and "Shakti"—a name meaning force, believed to represent Shiva's feminine side, his stronger half. Vishnu speculated they were using the code name Shakti for a secret project.

Dhotia tapped Vishnu on his shoulder. "I'd like you to interview our five-member board," Dhotia said. "The *panchayat*, we call them in the villages, 'municipality' to you. Write that up for the first issue of our newspaper, would you?"

Addressing the crowd Dhotia said, "The rest of you stay with me. We have work to do."

A squat man whose narrow eyes disappeared in the folds below his eyebrows motioned Vishnu to an adjoining room. It was a tiny alcove with a window, a table, and two chairs.

"My name's Tilak," the party elder said as they positioned themselves in their seats. "I don't know how much you know about us. We make up a large percentage of the population in the northeastern part of the state."

"I'm aware of that."

"But we hold very little economic or political power. Hindu and Muslim landowners, greedy pigs' sons, come to our village with their private armies and loot our property. They call themselves 'freedom fighters.' Do you know that the police collaborate with them? If we fight back, they say we're trying to overthrow the government."

Serious charges, some of which were probably true. Vishnu peered through the window to distract himself for a moment and saw a spindling tree with a red kite snared in its branches.

"That's a *pipul* tree," Tilak said.

"Oh?"

"Do you city boys even know about trees?"

Vishnu swallowed the jibe and managed a weak smile before saying, "I'm a village boy, too."

"To us, trees are everything. Teak, bamboo, sandalwood, each serves a purpose in the life of our people." He gazed down at the table, touched its surface with his palm as if to determine what kind of wood it was made of, and added, "Our ancestors were living in the Kasun forest, east of here, when the Aryans arrived. They believed that Lord Shiva, the creator of the forest and all that lived in it, resided there himself. When I was a kid, we used to gather teak and sandalwood for furniture, bamboo for building houses and basket weaving, and all kinds of twigs for cooking and heat. But we didn't take any more than we needed. Now the government is cutting down entire forests to supply the cities with timber. They build roads which bring in more people and push us from our land. We are forced to pay high prices for permits from the Forest Department to harvest what was given to us by Lord Shiva. All this is leading to the destruction of our tribe. In fifty years we shall cease to exist. How can we accept that? Of course, we shall fight."

Vishnu couldn't disagree with any of it. "You make a strong case."

"Write that down," Tilak urged. "We want the government to stop cutting down the natural forests in the Moxan areas."

Vishnu did as he was told.

Tilak went on. "We want nineteen thousand square kilometers of land."

This, to Vishnu, was unrealistic. It was a sizable part of the state.

"Tihili should be recognized as an official language by the government."

How ridiculous. So few people spoke it. They didn't even have a dictionary.

"The first choice for any job opening in our part of the state should be a Moxan."

First choice? No problem with that except Vishnu didn't think there were enough skilled Moxans to design a dam, teach college, or run a hospital.

"These we insist on," Tilak said. "They are nonnegotiable. And we shall strike if they aren't met. A total boycott. You understand?"

Vishnu said he understood.

It was late evening when he finished talking to all five board members. He was glad to finally get up from his chair and leave. As he walked toward the elevator, Dhotia stepped out of one of the rooms. He gushed his appreciation for Vishnu's help, then added, "Show me a draft of the issue when you're ready, will you? And come see me if you need anything."

Vishnu mumbled a good-bye. Out in the open, he sensed that few people dared to walk this empty lane at night. If there were thugs anywhere in Calcutta they would be lurking here. The pulse in his temples began to throb like drumbeats. A creeping sense of panic made his legs feel leaden; he moved rigidly like a toy soldier. He had somehow managed to end his first day on the job with a splitting headache, and in fear of his life.

What a contrast to the dreams he had for himself as a journalist. That truthfulness and honesty would be his principles. That by reporting impartially he'd unite people who were divided. How had he ended up in this situation?

Then he emerged from the darkness onto Chowringhee Road, a familiar well-lit avenue, and felt a rush of relief. In a sudden burst of optimism, he decided he'd do a fair, credible job for the Moxans.

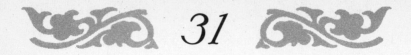

31

The workday had been long and weary, with a gritty feel to it. But now all that remained on Meena's agenda was to check any new e-mail that might have arrived. As she waited for the computer to respond, she looked up out of habit at the travel poster on the wall across from her oak desk.

After she had bought this image of Shiva with a serious face while shopping with Claudette, she had framed it herself and hung it the next day. It served, as she had hoped, to break the sharp straight lines and the cool monotonous beige of her office space. But today the image seemed to do more than that. As she gazed at it, it emanated an aura of power that imbued her with an unsettling, yet expectant, mood. The small caption WHY NOT VISIT INDIA THIS YEAR? seemed to be directed at her personally. She snatched her eyes away. Better concentrate on the here and now. She opened her e-mail box.

There was only one message, whose unfamiliar address of CAL-CUTTA.COM made her glance at the bottom for the sender's name. Vishnu. Vishnu? She jumped, then sat down again. A jolt of elation tinged with apprehension shot through her as she began to read.

Dear Meena,

What a surprise to receive your e-mail address from my friend, Asha.
In case you're wondering if I'm the right Vishnu, let me remind you that you like marigold flowers and *laddoo*

sweets and dancing barefoot on the sand. And I'm sure
you remember our favorite meeting place in the dunes.

The screen blurred momentarily. Who else but Vishnu would remember her three childhood favorites? So, Laxmi had finally gotten hold of him. Meena couldn't contain her delight at the quickness of the response. She pictured the small boy, the same height as she was, slim, immaculate in white, his eyes glowing with the ecstasy of seeing her again. She didn't know what the grown man would be like and it didn't matter. The essence of Vishnu would always be the same, that she knew for sure. She scrolled down and read a little more.

I have looked for you everywhere and never given up
hope. I'm overjoyed to hear that you are well, that you are
a success, and most of all that you still remember me.
I'm not married either.

Was this really happening? Really true? It sounded as if he wanted her back! The euphoria that filled her heart was not a Western emotion. It was that of a young Rajput bride consumed by the desire to reunite with the husband from whom she had been so cruelly torn. Their deep love, their shared childhood experiences, their marriage vows were far more powerful than the feelings of despair and loneliness she had suffered during their long separation. And paging down farther . . .

Please come to Calcutta as soon as you possibly can. My
address and phone number are below.
Most anxiously awaiting your arrival.
Lovingly yours,

Vishnu

She read and reread the note until she had committed it to memory, until the words felt as real as though Vishnu were saying them himself. She hit the Print button. When the printer had finally clattered to a halt, she snatched the sheet from it and devoutly touched it to her forehead as if it were good fortune bestowed by the gods. She looked up at Shiva's image and, yes, he was attempting a smile.

As the initial wave of emotion subsided a bit, Meena experienced a sense of uneasiness. There was an urgency in the way Vishnu had asked her to come to India. Why? Was it love? Was it memories? Or was there something else?

Her discomfort vanished as she was overcome again by her feelings. She could no longer think of anything but to answer him immediately. Her hands trembled as she composed a reply.

Dear Vishnu,

I don't have words to tell you how happy I am to receive this message. I'm just now realizing how long I have been wanting to see you, my family, my village, and my country. Love and caring have a way of reuniting people across time and distance, of this I'm sure.
I can't give you an exact date yet, but rest assured that I'll be visiting you at the earliest possible time. My first stop in India will have to be Karamgar. Could you send me precise directions for traveling there? Then I shall join you in Calcutta.
Please don't say anything to anyone in Karamgar. I want to arrive there unannounced.
With much love,

Your Meena

E-mail was just the right vehicle for this purpose, Meena told herself contentedly. Here she could be spontaneous and unedited. If she called Vishnu now, she'd be a complete wreck. If she tried writing a letter, she'd have wasted a whole ream of paper.

She got up from her chair and looked out the window. Even with darkness approaching, the western sky was shimmering with an ethereal light that filled her with hope. A whole new life was waiting for her in India. Her office suddenly seemed dreary and cramped. It wouldn't be able to imprison her exuberant spirit much longer, she knew.

32

The room in Denver's Mayflower Hotel annoyed Antoine the moment he and Liv walked in the door. Every detail from the ashtrays in a supposedly no-smoking room to the ostentatious gold-foiled chocolate coins on the pillows grated on him. A coy little card saying "Now you're sleeping with the best" was the final straw.

As his eyes fell on the portrait of a cat with a red ribbon on its collar hanging on the wall above the bed, he said acidly, "They even provided a cat," then remembered how Liv adored her two Siamese.

"Well, at least it's clean," Liv said, as she reached for the phone.

Antoine looked out the window to see a bleak late-night sky above and harsh city lights below. He was vaguely aware of Liv talking to her mother about their upcoming visit for a few minutes before hanging up. He stole a glance at her as she changed into a bluish nightgown with lots of frills, but she was turned away from him.

"I'm exhausted," she announced, kissed him without ardor, and collapsed into bed.

Antoine undressed, put on his pajamas, slid under the covers, and turned off the bedside lamp. Voluptuous Liv was lying inches from him. He touched the warm skin of her arm. He wanted to draw her closer, but she was already in a deep slumber. He closed his eyes, took a long breath, and tried to relax his body. Light from the hallway seeping under the door nagged at him. Maybe he should get up and do something, but he didn't know what. All he could do was ruminate.

This was his second crack at marriage. The first one had lasted only two years. Was this turning out to be a mistake too? Sometimes a question all by itself is answer enough.

Eventually he fell asleep, his mind weary of the struggle. He dreamt of Liv. In black and white. She was standing only a few feet away from him, but her face and figure were a blur. All he could see was one huge tear sliding down her cheek. He woke with a start.

Daylight was streaming into the room. Liv was still asleep, her breathing deep and even, her lips slightly parted in a smile. When was the last time she had smiled at him like that? Who had changed, Liv or him? Or both?

By now the room was overheated and he was sweating. He checked his watch on the nightstand. My God, he had less than an hour to get ready for the book signing. He got out of bed and picked up the *Denver Post* from under the door.

There he was on page three. The bold headline AUTHOR TAKES US ON A JOURNEY OF SELF-DISCOVERY and his smiling face. Self-discovery—how pretentious. Who am I, he asked himself, to be guiding others at this point in my life? But this half-page article would probably bring out a good crowd. He shaved and showered, then brewed coffee in the coffeemaker. He poured a cup. Ugh. Hot water with a bitter taste. He set the plastic cup aside and was combing his hair when the phone rang. A glance at the clock radio indicated only twenty minutes before the book signing. Perhaps Liv's sister calling. Let Liv answer it. He stepped out into the dressing area, quickly donned his corduroy slacks, a light blue cotton shirt, and a navy blazer, and returned to the bedroom. Liv was lounging on the bed, eyes on the ceiling, whispering into the phone, laughing. When he reached for his watch on the nightstand, she started, cupped her hand around the mouthpiece, and raised an eyebrow.

"It should be a good one," he said. "I'll be back by one."

"Okay," Liv said.

Antoine snatched his topcoat from the closet and headed for the elevator.

He arrived at Cover to Cover bookshop to be greeted by a larger than usual crowd. A forest of expectant faces waited in a line that began at the back of the room, wound down the aisles and out the door, and extended around the block. The store manager guided him to the signing area.

Antoine's thoughts were still occupied with the remnants of the dream and the state of his relationship with Liv, but as soon as he took his seat at the autograph table he slipped into his public persona. Holding copies of *Parallel Lives* in their hands, introducing themselves, his fans approached the table one by one. He glanced at each, seeing only a blank face. He scrawled a personal message in each book, followed by his usual flowing signature.

It was about twenty minutes into the signing when a pale woman edged along the table and said, "My name is Lynn, spelled L-y-n-e. You've helped me come to terms with my brother." She gave him a mug with a map of Denver and pointed out LoDo, the lower downtown area, where she lived.

By now Antoine's fingers were cramped and his caffeine-starved body clamored for a good cup of coffee. "I was hoping that mug would be filled with hot coffee," he muttered.

How could he make such an inappropriate remark? It was too late. He bit his tongue as he signed her book.

The next woman, with smoldering eyes and lips the shade of orange marmalade, scanned his chest and below, silently put a long-stemmed red tulip before him, then glided away, hips swaying, tossing another steamy look over her shoulder. At least she'd be uncomplicated, Antoine said to himself as he contemplated her derriere. Should he beckon her back?

What had come over him? Would he even be able to stoop this low?

As soon as the last buyer of his book got her signature, Antoine rose from his chair and stretched. The store manager, waiting at a discreet distance, moved closer and had started to say something when yet another woman came rushing up clutching a copy of his book. She had unkempt hair, a coat that had seen too many snowy days, and an obviously unhappy little girl in tow.

"I've read your book," she said breathlessly. "This copy is for my brother. Please, stay one more minute and sign it."

Antoine put aside his fantasy of a steaming hot cup of Starbucks Sulawesi coffee. "With joy," he said automatically.

"That reminds me of my favorite line in your entire book," she said. " 'Follow your hidden joys.' And I took your advice. I'm a single mother with a full-time job. I have very little time for myself. My hidden joy is painting. After reading your book I went back to my studio. My art has changed my life."

Antoine fixed his gaze on her as she gave voice to her gratefulness. Her cheeks were flushed. Her face held a beauty that he knew surfaced only on rare occasions. He leaned over the table and signed with great care. "Thanks for reminding me," he said. "Maybe I should seek out my own 'hidden joy' now. A good cup of coffee." He meant that as a joke, but immediately asked himself: Had he ever stopped to think what really were his hidden joys?

The store manager approached again. "How about some lunch?"

"Sorry, I have to get back to the hotel," Antoine replied. "My fiancée is waiting for me."

"We get big names here all the time," the store manager bubbled. "But yours was the strongest signing we've had in ages. We'd love to have you come again."

Back at his hotel, Antoine went directly to the coffee shop and retreated to a quiet corner, where he sat with an espresso, musing about his failed loves. Was the fault his? Did he need to be more open, caring, sharing? *Could* he be? He felt a frustration building within him as if he had been trying to open a jammed door and was now ready to kick it in. Hidden behind that door was self-awareness. He must find it.

The coffee seemed insipid, barely drinkable—or was it him? In a perverse sort of way, it took him back to his first trip with Liv and the coffee shop on the Plaza in Santa Fe where they had sat. It was a crisp clear morning, and as they gazed at each other across their morning espresso, he brushed her face with his fingers. She responded with a wisp of a smile. Eyes, touch, smile. The coffee had been splendid that morning.

It was five years ago that Liv came into his life. He saw her—this tall and attractive woman in a black dress and boots—standing across the room at a friend's house. He wanted to get to know her. And he did. They were together every single minute of their spare time for the next three months. She was an up-and-coming executive in a high-powered advertising firm. He admired her business acumen. He had difficulty managing money; to her it came naturally. She was dedicated to her mother and siblings in a way he wished he could have been. She met his basic needs and relieved him of petty daily annoyances like having to make a dental appointment. To their relationship she brought a focused energy and talents he didn't possess. She had a lively social life and entertained often, though she invited mostly colleagues and had the food catered. Her passion in life was shopping. Vacations consisted of trips "back east" to visit her mother in Des Moines, Iowa.

If her life was monochromatic, he had entered it with eyes wide open. She was ever the even-tempered one. With a career of her own, she didn't make draining emotional demands on him. This was one of his introspective and creative phases. He tended to be moody and irritable, and Liv was the only one who could tolerate the artist in him. Looking back, it had been a well-run existence, but ultimately sterile.

Antoine now found himself thinking back to Shanti. He had married her—though it hadn't been clear to him at the time—as an act of rebellion against his parents' stifling upper-middle-class values, which consisted of maintaining appearances and accumulating material goods. But with the initial passion fading, he found he couldn't share his deepest self. Only recently had he realized that she simply wasn't enough of a person to draw that out of him—that she didn't have the intellect and depth of character upon which to build a lasting relationship.

The whole Shanti experience left Antoine leery of women. In the years after their breakup he had several brief affairs, none of any importance, until finally he met Liv. His parents took an instant liking to her, relieved that he hadn't chosen another Marin County flake. Liv was nothing if not stable, and she didn't demand a fusion of souls like Shanti. To Liv, Antoine was multitalented, sexually attractive, possessed of a magnetic personality that dwarfed the sallow-faced, single-dimension business types she dealt with at the office. He was a total package—and he enhanced her social life, where an attractive male companion was a definite plus.

The turning point came with the birth of his second novel. During months of intense effort he became slowly aware that he was in the midst of a period of great personal change, that the polar expedition he was writing about in *Parallel Lives* was a metaphor for his own inner journey of exploration, and his only guide was a sense of dissatisfaction with his present state. What a shame, he thought, that he had not begun this adventure earlier. Each sentence he put down on paper forced him to reexamine lifelong beliefs and assumptions. Every love scene in his book hinted at his own suppressed passion. He felt on the verge of integrating the disparate fragments of his life. And he knew that the intensity with which he intended to live that life and the values that would give it direction weren't the same as Liv's. His writing had taken him on a different course.

Liv must have come to some conclusions of her own, for she began to travel on business for extended periods. It was then that he met Meena.

Meena was different from any woman he'd ever encountered. She seemed content in a give-and-take relationship where roles were not rigid. It was obvious she was interested in him, and he found himself spending time with her—training for a race, going to cafés, flying kites, surfing the Net—even though he knew at some point he'd have to come clean with her. Several times during their last few jogging sessions he had been on the point of telling her of his engagement. But time always seemed to run out before he could marshal his courage.

Lately Liv seemed remote and preoccupied. Or was that wishful thinking on his part? At their engagement party when he noticed her flirting with her boss, it had merely amused him. Why hadn't he been more offended? Perhaps because he had already concluded he no longer loved her—if indeed he ever had. Of course, he wanted Liv to be happy. His conscience couldn't bear another wounded woman. By now, she probably suspected his heart didn't belong to her. But did she have to know that it belonged to someone else?

Oh my God! Had he just admitted to himself that this was so? In a moment of clarity he knew he could deny it no longer. He'd have to go to Meena and express his true feeling for her. He could only hope that it wasn't too late.

A bellhop came up to his table holding a copy of his book. "Uh, Mr. Peterson? Would you mind signing this? It'll go in the prominent author collection in our second-floor library."

"Not at all." Antoine got his pen out, drew a media-happy smile on his lips.

"I knocked on your door half an hour ago," the bellhop went on. "Your wife said you weren't back from the book signing yet. Then I noticed you sitting here. I recognized you from your picture in this morning's paper."

Antoine returned the autographed book. As the bellhop retreated, his words lingered. Soon Liv *would* be his wife. Walking toward the elevator, Antoine knew the time had come to act. His decision to call off the engagement had gathered strength inside without his knowing. No more procrastination. Even imagining Liv's pained expression, the argument they would have, none of it would dissuade him this time. His only regret was that he hadn't reached this point a lot sooner. He was suddenly feeling more alive than he had for years.

33

Meena drove down San Pablo Avenue taking in familiar sights. There was the Internet Literacy Center where she volunteered twice a month, the hair salon named Shear Madness run by an ex-con who had often tried to lure Meena inside to cut her hair short, and the sari shop with a window displaying incredible colors and patterns. Finally she came to Juanita's Café. She parked her car on a side street at 8:55 A.M., five minutes before her appointment, and walked a block. At the entrance she paused to view a rockery of wildflowers and spend a leisurely moment preparing herself.

The soft music inside made her want to go wandering in the foothills of the Sierras. Only the huge bulletin board with thumb-tacked cards announcing cat-sitting services, Zen handyman avail-ability, and a support group for cockatoo owners reminded her that this was Berkeley.

She had just sunk into a chair when Jim "Attila" Lanigan of Gamma Solutions entered. He was at least six feet tall and well over two hundred pounds, with round black-rimmed glasses and the look of mild disorientation that characterizes programmers away from their keyboards.

Jim set his briefcase on the floor, shook her hand, and sat across from her. "You're just as I remember from the first time we met, five years ago." He spread his huge arms on the table. "Work keeps you young."

Meena smiled. "Hope this isn't too much of a bother."

"Not at all," Jim replied. "I'm on vacation, staying home with my kids. Glad to get out for a while." As he leaned back, the chair made a disturbing creaking noise. "And you're not the only reason I drove down to Berkeley. I have a job interview with an outfit here later this morning."

"You're leaving Gamma?" Meena pretended to be surprised. She wanted to hear his reasons firsthand.

"Yes. It's my yearly job search. We computer geeks are on a carousel." Jim's finger traced a pattern on the table surface. "We know the entire industry because everybody has worked with or for everybody else. We're loyal to our profession, not to our companies. I'm glad to spend my whole day in front of my screen. The computer spits back answers. It doesn't argue with me. But I get fed up with a company pretty fast. Rules, politics, bitchy people. The next job will be my seventh."

"I've been with the same outfit ever since I graduated." Meena sighed. "Over ten years. Too long, I guess. I've always wanted my own software business."

"You could call it Meenaware," Jim said.

Meena chuckled softly.

"I never got around to thanking you." Jim's tone became serious. "You helped me find my current job. Remember? You gave me the name of Stan Schumacher at Gamma. He hired me on the spot. I owe you one." He looked up at the waitress who had come to take their orders. "One tall black, please."

"How about some breakfast?" Meena asked. "It's my treat."

Jim seemed to perk up. "I didn't get my size by not eating." Turning to the waitress, he asked, "Any doughnuts?"

"No." The waitress smiled brightly. "But we have great biscotti. Double-sized."

"You just talked me into it."

"And for you, ma'am?"

"Assam tea and wheat toast, please."

When they were alone again, Jim said gloomily, "But now they want me out. The big wheels at Gamma would do anything for a buck. They're cutting corners on quality, and when I call them on it, they make things difficult for me. My printer broke down. Wasn't fixed for ten days. I've been coding twenty years, and they hire some brat with only two years UNIX experience at three thousand more because he's got a Ph.D. I took the hint."

Meena drained her glass of ice water. "Perhaps you should interview with SIC—we always have some turnover."

"Thanks, Meena." Jim looked straight into her eyes. "You're a technical giant. But I wouldn't come to work for you."

Meena was taken aback. "Why not?"

"Your own position isn't too secure."

"What are you talking about?"

"I'm talking about the COSMOS spec being sold under the table to selected clients before its release. Word's bound to get out." Jim reached into his briefcase and slapped something down on the table. "Does this look familiar?"

"Sure does. It's a Xeroxed copy of the COSMOS design document." It was like finding a rattlesnake in the mailbox. Numb, her throat dry, Meena put her mind to work. She examined the encrypted date on the top right-hand corner of the first page. Thank God, the version was outdated. She looked up, trying not to show the feelings jostling inside her. "Where did it come from?"

"My boss got it for me a little while ago. He asked me to keep it hush-hush. You didn't sell it to him?"

"Of course not." Meena flipped the pages with stiff fingers. A square green sticky note was posted on one page. She read the hand-written message: *"May not be the final version. The interfaces should work."* Whose handwriting was this? It looked familiar.

The waitress came back with a tray balanced on the palm of her hand. A foot-long biscotti jutted out over the edge of one plate.

Jim picked up the biscotti like a club. "My sons would love to fight with this."

The waitress laughed. "My Tommy too."

As Jim flirted with the waitress Meena quietly removed the note and put it into her purse. She was sure Jim saw her doing it, but he said nothing.

The waitress departed. Meena handed the document back to Jim and sat facing him with assumed cheerfulness.

"This early information has helped," Jim said. "I got my testing done way ahead of schedule. Now Gamma's going to beat out Sawoya's next spreadsheet offering. Too bad I won't be there for the bonus. But wait till Mr. Sawoya finds out your company is giving Gamma preferential treatment. He'll raise hell. He might even sue you."

Meena drank her hot tea so quickly it burned her mouth. "How did the document get to Gamma in the first place?"

"Somebody at SIC sold it to my manager." Jim took a huge bite of his biscotti with visible pleasure. "If you don't know about it, then whoever is doing it is trying to sabotage you."

"What else do you know?"

"That's all I can tell you." His eyes wandered off into space.

He was holding something back. She let it slide for the moment. She remembered that Dad in his circle of academic friends never pressed for information. He would often shift the subject, come back to it later from another angle. So she talked about chip technology and where it was heading, then turned to the pros and cons of people with MBA degrees managing the computer industry. "Brett Watson, my peer, has an MBA."

"I know Brett," Jim said. "He came to Gamma a lot when he was dating our office manager, Claudette. Brett and I work out at the same gym. We go out for a beer afterward occasionally. If you want my opinion"—he wiped the crumbs off his fingers with his napkin—"he's running scared. He's found out he can't manage a software project without being a techie. He gets snowed by people under him all the time. He's having a tough time. You were a programmer before you became a manager. He envies you for that."

Meena lifted a slice of toast to her lips and took a bite. Think, she commanded herself as she mentally toured the cubicles and offices of SIC looking for the culprit. She came up with no name.

"Just the same, you have to watch your step," Jim said. "In our industry women aren't discriminated against, either for opportunities or for dirty tricks. Some of the best programmers I've worked with have been women. They handle details better than men, if I may generalize. But they don't always get the best positions. There are cliques, you know. Men band together to protect themselves and their interests."

How Meena hated such political maneuvers: doing favors, then cashing them in when needed; forming an alliance only because it could do you some good. But this was one time when she would just have to play the distasteful political game.

Jim tilted his coffee cup, draining the last few drops. "Hope I didn't upset you."

Meena smiled pleasantly. "Actually," she said, getting to her feet, "you've been a great help."

34

As she drove back across the Bay Bridge into San Francisco, Meena kept wondering who could have sold the COSMOS spec to Gamma. By now it was late morning. The fog had lifted, unveiling the high-rises of the Financial District. Tall, slim boxes arrayed perfectly, giving an impression of excessive orderliness in a chaotic world. Their tops seemed to conspire to block out not only the sky but the human spirit as well.

Alone in her office, Meena examined the handwriting on the green adhesive note. The loop on the y was rounded, the t crossed, in a characteristic way. It was almost certainly a woman's writing. Thanks to that handwriting expert, her beau of two years ago, she had learned about handwriting styles. Then a wisp of suspicion passed through her head. She went to her file cabinet and pulled out one of Joy's memos sent some time ago. The y of "Joy" exactly matched.

"My God!" Meena said to herself. "I don't believe it."

How could Joy do such a thing? Not just to Meena but to her own employer? Selling top-secret material ... well, maybe not selling exactly. Maybe Joy was just doing a favor for someone—a man, of course—either at Gamma or here at SIC. Every transaction had at least two parties, and Meena meant to find out more.

She phoned Claudette at Gamma.

"I was hoping you'd call," Claudette said. "How about a run this week?"

"The weekend would be better. It's supposed to get warmer." A pause and then, "I need some help ... a favor to ask of you."

"Shoot."

"Can you trace a payment for me?"

"Honey," Claudette said, "I'm just the office manager. I'm not supposed to poke around the accounting area. What do you want to know?"

"A person from SIC sold a COSMOS spec to Gamma a little while ago. As the project manager of COSMOS, I'm responsible for its confidentiality. So I need to know who, and I need to know now. A check was probably made out to that person."

The line was silent for a moment. "Someone else handles the money side of things," Claudette said. "And that type of payment is usually done in cash, you know."

"Maybe not this time," Meena said. "And if it was company money, even if it was cash, wouldn't there be a record of who it was for?"

"Who do you suspect?"

Claudette would secretly want to hurt Brett, Meena knew. "Brett, of course."

"Well . . . now that I'm not seeing him, I could dig into his character, couldn't I? I used to date an accounting guy too. I don't talk to him much anymore. But maybe just this one time . . . I can't promise anything, though."

"Thanks," Meena said. "And let's squeeze in a run this Saturday down around Fisherman's Wharf."

Two hours later the phone rang. Meena picked it up promptly.

"Guess what?" Claudette said. "A ten-thousand-dollar check was made out to a Joy Preston for 'consulting services rendered.' I recognized the name because Brett mentioned her. I've never met her, though. Weird, huh?"

So—Joy really did sell the COSMOS design document. Meena was at a loss to understand why. Was it greed? Simple jealousy? Had Brett won her allegiance?

"Thanks, Claudette," she said. "I'm a little upset. She's a colleague who I thought was a buddy at one time." Meena hung up the telephone and sat silently.

She went back over what she knew, trying to make sense of it. First, and this according to Carlos, Joy had bought a condo in Mexico. The timing would fit. And if the money for it came from this payback from Gamma Solutions, that would explain why Joy hadn't told her about buying the condo. Second, now that Meena remembered it, during their dim sum lunch Joy had sniped at her, disparaged "techies," made envious comments about her looks. So yes, jealousy could be another motive.

She marched down to Joy's office and burst through the door without knocking.

Joy was lounging at her desk, a paperback mystery novel open before her. She was pulling a strand of her hair and examining it absentmindedly. She looked up and pasted a big smile on her lips. "Meena . . ."

"Thief!" Meena raised a finger at her. "You stole the COSMOS spec from Dave's desk and copied it and *sold* it."

"What are you talking about?" Joy was a picture of innocence. "I've never seen you this angry, Meena. What happened to that pretty face the famous authors in this town love?"

"Don't change the subject."

"What makes you think it was me?"

"I have your handwriting as proof. I also know how much you got paid and what you did with the money—"

"A regular little private eye, aren't you?" Joy had a smirk on her face. "Well, don't try crying to Alex, he won't listen to you."

So there was something extracurricular between Joy and Alex. Meena had suspected that. "For chrissake, what made you do such a thing?" Meena said. "Does money mean that much to you?"

"No, it's you I wanted to get." Joy's voice echoed in all the walls of SIC. "I hate you. You, the star. You get all the attention from the men." Her face cracked and creased in agony. "And me"—now she was whimpering—"I get only the married creeps. . . ." She broke up crying.

"That's not all you're going to get. You made a major mistake, Joy. You'll have to live with the consequences, I'm afraid." No need to carry this any further, Meena thought as she ran out of the room. Her heel caught a tear in the hallway carpet and she almost stumbled.

Back in her office, Meena sank into her chair. Her reputation was on the line. But Joy's betrayal had shaken her even more deeply. She now realized being attractive and competent—both matters of perception—could become a handicap in business. Funny thing was, she never thought of herself as quite so special.

Alex would be back from his European trip today. From all indications, he'd protect Joy. Meena shuddered to think that she could even get *herself* fired on the grounds that she had let the confidentiality of her project be breached.

At that moment Dave stuck his head in her door. His eyes had their usual bleary look from staring at the screen too long. "What's the matter, boss?" he asked. "You seem upset."

Meena shuffled papers for an instant. "Remember the COSMOS document that was copied from your desk?" she said. "It showed up at Gamma Solutions. Somebody sold it to a manager there."

Dave walked in, dropped into a chair. "Good heavens. Who sold it? Brett?"

It took several seconds for Meena to reply. "No, it was Joy, damn her. She screwed me over."

"I thought you were friends."

"Shows how naive a person can be."

"You need to get to the management right away," Dave urged. "It's a crime, you know, to—"

"I'm afraid Alex won't do anything. He and Joy are pretty tight. As for going to the top—I don't know Lou Cassidy well enough to say how he'd react. Right now I'm the one who looks bad."

Dave shook his head. "It's awful. What are you going to do?"

"COSMOS will go out the door in a matter of days. I'll stay with the project till that's done."

"I like working for you, Meena. We have an excellent team. For the first time in my career, I've felt like I belonged to a group." Dave rose slowly to go. "Hope it all works out."

Meena closed her eyes for a moment. Her team of programmers was still loyal to her. Perhaps all wasn't lost. If she could—

The phone rang.

"Could I see you right away, Meena?" Alex sounded deliberately gentle and courteous. His voice gave her a ray of hope.

"I'll be right there."

On the way she decided not to say anything to him about the Joy incident yet. Unless, of course, he brought it up himself. Joy might have gone running to him the moment Meena left her.

Alex was getting a folder out of a file cabinet. "Close the door, Meena. Have a seat."

Meena noticed the remote expression on his face. "How was your trip?"

"It was productive. I pitched our products in Holland and Germany. Got some enthusiastic responses to . . . Actually, I wanted to see you about another matter. Corporate downsizing. You might have heard rumors of layoffs."

"You mean they're true?"

"I've been asked to bring my budget down by twenty-five percent."

"You're not going to ask me to let any of my people go, are you, Alex? With the COSMOS release date coming up soon I need every single one of them. And they all have worked very hard this past year."

"We can keep the programmers, Meena. But . . . It's hard for me to say this. I remember you from the day you walked in as a college hire. It's . . . it's you I'm going to have to let go. We're calling it a 'career reshaping opportunity.' "

"What? Lay *me* off?" Meena sat stupefied for a second. "I've been with this company for twelve years, Alex. I've written half the code—"

"I'm sorry, Meena. No one would question your intellectual abilities. It's not your competence that's in question."

"What, then? And why me? Are you keeping Joy and Brett, who have yet to produce one goddamn thing?"

"Both Joy and Brett need at least a year more to finish their projects. COSMOS-1 is done."

"You bet it is, Alex. Done fully and done fast! And COSMOS-2 will—"

She caught herself up abruptly. This business bozo had everything backwards. Her project was achieved, so *she* was obviously dispensable. She shifted tack.

"Do you know that Brett's programmers have no respect for him? They come to me with their technical questions. And Joy reads mysteries at her desk. These are the managers you want to keep? That's rewarding incompetence, Alex."

"I know you're extremely upset, Meena. You have a right to be. But—I have no choice. These are orders from above. Times are hard. The company needs to tighten its belt. And you're expensive."

"Didn't you tell me a week ago our president was worried about me leaving?"

"Lou's staying out of it. He doesn't know my staff as well as I do. He told me I could handle it however I want."

Alex was being given free rein to get her out, to protect Joy, and to give Brett more responsibilities.

"I can't accept it, Alex. I just can't. I have to speak to Lou."

"He's off to an executive productivity seminar this afternoon. He'll be gone for a couple of days."

"I'll wait."

"Go see Jean. She's handling the paperwork. She'll give you an exit interview and listen to any grievances you might have."

Meena knew she wouldn't win this round. Alex had it in for her. She would have to get past him to higher-ups.

Alex continued, "Look at it this way. We're offering you a good severance package. Six weeks' pay. And all the vacation you've earned. You haven't taken any vacation so far this year, have you?"

"I didn't take a vacation last year either, Alex. I was working on COSMOS. Remember?"

"The company appreciates your contribution, Meena." He pushed a sheet of paper toward her. "Now if you'd sign at the *X* here."

"So my signature is still valuable?"

"This says that in consideration of the severance pay you will not sue the company—"

"Sue the company?"

"Or sue me. It's standard legal procedure these days. You know, cover your ass. . . . Now go see Jean. She'll have your paychecks ready. And, oh, you have an hour to clean out your desk." He looked at his watch. "Of course, you'll leave all company materials here."

"One hour?"

"Yes, Meena. I'm afraid that's it. But you know you can get a job anywhere in the Bay Area. Lots of companies will hire you. You're so attractive—"

"And you're such a great manager." Meena realized she was almost yelling. "Stuff it, Alex," she added gleefully. "You can't lay me off. I quit. And don't call me to fix bugs in the programs around here."

She tore up the form, threw it on his desk, and slammed the door as she stormed out.

With her head floating in space, her legs shaking under her, Meena walked down to the Pencil Czar's cubicle. Jean was half dozing at her desk, or perhaps in an alpha state. A mud brown muffin in a wrapper marked "day-old" was within arm's reach. The silk roses in a plastic vase before her looked wilted. The Pencil Czar woke with a start and blinked.

"Sorry to disturb you," Meena said sarcastically.

The Pencil Czar's eyes flicked over Meena. She opened a drawer, picked up two checks, and thrust them at Meena. "This one is your paycheck. And this other one's the severance—"

"Just the paycheck, please. I am resigning. And I'm refusing an exit interview."

Back in her office Meena told herself her first priority was to regain her inner equilibrium. Nothing had prepared her to deal with something like this. But unbearable as it seemed, she felt confident that she'd find the strength to deal with it. She had the tool: a five-minute meditation. Eyes closed, she inhaled deeply, held her breath for a moment, then exhaled slowly. She repeated this several times and still found herself jittery. Never before had this routine failed to transport her mind to a state of tranquility and mental clarity.

Next, she tried to picture herself standing barefoot in a vast arid field in Rajasthan, arms by her sides. Almost immediately the sun touched her forehead, the earth rooted her feet in the soft sand, the breeze caressed her limbs. She became part of the hills, the trees, the atmosphere. Minutes later when she opened her eyes, her mind was "where it belonged," as Guru Kailash would say. She knew just what to do.

Confidently she walked to Lou Cassidy's office. Through the plate glass she could see the company president in an off-white shirt and blue tie, his hair the color of birch bark. He was speaking on the phone and tapping his keyboard at the same time. Good. He hadn't left yet. She could still catch him for a few minutes.

His secretary stopped her with a wave of the hand as though guarding a vault of gold. "Where are you going?"

"Got to speak to Lou. It's urgent."

"He's on long distance."

"I'll wait."

The secretary checked the clock on the opposite wall. "He has a meeting down the peninsula in half an hour. He'll have to leave as soon as he gets off the phone."

At another time, Meena would have pressed on. Today she didn't have anything left. She turned, walked slowly back to her office, and simply sat there.

Where did she go wrong? she asked herself. She had put her whole self into this job, made it the focus of her life for twelve years, and what had it gotten her? Now she'd have to find another position—another passion.

Passion ... There were important things in life she had been neglecting. Perhaps, she told herself, in the long run she'd be grateful this had happened. But the pain refused to let up. It was as acute as on that terrible long-ago day when she had been carried away, still in her wedding finery, from the only life she knew.

All at once Vishnu leapt into her consciousness. What a perfect opportunity this termination had given her. She had been worried, ever since she received his e-mail, about getting time off to see him. Now she had all the time in the world. Things weren't altogether bad after all. She broke into a tremulous smile.

But first things first. She began composing a letter of resignation to Lou Cassidy on her screen. Eyes misting, she explained how a programmer from a client company had shown her the COSMOS design document that Joy had sold them, how an atmosphere of mistrust had made her work impossible, how a highly damaging, criminal act had been concealed, how she had been fired without just cause. She could only hope that he would delve into the matter and punish the guilty parties. She finished by saying:

"I am leaving for India in a few days to pursue personal and professional goals. I can be reached through my home e-mail address, which you have. Feel free to contact me with any questions or problems regarding COSMOS. And the day COSMOS hits the market, I'll be here in spirit."

The last twelve years had boiled down to a single page.

She printed the letter, signed it, attached the note paper from the stolen COSMOS spec with Joy's handwriting. A secret "gotcha" feeling filled her with perverse delight. Lou Cassidy had a reputation for being fair. He'd act on this, she was sure. She put the letter in an envelope with Lou's name and home address, marked it "Personal and Confidential," affixed a stamp, and dropped it down the mail slot.

What a pity, she ruminated, that he wouldn't receive this letter until after she had set off for India.

She did one more thing and that was to pack the COSMOS-2 folder in her briefcase before walking out the door.

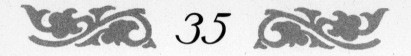

35

Getting canned wasn't something Meena had ever envisioned. She had always prided herself on being efficient, hardworking, and loyal. So how could this most humiliating experience have happened to her?

In the days that followed, she felt tragic and bitter. She couldn't sleep at night and was utterly exhausted in the daytime. She didn't touch her books, listen to music, even tend her plants. Her wastebasket was filled with empty Pepperidge Farm cookie wrappers—that was about all she could eat. All except for the homemade tamarind pickles Shaheen had left at her door. Tart at first bite but with a warm and satisfying aftertaste, the pickles eventually teased back her appetite.

Finally today she went running, ten miles through the woods and meadows of Golden Gate Park. Nature healed. Her body became drained of all tension, her mind calmer. Her strength was there, waiting to be tapped. When she returned home, she found she could appreciate her unfettered life and the free time that came with it. She picked up the phone and called her travel agent. Then she phoned Kazuko.

"Guess what?" Meena said. "I'm finally going to India." Saying the words made it all seem more real. Her voice gained enthusiasm as she outlined her plans.

"Perhaps I was wrong," Kazuko said. She sounded down. "I'll miss you, Mee-chan. I'll miss you very much."

Within the hour Carlos called, his voice distressed. "I'm in a state of shock. You're really leaving for India? How will we get along without you?"

"It's sudden for me as well," Meena said. "But a lot of things have happened lately and the blowup at SIC was the last straw."

"Kazuko said you are subletting your apartment."

"Yes. Do you know of anyone—?"

"Me."

"You? What about your own place? And your Japanese *amour?*"

"Yoko . . . went home." He sighed audibly over the phone. "Just left. And coincidentally my lease is up for renewal. I want to get out of here—too many ghosts."

"I'm sorry, Carlos. I know how much it can hurt. Sometimes things just don't work out the way we want. But things will look different after a while. Just give it time."

"I'm so weary. I just don't feel like looking for a place."

"You don't have to," Meena said. "I'd love to have you sublet my apartment. My landlord has already said he'd prefer it if I could find a reliable friend. I'll give him a call. I'm only taking some clothes with me, so I can leave the furniture and all the kitchen stuff for you. All you need to bring is your personal things."

"Gosh, Meena. That'll be great. It's just what I need—to be in a place full of pleasant memories for a while."

Today was her last day in San Francisco. With her heart paining, Meena opened the Roman shades in her living room. The sun was just burning through the morning fog. Only San Francisco had this special beauty. Its endless sky had filled little Meena with hope from the day she arrived here as a frightened seven-year-old. Over the years the city had nurtured her, shaped her attitudes and tastes, given her many happy moments. She was attached to it by a strong tie that she'd now sever for good.

The phone rang. She heard Carlos say, "Could I take you out to lunch today?"

"That would be lovely."

"At noon then."

Meena packed the last of her clothes, the gift she had chosen for

Vishnu, her laptop with its internal modem, a power converter, and the 800 number of her Internet service provider. As an afterthought, she tucked *Parallel Lives* into her carry-on bag. Only twenty more pages to go.

The doorbell buzzed. The Rasul family stood there with a giant placard that said "We'll miss you, Meena," signed by the whole bunch and sad faces drawn in charcoal by Sonny.

"Auntie Meena," Sonny cried. "Would you visit us in Bombay this summer? We can fly kites on Chowpatty Beach. I'll take you to my favorite street magician afterward. He has sparrows flying out of his mouth."

Meena bent to hug him. "Fly kites in Bombay? That's a promise."

"It's such a long journey. The plane food is abominable." Shaheen handed Meena a big packet of *dalmut*, adding, "Keep this in your purse for the inflight movie."

"You've been like family to us, Meena," Ahmed's mother chirped. "I'm so very sad to see you go. When are you getting married? Let us know in advance, will you? We'll try to be there. I'll help you get dressed on your wedding day. All that beautiful hair you've got. I know just what to do with it. I'll color your lovely hands with henna—"

"One day at a time, Mother." Ahmed laughed. "First we have to get Meena to the airport."

"Write to us," Shaheen said.

The family was still at the door when Jim Lanigan and Claudette, looking quite happy together, came out of the elevator. Meena thought they would make a good twosome.

"Captain COSMOS!" Jim playfully grabbed Meena by the shoulder as she led them to the living room.

"Now I'm just plain Meena."

"The word's out that you left SIC." Jim snickered. "Everyone's gossiping. The politics there stank. SIC will have to make some changes if they want to get their reputation back. I have a job lead for you, by the way—"

"I want to try something new, Jim," Meena said quickly. She walked the length of the room to open the patio door and pointed to the rows of lush green plants in ceramic urns and wooden planters. "Come, take a plant from my arbor."

"It has to be something that doesn't need much care," Jim said.

Meena handed him a cactus and an ivy.

Turning to Claudette and motioning toward the ginger plant, Meena asked, "Remember this?"

"Of course," Claudette said. "We bought this together near Union Square. It's grown so big."

"I'd like you to have it."

Claudette took the plant, caressed its leaves, and said, "Can you imagine? It survived this foggy climate and now it's going to flower." She held the plant tenderly. "I'll send you an e-mail the day it blooms."

The rest of the morning passed like a dream. Every chore Meena did was for the last time. Mindfully, she scrubbed the kitchen floor, polished the coffee table, and dusted the windowsills. She thought about Vishnu. What would their reunion be like? She was both excited and apprehensive.

At noon Carlos arrived. "I have strict orders from Kazuko to take you to her place for lunch."

Of course Meena would be delighted to spend her last afternoon with Kazuko, Henry, and Carlos. But the closets still had to be cleaned. "Looks like I won't be able to straighten up this place for you."

"Don't take every bit of yourself out of here, Meena. I want to be able to say, 'That piece of paper in the wastebasket, crumbled to a perfect round. That was Meena. The slight tilt of the eucalyptus branches in the vase. That's Meena. The haiku book on the coffee table with a peacock feather sticking out. That can only be Meena.'"

Meena laughed. "Are you turning into a poet?"

"Everyone's a poet when the wound is deep, you know. In my state of mind, I could be a Sufi."

Meena stopped dusting the bookcase for a moment. Carlos had always been there for her. Her heart reached out to him. To think she might not see him again . . .

"Sure will miss your company, Carlos."

He crossed the room and stood a few paces from her. "Me, too. I couldn't ever count on the women I dated. But you've been a friend."

"Odd how we came from such different parts of the world. Our interests weren't the same. Our tastes were sometimes poles apart. Yet we have become the best of buddies."

"There's hope for the world." Carlos moved toward her, held her hands.

"You'll probably never understand how fast everything moves in computerdom," Meena said, "where you count significant events not in days or hours or even minutes or seconds, but in billionths of a second. You never stop to appreciate what you've done or the people around you. The present is imperfect. You always wait for the next version, the next great enhancement. And I've lived my life that way for a very long time. But today I'm happy just for these few perfect moments with you."

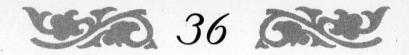

36

Oh, the joy of returning home, Antoine thought as he arrived at his house in Corte Madera. After his book-tour stay in Denver he had gone on to Boston, honored his book-signing commitments, and spent some uncomfortable time with his parents explaining why Liv was not with him. Des Moines had, of course, been scrubbed.

He was still recovering from the trauma of breaking up with Liv. Their last afternoon together had drained him completely. Her outburst of abuse and recriminations came like an endless freight train. She told him that he was a self-absorbed jerk and that her boss, D.J., was a better lover. He didn't know which accusation hurt more. She slapped his cheeks with such force that he saw darkness. Her tears came in gusts, and he had shed a few of his own. She stormed out of the hotel. Watching her go, he saw more desperation on her face than love. He didn't follow her.

It all had ended about as badly as it could. Now Antoine was ready to settle back into the quietness and familiarity of home and, however injured, to start again.

He unlocked the door, flicked on the light switch. The message light on his answering machine was blinking nervously. He touched the Play button.

"This is Deepak in Jaipur. I've got some important information about Vishnu Chauhan. Call me ASAP."

The message was two days old and sounded urgent. Antoine put his suitcase down and dialed the international code for India followed by Deepak's number. The phone kept ringing at the other end. Of course it would. It was early afternoon here but the middle of the night over there. Antoine was about to put down the phone when Deepak's drowsy voice came on the line. "Hello."

"Antoine here. Sorry to call you at this ungodly hour. Just got back from a trip—"

"That's all right, Antoine. Let me turn the light on."

It had been twenty-two years since Antoine had stayed with the Naj family as an exchange student. Yet Deepak Naj, his classmate in Jaipur, had remained a friend and always seemed happy to get a letter or call from him—even at such an hour.

"Let me think for a sec what I called you about. . . ." Deepak had returned to the line. "Oh, it was about Vishnu Chauhan. A police officer in Calcutta, who happens to be a friend of my father's from college, tracked the man down. This information, by the way, is confidential. The police are watching him."

"Why?"

"He's writing for a tribal group. The Moxans. A northeastern tribe who want autonomy. So far they've stayed away from violence. But some of the younger Moxans are believed to be extremists."

Antoine found himself frowning. "What does that mean?"

"The police think they're planning an attack on a police station. They might be making bombs, too, in their Calcutta office. A kidnapping a year ago has been linked to them, though nothing has been proven so far."

"What's Vishnu got to do with any of it?"

"Nothing, at this point," Deepak said. "He appears to be an innocent hired hand. But Father says once he's in, he'll know too much about the party. He'll never be allowed to leave his job alive."

"Oh, swell," Antoine said. "Thanks for the news. Now go back to bed."

"Call back if you need more information. Father says he's curious and will keep me up to date on any developments."

With a copy of his book of poems, *Dream Mask*, in his hand and a heart that was on a marching drill Antoine rang Meena's doorbell. He pictured her taking off the orange-red wrapper and the gold bow—

he'd taken that much trouble to make his gift attractive—and her face brightening. His poems would speak for him. He'd read them throughout the evening, starting with the one titled "You, by the Jasmine Bush." They'd tell her how he felt about her and make her understand why it had taken so long for him to come to her. And he'd give her the news about Vishnu. He smoothed his hair, straightened his posture, and brought a slight smile to his face just as the door swung open.

Carlos stood framed in the doorway. Around his neck hung a shimmering gold chain that reflected dots of light on the hallway wall. His opened shirt displayed his muscled chest to advantage. His jeans fit his lithe body too snugly. He was the kind of man who always smelled of fine cologne. If Antoine had had a sister he'd have advised her to stay away from Carlos. And now Antoine wondered how actively Mr. Mango was buzzing around Meena. He felt a burning sensation on his face.

Carlos stiffened visibly. "What can I do for you?"

"Just got back from my trip," Antoine mumbled. "I cut it short. I came to see Meena. Is she in?"

Carlos smiled sarcastically. "Meena's gone to India. I'm subletting her apartment."

"She's gone?"

Carlos turned away as if to close the door, then seemed to change his mind, finally saying in a tentative voice, "Come on in." He picked up the painter's easel that had partly blocked the entryway and headed toward the kitchen. "My girlfriend, Anna, paints."

In the background a lone guitar was pouring out a melody of love unfulfilled. Antoine crossed the room, recalling time spent here with Meena, noticing the changes. Magazines littered the floor, the coffee table had a film of dust, the ochre sofa had lost its luster.

"Can I get you some coffee?" Carlos asked.

Antoine gave a low "yes," then noticed that Meena's own painting *Options* still remained on the wall. As he studied it, the assertive splashes of blue and red seemed to vibrate, then undulate. He could almost see Meena jogging, her slender but well-muscled dark legs flowing across the canvas.

Carlos emerged from the kitchen with two steaming mugs of coffee and handed one to Antoine. They sat down across from each other, maintaining a wary distance. The air between them had a definite chill to it, Antoine thought.

Antoine took a sip and immediately recognized the strong rich Sulawesi flavor. Carlos did have good taste, and not just in women. "Nice coffee," Antoine said, and wondered at his own tone, for his mood was dark enough to be thinking, "but I could punch you in the mouth." He asked casually, "Have you heard from Meena since she left?"

"Yes." Carlos yawned as though he had better things to do. "She called from Seoul. She stopped there overnight."

"What's the rest of her itinerary?"

Carlos rubbed his eyes and changed his position. "I don't have it memorized."

"Has she e-mailed you?"

"Not yet." Carlos sighed.

Antoine tried again. "I was thinking of going to Calcutta."

Carlos caught his eye. "With Liv?" There was an edge to his voice.

"Liv and I broke up." Antoine felt his body sagging onto the sofa.

Carlos got up and turned off the music. With his back turned, he said, "That's too bad."

"It's okay. She and her boss had a thing going, but the truth is I wanted out."

"Really?" Carlos said in a tone that bordered on disbelief.

"Now that I'm free . . ."

"I'm not sure Meena will want to have anything to do with you. She's on her way to meet her husband."

Antoine chewed on his lip. "When," he asked, "is she reaching Calcutta?"

Carlos, his back still turned, said nothing.

Antoine was getting impatient, but he was careful not to show it. "Which hotel did she book into there, could you tell me?"

Mr. Mango now turned and stared at him intently with obsidian eyes beneath furrowed brows. His complexion darkened and his voice was knife-sharp as he said, "You ask a lot of questions, amigo."

"Look, Carlos, you don't like me and I don't like you. But you better level with me. Her life might be in danger."

"What are you talking about?"

"Vishnu has gotten himself involved with a bad bunch, a group of tribal rebels called the Moxans," Antoine said. "I just found that out from my college roommate Deepak, who lives in Jaipur. That tribe wants its own homeland. They'll stop at nothing. They kidnapped a tourist a year ago, or so the police think. Now they're into making bombs. The police are watching Vishnu. And if Meena's seen with him . . ." Antoine broke off.

Carlos's face betrayed his inner turmoil as he stared at Antoine in silence.

"She's a real bright lady," Carlos said eventually. "She'll figure things out in a hurry." Then he blurted, "Do you know how badly you hurt her?"

Antoine's hands shook as he put his coffee cup down.

Carlos began again. "She had strong feelings for you. I've never seen Meena get so excited about a man. And what do you do? You build up her hopes, then dump her the day Liv comes back. Pardon me if I'm getting a little emotional. But Meena's my friend. It hurts to see her cut up like that."

"I didn't mean to hurt her. My situation is different now."

"It'd better be," Carlos said. "Where I come from, we don't treat a woman like that. Don't go anywhere near her again unless you're serious, understand?"

"You don't have to threaten me, Carlos. I'm as serious as anyone can be. Look, I made a big mistake with Meena. But I had to spend a little more time with Liv to know for sure."

"You had to spend so many years with Liv to know?" Carlos sounded bitter.

After a moment of silence Antoine said, "I brought this for her." He removed the wrapper and held the poetry book up. What a fool I am, Antoine thought to himself a moment too late. Here he was admitting his feelings for Meena to a potential rival.

Carlos studied the cover and said, "You're going to try to bring Meena back safely?"

"Yes."

"She gets to Calcutta late Monday night." Carlos stared blankly at the coffee table. "A suite is booked for her at the Grand Bengal Hotel. She intends to stay there . . . oh, for a while . . ."

Meena might choose Vishnu over him? No way could Antoine let that happen.

"I know Meena. We're very much alike," Carlos said.

Antoine didn't like the comparison. "How so?"

"We're both Americanized outside. Inside we're something else."

Antoine picked up his coffee cup and sipped at his Sulawesi.

"But we wouldn't be good for each other." Carlos sighed. "I miss her, though. She was part of my life." His eyes wandered the room. "I wish I wasn't staying here. Every damn thing reminds me of Meena."

For the first time Antoine felt a kinship with Carlos. Mr. Mango had dragged out feelings Antoine hadn't voiced even to himself. "I'd better go home and call the travel agent. By the way, please don't mention anything about my coming here to Meena. I want to surprise her."

Carlos walked him to the door, stopping at Meena's phone table. "Her former boss called here the other day," he said. "A man by the name of Lou Cassidy. Sounded like he had important news for her. You might want to talk to him before you go. Here's his number."

Antoine took the slip of paper and put it into his breast pocket.

His dark eyes misting, Carlos said, "I'll be hoping for the best. . . ."

Antoine gripped his hand. "Thanks," he said. He looked a long time at Carlos before turning away.

How did Meena attract such loyal friends as Carlos and Kazuko? They set a high standard for Antoine to measure up to. But measure up he would.

At home Antoine called Deepak right away. It was morning in Jaipur and, thank God, Deepak answered promptly.

"I'm concerned about a friend of mine, who's on her way to India to renew a childhood acquaintance with Vishnu," Antoine said. "Her name is Meena. I might have mentioned her before. I'm sure she knows nothing about the Moxans. Might she be in danger?"

"She could very well be. The Calcutta police will trace all calls Vishnu makes, which automatically makes her a person of interest. Also, people in Calcutta may have ill feelings toward the Moxans because of that kidnapping they did. If violence breaks out and Meena happens to be with Vishnu, she'd be a target, too. By the way, Antoine, what's she to you?"

"A friend."

"Not romantic, old boy?"

"Well . . . it wasn't initially. I meet women all the time, but Meena's different. I admit there was a strong attraction from the beginning. But I was with Liv then and I thought it was mostly physical. Then as I got to know her, I found out that she's quite exceptional—really the most exciting woman I've ever met. The contrast between her and Liv made me reexamine my whole life. And in the process I think I've discovered who I want to spend it with. I can't lose Meena now."

"What about Liv?"

"I broke off with her a couple of weeks ago. Seems like ages now—"

"No wonder I haven't heard much from you these past few months," Deepak said. "You obviously have been going through a lot. Now that I've been married for fifteen years, I've forgotten what it's like to be single. In any case, as you know, when it comes to romance we do things differently here. We move a lot slower. When I was growing up, there was very little dating. I used to meet a classmate of mine in the college library to study together. Then we'd take a walk in the park. That went on for a long time. Then one day I got enough courage to hold her hand. There was something in her touch. I knew my life had changed. I stayed up all night just thinking about her. We got married five years later. You see, we Indians are sentimental people. We tend to follow where our hearts lead. It worked for me. My marriage has been happy. And it seems to me that's the direction you're taking too. Maybe your time in India wasn't wasted after all." Deepak's chuckle was audible.

Antoine smiled in spite of himself. Deepak hadn't changed a bit. "Right now my heart is leading me in the direction of Calcutta."

"You'll have to act quickly. The Calcutta police expect the Moxans to stir up trouble pretty soon. When all this is finished, be sure to stop in Jaipur. My little ones can't wait to meet Uncle Antoine from America. We'll all be waiting for you. And be careful, old friend. Life is cheap to the Moxans."

"I'll catch the next available flight to Calcutta," Antoine said. "Once things settle down there, I'll come and visit you. We have a lot of catching up to do. And the idea of being an uncle is already growing on me."

As soon as the connection was broken, Antoine dialed an 800 number, silently thanking his mother for providing it—though Lord knew this was not the purpose she intended.

Against a background of sitar music, a woman's melodic voice delivered a recorded message: "For honeymoon, anniversary, or simply a break in your routine, there's No Place Like India. . . ."

A man with a strong Indian accent cut in. "No Place Like India Travel Agency. Pran speaking."

"My name is Antoine Peterson. I want to make a reservation."

"You're Sybil Peterson's son, aren't you? Your mother said you're honeymooning in India. So glad you called. I have an excellent deal for you. If you want to impress your new wife, reserve the master suite in Jaipur's Sitabagh Palace. It's the best. I have the screen in front of me. Let me read it to you: Marble bath, moonlight serenade, peacocks on the grounds . . ."

"Forget the honeymoon," Antoine said. "The wedding's off. I just want to go to Calcutta. When is the next flight?"

"Sorry to hear that, Mr. Peterson. Wait just one moment, please. Let me call up the chart of . . . Ah, yes, I can get you on tomorrow afternoon's flight from San Francisco International. It'll arrive at Calcutta early Monday evening. Do you need a hotel, too?"

"Yes, the Grand Bengal Hotel."

"Sorry, Mr. Peterson. The Grand Bengal's all booked. They're having an international film festival in Calcutta this week."

Antoine thumped his fist on the table. One would expect a film fest in New York or Cannes, not in Calcutta. Then the next moment he thought, how could he forget the Apu Trilogy of Satyajit Ray? Yes, Calcutta was a big cinema town with a fine reputation for producing art films. "Get me the closest hotel, then," he said.

"That would be the Park. About a ten- or fifteen-minute walk. Anything else, Mr. Peterson?"

Antoine sat in thought for a moment. "Book me a flight to Jaipur the following week and . . . uh . . . reserve that suite. I could cancel it, couldn't I?"

"Sure, Mr. Peterson. Just fax the hotel. They don't have e-mail yet, but they soon will. They'll reserve a chauffeur and a car for your use twenty-four hours a day, if you ask. But if you want to use a camel for your transport, arrange that when you get there."

Antoine laughed. "A camel sounds better."

Pran completed the formalities and wished him a pleasant journey.

Antoine put the phone down with a feeling of anticipation mixed with accomplishment.

This flight would put him in Calcutta a few hours before Meena's arrival. With luck he'd be able to catch her right away and alert her to the impending danger of associating with Moxans—and with Vishnu Chauhan.

37

For the last five hours Meena had traveled huddled in the backseat of a car through a hot, dry, featureless landscape in shades of yellow and ochre and brown. Along the way she'd seen occasional hills or villages or ridges of sand dunes, but mostly open spaces dotted with dry scrub, cactus, and babul trees. Their car would occasionally swerve off the road, to avoid trucks that rampaged toward them. Every two hours they'd stop at one of the roadside *dhaba* cafés to have *chai*, samosa, and newspaper-wrapped roasted chickpeas. Now they were jouncing over a potholed two-lane road that she remembered as no more than a narrow track through the desert. But the heat hadn't changed. It blurred her vision and made her drowsy.

She was frazzled from the three days of travel that had begun with an exhausting flight from San Francisco. Overnight in Seoul, then a direct flight to New Delhi where she had immediately caught a night train to Bikaner—the same train she had taken decades ago with the bandits, only going in the opposite direction. She hadn't slept in the train this time either, being filled with the same anguished thoughts. Once in the bustling town of Bikaner, she hired a man to drive her to Karamgar. The obsequious man with oiled hair proved to be a cautious driver and seemed to know his way across the desert. He spoke English fluently except when it came to masculine/feminine forms. He kept calling her "sir." With him guiding her, she was about to complete the final leg of a journey twenty-eight years into the past. It was an eerie feeling.

"That's Karamgar." The driver nodded toward a cluster of houses far away.

Meena jerked upright at his words, neck stiff from leaning against the car window. Her hair was pinned up in a chignon and she was aware of its weight. She was thirsty. Eyes burning, armpits stained with sweat, she felt completely miserable. Her ankle-length skirt, supple and smooth just hours ago, was as limp as a day-old crepe.

She felt a sense of elation at the somehow familiar sight of a young herdsman, stick in hand, cajoling his floppy-eared goats across the road in front of their car. The car screeched to a halt and the driver muttered a curse. Her mood brightened even further as they passed a camel-pulled cart bearing a dozen village women who stared curiously at her. A flash of dark skin, dazzling colors, veiled faces. How they resembled the people she grew up with. The smell in the air was familiar too. A mixture of sun-baked animal dung and urine and desert dust. Thin-bodied pilgrims trudged along with bundles balanced on their heads. Meena wondered at how seemingly oblivious they were to the blazing sun overhead.

The driver, who obviously had seen it all before, was nearly as energetic as when the trip had begun. A colorfully decorated truck came toward them belching a cloud of fumes. As it careened past, horn blaring, it nearly sideswiped them. Meena caught a glimpse of a painting of Lord Shiva glued to the hood with the word *om* inscribed below. Just at that moment, her driver avoided certain disaster by swerving onto the narrow shoulder of the road.

He smiled in relief. "It's okay, sir, not to worry," he said. "Lord Shiva saved us. Do you know about Lord Shiva? He's our highway god. Every morning before I start, I pray to him: *Om namah Shivaya.* Is this your first time here?"

"It's my first time back," Meena said. How strange that sounded. Until now she had always said she was a San Franciscan.

He looked over his shoulder and glanced at her inquisitively. "Many people leave their village, go to big cities. Few return."

Meena was puzzled by his words. Karamgar was India to her. She wanted to breathe the air, smell the earth, absorb the place again through all her senses if only for the memory.

A village sprang up from nowhere. "We're passing Vijaygar on the right," the driver said.

Vijaygar. That was as far as she had ever gone as a child.

The driver turned off the main road, making a screeching turn to the left. And there it was. Whitewashed houses loomed up before her, and shrubbery dusted a golden brown by the desert sand. The throaty music of a frog rang in her ears.

The driver pulled over under the partial shade of an overgrown babul hedge and came round to her side to help her out of the car. She started to put her foot on the ground and almost stepped on what she thought was a clump of soil but proved to be a tiny snake. It slithered away. A simple snake. She relaxed a little, straightened the cotton skirt that clung to her legs, and found herself stumbling on a heap of dried camel droppings. Of course, camel droppings. Her whole childhood came flashing back to her. The breeze that always rose up in the afternoon and tasted of desert dust now filtered through her hair. The sun that was once a loving god warmed her forehead. How right everything was. How perfect.

"Do you know where you want to go?" the driver asked.

She shook her head. She knew the bushes, the rocks, the hills beyond. But the village ahead looked no different from the ones seen on the way—mud and redbrick houses scattered through an open land, buffaloes roaming. Nothing to make it distinctively Karamgar.

A young schoolboy with enormous eyes ran along the dirt path carrying his books in a shoulderbag made from a grain sack. That was the way Vishnu used to go to school. The boy stared at the taxi, then at her, eyes bulging in awe. He asked in Hindi, "What do you want?"

Meena stammered an answer in Hindi, but the boy just stood there staring at her as though something were missing in her speech. Hindi and Rajasthani—those used to be her mother languages. Now they sounded strange coming from her mouth. "Please tell him I'm looking for my mother, Gangabai Devi," she said to the driver in English. "She was a seamstress."

The driver and the boy exchanged words, heads tilting, eyebrows rising, hands gesturing. Meena listened hard for any phrase whose meaning she could catch. Finally the boy shook his head in a vigorous no.

The driver spoke. "He says he hasn't heard that name."

"My mother made clothes for the kids. She embroidered their names in their baby saris. Everyone in the village came to her."

The driver talked to the boy.

"His mother buys readymade clothes for him. But he'll take us into the village."

They walked up the path with the boy in the lead and the driver scurrying along by her side. Off to the left was a new temple with a concrete cone top. On the right was a long block of brick buildings with no character. Ahead was an asphalt road lined with tin shacks and mud dwellings with roofs thatched in pampas grass. In her absence the village had doubled, maybe tripled in size. Where was the one-room school building? The old yellowstone temple whose top radiated a golden aura at sunset? The millet fields that should be turning green by now?

Meena said, "Our house was by the well."

The driver talked to the boy. "He says there's no well."

No well? The well was at the center of everything. It was a circular opening in the ground, barely three feet in diameter, walled with brick. Every morning the women gathered there to draw their daily supply of water. Barefoot with bells at their ankles, they'd be swathed in full skirts of outrageous red and orange and yellow that glowed in the sun. Their dark hair and flashy earrings peeked through the sheer iridescent scarves that covered their heads. They filled the pitchers with water, their minds with news and gossip. With graceful steps they returned to their homes, shiny brass vessels heavy on their heads, eyes straight ahead. Meena had watched the procession and dreamed of the day when she'd grow up and carry water. Only then would she be allowed to move in with Vishnu and his family. Already Mataji had taught her how to balance a pitcher on her head.

On the opposite side of the street there stood a long-handled pump barely three feet high. "Tubewell," the boy said, pointing. He rushed to it and levered the handle until water gushed out. Meena made a cup of her hands, drank deeply, and splashed the remainder on her face. As she did so, she went back in time to when she was tiny. Mataji would hold a glass of well water to her mouth to sip from. This clear earth-water tasted the same.

She had missed it. Without knowing it, she had been thirsty all these years.

Now they paraded past a brand-new two-story structure with a mud fence and wrought iron gate. Curious young eyes peeked out of latticework grilled windows on the second floor. So that was the school building. Meena lingered.

From the grocery shop next door, the perfume of newly harvested rice wafted on the breeze. A man sat cross-legged on a mat, weighing lentils on a scale, a bundle of old newspapers beside him to wrap the purchases. Meena remembered huddling with Grandfather to listen to the news that someone read from the single newspaper that was brought to the village.

A teenage boy in dark polyester slacks and short-sleeved shirt came out of the shop. Maybe he could direct Meena where she wanted to go. She turned to the driver, who talked to the teenager for a minute. The boy yelled at someone and soon several men emerged from shops and houses lining the road. They tagged along with Meena and the driver, chatting animatedly and waving their hands to embellish their points. It was as if having this stranger in town was a big event and they would forsake their daily chores to be a part of it. Still no one had a clue as to where Meena's house was.

"Perhaps if we asked some of the older people here," Meena offered.

A young woman passed by. At the sight of the men she quickly wrapped her shoulder scarf over her head and across her lower face. Without conscious thought Meena pulled a scarf from her purse and did the same. Mataji had taught Meena how to use face veils when she was barely able to walk. Often viewed by Westerners as exotic and mysterious, they had a practical use after all, Meena well remembered. The sheer fabric reduced unwanted attention from men, giving a woman her serenity, her privacy even in a crowd.

They came to a small rose-pink brick house. Plain as it was, it dazzled in the sunlight. The yard had a homey feel: a clothesline, scattered bushes with flowers blooming, an ox bellowing. An old woman sat on the front steps. A desiccated, leathery face was all that was visible among the folds of her widow's all-white sari. Her skin had an unhealthy grayish cast to it. But her eyes were two pieces of black onyx set deep in their sockets. At the boy's urging the driver approached and began to query her. As he did, she glanced at Meena again and again. Suddenly a smile broke through the thousand lines that mapped her weather-beaten face.

Meena drew nearer to the woman. Her entourage of men retreated to a respectful distance save for the driver.

"She is your father's cousin," the driver said. "She remembers your mother, Gangabai. You were such a pretty little girl, she says. All these years she has been waiting for you."

Auntie Teelu. Of course.

The woman rose slowly, supported by the boy. The pain in her face indicated that her body was failing. Straining forward, she took Meena in her thin arms and held her. It had been twenty-eight years since Meena had been embraced by a blood relative. At first she felt an awkwardness, but it soon melted away. A certain and absolute joy rose from deep within.

Auntie Teelu gestured Meena to take a seat by her side, saying softly, "Meena dear, I knew you'd be back before I died."

"And my mother," Meena burst out eagerly, "where is she?"

Auntie Teelu averted her eyes and dabbed at them with the fall of her sari silently.

"Auntie, would you please tell me where my mother is?" Meena said with a trace of impatience. "I came all the way from the States for her."

Now Auntie Teelu spoke rapidly, her voice betraying a trace of anger. The driver translated, "My dear little niece, didn't you know those bandits killed your mother? And your grandfather was so heart-broken he died within a month. He talked about you all the time. Where were you? Why couldn't you have come back sooner?"

Shocked and dizzy and crying inside, Meena said, "I wanted to, but I didn't know my way. I couldn't even find Karamgar on a map. And nobody I asked had ever heard of this village. You must forgive me, Auntie Teelu."

She wondered about their house, which Mataji used to call Meena Kumari Cottage. Where was it? As the sole surviving member of her family it was her duty to touch the soil, to honor her ancestors who had passed their days there. She asked, "How far is our house from here? I want to go there at once."

The driver talked to Auntie Teelu, then translated, "Your house was where the school building is now."

How foolish Meena had been to hope that her house would still be there, that she would be able to stand on the plot, to her the most precious on earth. She had been raised in a Western culture. Yet the invisible bond to her family and place of birth was so strong that she had tracked both down after all these years—only to find that not a trace of her people or her house remained. Suddenly the afternoon light looked too bright. Meena buried her face in the scarf to hide her tears.

Auntie Teelu touched Meena's hand and spoke to her more gently. Meena barely understood and yet she knew what Auntie Teelu was saying. "All gone, my child. Time has taken everything. We cannot fight time. We can only remember."

Auntie Teelu whispered to the driver, who translated. "She's asking if you'd honor her by going inside."

Visit Auntie Teelu's home? Of course Meena would. Nothing else was left in this village that she could own, relate to, cling to. And she needed something to help her recover from the tumult going on inside her.

"I'll wait just outside," the driver said. The men and the boys were milling about in front.

Following Auntie Teelu's example, Meena took her sandals off and deposited them by the entrance. A perfume of cumin emanated from the kitchen in the back. The sitting room was spotless and, with windows shut, cooler and dimmer than outside. The floor was covered with a woven cane mat that felt smooth under her bare feet. A stool, a hard-backed chair, and a bed with a paisley print cover were the only furniture. On one wall hung a framed picture of Lord Rama with a fresh marigold wreath draped in a semicircle over it. A simple life, yet lived with grace, Meena thought.

Auntie Teelu gestured toward the chair Meena knew was meant for the most important guest. As she settled herself, Auntie Teelu called out to someone. A young woman, possibly her granddaughter, appeared in the doorway. She was tall, with gray-green eyes, high cheekbones, and hair down to her waist. Meena was seeing a younger version of herself. This was her family.

"My name is Nishi," the woman said in halting English. She knelt and lowered her head before Meena in a gesture that showed respect to older family members. Her right palm swept Meena's feet. Nishi then touched her own forehead with the symbolic mote of dust. Now Meena was the elder, to be honored with this ritual. With hesitation, she placed her hands on Nishi's head to bless her. Her mind went back to the days when, as a child, she herself had acknowledged her elders this way. Three decades later it still felt natural. Nishi rose slowly.

Sitting on the stool grinning, Auntie Teelu spoke. The driver who had camped in the doorway translated. "I missed you very much. All this time where have you been?"

"An American couple found me on a train," Meena said. "They took me with them to San Francisco."

"How lucky. Were they rich? Did they take good care of you?"

Speaking in bursts of small sentences Meena gave Auntie Teelu an outline of the events of her life in the U.S. Auntie Teelu kept nodding. She understood and accepted her story, she seemed to be saying, as though that were the only logical way things could have worked out for Meena.

"What work do you do?" Auntie Teelu asked finally.

"I work with computers."

Auntie Teelu's face brightened. With the affection of a mother whose child has won a trophy she said, "How proud I am of you. How proud your mother would have been. I'm so glad you're back." Then in a wavering voice, "My health isn't good. Now that I have seen you, my child, I can die in peace."

"No, Auntie Teelu, you must not die," Meena cried out, but almost immediately understood that death held no fear for Auntie Teelu. It was simply passing on to another phase in the cycle of life.

Nishi left only to return toting a pale blue quilted bundle. "A boy," she said, proudly exposing her son's face. Meena held her arms out. She felt alternately buoyant and nervous holding a baby of her own blood. The red, wrinkly boy, who looked well cared for, was only a few days old and had a milky-sweet baby smell. As she listened to his breath, tender motherly instincts surfaced that she didn't know she had. He opened his eyes, regarded her face, gurgled, reached out with one hand, then let out a howl.

The driver said, "A singer in the making."

Everyone laughed. The baby became drowsy again and Meena handed him back to Nishi. She disappeared, but came back shortly carrying a tray of steaming teacups. Ah, a brisk and fruity-flavored tea. As Meena sipped it with gusto, she noticed a woman clad in a sunflower yellow sari appear in the doorway. Two teenage girls stood beside her in long flared skirts, silver chains on their ankles. The woman looked vaguely familiar. From the vermilion dot on her forehead and the matching daub in the part of her hair Meena could gather that she was married and a Hindu. Her features were on the plain side, her cheeks pockmarked from childhood acne. But she carried herself well and wore the contented expression of someone who passed her days without complaint. One of her daughters handed Nishi a tray of curd and golden *laddoo* balls. Meena watched as a small table appeared from nowhere and was placed before her. The woman arranged the food on the table and smiled brightly.

"Do you remember her?" the driver asked. "Her name is Janu. She was married at the same time you were. You two sat across from each other at the wedding."

The memory of Janu, a childhood neighbor, flashed before Meena's eyes. The tiny bride who had jumped out of her seat, crying just before her wedding because she hated her bully of a groom. And here she was, showing Meena an image of what life could have been.

Meena and Janu beamed at each other and clasped hands. Janu proudly introduced her two teenage daughters. One of them brought a basin of water, washed Meena's palms, and for the next half hour painted intricate designs on them with brownish green henna paste. "Look, the paste is turning red." The teenager drew everybody's attention.

"Do you know what that means?" Janu asked Meena. "Somebody loves you."

Meena knew she was blushing, but noticed how everyone was enjoying her presence and participation.

Next, the teenager varnished Meena's toenails a red ochre with a natural dye. Just what Mataji did for her on her wedding day. In her mind Meena smelled the sandalwood incense, heard the bells of her anklets, felt the silken touch of her wedding skirt. She wanted to dance.

The other daughter squeezed Meena's hands and slid a cluster of beaded bracelets past them onto her wrists. When Meena moved her arms, her bracelets jangled, the gentle sound taking her further back into her early years.

Neighbors came and went. The room swirled with sari colors so bright as to chase away any trace of gloom from the corners. Most, as it turned out, were aunts, cousins, or old friends Meena could barely remember. A few strangers came too, out of curiosity, just to look her over, Meena knew. She was getting the biggest welcome of her life from everyone. Well, almost everyone. A woman in a coarse brown sari was throwing hostile glances at her from the back. Who was she?

The driver was still in the doorway. He was too shy to share the mat with the women who had formed a circle around Meena. They nudged and jostled each other, tried to speak to her all at the same time. "Meenu, Meenu," they called her, using an endearing form of her name. Meena pushed her chair aside and joined them on the floor. She answered by smiling and linking arms. A woman produced notes on a harmonium and the whole group began belting out a happy folk song.

"They are welcoming you," the driver said. "The same way they welcome the monsoon and the full moon."

Meena hummed along at first, then poured her heart out. Her head swayed from side to side, her hand pumped the air. They helped her when she mispronounced the lyrics. For she had reestablished herself as one of the clan, bound by music, by culture, by blood. Her voice was in harmony with those of others, if not all her words.

Children carrying schoolbooks poured through the door. Alive faces, open eyes, eager movements. The driver explained they had been given a recess so they could meet a former resident of the village, a computer expert who had returned.

"Hello, how are you?" In cheery tones they took turns practicing their schoolbook English.

"Very well, thank you," Meena affected a schoolgirl tone.

Notebooks opened up before her. "Your name, please . . ."

"What city?" one boy asked. "New York?"

"No, San Francisco." Meena had to write that down too.

A round-faced girl appeared, pinned a tiny flag of India on Meena's left shoulder, then scurried away to hide behind other children. Just the way Meena would have acted in her own shy, sweet days of youth. Her mouth widened into a warm smile, her cheeks became slippery with tears.

The children were seated. Nishi brought out more refreshments and everyone joined in the celebration. Meena picked at a *laddoo*, sweet, filling, and crunchy. After all these years it was her most favorite confection still.

"You're an American," a woman said, "but you feel the same way we do."

"But she's too skinny," another teased. "She should eat more *laddoos*."

The children giggled, teacups clinked, laughter erupted. Then it struck Meena that no one had mentioned Vishnu or his parents so far. With Mataji gone, they'd be like her parents. "How are Mr. and Mrs. Chauhan?" Meena asked Nishi. "I was married to their son, Vishnu."

"Vishnu is well," a woman announced. "He's a good boy. He sends his mother a money order every month. He has built a new temple for us."

"He writes for a big newspaper," another offered. "His stories are about people who have very little. Like us. He has never forgotten where he came from."

The room was alive with praises for Vishnu. Everyone was wishing him a long, healthy life. Meena took comfort in that. She definitely wanted to visit Vishnu's mother, whom she had always liked. She took a bite of another *laddoo* and asked, "How is Mrs. Chauhan?"

The room grew silent. No one responded. Several women looked furtively at the brown sari. When the driver persisted, Auntie Teelu waved a dismissive hand and spoke tersely. Meena put her half-eaten *laddoo* aside and turned a questioning eye to the driver. He said, "Mr. Chauhan died years ago. Mrs. Chauhan lives at the other end of the village. She has caught malaria."

Malaria? That was how Meena's own father had died. She was filled with concern. "Could I visit her?"

The driver repeated her words in Hindi to Auntie Teelu, who clenched her jaws. He probed further. "Mrs. Chauhan will not receive you," he said at last. "She curses you because you deserted your husband." He coughed and looked off into the distance.

Deserted her husband? Meena lowered her eyes in dismay. Bandits had kidnapped her. She didn't leave on her own. How could they have held a seven-year-old responsible all these years? Her only consolation was that half the village, at least the people in this room, hadn't rejected her.

The woman in brown stood up, pointed a crooked finger at Meena, bared yellow teeth, and yelled, "You've ruined your family name. And you have the nerve to come back." She began hurling insults so loud that a little girl started to cry and was carried out of the room. The driver threw his hands up in the air and quit translating.

Family reputation, that always came first, Meena realized. Perhaps her relatives like Auntie Teelu had also been chastised. Meena could see that the village had progressed much, but old attitudes, meaningless traditions still gripped its residents. Now furious, she stood up. "Be quiet, you spiteful old crone," she said to the brown sari. "What do you know? Was it you who was kidnapped, you whose wedding day became a nightmare, you who were alone in a vast city with no chance of finding your way home? *I* did nothing shameful. You're the one with nerve." The anger inside now burst forth lavalike in a torrent of words. She didn't know how long she spoke or whether anyone understood what she said. "I'm meeting with Vishnu in Calcutta after all these years. . . ." she muttered, breathless.

Meena sat down again, sweating, her heart palpitating. But she felt liberated, coming full circle, having explained it all, releasing the shame and anguish of the kidnapping from her heart.

Someone shoved the hostile woman out the door. "She's Vishnu's aunt," Nishi whispered. "Don't mind her. She has a sharp tongue, but she's harmless."

"Doesn't matter what she says," Janu added. "You'll always have a place in this village."

That was doubtful. Meena couldn't have lived peacefully in this tightly knit community even if the Gossetts had brought her back, it was now clear to her. She wouldn't have been accepted. She silently released Mom and Dad from any reproach.

The women chattered among themselves. The children fidgeted. Amid the din the driver reminded Meena that it was now two o'clock, time for her to get back to Bikaner to catch the overnight train to Delhi.

"No, no, don't go," the children clamored.

The women groaned, looking disappointed. "They want you to stay here tonight," the driver said. "Nishi says this is your home."

Meena reflected for a moment. It was hard to pull away. She could see the welcoming eyes, the kindness and simplicity in the faces around her. But she had intentionally planned a short visit here the first time around. She couldn't alter her schedule now. Vishnu was expecting her in Calcutta. With a sigh she rose. "I have to go. But I'll come back. I'll come back."

Auntie Teelu, assisted by Nishi, handed Meena an old and wrinkled sari, whose original white color was now a sad gray, its silver borders frayed. "This belonged to your mother," Auntie Teelu said. "She wore it on your wedding day. I saved it in her memory. It's now yours. Touch it. These threads still hold her life force." All the women bowed before the sari.

Meena drew the sari to her chest. Mataji's love enveloped her once again. Mataji had never left. An invisible support, she had helped Meena get to where she was today.

Stepping outside, Meena turned and waved a farewell. Auntie Teelu stood there gripping the doorframe, her eyes overflowing with tears. It was her final good-bye, Meena knew. She tore herself away.

The women and the children steered Meena down the road. They stopped at the schoolhouse just so Meena could spend a minute in silence recalling memories of her family. She felt a certain movement in the air, saw the wave of delicate cotton, the flash of a brass pot. Like Mataji passing by.

"You work with computers?" A boy with puffy cheeks interrupted the rush of thoughts in Meena's head. Other expectant young faces now surrounded her.

Meena must put her grief aside. She realized computers were omnipresent in big cities in India, but villages had yet to gain access to them. She had a sudden inspiration. What if she brought some portables and taught these children how to use them? That would be giving something back to her village. And it'd be a way to pay respect to Mataji and Grandfather.

The womenfolk and the children guided Meena to the "tubewell" so she could get a drink before returning to where the taxi was parked. The afternoon sky was showing its best golden-blue light and the breeze was still pleasantly warm. Meena felt the solid earth under her feet, raised her head to catch the sun's rays on her face, took a deep breath, and waved as she climbed into the car. The children jumped up to steal one last look at her through the window. "Come back soon," they cried.

"I will," she murmured, touching their hands. "I will. . . ." Her heart swelled so much she could say no more.

38

Late Monday morning found Vishnu bent over the keyboard on his desk cluttered with books, pamphlets, and newspaper clippings. His office was located in a remodeled room on a floor entirely occupied by the Moxans. Though not particularly spacious, it was furnished with a large round table, rickety stools, and a television. Occasionally a young Moxan would come in, take a seat, read the newspaper, watch television for a few minutes, then leave. Vishnu was finding it difficult to concentrate, but he was in no position to complain. The rough draft of the first issue of the weekly *Tribal Express* was due today. He had plenty of material, but no focus. Now and then he thought about Meena's imminent arrival and how nice it would be to finish this work and get ready to welcome her back.

He had spent the past week interviewing people, visiting the National Library and the State Archives, and plowing through the Archeological Survey of India in an exhaustive search for information on tribes in general and Moxans in particular. Reliable facts about Moxans were scarce. He had browsed through the tribe's own library, which included a considerable shelf of propaganda literature. To his surprise, he had come across a manual on RDX explosives. He quickly put it back before anyone noticed. He had felt as if he had touched a burning iron rod by mistake.

During his college years he had paid little attention to the suppressed tribal groups—"others," as they were called. Later his college degree and position as a newspaper reporter elevated him to a relatively high status in Hindu society. At parties he attended it was fashionable to talk about the cinema, water pollution, and latest models of cars, but not the plight of the four hundred or so indigenous groups who had lived in India since long before the Aryan invasion that had relegated them to the fringe of Indian society.

He had learned that the Moxans, one such indigenous group, were racially different from the dominant Hindu majority. Yes, they worshipped Lord Shiva, a Hindu god, but genetically, linguistically, and culturally they were much closer to the peoples of Myanmar and Thailand to the east.

He thought of his own forebears, the Sadras, a group of nomadic Rajput goatherds who had traditionally migrated with the changing of the seasons. Then climatic disruptions and the conversion of precious grazing land to agriculture had forced them to settle in Karamgar. Were Moxans that much different from Sadras? Both clung to a traditional lifestyle totally at variance with that of the Hindu majority bent on industrialization. Both married young and valued large families. Modern Hindus all over India frowned on this practice. Yes, Vishnu could feel a kinship to the Moxans.

Still he found himself unable to organize his thoughts. He was shuffling papers aimlessly and chewing his pencil in frustration when a young woman came by with tea. Oh, for heaven's sake. Another interruption. No choice but to put up with it, Vishnu thought. He looked up wordlessly. Gopa, the Bollywood Beauty, seated herself on the edge of a chair and tugged at her forest green chiffon sari to keep it modestly in place. Her shining hair was tasseled around her smooth cheeks. Vishnu thought again of Meena. Would she be wearing a beautiful sari like this? Be this modest? This beautiful?

Gopa finally looked expectantly up at Vishnu with her deep brown almond eyes. Suddenly he was glad to have an opportunity to speak to a Moxan woman, a pretty one at that. Head respectfully low, eyes averted in the old-fashioned way, Gopa whispered in Hindi, "I'd like to tell you about my project."

"I'd be most interested," Vishnu replied.

"To improve the deplorable condition of our female babies."

A pleasant change from the incessant talks about bombing and raiding. Vishnu found himself paying close attention.

"You see, the mortality rate for our female babies is much higher than that of the boys. Almost double."

My God. That had also been true in his village when he was

growing up. He remembered that his mother had lost twin girls shortly after birth. In recent years conditions for women in his village had improved. Still he couldn't help but think that, had Meena been with him, they'd probably have had five kids by now and, most likely, only three would have survived. Though the loss of Meena was a terrible one, perhaps it was just as well they hadn't stayed together.

Gopa's voice broke into Vishnu's thoughts. "Baby girls don't get vaccinated," she continued. "Parents don't feed them enough, don't take them to the doctor when they're sick. They're not sent to school. Ask any Moxan villager what kind of children he wants, he'll reply, 'Three boys and less than half a girl.' I'm reminded of the famous phrase by our beloved poet Uma Joshi. You know it, don't you?"

Vishnu had to admit he didn't.

"She called them 'secondhand sorrow,' because no one cries much if baby girls die." Gopa added that her job was to travel from village to village, advising Moxan mothers about proper diet and medical care for girls. Dhotia backed her. Many Moxan women had volunteered for her project. They all realized that change was long overdue.

Vishnu cringed when Gopa began reciting a litany of pitiful statistics from a document she had in her hand. And as he listened, there were times when he simply got lost in the passionate expression that suffused her copper face.

Abruptly she stopped. She rose with an embarrassed look on her face, as if she realized she had spoken too long. After a moment's silence, eyes still averted, she tentatively offered him her report. Vishnu accepted it in silence.

"You're most kind," she said softly and left.

Lord Rama, Vishnu said to himself as he looked at his watch. It was one o'clock and he still didn't have a draft ready. He put Gopa's document down on the table and turned to his keyboard. Furiously he began to type an article entitled "Where Are Our Little Girls?" The lead paragraphs were the story of his own two sisters and his mother's anguish at their untimely death. His words formed images so evocative they seemed to dance on the page. Finally, he had something to say.

How good it felt to be writing again. When he looked up, it was five o'clock. Vishnu scanned the finished draft and smiled to himself. This was one of the best pieces of writing he'd ever done. It would be sure to grab people's attention. The reporting was Gopa's and he gave her a byline too. Proudly he walked to Dhotia's office with the draft in hand.

Karun Dhotia sat hunched over his desk, eyes narrowed, worry furrowing deep creases into his forehead. He raised his eyes and said warmly, "Our group is happy to have you with us, Vishnu." He took the papers and glanced at the headline. "You're not ashamed of us, I hope."

"Quite the contrary," Vishnu said. "Gopa and what she's trying to do can only make the Moxan case stronger. By treating all children equally, your group will assume its rightful place in the world. If you hope to have support from the West, equality for women will be important to achieve."

Dhotia scanned the pages and turned at last to Vishnu with a big smile. "Just the kind of writing we need. Very good, very good . . ."

Pradip bustled into the office. Seeing them in close proximity, Vishnu couldn't help but compare the two. Pradip was clearly the lesser man, lacking both Dhotia's intelligence and his intensity. Vishnu thought Pradip was caught between the caution and wisdom of the older generation and the aggressive militancy of Moxan youth. It seemed he was still trying to find his own niche.

Ignoring Dhotia, Pradip said to Vishnu, "I need to speak to you before you leave."

"I'll be sure to catch you," Vishnu replied.

Pradip rushed out wordlessly.

Dhotia shook his head sadly. "These hotheaded young chaps," he said. "I have to deal with them all day. They still think that the road to Moxan independence will be littered with bombed-out police stations and dynamited railroad tracks."

Vishnu's latent worry surfaced again. "You won't let them do those crazy things, will you?"

"I'm doing my best, but my control is not absolute. Our cause is just, no doubt. And they are young and impatient. The government's refusal to consider our demands is not making this any easier."

"Aren't you meeting with the state government soon?"

"I have a joint meeting with the state government and the Center next week."

Vishnu knew the Center meant the national government in New Delhi. "Here's your chance," he said. "I can draw up a list of requests for them to consider—"

"Why should the Center make concessions to Moxans?" Dhotia's voice had a bitter edge.

"The election," Vishnu pressed on. "They're in a tight race and they need every vote they can get, even the tribal vote. Tell them you'll get every eligible Moxan to the polls this time. I have done a lot of digging into the whole tribal situation. My statistics show that if you form a coalition with other tribes in the state—" Vishnu quoted some figures.

"A lot of people talk like that."

"With a good newspaper it can be done," Vishnu said. "Show them the first issue of the *Tribal Express*. They'll see it speaks with a common voice for all tribes."

Dhotia's face brightened. "You may be onto something, Vishnu. It's certainly worth a try, considering the alternative."

Vishnu knew he was putting his own neck on the line by being associated with the Moxans and appearing to be antigovernment. "But you must understand, Dhotiaji, the minute these boys start getting violent, I leave."

"I'll do my best to keep them under control," Dhotia said. "But if it comes to that, you have my understanding and consent. You're not one of us, after all."

Vishnu rose from his seat hesitantly. "Do you suppose," he stammered, "I could get an advance on my salary? My mother is ill and . . ."

"Of course, of course," Dhotia said immediately. "I'll see to it right away." He left the room and returned in minutes with a stack of fifty-rupee bills which he slapped into Vishnu's palm.

Vishnu pocketed the money feeling more than a little discomfited. He hated to borrow money, even a two-week advance on his salary.

Just outside the door Pradip was talking to a young man with baleful eyes. At the sight of Vishnu their conversation trailed off. The young Moxan turned abruptly and strode off.

"What's going on?" Vishnu asked.

Pradip sidestepped the question. "How're you coming along with the newspaper?"

"The first issue is done—"

"Since you won't have another one to worry about for a few days," Pradip said, avoiding Vishnu's gaze, "it's time I got you involved in other projects."

Gopa passed by. The green train of her sari, embroidered with metallic threads, illuminated the dark narrow corridor like a shooting star.

Vishnu asked, "What other projects?"

"We'll talk about that later," Pradip said. "Meet me here tomorrow afternoon at five."

That late? Vishnu hesitated. He regularly worked till six. But Meena's latest e-mail said she'd arrive in Calcutta late tonight. He had planned to spend tomorrow evening with her. Still, he was new at his job and Dhotia had just given him an advance on his salary. "For how long?"

Pradip's pupils narrowed to beams of torchlight before his face assumed a noncommittal expression. He said smoothly, "Oh, only for a couple of hours."

39

Twenty-one exhausting hours in the air. It was Monday evening when Antoine watched through the window of his plane as it landed at Calcutta. The flight had been uneventful, routine, until he flicked to a certain page in the copy of *India News* he had grabbed from the plane's magazine rack. He'd planned a casual look through the paper to help pass the time and bring himself up to date on the big stories and scandals of India. He stumbled on a paragraph about a tourist, a possible informant for the police, being beheaded by a tribe somewhere east of Calcutta. Antoine didn't expect to be horrified by the news of this medieval-type killing. But he was. The next story, which was about the Indian Institute of Astrophysics conducting experiments to determine how solar energy worked, could hold his attention only temporarily.

Disembarking, he spotted the tricolored Indian flag hoisted on a pole, saffron for the Hindus, green for the Muslims, and white for the other faiths, fluttering in the evening breeze. In that moment his mind went back twenty-two years. He was once again the footloose college junior to whom India was a tragicomic street theater with no interval between performances. Anything could happen here and often did.

This was his return visit to India, his first ever to Calcutta, the biggest metropolis in the country. Whatever its reputation, he'd heard Calcutta was a city with a soul. He arrived fully prepared to open his own in return. But first things first. He'd check in at his hotel, unpack, shower, and grab a nap. He had flown halfway around the globe for Meena. From what Carlos had told him he had a few free hours before she was scheduled to arrive. Better to get whatever sleep he could.

The baggage claim area was an ocean of dark faces, all pushing and shoving. Relatives waiting at a distance in a roped-off area shouted greetings. Soldiers with rifles on their backs tried to maintain order by simply looking stern. Feeling quite alone, Antoine began scanning the faces. He couldn't tell the difference between Hindus, Muslims, tribals, and troublemakers. Just the same, fear of ethnic strife filled him with apprehension.

He stepped outside with his luggage. The weather was sticky, the temperature in the high eighties.

"This way, sir." Several taxi drivers spoke to him in unison.

"I have the best taxi," one man said. He was small and fine-featured with a blackberry sheen to his complexion and friendly enough manners.

Antoine let himself be led to a waiting taxicab. The cab's cream-colored top had turned café au lait from dust and soot, but the interior was a miniature temple complete with bells, incense, and figurines of Hindu deities arranged on the dashboard. Antoine was overpowered by the rich, cloying scent of sandalwood mixed with the smell of cow dung rising from the street. Yes, he had arrived in India.

The taxi driver swung around. "Where do you want to go?" His English, though accented, was easily understood, as though he had adopted the foreign tongue and made it his own offspring.

"The Park Hotel."

"Where are you from, sir?"

"San Francisco."

"Welcome to Calcutta," the driver said. "You're arriving here on a very special day. It's *Ram Navami.*"

"What's that?"

"The anniversary of the birth of Lord Rama."

Antoine said, "He killed Ravana, the enemy who stole his wife, Sita, didn't he?"

"Oh yes. And he was the seventh incarnation of Lord Vishnu."

The name startled Antoine. He thought of the other Vishnu, the human one, Meena's husband—if he could be called that. It was he, after all, who had indirectly brought Antoine back here.

Suddenly they turned onto a major thoroughfare and the noise level rose. The honking of cars, the jangling bells of the cycle rickshaws, the thundering of the motorcycles, all blended into a single discordant roar. Antoine's taxi weaved its way through the stream of traffic past several shantytowns, then through a middle-class suburb, dodging pedestrians and animals and vehicles all along the way. A wild-eyed bull bolted into the road and came to a halt right in front of the taxi, rigid with fear. The driver blasted his horn, then yelled in Bengali at the bull, which seemed to come to its senses at the sound of his voice and lumbered off to the side of the road. Antoine was at first amazed, then amused at the idea of a Bengali-speaking bull.

"He does this every day," the driver said. "He isn't a bad bull. He just gets confused."

It must have been this way for centuries, Antoine thought with a chuckle. People and animals living side by side like quarreling brothers, each knowing it couldn't do without the other. Antoine resigned himself to a long ride to the hotel. He sat back as he took in the vibrant street life unfolding around him like scenes from a slow-motion movie.

A procession came toward the taxi, its main focus a life-sized statue of a god in the back of a pickup truck. A bare-chested boy twisted sinuously forward and back in dance movements before the statue. The crowd behind clapped rhythmically in a ritual that, Antoine perceived, lifted their lives from the mundane.

The taxi slowed to a near halt as a tall laborer with snarled hair, naked except for a loincloth, crossed the street with a bundle of sugarcane sticks, six feet long with spiky ends, on his head. He strolled serenely, a sadhu out of rhythm with the procession. Amazingly, he hit no one with the sticks. This chaos didn't reach him at all. Antoine wished he possessed the man's secret.

The car stopped at a traffic light. Music erupted from a loudspeaker mounted above the entrance to a shop and assaulted Antoine's ears. The Hindi film song, probably lip-synched by some curvaceous cinema actress, was laughable in its overdone eroticism, not warmly arousing as it was intended to be. Antoine's eyes watered as acrid charcoal smoke from a clay stove on the sidewalk drifted in through the open car window. Along with the smoke came the smell of freshly baked flat bread. A young woman in a yellow-orange sari browned the puffy *roti* rounds over the fire. Her deep eyes and rhythmic gestures reminded him of Meena. He yearned for fresh bread made just for him.

He was seeing Calcutta life as it was—in black and white, red and gold, in the mixed bright colors of reality. The truth wore no clothes here.

Could he drop the excesses of his California life and get down to basic living in a place like this? Antoine wondered. Just him and Meena and India?

Nearer the heart of the metropolis, the taxi gained speed. There came wide paved roads, sorbet-colored colonial buildings, flickering neon signs mounted high above the street advertising everything from shoe polish to computers. Computers. That was synonymous with Meena in Antoine's mind. And there were billboards on every street corner. One that caught Antoine's attention said, "Why not forget everything and go to the film fest?"

Now they were passing through a neighborhood street with buildings that had a faded, ancient look. At this evening hour, many businesses had shuttered their doors, but the sweetshops—and there seemed to be one on every corner—still stood wide open. Antoine could see those famous Bengali delicacies in the display cases, jewel-like in white, yellow, and maroon shot with silver flecks. Shoppers rushed in and out with faces that bore some degree of seriousness. Sweets were not to be taken lightly. Antoine had tried similar ones while living in Jaipur. He remembered his pleasure even though he couldn't remember their taste.

His large modern hotel was located on a boulevard packed with shops and restaurants. The hotel lobby was calm and orderly in contrast to the streets. Registering took but a minute. A hollow-jawed bearer with sandals that flapped at each step picked up his luggage and led him toward the elevator. The man's face was impassive. Antoine couldn't tell his age or anything about him.

His room was austere. Nothing but a double bed, a dresser, a desk and straight chair, a closet, and floors that gleamed in the light from the ceiling. Indians kept their floors dusted and polished. Antoine liked that.

The bearer set the luggage down and said, "The restaurant is now open, babu-sahib."

Babu-sahib, that was a doubly respectful address. Antoine took a wad of rupee notes out of his wallet and pressed a few into the bearer's palm. The man touched his forehead with the colorful bills in salutation, then backed away. Antoine examined one of the bills. The amount was written in thirteen languages, including English.

He unpacked, showered, and changed. Should he call Meena? He looked at the clock on the night table. No, she hadn't arrived yet. And when she did, she'd be exhausted. He decided to visit her first thing tomorrow morning.

For now he went to the desk, picked up a notepad and a pen, and switched on the reading lamp. Time to work on his Munich novel. He hadn't touched it for weeks. He started a sentence, hoping more would follow. He completed a paragraph, corrected a couple of words, crossed the whole thing out and stood up. Everything he had written was crap.

He couldn't face a blank page again until he had some coffee. No, tea would be easier on his nerves at this hour. *Chai*, and time to collect himself. Calling room service seemed like a big production, so he headed downstairs.

The large ivory-colored dining room had whirling overhead fans. It was ten o'clock on a weeknight and the place was still buzzing with patrons. Antoine was reminded that Indians dined late, when it was cooler, much like himself. He was invariably at his creative best as the day wore on. A tall waiter, whose milky white turban rose above his dark features like a dove, seated Antoine at a table for four. Two Indians, a man and his woman companion, were already there, lingering over the remains of their meal.

The man, about thirty and dressed in fine cotton, had a robust laugh and confident manner. Alternately speaking in Hindi and English, he turned to share jokes with the patrons seated at the adjoining table. His sari-clad companion tossed her licorice black hair as she joined in the laughter. They were obviously having a wonderful time and Antoine, still disoriented from the long flight and more than a bit lonely, found himself listening unabashedly.

The woman opened her pack of Wills filter-tipped. As the man lit her cigarette with his lighter, the ruby ring on his left middle finger flashed a red highlight. "Wouldn't it be nice if we," he said in English, then finished the sentence in Hindi. The woman nodded her agreement. Antoine was dying to know the rest, but he could only guess at the meaning.

The waiter took Antoine's order for tea, then spoke questioningly to the man in a language that sounded different from Hindi.

The man turned to face Antoine. "You ordered *chai*, didn't you?"

Antoine said yes.

"Shall I tell him to bring real *chai*, which we call ready-made *chai*, or hot water and a teabag? Most foreigners don't care for tea the Indian way. The waiter wants to make sure. He speaks Bengali. His English is very limited."

"A teabag!" Antoine gasped. "That's what I use in San Francisco. Here I want the real thing."

The man grinned and spoke to the waiter, then turned back to Antoine. "So, you're from the States. My uncle lives there. He's a senior research scientist with AT&T. He's constantly asking me to move there, but I tell him we've got plenty of opportunities here."

"It seems a lot has changed recently," Antoine said. "I lived in Jaipur for a year when I was going to college. There weren't as many opportunities then."

Almost instantly the waiter arrived. He set a white porcelain cup on the table along with a teapot whose handle was pointed straight toward Antoine—must be the correct way to place it, Antoine guessed—and grandly gestured toward an accompanying plate of white fudge, saying in halted English, "Here some *sandesh*."

Antoine took a slow, appreciative sip of the spicy tea, then bit into the fudge, which turned out to be filled with mango puree. He closed his eyes in delight.

His tablemate apparently still wanted to talk. "My name's Saat, short for Satya. And this is my friend, Kalpana."

Antoine vaguely recalled that satya was an important word in Sanskrit, meaning truth, part of an ancient phrase. Truth, Shiva, Beauty. Finally he said simply, "I'm Antoine Peterson."

"Your name sounds familiar," Kalpana remarked. "What do you do?"

After a moment's hesitation Antoine said, "I'm a novelist."

"How interesting," Kalpana said. "Are your books available here?"

"I don't know," Antoine said. "But I can give you the names." He named his two books.

"Oh, my goodness. I've seen those titles in a College Street store window," Kalpana said excitedly. "I must pick them up."

Her interest seemed genuine. Antoine's initial discomfort with the unsolicited conversation eased. He said, "Tell me, is there much of a market for American novels here?"

"Most educated people in India have studied English since childhood," Kalpana said. "They have a voracious appetite for almost any book written in English. And there is a growing interest in fiction by American authors."

He was mulling that over when Saat asked, "How long are you going to be here?"

"Hard to say," Antoine replied. "I'm here to meet a friend from San Francisco."

Saat asked, "He lives here?"

"It's a she. She's traveling here. She's a software engineer."

"That's my field, too," Saat piped up. "I'm a salesman for an up-and-coming software firm."

"Is there much of a market for computer software here?"

"Oh, yes. There's a tremendous demand for personal computers and software. It's primarily due to our newly affluent middle class, which is almost the size of your entire population, you know. And every one of them seems to want to have a computer and get on the Internet. An enterprising fellow can make a fortune. No need to go to America."

Antoine, more than a little surprised, could only manage, "I didn't realize that."

"And Calcutta might become the multimedia capital of India," Saat said, warming to his subject. "Our first national CD-ROM conference was held here recently. Even my two cousins, who have been working in Silicon Valley since they graduated from Berkeley, are moving back. A reverse brain drain, you might say." Saat chuckled. "If your friend ever needs a job . . ." He fished a card from his shirt pocket and handed it to Antoine ceremoniously. "My company is always looking for competent software specialists. We're especially interested in U.S.-trained people."

Saat's exuberant manner was infectious. Antoine rolled his shoulders to release the tension that had built up from the long flight, sat back, and asked, "What types of software does your company specialize in?"

"Many kinds. Currently our most popular offering is a horoscope analysis package. HAPI—Horoscope Analysis Program International. I use that program myself to predict my good and bad days. Recently we added a new feature that would chart a prospective mother-in-law's luck." He grinned broadly and winked. "As you can see, we have a diverse clientele."

Antoine laughed heartily. At that moment the waiter brought the checks. Over Antoine's protests Saat grabbed his too.

"Oh no no, please. You've been our guest tonight." Saat slipped a stack of rupee notes into the waiter's hand, then checked his gold watch. The wide watchband was intricately carved with stylized images of humans, animals, trees, and flowers, likely an illustration from Hindu mythology. Turning back to Antoine, he added, "By the way, would you be interested in coming to our chummery party Saturday night? It would be an excellent opportunity for you to re-acquaint yourself with India as it is today."

"Chummery party?"

"I share a flat with Kalpana and one other roommate. The newspapers call that type of an arrangement a chummery, from the word 'chum.' "

"You're right," Antoine said, surprised. "India has changed. And I do have some catching up to do. I'd be delighted."

"It's quite common in big cities for men and women to share accommodations," Saat said. "For us it's working out quite well. Strictly platonic, of course."

"I suppose you think we're getting more and more westernized," Kalpana said, puffing on her cigarette. "But we keep our old ways, too. Tomorrow night I'll visit my parents. My mother will sprinkle water from River Ganga on my head and I won't smoke there. Smoking in front of one's elders is a sign of disrespect."

"India has somehow managed to retain its old traditions when so many countries have abandoned theirs," Antoine said. "When I'm here, my initial impression is I'm in another century. Then I see how Indians are taking modern ideas and new technology and adapting them to their own ways. It's all very fascinating."

"Hope we get a chance to talk some more," Saat said. "We really have to go now. It's getting late and I have to be at work early tomorrow morning." He rose, shook Antoine's hand. "The address is on my card. Just tell the taxi driver you want to go to Gol Park."

Kalpana smiled warmly. "Very nice meeting you." Her sari rustled and its gold embroidery reflecting the light from the candles on the tables cast an undulating flaming pattern on the walls as she walked away with Saat.

Antoine lingered over his tea for several minutes, then eased out of his chair and headed for the elevator. An Indian family of four got in just as the door was about to close. The woman wore an exquisite lavender sari set off by finely tooled gold bracelets, several on each arm. Her little girl in a lacy white frock gawked at Antoine, conveying how odd he must appear to her. The boy whispered something in his mother's ear in yet another language that Antoine didn't understand.

Back in his room, suddenly exhausted, he went straight to bed, but a stream of images kept passing through his head: Meena moving gracefully about in a sari, Meena meeting men, a smart young computer salesman like Mr. Truth who, given a few minutes and a cup of tea, might knock her off her feet. Antoine couldn't sleep.

His travel alarm clock, still on Pacific Daylight Time, said it was late morning in San Francisco. Time to write. He got up, switched on the lights, returned to his desk. Suppose he embarked on a novel about India. Not the India of Moghul kings or the British Raj but India as it was today, with a population of nearly a billion, people speaking hundreds of languages and dialects, four hundred tribes, a pantheon of religions, the second biggest railroad system in the world and the fourth largest army. India, the world's largest democracy, where grinding poverty and unimaginable wealth lived side by side, where goddesses and gods were worshipped with equal fervor. India, a land of constant ethnic strife, yet which gave the world Gandhi. He didn't fully understand this culture, never would, but he could at least attempt a story about it.

Now that he thought about it, India had been in his blood since his junior year in Jaipur. How strange he'd never used his experiences in his writing. He had been caught up in his California middle-class angst while this rich material had fermented inside and taken on a form ready to be used—themes and ideas that were larger and more powerful than anything he had ever put on paper. He now knew he wasn't here for Meena only.

He picked up the pen, filled a page, then another, then . . . Sleep didn't intervene; caffeine wasn't necessary. The bareness of his surroundings seemed to prod his imagination. Words came tumbling out. Why was it so easy?

He finally had the answer.

He had been writing the wrong book.

40

It was past midnight and here was Meena taking a taxi to a run-down area that had once been one of Calcutta's finer neighbor-hoods. Rising above dilapidated houses, makeshift sidewalk shops, and a huge "Resist Malaria" billboard, there appeared the Grand Bengal Hotel sign. It was an enormous, freshly painted colonial edifice that stood like an overdressed matron distributing alms to the needy. Meena was shocked and already uncomfortable about her stay here.

The lobby was large with stark white walls, a registration desk, a seating area cozy enough to be a tea nook, and a door open to what in the dim light appeared to be a courtyard. The night manager, well dressed but with a humorless face, straightened his tie. He checked her passport and raised an eyebrow. "You're from the States?"

She nodded, too weary to speak.

"Will you be staying here for a while?"

"I don't know for how long."

"Our hotel is quite modern. Continuous hot water, telephone, fax—I can provide you with everything. And there is a lift for every fifteen rooms."

Meena just wanted to go to bed. All she needed was a clean room. The next moment she chided herself for thinking like an arrogant, impatient tourist. And that in her own country.

"Internet, too." He handed her a brochure on Internet connection, then kept on. "Our service is personalized. I'll assign a boy to your room. He'll take care of anything you might need." He handed the passport back to her, then yelled, "Boy! Bearer!"

The boy, actually a frail elderly man dressed in white from his turban to his trousers, shuffled in. He touched his forehead in a gesture of salaam but didn't offer his name, as if his job had reduced him to being "bearer." His eyes were watery, his face so thin and angular that it could have been sketched in a few straight lines. Yet he picked up her luggage easily, saying, "I'll take you to your room."

He walked with the care that came with age, his alert eyes moving well ahead of his body. He guided her out of the elevator to an ornate teakwood door. Unlocking it, he turned the brass knob and let her into the front room. It had a sofa, a coffee table, and a magazine rack overflowing with yellowed publications. A black-and-white drawing of a cat, fuzzy and indeterminate, hung on one beige wall. Altogether modern, she decided. Depressingly so.

The bedroom had a queen-sized bed draped with a turquoise spread made of brocade. Now that's decadent, Meena thought, remembering the tiny rope bed in which she slept as a child in Karamgar. As the old man turned down the bedcovers, she moved to face a full-length mirror on one wall. Another luxury item. Her mother only used a hand mirror in her cottage. For now Meena ignored her image and said, "This will do quite nicely."

"Every morning I'll bring you your mail." The old man sounded as though serving her were the primary responsibility of his life. "I'll wait outside your door just now. If you need anything . . ."

"That won't be necessary." She drew several notes from her purse and put them on his palm. "It's late. You should go home now."

"This is my home, memsahib. Good night."

She too was Indian, and certainly not rich by birth. Yet here she was staying in a hotel whose daily rate probably exceeded the man's monthly salary. It felt utterly strange.

She went to the bathroom sink and splashed water on her face as if to rinse away the sudden fear that was welling up from inside. Could she ever make India her home again? She pressed her face into the thick white towel, stumbled across the bedroom, and toppled onto the bed covered with creamy smooth silken sheets . . . and lay there wide awake. The overhead fan droned on, children wailed to their mother out in the shacks behind the hotel, and a dog yelped in pain as though someone had kicked it. The decadent bed lost its appeal.

Eventually she got up, plugged in her laptop through the power converter, dialed the number to connect with the Internet, and sent a note to Carlos.

Arrived at Calcutta. Hope to meet Vishnu tomorrow.

Meena

Then she stood, yawned once, collapsed onto the bed a second time, her eyes already closed, and was instantly asleep.

She awoke at daybreak. Tired body, an ache in every bone. Outside her window two crows pirouetted on the electric lines and stabbed at each other peevishly with their beaks. A shoeshine boy, maybe twelve years old, began setting up his shop beneath them on the sidewalk. What a life for such a young boy. Across the street, day laborers huddled in a shabby shop, chatting and drinking tea. They looked just like people in her village, but she knew she couldn't walk in there now. She wasn't one of them.

A mother, Meena's age, waddled up the street wearing fine chiffon and pearls and amethyst, her belly bulging out of her sari. Her two boys, neatly dressed in identical school uniforms, trailed along behind her lugging their books in shoulder bags. They were obviously well-to-do and strode with a certain self-assurance, now and then throwing a haughty glance to either side. Thank the gods, Meena wasn't one of them either.

Meena passed by the floor-length mirror in her dressing gown and scrutinized her face: eyes puffy, lips swollen, hair tangled. What a hellishly long journey. Still she managed a smile. Today she'd reunite with Vishnu. She'd call him at a more respectable hour. His apartment address and telephone number were secure in her purse; she checked again to make sure.

Vishnu. She remembered his touch.

A knock came at the door. She opened it a crack to see the bearer standing there with a tray in one hand, a copy of *India News* in the other.

"Bed tea, memsahib?"

She motioned him to enter. "Please."

He set the newspaper and the tray on the coffee table and poured her a cup.

What a lovely custom, Meena thought.

"Will you have some breakfast, memsahib?"

"No, thanks."

The bearer looked a little worried. "Taxi?"

"No, thank you." She hated to disappoint the old man, whose existence depended on providing her service.

"You rest now, memsahib. I'll be around if you need anything." He bowed his way out, closing the door gently.

Memsahib, upper-class woman. In the beginning she had been a simple Rajasthani village girl abandoned on a train. Now that she carried a U.S. passport, she was someone to be deferred to.

She went back to bed, her brain summoning slumber. When she woke it was already afternoon and she felt disoriented. She went to the shower.

Time to get dressed. What to wear? The big question. She opened her suitcase, put aside her jeans and tee shirts and took out a scarlet sari whose exuberant shade and deep glow had reminded her of her wedding dress the moment she saw it in a San Francisco store window. The fabric was delicately embroidered with peacocks and glittered with *zari* threads. It came with a matching *choli*, or short blouse. In San Francisco the ensemble would seem gaudy, and she had never worn it there. But here in India color and glitter were everyday necessities, a legacy of the kings, an integral part of this sensuous culture, perhaps also what made life bearable for many.

She ran the fabric through her fingers to savor its feel and the slithery silk created a luxurious mood. She wrapped it around herself, powdered her face to take the shine off, braided her hair, and applied lipstick, all the while wondering if she wasn't affecting a disguise. Finally she looked at herself in the mirror close up. Conventional? No, only modern and foreign. Doubt and apprehension showed in the blinking of her eyes and the quickness of her breath.

Time to call Vishnu. She dialed his number, her heart doing a tabla beat, and was a little relieved when no answer came. For all her Western upbringing she wasn't quite prepared for this meeting. Was she throwing herself at a man whom she hadn't seen in twenty-eight years? Was the story about him having a girlfriend accurate?

To give herself something to do, she checked her e-mail. It had been daytime over there when she sent her message, and Carlos had responded.

Hope you're spending all your time with Vishnu, lying flat, looking up at the ceiling.

Carlos

How like Carlos. Meena smiled to herself.

She put her laptop away and from her carry-on bag took out *Parallel Lives*, the book that bore a written note from Antoine. She sat on the sofa and opened the volume to a bookmark. These last twenty pages turned out to be mostly a monologue from the protagonist, who was facing a major decision in life. She could actually hear Antoine speaking to her: "The time may not be yet. But when the hour strikes, I'll be fully prepared with all the love and wisdom I possess." Stop dreaming, Meena reminded herself. He was just another author.

Now she was on the last page, the final moment in which the protagonist embraces the path of daring and discovery, leaving a comfortable life behind. She was rooting for him, was satisfied by the choice he made, and was as anxious as he might have been. She finished the book and put it away for the last time.

Someone rapped at the door. She got up and answered it quickly.

The bearer was standing there. He announced, "A visitor for you, memsahib."

"A visitor?"

"You can see him from your balcony."

She hurried to the balcony and peered down below at the green courtyard. Standing under the shade of a tree and looking up at her was an Indian man of average height in white cotton trousers and shirt. In his hand he held a flashing yellow marigold garland. There was gentleness, refinement, and humility in the way he stood. His head was straight, proud, Rajput-like, but not stiff.

"Meena!" the man cried out. "I'm Vishnu."

Meena couldn't answer. She felt like laughing and crying both. Staring at him once more, then drawing in her breath and composing herself, she walked slowly the length of the balcony. Her sari didn't allow her to move any faster, which was just as well. She descended the exterior staircase, emerged into the courtyard, and stood face to face with Vishnu. Magnificent Vishnu. She gazed at him the way she used to as a seven-year-old. Time had no boundaries. The flower bushes, the building, even the sky all receded into the background.

He was the same height as she was. His gaze was direct and clear, emanating from deeply etched eyes. The handsome boyish countenance that she vaguely remembered had been only slightly weathered by the years. Vishnu had faced challenges, learned to be resilient, lived in moderation. His attractiveness went far beyond his fine features. He was the sort of man an Indian mother would love to introduce to her daughter.

Vishnu seemed perfectly at ease as he moved toward her and draped the garland around her neck. Her arm reached out to him, whether for a hug or a handshake she didn't know. All these decades of being apart vanished, leaving behind the affection she had felt toward him when they were children.

She noticed Vishnu drawing back.

"Come see the theater," she heard a man call.

As if waking after a deep slumber, she immediately became alert. Tilting her head up, she saw hotel workers staring from the balconies that were stacked like opera boxes on each floor. How could she have forgotten that Indian couples dared not touch in public? Intimacy could be the subject of stage plays, Hindi box office hits, or the latest trashy novel, but never of real life. What a sight it must have been.

Embarrassed, trembling inside, she stepped back.

Vishnu threw an angry glance toward the servants and they scurried away. "Do you suppose we could go upstairs?" His English was clipped but fluent and he spoke confidently.

She nodded and they mounted the stairs to her balcony.

"Come in," she said at the door.

"Hmmm." He stepped into the living room.

She left the door ajar. They both stood awkwardly in silence.

He surveyed the decor and said in a clear warm voice, "Nice room you've got."

She took her garland off and smelled the hint of fragrance rising from the flowers. She placed it on the coffee table gently so it wouldn't be crushed. "Please sit down." They took seats at opposite ends of the only sofa.

He stretched and turned to face her. "Welcome back, Meena." He spoke as though she had been away only a week.

She tugged the trailing end of her sari and wrapped it around her right shoulder the way Indian women do when around men, a gesture that came naturally to her now. "How did you know I was staying in this hotel?"

"I started calling all the first-class hotels this morning. You had to be in one of them. And it turned out to be so."

"That's clever," she said.

He laughed. "It's routine for newspaper reporters."

After a time he began again. "Isn't this a miracle? Twenty-eight years have gone by. All this time I've hoped you were somewhere safe—"

"It's a long story, how I ended up in the U.S." She'd fill him in about her life later. For now, she was occupied with finding what was familiar in him: his reassuring manner, his neat reserved posture, his way of gripping the top of the sofa with his long slender fingers. "I'm just so happy to be back here," she said. "By the way, I made a stop in Karamgar."

"You saw how the place has changed," he said proudly. "People there live differently than we did. Our day began with sunrise and ended with sunset. Now they have electricity. And did you happen to see the new temple? I paid for most of the construction."

"Yes, I did." She went silent for a moment, lamenting to herself that the hundred-year-old temple was no more. It held the silent cries, the whispered confidences, the unfulfilled hopes of her ancestors. "I must say I liked our old village. That's one reason why I came back. A part of me stayed with it, probably died with it. I had a hard time connecting with the new village at first. That changed as I spent time with my relatives and friends. We chatted. We sang. I felt close to them. But to tell you the truth, it would never be the same for me. . . ."

"I can understand that."

"I envy you, Vishnu. I've lost some precious things. My mother. My house. My Rajput self. I have lived in the lap of luxury in San Francisco, yet I feel quite incomplete. . . ." She choked and had to cradle her head in her hands to hide the tears. When she recovered she found him edging a little closer to her side. He wiped her tears with his handkerchief and pushed a lock of hair away from her forehead.

"Meena . . ." Vishnu said softly, his voice trailing off.

She raised her head to see his large eyes glowing, his face dissolving into tenderness. "Yes, Vishnu . . ."

Just then the bearer knocked and entered without waiting to be bidden. Vishnu slid quietly to the other end of the sofa. So society here still frowned on a couple being intimate even in their own room, Meena concluded.

"An American gentleman was here asking about you, memsahib," the bearer said.

"An American? There must be a mistake."

"He did not leave his name." The bearer paused and asked, "Tea for two?"

How could she have forgotten the custom of serving tea and sweets to guests as soon as they arrived? She bit her lip.

"Not for me," Vishnu said. "I just had tea. But thank you."

The bearer bowed from the waist as he closed the door. Bright naked sunlight filtered in through the window.

"Who were you expecting?" Vishnu asked, apprehension making his voice husky.

"Nobody. I don't know a soul here in Calcutta other than you."

Vishnu regarded her thoughtfully, then glanced at his watch and suggested, "Want to take a stroll in the Maidan? It's only a block from here."

It might be safer to get away from here for a while. "I'd love to," she said eagerly, rising from the sofa.

He led her along the balcony and down the stairs to the courtyard. "I have to go back to the office in an hour," he said as they reached the gate. "I was hoping to take today as a holiday, but it didn't work out that way."

Meena sighed gently, sharing his disappointment. "Do you still work for *India News*?" she asked. "I enjoyed reading the article you wrote about object-oriented programming."

He closed the iron gate behind them with a sharp click. "No, I—I lost that job."

Meena could see anger and sadness in the creases of Vishnu's eyes. She must not let him feel embarrassed. "I lost my job in San Francisco, too," she said quickly. "But an opportunity has opened up for me in Bombay. I might pursue it."

They emerged onto the main street. The roar of the vehicles hammered at her so that she felt disoriented. A beggar with a leathery face sitting on the opposite sidewalk shrieked unintelligible words at her. She could neither respond to him nor ignore him.

"You might want to take a little time to tour this country, Meena." Vishnu looked into her eyes as they waited at the street crossing. "From what I've heard you've done well in the States. You're pretty and wonderful and smart. I'm sure people in our village are proud of you. And you're staying in one of the costliest hotels in Calcutta." His voice lightened. "The servants probably think you're either a foreign dignitary or Miss India."

She blushed. She felt seven years old again, warmed by Vishnu's compliment and attention. It was pleasing to note that his attraction to her was as strong as ever. "And you?" she asked. "How's life been for you?"

"My new job is writing propaganda for a tribal group. The Moxans."

"The Moxans?" She found herself frowning. "Of course, we don't get all the news in the U.S., but I remember reading about them kidnapping a tourist."

"There's no proof they were in any way involved in that case," Vishnu said.

A traffic policeman, standing in the middle of the intersection, directed the vehicles and pedestrians with a gloved hand. He blew his shrill whistle and cars, buses, rickshaws, and scooters screeched to a shuddering halt. Meena and Vishnu jostled other pedestrians as everyone rushed to cross the road.

The Maidan, a lush green park, would make a perfect running course, Meena thought, had it not been filled with yoga practitioners, on-the-spot masseurs, arm-in-arm young lovers, and of course many children. Office workers on a break sat on the grass playing cards nonchalantly, as if on a family outing. Two shoeshine boys were arguing loudly, drowning out the music of a flute player that Meena wanted to hear. A coarse-looking, muscled man bumped into her— intentionally, she was sure. Another man standing on the sideline leered at her with eyes in a lustful daze. Even in a sari, she lamented to herself, she couldn't blend with the crowd, couldn't pass as a local product. Vishnu must have noticed, for he stared at the man hard. The creep finally averted his gaze.

It was fun to watch the food vendors busy with their afternoon activities: roasting nuts, grilling corn on the cob, deep-frying battered

vegetables. A thick smell of hot oil and spices and the clatter of utensils teased Meena's senses.

"That chap over there roasts his groundnuts in hot sand," Vishnu
said, pointing as they strolled along the line of stalls. He bought two
paper cones of roasted peanuts, still smoking hot, and handed one to
her. "His are the best in the city."

Meena shelled a nut, popped it into her mouth, tasted its fresh
roasted flavor. At the same time, she probed her initial impressions of
Vishnu. Her first reaction: Vishnu was savvy. He took charge with
ease. He made her feel comfortable.

They continued their promenade, talking about nothing special,
laughing and munching like two old pals who were happy to be
together anywhere on earth. The affinity between them had definitely
returned. Then came her second reaction: Alas, this wasn't the same
flush of excitement she had felt with Antoine.

They turned a corner and Vishnu pointed to a monument with a
gleaming white exterior, a Taj Mahal look-alike. "That's the Victoria
Memorial over there. It was built before India's independence, of
course. And that chap sitting there," he indicated a man in tattered
clothes who had stationed himself on the steps, "is what you call
'homeless' in the States. He'll stay there until the police chase him
away. I save all my old clothes and shoes for him."

Vishnu's concern for the unfortunate man touched Meena.
"You seem to know what goes on in every little corner," she said
affectionately.

"I love Calcutta," Vishnu went on. "It's quite a city. People are
neighborly. But things are changing here, too. In the old days everybody would be out in the streets. Now the Indian middle class has
buying power. They're getting refrigerators, televisions, VCRs, computers. They stay home more. The crime rate's going up. Needless to
say, the pollution's pretty bad. But I still roam around and take the
pulse of the city. And our local council—" Vishnu talked excitedly
about the present government, the parliamentary election that was
drawing near, the recent surge in the economy, and the dawning of
an electronic era in India.

Meena could see that Vishnu was very much a citizen of this land.
He and his country were inseparable. She was feeling overwhelmed
by the crowd, the noise, and the heat. Calcutta, to her, possessed the
same violent energy as New York, a city she only occasionally visited.

Now they stopped to watch a cricket match that was going on. Vishnu seemed entranced by it; Meena didn't understand the game at all. Hearing a pounding sound, she looked around and saw three uniformed policemen canter by on horseback.

"They're having a big football match here this afternoon," Vishnu said enthusiastically. "That's why you see so many police. You call it soccer. Everybody here loves football regardless of caste or religion."

As they began walking again, Meena drew him out about popular attitudes toward lower-caste people and tribals and his own work on behalf of the Moxans.

"It's only a job, and it may not last all that long," he concluded. "In the meantime, I have a nice office in the Moxan headquarters. Why don't you drop by this evening? You might find it interesting. I'll be there till seven."

"You work that late in India?"

"I do, tonight. I have no choice. I've been asked to take on a new project and I have a lot of catching up to do. By the way, would you like to have dinner with me afterward? There's an excellent restaurant a short distance from my office. They specialize in the fish dishes this region is so famous for. People from all over Calcutta go to that restaurant. The place reminds me of an ancient Bengali poet who said: 'Fish is created by the gods for their own dining pleasure.' I sometimes think the gods must hold that restaurant in high regard."

Meena chuckled. "You make it sound irresistible." Sampling the local cuisine would be exciting. But even more urgent was her longing to reconnect with Vishnu. So many years to be filled in. "Where's your office located?"

"About a fifteen-minute taxi ride from here. Tell the driver you want to get off at the vegetable market in Shambazaar. I'm in the five-story office building right across from the market. I'll meet you outside at seven."

They made their way back to the Grand Bengal Hotel and at the entrance Vishnu came to a pause. "Try to get some rest, Meena. I'll see you a little later."

"Thanks for the guided tour, Vishnu. You showed me a side of Calcutta I might not have seen on my own."

"Maybe tonight we'll remember Karamgar together." He fumbled in his pocket, pulled out a marble incense holder and a packet of incense sticks, and presented them to her. "The incense will make the hotel room seem less sterile, more like home," he said. "And it will keep out the demon, too—remember how we used to say?"

She accepted the gift with gratitude and smiled her thanks. Then she reached into her purse for the Polaroid she had brought and offered it to him. "Here's a souvenir from the States."

"A camera?" His face lit up as he took the case in his hand. "Thank you, Meena. Mine disappeared with the last job. I like taking pictures. I'll have to take one of you later. That sari is very becoming." He gave a happy little laugh. "See you in a few hours." He turned and was immediately swallowed in the crowd.

On the way to her suite Meena stopped at the reception desk. The manager smoothed his shirt, patted his breast pocket for his pen, and said in a cool voice, "Yes, madam."

"I was told an American man was asking for me. . . ."

"Any problem?"

"Well, I don't know who it might be. I don't know anyone here and—"

"Don't worry, madam. I've been in the hotel business for more than twenty-five years. I have handled all kinds. Rest assured that henceforth we'll not give out any information on you to anyone."

Meena thanked him, then went slowly to her room, her head bursting with thoughts and impressions of the day. She lit the incense and sat in its aromatic air for fresher, clearer instincts to arise from within.

The reunion with Vishnu had gone as well as could be expected. He had introduced her to his city charmingly. He'd come a long way from an obscure village, yet remained true to his humble beginnings. No doubt he would be a genuine friend, an ideal companion. All the wonderful traits with which she had endowed India were there in him. But the meeting just wasn't . . . exciting. With Antoine she used to feel giddy, intoxicated, feverish, wild thoughts running through her head.

Was she being fair? Could her reaction—her decision, really—be so immediate? It must be partly the result of years of quick bit-on/bit-off programming decisions. Vishnu was a man of great quality and appeal. But living in India had molded him, and it would shape her too. He'd expect her to take on the role of an Indian wife: preparing the meals, cleaning the floors, hanging up the wash, visiting relatives. She'd think of herself only secondarily. After all those years in the

U.S. she needed more from life. How easy it would be if she hadn't changed—was that innocent Rajput girl again.

Then too, her favorite attire of jeans and tee shirt would shock him. She would always have to wear a sari and adapt to cultural norms that might well offend her. And she could never reveal parts of herself that she could show to Carlos or Antoine. Only the Indian side of her personality would be acceptable to Vishnu, and by now she was beginning to realize how little Indian she was.

Time had tested everything, upset everything, snatched away what was once most precious.

41

The afternoon was particularly humid. On the way to the Grand Bengal Hotel, Antoine's taxi had battled with the evening rush-hour traffic. He had meant to catch Meena early but, still tired from a day-long flight followed by an all-night marathon writing session, he had fallen asleep near dawn and hadn't wakened until late in the afternoon. The ten-minute ride took twenty-five, and he felt nauseated from the combination of car exhaust, noise, dust, and heat. Now seated in a corner of the Grand Bengal Hotel lobby on an aged upholstered couch, he looked out at a courtyard of trees, flower bushes, and a gazebo. After a minute he began to compose himself to see Meena.

The bearer he had dispatched to announce his arrival to Meena reappeared before him. Speaking in a hushed tone as if he were privy to a secret, and with a smile that was probably rare on that face, the man said, "Memsahib is with another gentleman."

"Do you know which gentleman she's with?"

The bearer stood there mutely.

Antoine got up and dropped several rupees on his palm.

"She called him Vishnu," the bearer said. "They were . . . you know . . . sitting close."

Antoine envisioned Meena alone in a room with Vishnu, their two bodies wound around each other, writhing in ecstasy.

Should he just go back to his hotel, pack up and leave? No, he told himself, he'd stay. He wanted to size up his rival. Besides, he must speak to Meena and warn her about the Moxans at all costs.

He asked, "Mind if I wait here?"

"No, sir." The bearer began dusting a table lamp.

Antoine picked up today's *India News* from a magazine basket at his feet and started scanning it. The brevity of the newspaper, the lack of padding, the colorful phrasings pleased him. He laughed at the story about an Indian cook who prepared lunch for a school and was sacked because his hot food made the young students rush out like "dragons blowing fire." On the Personals page, which they called Matrimonial here, he caught some prospects. "Proposal invited for a beautiful Rajasthani woman from a professional gentleman age 35–45. Must respect women, adore children and enjoy traveling." Antoine smiled to himself. He would qualify.

His smile changed to a frown when he read a news story about the Moxan tribe. Their leader, Karun Dhotia, had met with government officials to voice his demands, but the central government hadn't budged. A local politician, interviewed for this article, expressed his fear of terrorism striking the city.

Antoine was only vaguely aware of the couple who had emerged into the courtyard until the bearer signaled him with a slight tilt of his head. There was Meena elegant in a scarlet sari, her walk languid, almost regal. He wanted to dash out to her, but Vishnu was there right alongside her. Antoine studied Vishnu from behind his newspaper. Vishnu was not tall—Antoine was suddenly aware of his own height, well over six feet—but gave off an aura of integrity. It was as though a *diya*, a tiny lamp, illuminated him from the inside. Was that the kind of man Meena wanted?

They approached the gate. Antoine stood up, eyes riveted on them. Just then a clutch of Westerners, chattering in what sounded like Italian, burst into the lobby and obscured his view. They each were dragging at least five pieces of luggage.

"The international film festival starts this week. That's the Italian delegation." Having dispensed this bit of information, the bearer continued cleaning the ashtrays.

Antoine wove his way outside, but by then Meena and Vishnu had disappeared beyond a cluster of kiosks. Dejected but not giving up yet, he decided to return later to the hotel.

On the sidewalk, a foot masseur approached him and offered to rub his feet in the park across the street. "Fifteen rupees only," he said. "You don't even have to take your stockings off, if you don't want. Your feet will feel so good, you'll want to take your wife out to the disco. . . . No wife? You want a woman? I can get a pretty one for you."

Antoine brushed him aside.

A stick-thin beggar approached him, saying, "No food. Two days. No *chai*. Three days."

If only they'd leave Antoine alone. His soul craved solitude and time to reflect.

He strolled over to a small shop across the street. Perhaps he wouldn't be hassled here. And he would be able to view the comings and goings at the hotel entrance.

"Hello, mister." The shopkeeper was a middle-aged man in a dhoti, his complexion a warm brown. His face seemed to light up at the prospect of a sale.

Oh no, not another salesman. Antoine nodded a greeting, then turned toward the shelves to avoid speaking with him. He saw stacks of small wooden molds with Indian-style complicated designs, and that was about all. Cookie cutters? Pointless objects? He could amuse himself here provided he didn't have to spend too much time.

"Where are you from, mister?" the shopkeeper asked from behind.

Antoine turned to see the man bare his teeth, red-stained from chewing betel leaves. "My home is near San Francisco."

"Did you leave your heart there?"

Antoine couldn't even manage a grin. His heart bled, wherever it was.

"My son plays Tony Bennett. That's how I know." The shopkeeper went on. "I sell molds for *sandesh*, our most popular milk sweet. I'm one of the few merchants in Calcutta who carry these molds. We give *sandesh* to family and friends whenever there's any good news to share. K. C. Das sells the best *sandesh*. It's about five hundred meters from here. Have you ever been to K. C. Das?"

Antoine had, in fact, already developed a weakness for the creamy white fudge he had tasted last night. But what would he do with these molds? He knew how to prepare some curry dishes. But he had never tried making Indian sweets. And he might never. It was best to keep a few mysteries in life. "No, I haven't been to K. C. Das," he said. He did make a mental note. "And thanks, but I don't want any molds. Just looking."

"Perhaps you'd like some tea?"

Who would ever think of drinking a hot liquid on a scorching afternoon? But tea was meant to open conversation, and though there were aspects of India he detested, tea drinking wasn't one of them. In fact, he could never get enough. "That would be splendid."

The shopkeeper sauntered into the back kitchen and returned with two steaming cups.

Antoine perched himself on a stool and took a swallow of the malty tea. A perfect cup. Every now and then he stole a glance at the hotel across the street, hoping for a sight of Meena.

"Biscuit?" The shopkeeper opened a package of cookies.

"No, thanks."

The shopkeeper began laying down the molds on a small table. Antoine was annoyed at his pushiness.

"See this one?" The shopkeeper held a piece out. "It's a lotus. The flower grows out of mud, but it's pure. The goddess Laxmi, our patron of wealth, sits on a lotus." He dunked a cookie in his tea, popped the softened part in his mouth, and seemed energized enough to sort through his collection and return with a two-inch tire. "And this one's a spinning wheel, a symbol of peace. You've heard about Mahatma Gandhi, haven't you? He spun his own cotton on a wheel like this. My son doesn't respect Gandhiji. They're a different generation. Even the sadhus—those are the saffron-robed people you see on the streets—are becoming politicians. They used to be holy men. Can you imagine?"

He handed a fish mold to Antoine. "This is the most important one. It stands for fertility. Do you have children, mister?"

"No," Antoine said awkwardly as he examined the fish.

"Then you must buy it."

Antoine was taken by the charm of the gadgets and the stories behind them, and decided to reward the man by buying one of each. They'd make a nice present for his mother. She had visited India years ago with his dad. Lately she seemed to be on an India kick again. And with the exchange rate for dollars being so favorable, he could buy these molds for a song.

The shopkeeper continued his tales. Still no sign of Meena. "How about a *paan*?" the shopkeeper asked.

"What's that?"

The shopkeeper returned with a betel leaf folded in a triangular shape and handed it to Antoine. "You hold it in your mouth and chew it slowly. I do after each meal. It helps digest food."

As Antoine chewed the *paan*, he got the inside story on the man's irresponsible teenage son. A little later Antoine laid down some money and pocketed his purchase. When he tried to pay for the tea and the *paan* the man said both were on him.

Antoine strolled the Esplanade section of downtown to locate the sweetshop called K. C. Das. He stopped there for *sandesh*, and finally made his way back to the Grand Bengal Hotel. By now the sun had sunk low on the horizon. He was only half a block away when he suddenly noticed a beautiful woman in a scarlet sari pass through the hotel gate and approach a taxicab.

"Meena!" he called. But a truck rumbled past and she apparently didn't hear him. She stepped into the waiting cab and it roared down the avenue.

Antoine jumped out to the curb, signaled a cruising taxi, hopped into it, and said to the driver, "Follow that taxi, will you?"

The driver, a scrawny teenage boy, turned around and smiled broadly. "Oh, just like the chase scenes in the cinema!" He sang a line from a Hindi song, undulating his body to the rhythm as he put the car in gear.

"Drive carefully," Antoine urged.

The boy eased the taxi, an Ambassador make, into the crush of traffic while Antoine fidgeted in the backseat. Soon the boy started jabbering about his five sisters. The oldest one was cruel, the second pretty, the third bright . . . Antoine half listened. Where was Meena off to? To meet Vishnu somewhere?

Antoine wasn't familiar with the city. He looked out the taxi's window. The dark lanes and alleys off the main road seemed full of intrigue. He imagined getting lost here and never being able to find his way out. He prepared words in his mind for Meena, warning her against venturing out alone. For now, he was glad to have this skillful driver who maneuvered the taxi and negotiated his way through other vehicles, cycle rickshaws, and pedestrians without losing sight of Meena's cab. He narrowly missed a decrepit jaywalking woman, who spat on his wheel and yelled from a toothless mouth. Antoine closed his eyes for a moment.

His taxi eventually arrived at a deserted marketplace, an area that probably teemed with shoppers in the daytime. Now at night, with the stalls closed, vegetable trimmings littered the sidewalk and fruit peels rotted in the gutter. It was dirty, desolate, and rancid in smell.

Meena's taxi was slowing across the street from a grayish white five-story building. Hung from the top floor was the Moxan Headquarters banner, one that eclipsed all other shop signs in the block by its size and vivid scarlet coloring. "Stop here," Antoine ordered the driver. As soon as he brought the cab to a halt, Antoine handed him some rupee notes.

A policeman in khaki uniform and beige belt and cap ambled by. He jabbed his baton on the sidewalk to exaggerate his importance, and glanced inside the taxi. Antoine opened the car door and jumped out onto the sidewalk.

"Should I wait for you?" the driver asked, peering out the window.

"Yes, I'd like you to," Antoine replied. "I'll pay you for waiting." The boy proceeded to park the car.

A breeze blew the Moxan banner to a precarious lopsided position. The streetlamp cast a harsh light over it. It seemed to Antoine that blood was pouring out of the red lettering onto the square below. Just a few yards ahead he saw Meena alight from her taxi in tiny sari steps.

"Meena!" he called out.

42

From inside her taxi Meena was looking out across the square toward a five-story office and residence complex. She was in the right place. The area was well lit and most of the ragged shops were shut down. But this was a bazaar, a place for stallkeepers, porters, and the inevitable ruffians. Even at this evening hour laborers were going in and out of the building. Meena felt alone and far from her hotel in a strange city. Her nose twitched, irritated by the smoke from burning coal hanging in the air. Her watch showed the time to be 6:55. Five minutes to spare. She tipped the cabbie, the scruffy-looking man with one hand whom she had hesitated to hire at first but who, despite her jitteriness, had driven her safely. She stepped from the taxi and started toward the building. Up above in the sky clouds rumbled.

A voice called out behind her. "Meena!"

The name Meena was common enough in India, but the voice and accent made her turn.

Antoine was standing under the lamplight, all six feet of him, his body slimmer, the sleeves of his shirt rolled up. The wind ruffled his hair, pushing it away from his forehead.

The air around her seemed to heat up. She wanted to drop everything, rush to his arms. "Antoine!" she heard herself shout as she moved toward him. Someone was standing beside him, an Indian teenager. She hesitated. Why was Antoine here? Shouldn't he be off somewhere with his new wife? Had he come all this way to see her? And how could he be *here*? No one except Vishnu could have known that she was coming to this obscure vegetable market in North Calcutta at this time of night.

"Antoine, what are you doing here?"

"I have to talk to you, Meena." Antoine's voice was full of urgency. "It's important."

She was facing the building and a dilemma. Two men, vastly different, pulling at her. Why did Vishnu work this late at night? And at this location? What did Antoine want? How did he come to be here? For now she managed to say, "I can talk to you later—but not now, Antoine. I'm already late for my appointment."

She heard her driver roll down his window. Concern sharpened his voice. "Do you want to get back in the car, madamji? You shouldn't be here alone. I'll take you to your hotel."

"I'll be fine," she said to the driver. "Come to my hotel tomorrow morning, Antoine. The Grand Bengal. We'll talk over tea—"

She was in the middle of the sentence when the right side of Antoine's face glared red. The sudden deafening roar of an explosion took her words away. The ground shook. A rush of heat seared her skin. Glass shards streamed past like bullets. As part of the building structure crumbled and began to sag, her runner instinct took over. "Run!" she bellowed. But it was much too late.

43

A young woman with a starched white nurse's cap perched atop her braided black hair put something cold and damp on Meena's forehead. It was morning. Sunlight shone weakly in through a dirty window in an attempt to cheer a room that was warm and stuffy with a medicinal odor. Meena found herself lying on a cot, a bedsheet covering her body. The nurse drew away, frowning, and said something in Hindi that Meena didn't understand. She tried to gesture and found her arm to be heavily bandaged. She stared at it and asked, "Where am I?"

"Eden Hospital," the nurse replied in her accented English. She looked like someone who had never smiled. "Please don't move. Maybe there's concussion."

Memories of last night returned in an amber fog. Meena remembered being brought here and falling asleep. Yawning, she asked, "Where are my two friends, Vishnu Chauhan and Antoine Peterson?"

"I know nothing about them."

Meena heard a cough, a wheeze. Turning her head gingerly, she saw a row of identical cots, each occupied by a woman. An elderly patient, head swathed in bandages, prayed softly. Beyond her another moaned, pausing only to breathe. Farther down the line a frail girl slept. Her mother sat beside the bed, eyes brimming with tears.

"How did I get here?" Meena asked.

"The police brought you here. You were not awake. Terrorists set off a bomb."

Yes, of course. Her fears about the Moxans had been justified.

How strange. Violence had expelled her from India in the first place. Now that she had returned here after thirty years, she had once again been caught in violence, though of a different kind. She forgot her pain and lifted her head. "What happened?"

"Many people died," the nurse said matter-of-factly. "How do you feel?"

Mentally Meena checked her body. Her knee joints ached, her back hurt, and she felt nauseated. Yet she had to find Vishnu and Antoine. Making her voice as solid and clear as possible, she answered, "Fine."

"We'll release you, then. We need the beds. They'll bring in more people." She paused and added, "But you'll have to see a doctor and the police first." The nurse turned to the next patient and went on about her business, leaving Meena to ponder whether she could, in fact, get up.

After breathing deeply, Meena pulled herself up to a seated position. When that worked, she funneled all her effort into getting her thoughts in order. But she had more fears than thoughts.

A maid came and offered tea. Meena guzzled hers, noticed how the elderly patient in the next bed was blowing on her stainless steel glass to cool it. A glum-faced doctor entered, took her blood pressure and pulse, gave a cursory look at her bruises, then left without a word.

A uniformed police officer approached—short, middle-aged, black hair corrugated into curls. His high cheekbones reflected a knifelike light from the window. He seemed more like a meek grocery clerk than a cop. He pulled up a chair, opened a notebook. "Your name and address?" he demanded in a routine tone without meeting her eyes.

"I'm Meena Gossett." She spoke slowly and distinctly in an attempt to appear normal. "I'm staying at the Grand Bengal Hotel."

The officer raised his eyes. "You're . . . a foreigner?"

All those years of checking the Other box on forms in the U.S. Here she was in India, still a foreigner. "I was born here," she said. "Moved to the States when I was seven. I just returned."

"To visit family?"

"I have no family left here."

The officer wrote it all down. "You," he said, "are what we call an NRI—a Non-Resident Indian." The voice became cheerful. "My brother is also an NRI. He visited me just last month. He lives in San Antonio. Mechanical engineer. What do you do?"

"I write software."

"And why did you come back?"

"To visit a friend from my village."

"His name?"

Meena hesitated. He waited, pencil ready. "Vishnu Chauhan," she said eventually.

"You know Chauhan?"

A chill rippled through Meena's body. "Was he hurt?"

"He broke his ankle, trying to rescue a man trapped in the building. He'll recover."

"Is he in this hospital?"

"He's under arrest."

She pleaded, "Can I see him?"

"Mr. Chauhan is not allowed any visitors."

"I've got to see him. I came here just because of him."

"Oh?" He shifted in the chair. "Madam, what were you doing with Vishnu Chauhan last night?"

"Vishnu asked me to meet him where he worked. I took a taxi from my hotel and was waiting for him outside the building when . . ."

The image of Antoine standing before the Moxan headquarters faded in and out of her mind. She wondered, not for the first time, why he was there and whether she had dreamt the whole incident.

The officer took copious notes. He wrote slowly.

"What are the charges against my friend?" Meena asked, anxious and shivering.

The man sighed. "He was in the Moxan headquarters when it happened."

"What happened?"

"Apparently his friends were building bombs. We nearly had a disaster. As it turned out, the troublemakers were killed. One radical leader, Pradip, fled the scene and is at large. But Dhotia, their top man, is safe in jail. What do you know of him?"

"Nothing."

"We can arrest you too, you know."

"That's insane," Meena said with anger. "Do you think I'd have been anywhere near that building if I knew a bomb would go off? I know nothing about your local politics. I just arrived here."

He stared at her in silence.

Meena said, glaring back now, "Look, I'm an American citizen. I don't have to answer any of your questions. I'm going to call the American Embassy."

The officer backed off. "When did you enter the country, madam? Which airline? What stops have you made?"

She gave him the information.

Closing his notebook, he said, "I suggest you remain in Calcutta a few more days. You were a witness and might be able to help us. Here is my office number." He handed her a piece of paper. "I can arrange for a taxi to take you back to your hotel now. Anything else I can do for you?"

"I still want to visit Vishnu."

He actually smiled. "Vishnu Chauhan is being kept in a room by himself," he told her. "A guard is watching him. But since you're from the States and our guest, I suppose I can authorize a few minutes' visit."

"Thank you. And do you know of an American by the name of Antoine Peterson?"

The smile vanished. He gave her an appraising glance. "An American at the building?"

"Yes. With me."

The policeman consulted his list. "Not in this hospital." The voice was pensive. "He could be in one of the others."

"I want to make some phone calls right away."

"Yes, madam. The nurse can show you where the telephone is."

"And I'd like to know about the taxi driver who took me there. He had only one hand."

"There was someone like that." He thumbed through his notebook. "A man with one hand. Yes. He went home this morning."

Meena was relieved.

"As for Mr. Peterson," the officer rushed on, "I'll call you. We're still finding bodies."

Finding bodies? No. That couldn't be. She remembered how the streetlight illuminated Antoine's face, his eagerness to talk to her last night, his resolute stance. And how she brushed him off. Did he know something was about to happen?

"Could I go there to look for him myself . . . ?"

"No, madam. We have cordoned off that area. The market's closed." He left abruptly, snapping his notebook shut as he went.

The nurse came back with some clothes, saying with an expression of disapproval, "Here's your sari."

Her exquisite sari, worn just once, was now tattered and scorched. It couldn't even be kept as a memento. Crushed, numb, she took the pieces in her hand.

"You can't wear it on the street," the nurse said. "We'll lend you this one." She handed Meena a flimsy voile thing, wavy in parts from lack of pressing. "Be sure to return it."

Meena got up and followed the nurse to a curtained alcove for dressing. The legs that regularly jogged eight miles were now tired from taking these few paces. Meena regarded her image in a small mirror on the wall: several small cuts on her forehead, one eye swollen, bruised cheek, scraped elbow. She'd worry about those later. She changed into the cheap sari and a short blouse with armholes so huge that a jet of air from the ceiling fan whipped right through. She placed the end of her sari over her head to hide her disheveled hair.

As she waited she mused about how fragile life was. She now wanted to follow only the truth that was inside, paying no heed to what was expected of her. She wondered if Vishnu could be a part of that picture. Her fleeting visit with Antoine last night had made her realize how much he still meant to her. Be serious, Meena, she told herself. Antoine could very well be married already. She wasn't sure of either man just now.

The nurse came back. Meena asked her for a telephone and was directed to a small office down the hall. Meena sat down, thumbed through a telephone directory that was years old, and proceeded to dial various hospitals. The lines were clear. She got wrong numbers, disconnected numbers, and was even told by someone he didn't understand her accent. She finally hung up and burst into tears of pain and frustration.

When she raised her head she saw an elderly maid with a face that could have been chiseled from granite. She was squatting on the bare floor just outside the office, eating her breakfast from a stainless steel tiffin box. A chair next to her remained empty. She stared at Meena dispassionately. Meena wiped her tears away.

"I'll take you to see Vishnu Chauhan now." The nurse had finally returned.

Meena followed her through the corridors, passing a young doctor and a dead body on a stretcher that was being wheeled out of a ward.

At the far end of the building a uniformed guard, half dozing, slouched on a stool outside one door. He awoke, exchanged brisk words with the nurse, and with a flick of his hand gestured Meena to go in.

The room was bare save for a cot. Vishnu was sprawled there, his left ankle in plaster, his eyes puffy and half closed. His cheeks marked with reddish pink patches of burned skin made Meena wince.

She stood at the side of the bed, touched him lightly on the hand.

He opened one eye, then another, and gazed at her for an instant, as if trying to focus. "Meena." His shocked voice, though fragile, had a tincture of hope. He tried to push himself up in the bed, but slid back weakly.

"How are you?" she asked softly.

"I'm so sorry."

"Don't apologize, Vishnu. I'm alive. How do you feel?"

"I have a slight fever. I get dizzy sometimes. My left ankle's all banged up." He frowned. "But with luck, I'll be out in a day or two. And you?"

"I got away with minor cuts and bruises."

"I should never have invited you to my office. Believe me, I had no idea what was going on there—"

"I'm glad it didn't turn out any worse than this."

"What a fool I was. I thought I could make the Moxans drop their plan. The voice of democracy and reason didn't work. They really were making bombs. My colleague Pradip and I were standing in the hallway arguing when the bomb went off. By accident, I guess . . ."

The guard outside cleared his throat.

"You should rest now," Meena said. Turning three-quarters she asked, "Is there anything you need?"

Eyes swollen, he seemed to study her expression. "Meena, maybe our marriage so long ago means nothing to you now, but could you ever consider . . ."

Though Meena knew that it was too late, that the gap between her and Vishnu was too great, she hesitated to add to his pain at this moment and kept her thoughts to herself. Her longings for Vishnu and India had been part fantasy and part voyage of self-discovery. Now that she had been here a while, she knew her earlier assumptions about fitting into the Indian scene were mostly wishful thinking.

"My life could be complete with you, Meena."

"Let's talk about that later. First you must get well."

"I'll show you India," he continued with increasing urgency. "There are parts of this country I haven't seen myself. Believe me, there's more to this country than you've seen. We'd grow closer together again in the process. I owe you that. . . ."

"Vishnu, you owe me nothing. I came here on my own."

"Don't you remember our beautiful wedding? Pundit said we're bound forever by the seven circles we made together. And my duty was to protect you."

At one time those words carried a lot of weight for Meena too. She just didn't know for sure if they did anymore.

"After meeting you yesterday, Meena, I realized I've been waiting for you all my life. Maybe that's why I didn't get married. I've met women who might have been suitable. . . ."

Meena said, "Asha?"

Perhaps he didn't hear her. "Just seeing you makes me feel so much better," he said eagerly. "My body was burning even a minute ago. Now my fever is going down."

She thought briefly of the young Vishnu, her first love. Yet now, standing before the adult Vishnu, she couldn't make any commitments. From nowhere Antoine's face flashed before her, a flicker of hope alongside it.

"I'll call you later to see how you are and if you need anything," she managed to say.

The guard appeared and motioned Meena toward the door.

"He wants me to leave," she whispered to Vishnu.

His eyes gleaming, his face flushed, Vishnu sat up and said deliriously, "Don't go, Meena. Please don't go. You left me once before. Please don't do that to me again." His chest rose and fell under the white sheet in spasms of agitation.

She wanted to hold his hand, to cry with him like they were still seven-year-olds. The face of the Vishnu she loved would always be in her heart.

She saw the guard glaring at her. Her lips trembling, she walked slowly away. Behind her she could hear Vishnu sobbing.

Feeling totally spent, she hobbled to the reception area. Wordlessly the same somber nurse showed her to a waiting taxi. Meena felt she was not regarded by this woman as one of her kind. Before Meena could thank her, she had whirled around and gone back inside.

A copy of *India News* lay outside her hotel room door. Meena picked it up, unlocked the door, walked in, put the paper on the coffee table, and collapsed onto the sofa. Thoughts about Antoine swirled in her mind. She called the police officer, but he wasn't there. She sat up groggily and opened the newspaper. Her eyes raced through the bold banner headlines on the first page:

BOMB BLAST IN VEGETABLE MARKET ROCKS CALCUTTA
Three Floors of Five-Story Building Pulverized
Six Known Dead
Vishnu Chauhan, Former *India News* Columnist, Injured

The pictures: a young boy sitting on the debris crying; several front rooms of the multistory structure reduced to rubble; ripped doors, shattered window panes, and cracked walls of adjacent shops. The report said the boy had lost his father, a laborer who was unloading a cartful of red chili sauce bottles. The whole square was splattered with blood and the red sauce.

Meena read on. The explosion was believed to be an accidental detonation of RDX explosives stashed in a secret room in the Moxan headquarters. The government described it as an attempt to instigate violence and had put the army on alert. Forensic experts were searching for further clues. Vishnu Chauhan's part in the scheme, if any, was yet to be determined. The names of the deceased were listed. There was, thank God, no mention of Antoine anywhere.

The story below was about a dengue fever outbreak in Delhi. Meena dropped the newspaper from her hand and shut her eyes.

In her dream, she saw Vishnu struggling up the stairs of his apartment building with bandaged legs. An extraordinary woman in a delicate sari waited for him at a window above, eyes wistful. She was weary of waiting, but her face was serene. Who was she? Meena was fascinated, but knew it wasn't herself. She was merely a well-wisher in Vishnu's journey. It was neither her choice nor her destiny to be Vishnu's destination.

Meena woke, her mind whirling with the snatches of the dream. She knew what to do next. She stripped off her sari, went to the bathtub, scrubbed her skin with a loofah sponge, dried off, smeared lotion on her face, and dabbed perfume on her wrists. Her body was still stiff, but much of the tension was gone. She pulled a tee shirt over her head, slipped on a pair of jeans, put on sandals and her wedding necklace, then dialed room service for lunch.

"Veg or non-veg?"

The question startled her. Not a choice she had had to make since Auntie Bimla's death. In retrospect, her family in Rajasthan typically ate meatless meals. How she had grown to nourish herself with a diet her family would never have approved of. She had moved too far away from her origins. "Veg," she said.

A young boy arrived shortly bearing a tray. He set it down on the table and stared at her with curiosity. His eyes said that the opulence of the surroundings was hard to bear. She summoned a smile, gave him a tip. He saluted her by lifting his palm to his forehead, then rushed away.

How famished she was. In minutes she polished off the spicy okra dish laced with chilis, the smooth and filling lentil soup, the creamy yogurt shake with cardamom seeds floating on top for tastes of her childhood.

Now restored, she donned a wide-brimmed straw hat and bustled down to the street. A cycle rickshaw squealed to a halt before her. "Where you want to go, madam?" the rickshaw-wallah asked.

She didn't like the leer on his face and waved a no. It was noon and felt as though someone had raised the sun's dial to the broiling point. The tar on the street had nearly melted. Her eyes burned from the glare. She put on her sunglasses and flagged a taxi.

"To Lake Place in Ballygunge," she said to the driver.

44

The door opened slowly on an exquisite young woman in a pale blue sari, her silken black hair in a coil that seemed ready to collapse. She straightened and wiped at a tear. How terribly young she was.

Meena felt a flutter in her stomach as she took a step back. Laxmi had mentioned in her e-mail that Asha Das, this child, was a close friend of Vishnu. She hadn't said the young woman was deeply in love with him. Meena hoped her impulse to visit Asha and give her the latest news on Vishnu didn't just upset her more.

"I'm Meena Gossett," she said. "Am I disturbing you?"

"Not at all, Meenaji," Asha said tentatively. "Vishnuda has mentioned you. When did you arrive?"

"Only yesterday."

Turning, Asha led her to the drawing room. Her sandaled feet took graceful yet small steps as if carrying a great deal of weight. "Do come in."

Meena sank onto one end of an upholstered sofa. Asha positioned herself at the other end. Thank God she's friendly, Meena thought. She's taking this better than I expected.

"My parents are inside," Asha said, looking candidly into Meena's eyes. "They're taking the news very hard. Father's never been particularly religious, but all morning he's been sitting in my mother's meditation room, crying and praying."

Asha's voice was even younger than her years. Her clipped English accent was charming to the ear. She was polished in a pure, unspoiled way. In her minimalist jeans and tee shirt outfit Meena felt vulgar and slovenly by comparison. Her hat and sunglasses that sat on the coffee table seemed like garish trappings, as did the wedding necklace that she wore around her neck. She felt an overwhelming urge to take it off.

Asha was tranquil, Meena noticed. No doubt she had been raised to accept people and situations, even a rival, with equanimity. She was someone who simply concealed her emotions beneath several layers of good manners.

"I just visited Vishnu in the hospital," Meena said. "They're still giving him pain medication, but the doctors say he'll be fine." She paused, wondering if anyone could be fine after what Vishnu had been through.

Asha looked up at her, perplexed, the jealousy suddenly evident. "But why were you allowed to visit?" she demanded. "We couldn't go in."

"I got special permission from the police." Meena had to check herself to keep from apologizing. "When the officer found out we were from the same village he let me see Vishnu for a few minutes."

Asha's smile was slightly bitter. "You're very special, it seems."

"You know I was in front of the Moxan headquarters last night when it happened—"

Voice rising, Asha said, "So you've already gotten together with Vishnuda."

Meena nodded a yes.

"You two were married, weren't you?"

"That doesn't mean anything now." Meena found herself on the defensive. "Child marriage is illegal here, isn't it?"

"What about tradition?" Asha could be tough when she needed to be, Meena could see that.

"I'd like nothing better than to see Vishnu happy. That's really what I want with all my heart." Meena added, "I came here because I knew you'd be worried and . . ."

Asha began to sob quietly. Meena wanted to comfort her, but she couldn't be a hypocrite. Asha might still be a rival.

With visible effort Asha regained her composure and said, "Last night I happened to run into him in the stairwell. It was about five o'clock. I asked him if he'd like to play cards with us. He seemed preoccupied. Said he was going back to the office. I was surprised. I asked, 'You're going to work in the evening?' He looked away and said, 'Just for a while. Pradip asked me to meet him there for something.' I'm sure Vishnuda didn't know they were making bombs. . . ." She rose slowly, wiping her cheeks. "I'll be right back."

Meena inspected the living room. The floor was immaculate and cool, the furniture modest except for an elaborate teak cabinet. *India News* was lying on the coffee table, creased from having been pored over too many times. The place clearly belonged to a family that consumed little in spite of good education and high income. On one wall hung a patchwork quilt of reds, blues, and oranges in a butterfly design against a white background. The overall effect was ascetic, yet tasteful. And except for the occasional squeal of car tires or blast of horn from outside the window an atmosphere of tranquility prevailed. A lot like her village used to be. Vishnu would feel at home here.

"Meenaji, please allow me to introduce my parents."

Meena rose, palms together in a position of greeting, as Mr. Das shuffled into the room. He looked pale and shrunken, though he had a cultured air about him. He seemed to have been dealt a severe blow. Raising the head of his cane toward her in a welcoming way, he said in a quavering voice, "Please sit down, Meena."

Meena settled back onto the sofa. Mr. Das lowered himself into a chair and set his cane to one side. Mrs. Das hovered by his side. She appeared to be in good health, but her rumpled sari was an indication of her preoccupation with the Vishnu situation. She was probably someone who wore clean and pressed clothes every day.

"Asha says you're Vishnu's friend." Mrs. Das kept glancing between Meena and her daughter. "And you've come all the way from the States?"

Meena nodded.

"We're so happy you came to visit us," Mrs. Das said. "Vishnu's like family. You're from the same village. Now you're family, too."

"This is a terrible misfortune." Mr. Das coughed. "Last night I got a call from a friend at the police station. He said a policeman had kept the Moxan headquarters under surveillance all evening. He saw Vishnu go in about five-thirty and made a note of it. Later he observed a couple of taxis stopping there and two passengers getting out. One was evidently a European or American man."

The man, of course, was Antoine. And those were the taxis she and

Antoine had hired to get there. Meena's heart pounded. She listened eagerly for any new information.

Mr. Das continued. "The Moxans are believed to have kidnapped an American over a year ago. So when the policeman saw that man, he called his station. A jeep full of plainclothesmen arrived just as the bomb went off. They were able to take the injured to the hospital right away."

"Any news on the man?"

"I haven't heard anything," Mr. Das said. "But I'll ask my friend."

"Imagine the Moxans planting those bombs in the city," Asha said. "I think Vishnuda risked his life to save thousands of people."

Mrs. Das addressed her daughter. "Would you make some lemonade, Asha?"

Asha sauntered to the kitchen.

"I don't mind telling you this, Meena." Mr. Das lowered his voice. "I blame myself for this mess. I was blind. I was trying to find a husband for Asha when this fine chap, Vishnu, lived right in this building. Vishnu has always liked Asha. I don't think Asha knew how much she cared about Vishnu until this horrible thing happened. Nor did we."

My God, the parents didn't know she and Vishnu were married. That was why they were treating her like a relative. Meena swallowed. It was hard to go on listening to Mr. Das, but she couldn't cut him off. Today he needed a sympathetic ear.

"I like Vishnu very much," Mrs. Das said to her husband. "But we've never met his family. Don't you think—"

"How foolish of me." Mr. Das cut his wife off. "I should have helped Vishnu find a job and arranged a marriage for them. Then he wouldn't be in this mess today." His voice cracked. He pulled a handkerchief from his pocket and ran it across his eyes.

Meena was still struggling with her own ambivalent feelings about Vishnu. The more time she spent here, the more she realized that he would be better off with Asha than the cosmopolite she was. As adults it was right for both Meena and Vishnu to find partners who suited what they had become. "You'll get your chance, Mr. Das." She drew in her breath. "Vishnu will be fine in a matter of days. I'm sure he'll be proven innocent."

"I work for the government," Mr. Das said. "I'm using all my influence to free Vishnu. He can stay with us as long as he needs to.

We'll take care of him. Once he's back on his feet, we can think about wedding arrangements."

Without Vishnu in the wings there would be a void. And yet Meena was arriving at a decision that seemed right.

"Asha said you were brought up in San Francisco." Mrs. Das switched the subject. "You've come a long way. I'm sure you've had many wonderful opportunities and experiences in the U.S. that we'll never have. But you see, our Indian women are enlightened too. Every family I know has a woman doctor or an engineer or a professor."

Asha entered bearing a tray. "An Indian woman is either illiterate or she's a member of parliament," she interjected.

"But I can tell from your eyes, from the way you talk to us, that you have a heart just like ours, Meena," Mrs. Das said. "You understand us."

Meena lowered her eyes. Mrs. Das touched her husband's forehead with her palm. "You're running a fever," she said. "I must get you to bed. Please excuse us, Meena."

Asha arranged lemonade and a plate of *laddoos* on the coffee table. Taking care of guests seemed to come easily to her. She was what Meena would have been if that long-ago kidnapping hadn't taken place. The side of Meena that had always remained Indian appreciated Asha for the woman she was.

To be polite, Meena should refuse the food at first, but she and Asha had passed the fence of formality. Meena dove into the *laddoo*. More than a sweet, it was a childhood love and memory and hope rolled into a ball. Asha resumed her spot on the sofa.

"How long have you known Vishnu?" Meena asked, wanting to know Asha better.

"Five years," Asha answered. "Vishnuda lives one floor below us. After I met him, I started to take the long way down the corridor to walk past his flat, just so I'd run into him. One day Vishnuda asked me, 'Asha, why do you walk so much?' I said, 'I need the exercise.' He laughed. I think he knew then I was interested. . . ." After a silence, she added, "I believe Vishnuda's totally innocent. He had nothing to do with bombs."

"Vishnu would never hurt anybody," Meena said slowly. Tear bubbles were slowly pushing behind her eyelids. "In Karamgar, when we were kids, we used to play a game. Watch a lizard come out of its hole. One—two—three, I'd count. The lizard would peek from its hideout and stare at us. Vishnu never tried to catch it like the other boys did."

They were both smiling a little through their tears. Meena realized how much they both loved Vishnu, though in vastly different ways. She couldn't be Vishnu's model Indian wife the way Asha could.

Patting Asha's hand in a sisterly way, she said, "You two have a fine life ahead of you."

Asha looked up with a question mark in her eyes.

"It wouldn't work between us," Meena said sadly. "Vishnu and I must remain childhood friends forever."

Was she giving Vishnu away too easily? Was she acting in haste? Out of nowhere an image of Guru Kailash's face formed in her mind. He shook his head in a no, smiled, and disappeared.

"Meenaji," Asha exclaimed. Her features became clear and bright and hopeful, like a child receiving the biggest toy of her life. "Could I ask you . . . why you're leaving Vishnuda? I thought you had come to get him back. The way he was ignoring me the last few days, acting like he didn't care about me, I must admit I was worried. . . ."

"We were inseparable as kids," Meena said. "I'm richer because of Vishnu's friendship. We were married at age seven, and this year we both completed our fifth cycle of seven. In our village both five and seven were sacred numbers. So it's no surprise that we met again this year. We recognized each other instantly. I felt an immediate connection with him."

"That sounds so much like Vishnuda. To remember old friends."

"But we've been apart for so long and lived in such different places that we've lost much of what was shared between us. After all, we're nothing but all the little things we do every day, the choices we make. They may seem small at the time, but they accumulate, gather weight, push us in new directions, and suddenly we find ourselves on unknown ground. We start all over again."

"Lord Shiva danced," Asha said. "And the world changed under his feet. He does this periodically to bring the world back to order, to get us out of our rut. That's what Mother would say."

Back home in San Francisco Meena wouldn't have given this explanation much thought, but today she was intrigued. "Vishnu and I are on two different paths now—" She cut herself off. "I guess I'll have to make a fresh start. Let my past go. You'll have to do the same with Vishnu's. The Moxan part."

"Meenaji, you're smart and dynamic. You have the looks, I hope you don't mind my saying so. You can have the whole world. But I'm very traditional. For me there's only Vishnuda. I couldn't think of marrying anyone else."

Meena felt one last wrench, painful and yet at the same time liberating. She closed her eyes to calm herself.

"Meenaji, what are you going to do?" Asha's genuine concern was evident in her voice.

"I'll stay in Calcutta a few more days. That's all I know right now. . . ." She rose to her feet. "I really should be going."

At the door Asha grasped her hand. Warmth and trust seemed to come naturally to Asha. "Visit us again before you leave," she said. "I never had an older sister. I'd like to spend more time with you." The pearly light of the late afternoon outlined her tender face, giving the appearance of a halo.

Meena didn't covet Asha's sheltered life, but she envied that look of serene contentment. "I know you and Vishnu will be very happy." She unfastened the gold necklace from around her neck and placed it in Asha's palm. It sparkled with highlights from the rays of the afternoon sun. "Wear this joyfully on your wedding day, as I did on mine."

"Oh, Meenaji," Asha whispered, a stunned expression on her face. "It's beautiful," she stammered. Then more clearly, "I'm honored. You're a very special person from Vishnuda's life. We'll both remember you. I hope you'll stay in touch."

Meena knew she wouldn't, not in the foreseeable future, her future being uncertain as it was. Her meeting with Asha had given her courage. Meena was now ready to tackle whatever came her way. She gazed into Asha's eyes for a moment, thanking her silently, and slowly walked out of the building.

Back at her hotel room, Meena picked up the phone and dialed Carlos in San Francisco just to talk to a friend. No answer. Oh, it was still nighttime there. She hung up, sank into a chair, and sat there for a time unable to get up. The legs that once ran marathons now wouldn't move. Her illusions were crushed, her sole connection to India broken. Inside her was the stunned silence that follows a car crash. Even time had made itself a prisoner and was standing still. Here I am, she thought in a paralyzing moment, a thirty-five-year-old woman. I've lost everything: Mataji, Grandfather, and now Vishnu. I have no home, no job, no friends. Nothing left.

The phone jangled. A glance at her watch revealed that only thirty minutes had ticked away since her return. She wavered, afraid to answer. Eventually, she did.

"This is Das," Asha's father said from the other end. "You asked about an American tourist this afternoon. My friend at the police station said that an American man was brought into the Gandhi Memorial Hospital last night from the bombing site. He could be your friend."

"Is he . . . all right?"

"That's all I know. And I have some more good news. Vishnu should be released by tomorrow night. We're very happy." He hung up.

The bearer came in with hasty steps. "You didn't go downstairs for lunch, memsahib. Are you all right? Can I get you anything?" The old man once again was looking after her like she was a relative.

Meena picked up the thin newspaper from the coffee table, bundled it, and shoved it in her purse. "I'm okay. Really. Please call a taxi."

45

"Antoine Pearson?" The man at the reception desk of the Gandhi Memorial Hospital scanned his ledger pages. "No one here by that name."

He must not have understood her accent. "Please look again," she said. "The name is Peterson." She spelled it. "P-E-T-E-R-S-O-N."

The man rechecked his ledger and after a moment his face brightened. "Ah, here he is." And he began to rattle off directions. "First, take a left down the corridor, then to the right, and another left. He's in the last ward on the right."

And there, indeed, was Antoine, slouched on a cot in a large, dingy room. He still looked huge next to the Indian patients. With his hair rumpled, a stubble of beard on his chin, and several stitches over his right eyebrow he looked more than a little disheveled. A shirt, clearly borrowed, was buttoned tight around his chest. He appeared to be weary, but definitely on the mend. At least he was alive and in one piece, Meena thought to herself. That was all that mattered.

He glanced up as she approached. "Meena!" His cry of delight echoed from the walls as he lurched to his feet. She flung herself into his arms.

She clung to his chest for several moments, then gazed up and sought his eyes. He kissed her for what seemed to be forever. His lips were full and warm against hers. They conveyed regret for time lost and the joy of reuniting. He murmured words in her ear, their meaning unimportant. At last she opened her eyes, inhaled, disengaged herself from his embrace, and stood back to look at him. "Umm . . . you look a little beat up. Are you really okay?"

"Well, I have a headache. My back's sore. And I could do without these stitches. But nothing serious. Most of all, I'm alive." He squeezed her hand. "I was going crazy all morning. The manager of your hotel said you'd checked out. When I asked where you'd gone, he gave me a hard time and basically clammed up. I called several other hotels and two hospitals, but you weren't in any of them."

"I can explain it all," Meena said. Then, noticing that several other patients were listening to their conversation, she added, "Let's go someplace a bit more private."

They drifted down to a tiny balcony at the end of the hallway and leaned against a rail made pleasantly warm by the afternoon heat. Around them grayish buildings in myriad sizes and shapes were turning golden in the rays of the setting sun. A crow flapped by, carrying a piece of paper in its beak as though it was a message of good luck. The twang of a sitar that drifted up from someplace unseen filled the silence until Meena was ready to speak again. "I've been worried sick about you all day, too," she said.

"I was pretty lucky—just a few cuts and bruises." He looked her over. "You okay?"

"Yes. What about the young man who was with you?"

"My driver?" Antoine sighed. "He didn't get off so easy. He got hit by a flying brick. For a while they thought he'd bleed to death. But the nurse told me just before you came that he's going to make it. I stuck around here for an extra couple of hours waiting to hear about the poor kid."

"Antoine, what are you doing in Calcutta?"

"Deepak told me that Vishnu was working for the Moxans. When he said they were terrorists, I figured you might be in danger. I came to warn you."

"Against Vishnu? He was trying to turn the Moxans away from terrorism."

At her defense of Vishnu, Antoine suddenly gripped her arm. With eyes that were full of love, he said in a low voice, "Meena, you mean the world to me. Please don't tell me that you and Vishnu—" He choked.

"What about Liv?" She barely whispered the words.

"Gone. Forgotten. I guess I woke up. And where's Vishnu?"

"He's in Eden Hospital." Meena plucked the newspaper from her purse and handed it to him. It was easier than explaining.

"My God!" Antoine said, taking in the headlines. "Vishnu's lucky to be alive."

"I visited him this morning. He's doing well. But . . ."

"But what?"

"Yesterday I realized he wasn't right for me. We're too different. But I needed to lay a few things to rest. After all, we were officially married, even if we were only seven years old. He's one of the few people who remembers me from when I was a little girl. We were going to have dinner last night. It was just a matter of luck—I was about ready to go inside the Moxan building. Then I saw you there and stopped to talk to you. And that split-second delay probably saved me."

Antoine gently touched her cheek. "My girl, when I came to your hotel yesterday and you refused to see me, I worried myself sick."

"The bearer only said 'an American gentleman.' "

"You didn't know it was me?"

"How could I have known?" she said. "I thought I was being followed. I told the hotel manager not to give out my whereabouts to anyone."

"I was so disappointed I almost packed up and left for Jaipur. Thank God I didn't." He had stopped looking at her. He swallowed before saying, "I love you, Meena. I love you very much. I fell in love with you the moment I saw you in Kazuko's house."

No mistaking the sincerity in his voice. She now realized how much she had misunderstood him, taking his hesitancy as a lack of interest, when all he needed was time. "The day we first met I started a new seven-year cycle."

"Oh?"

"Now I believe what the people of my village used to say. Every seven years we reach a decision point. From my thirty-fifth birthday you took over my life. You became my whole life." Her words were hushed. "I love you, too, Antoine." A pause and then, "Now and forever."

A woman in a tunic, loose pants, and a long scarf about her neck appeared and began to sweep the hallway with a short grass handbroom. Each time she bent, the end of her scarf brushed the floor. She'd pick it up, wrap it back again, and continue her work.

"Let's get out of here," Antoine said.

"I need to go back to my hotel," Meena said. "Will you come with me?"

"I'll follow you wherever you go," Antoine said. "But no bombs, please."

Evening was closing in, soft and gentle. It was lovely, Meena thought, to sit across from Antoine and enjoy a leisurely dinner in the privacy of her room at the Grand Bengal Hotel. One delicious mouthful after another. Rich, subtly spicy, occasionally hot, with its many textures the food was a sensual experience.

The bearer returned with dessert and shot a bewildered look at Antoine, perhaps wondering where Vishnu was. How could she explain this bizarre set of circumstances to him? Even to herself? She bit into a creamy, juicy *ros malai* ball and mentally shrugged.

She was beginning to feel drowsy—undoubtedly the effect of the meal combined with the events of the last two days. Yet the slightest sound or movement from Antoine snapped her back to attention.

Antoine was saying, "India was definitely the right place for us to get back together."

"I see myself more clearly here," Meena said. "Away from my usual routine. In familiarity there is illusion and deception, I now know."

"I know what you mean," Antoine replied. "This complex culture, so alien to my Western experience, tests all my beliefs. I have to change so many of the assumptions I base my life on. I feel a bit naked, really."

Naked? She rubbed her eyes.

"And I can see you've stripped down, too," Antoine said, "peeled away some layers." He paused. "Not literally, of course."

They smiled at each other. Antoine had a look in his eyes that needed no interpretation. He brought his chair closer, removed the bobby pins from behind her ears, and let her hair cascade down over her shoulders and around her face. Their knees touched and that made her tingle all over. When the bearer came back to collect the empty dishes, she never even noticed.

Meena slept finally, her face resting on Antoine's chest. The same dog barked, the same children cried, yet the usual sounds were blotted out by their heartbeats as they lay in a tangle of limbs. A brush with death can be an aphrodisiac, and Meena abandoned her inhibitions as if this lovemaking might truly be the last act of her life.

Happy. Secure. Satiated. This night, a lifetime.

She opened her eyes to a glorious morning, and with Antoine lying in a deep sleep next to her it all suddenly came together. Her confusion about Vishnu, the senseless bombing, the chaos afterward were like the earlier pages of a book. None of it had ever been necessary, yet the sequence of events had pushed her into a new phase of life.

Now they were sitting in a secluded section of a park under the shade of an enormous banyan tree whose sprawling branches had dropped to the ground and taken root again. The morning sun filtered through the leaves in a gentle spray, just right for her bare arms. Off to the left a cluster of children screamed with laughter as they chased each other.

"By the way, before I forget," Antoine said, "I have a message from Lou Cassidy."

"That was another life." Meena felt herself frowning. "What does he want?"

"He wants you to know that COSMOS-1 is selling well and making tons of money for SIC."

"I bet he wants me to do COSMOS-2," Meena said with a laugh. "Eat your heart out, Lou Cassidy. I'm gone. I want a lot more out of life than a career at SIC." She turned to him. "What about you? What are you after?"

"I'll stick around for a while." He chuckled. "There's a lot more to India than I've seen in the last couple of days."

"The trip to my village was wonderful," she said. "I love the people. I'm proud to have been born here. But I know now I'm not cut out to live here."

"You think you might go back to the Bay Area?"

"Eventually. I'm not ready to make a choice between East and West. I'd rather take the good from many cultures. It's like I feel I don't belong anywhere. If I went back to San Francisco, I'd just fall right back into the same fast-track lifestyle and always feel a little dissatisfied. I feel like a stranger any place I stay."

"Sounds a lot like me. We're both wandering in search of a home, or maybe ourselves." Antoine smiled into her eyes. "You're an independent woman, Meena. I hope you don't think you have to travel alone."

With Antoine by her side her restlessness seemed to evaporate. She had a sense of being where she should be, having what she needed. The past was not a burden but a series of celluloid images on fast-forward leading to this instant.

"Do you suppose—we could just sort of wander?" Antoine asked.

Meena reflected for only an instant. "Oh, yes, Antoine."

"Being around you has already helped me to see India differently," Antoine explained. "And I seem to write better here, too."

A beggar girl of about five in a tattered frock approached Meena with wistful eyes, one outstretched hand holding out a jasmine bud. Her mother, also in ragged clothes, stood guard. Meena fished into her purse, picked out a ten-rupee note, gave it to the girl. The girl broke out into a joyous giggle, dropped the bud in Meena's palm, and raced away.

Meena breathed in the sweet smell of jasmine, then asked, "So you've gotten back into your novel?"

"I'm going to do a different book. My mind went totally blank for a while. Couldn't seem to get anything down on paper. That all went away after I got here. This new book is going to be about India. There are stories here on every face, every street corner, down every dark alley. Such a vast range of human experience. So much diversity. Funny, in the West we think all Indians are alike. We miss so much. Being here will take my writing to another level. But it's not going to be easy. I'll have to learn to look at things from an entirely different point of view. I'll probably be at it for the rest of my life."

"Me too." Meena smiled. "I'm glad you want to stay here for a while. I've been thinking about going back to my village anyway. There's a UN-sponsored program called Peace through Computers that my dad was involved with before he died. It teaches kids computer basics, connects them with other kids around the world. They have a branch office in Delhi. I'd like to introduce that program to my village. I really need to do that before I leave. It'll only take a couple of months."

"Great," Antoine replied, "I'll have a chance to get to know village India—and to understand you better."

Meena caught a glimpse of the future. Her own software outfit in San Francisco, ties with companies here, a few trips back each year— Wait a minute. She didn't have to plan it all out right now. "The most important thing," she said emphatically, "is you, my love. And our life together."

"On my bad days I'll hold your hand, look into your eyes, and say, 'I have it so good.' "

The moment was full, complete. Meena lowered her eyes and watched a black ant scurry about on the ground. She marveled at the strength and purpose with which its tiny legs moved. "Life's so fragile, so precious," she said. "These last few days have taught me that I want to live it to the hilt here and now."

"What if we took a vacation first?" Antoine asked. "I know just where I want to take you."

"Where's that?"

"Jaipur. I'm dying for you to meet my wonderful friend Deepak. He probably saved your life. And if it weren't for him, we might not be together today."

"I'm game," Meena said. "But there's one more thing I've got to do before I can leave Calcutta."

"What's that?"

"Say good-bye to Vishnu."

The maidservant in a cool blue sari walked ahead of Meena down the hallway of the Eden Hospital. Meena noticed her own drab print skirt was creased with the strains of travel. Yet for once she didn't feel she should have dressed differently.

The stool was still there outside the door, but no guard this time. The maid motioned Meena in, then left. Meena's heart skipped a beat as she pulled herself erect and stepped in.

Vishnu was in bed reading the *Hindustan Times*. His leg was still in plaster, his face unshaven, but his eyes held a spark. "Meena!" he cast the newspaper aside and raised himself up energetically. He seemed to gather strength at the very sight of her. "What a pleasant surprise. I thought you'd gone."

Meena sat on the edge of the bed, smiling slightly. "Told you I'd come to see you before I left. How're you doing?"

"Much better. My fever's gone. I went through hell for a couple of days. I'm supposed to leave the hospital this afternoon. Mr. and Mrs. Das are coming to get me."

"I'm glad you've gotten your spirit back."

"Meena, I'm so sorry for what happened the other day. I'm ashamed of myself. I must apologize."

"Vishnu, you needn't—"

"I have to tell you something. When I saw you for the first time after twenty-eight years I thought . . . maybe I'll get back the life I've always dreamed about. You know how you can look back and see everything as rosy. But in the last couple of days I began to realize that could never be. We had some very good moments, Meena. I get a lot of strength just thinking about our life in the village. No bandits or bombs can ever take that away from us. I'll carry those memories of you for the rest of my life."

The maid poked her head through the door.

Vishnu turned toward her and spoke rapidly in Hindi. Meena understood he was ordering tea.

The maid nodded and hurried away.

"Things are looking up for me, Meena. I got a call from the *Hindustan Times*. It's a big paper. They're offering me a position in Delhi. I don't really want to leave Calcutta, but how can I refuse? I don't like the idea of flying to Kashmir either."

"Kashmir?" Meena paused to accept a cup of tea from the maid. "Isn't the area unstable politically?"

"Yes. It's a bit risky to go there. But . . . no choice. At least for a year." Vishnu sighed.

"Be careful, will you?"

"Asha doesn't want me to go either. She has one more year of college. We'll see what happens after she graduates." His eyes met hers. "Will you be staying in Calcutta a little longer?"

"Just a couple more days. I wanted to hang around here until you got out of the hospital. Now that you are well, I can be on my way."

"Where are you off to?"

"I'll be traveling with my friend Antoine for a while. We want to see as much of India as we possibly can."

"Antoine? Is he French?"

"No, he's an American."

"That's good. You're very American, Meena, if you don't mind my saying so."

"Americans think I'm from India and Indians think I'm from America. That's the story of my life." Meena laughed as she rose. "It's been a good visit, Vishnu. Maybe not what I expected. But what the heck, my life got changed for the better. Antoine and I got back together."

"He's a lucky man. Tell him I said so. I'd like to meet him someday."

At the door Meena turned. A smile, a tear, a chapter closed.

"Send us postcards, Meena. And by the way, Asha and her parents wanted me to tell you, the next time you're in Calcutta, you can stay with them at Hotel Das."

Four days later Meena and Antoine, wearing identical Kimochi 8K tee shirts, caught a train bound for Jaipur from Calcutta's Howra station. A porter brought their luggage and stacked it on the overhead rack of their first-class compartment. As they took their seats, Meena by the window and Antoine next to her beside a wide aisle, Meena felt happy and secure to be finally together. She looked around. The car was less than half full. The journey would take all day, but that wouldn't matter, for she'd spend it with Antoine. She could ask no more than that.

"We'll have a blast in Jaipur," Antoine was saying. "The suite I have reserved at the Sitabagh Palace is supposed to be fabulous. We'll chase the peacocks, ride a camel, go to the bazaar. . . ."

"Can we have mangoes?" Meena feigned seriousness.

Antoine smiled mischievously. "I'll pick an especially ripe one for you."

Meena peered out the window. On the platform, two porters were engaged in a dispute over who was to carry a passenger's luggage, a vendor with a basket on his head was hawking *jilebi*, and scores of people intent on reaching their destinations were jostling each other. It was the kind of scene that had terrified her as a seven-year-old. Now it was familiar, even a bit endearing.

The train groaned and shivered, then began to move, leaving behind the bomb, the hospitals, Asha and Vishnu. "I'll never forget Calcutta," Meena said. "It's where we finally found each other. We must come back here from time to time just for memory's sake."

And in the next breath she was reliving her bittersweet farewell to Vishnu. A shadow of melancholy passed over her and vanished quickly, dispelled by the rhythmic motion of the train. The clacking noise of the wheels reminded her of a dancer tapping out a staccato pattern on the floor.

"Yes, truly, Shiva must have been dancing," she exclaimed. She laughed merrily as she recalled Asha's observations about life changes. "And see what he accomplished. He helped me turn my life around and bury the past. Now I can look forward to the future. Who can tell what exciting things are around the corner? All that I've struggled to be—a Rajput warrior, a software techie, a runner—are just parts of me and I won't ignore them. They helped make me what I am. But now I know my happiness and fulfillment come from being a whole person, a woman, with no baggage from the past, nothing to prove. And from being with you."

"Just be Meena," Antoine said, squeezing her hand and looking at her, eyes swelling with love. "And just be with me. That's all I'll ever want."